FRANKLIN HORTON

ALSO BY FRANKLIN HORTON

The Borrowed World Series

The Borrowed World

Ashes of the Unspeakable

Legion of Despair

No Time For Mourning

Valley of Vengeance

Switched On

The Ungovernable

The Locker Nine Series

Locker Nine

Grace Under Fire

Compound Fracture

Blood Bought

The Mad Mick Series

The Mad Mick

Masters of Mayhem

Stand-Alone Novels

Random Acts

ABOUT THE AUTHOR

Franklin Horton lives and writes in the mountains of Southwestern Virginia. He is the author of several bestselling post-apocalyptic series. You can follow him on his website at franklinhorton.com.

While you're there please sign up for his mailing list for updates, event schedule, book recommendations, and discounts.

BRUTAL BUSINESS

1

R oss County, Ohio

JUST NORTH OF CHILLICOTHE, Ohio, Thomas pulled his truck up to the gate in the chain link fence and grinned. An ominous sign read: *Looters Will Be Shot.*

"We'll see about that." He killed the engine, popped his door open, and stepped down. By the time his boots hit the gravel, more trucks just like the one he was driving fell in behind him. They were mostly military surplus M54A2 cargo trucks with few M35A2s thrown in. All ran multi-fuel engines capable of running on diesel, jet fuel, kerosene, home heating oil, and, in a pinch, even gasoline.

The need for fuel was what brought this special convoy to the Buckeye Farm Supply. Rumor was they still had a decent supply of kerosene and home heating oil put back in case things got worse. Of course, that rumor was extracted under duress, what some people might call torture, but Thomas had no qualms about employing such means. Someone had to do it. Someone had to lead in the group.

Someone had to find the next cache of fuel and keep the convoy rolling. That someone was him.

Thomas left the line of trucks, a grin on his face, and walked toward the tall rolling gate. He studied the sturdy chain and the serious padlock. He also noted the bloodstains on the dry gravel beneath his feet. Rather than scaring him, he actually found that to be an encouraging sign. Somebody had something here they felt a need to protect.

"Keep moving, soldier!" barked a voice from somewhere inside the farm supply.

Thomas searched the windows and doors of the main structure. He didn't see anything open, no heads sticking out. He decided he needed to keep them talking in order to get a better fix on the speaker.

"We're just searching for fuel," Thomas said. He was trying to sound both official and innocent, a poor stranded soldier out there saving souls and keeping the peace.

"Guess you haven't heard but there's a shortage," the voice replied.

The man was being a smartass and Thomas hated a smartass. Disrespect was one thing he would not tolerate. He'd worked hard to earn the respect he held and he wouldn't let anyone talk to him that way without paying a price.

"Yeah, we've heard about the shortage. We just want to take a look around. I'm certain you got something in there these vehicles can run on. Why don't you come on out and open the gate?"

"This official business?" the voice asked.

Thomas detected a flicker of concern in the voice. The guy was a law-abiding citizen who didn't want to do anything that might get him in trouble. "Official?" Thomas said. "What exactly do you mean by *official*?"

"I mean, is this official Army business? Government business?" the voice asked. "You're in Army trucks, wearing Army clothes. Figured you must be doing Army shit."

"Does it make a difference if this is official?" Thomas asked. "That help you make whatever decision you're in there trying to make?"

"Not really," the voice replied. "Just like to know who we kill. Helps us know how deep we need to bury the bodies."

Thomas had to laugh at that. The balls on this one. He hoped the man's laugh was a good one because it would most certainly be his last. As he was laughing, he was also searching, trying to find the man addressing him. Then there he was. A flicker of movement behind an enormous round bale of hay. Someone had turned several bales onto their flat end like giant soup cans and scattered them around the property, presumably to provide cover for situations like this one. In most cases, that bale would have protected the hidden man, at least for a little while.

Thomas spoke into his radio. "Mingo, you listening?"

"Yeah, T," came the response.

"See that hay bale with the white wrap around it? The one by the forklift?"

"Affirmative."

"Grenade launcher. Smoke that motherfucker," Thomas whispered.

Mingo popped up from the bed of Thomas's truck and fired a shot from his M203 grenade launcher. Thomas ducked behind the hood of his truck just in case fragments came flying his way. The round embedded itself in the hay bale before exploding. Strands of burning hay floated down on the scene like a snowstorm in Hell. The emerging cloud of smoke gave Thomas a slight tactical advantage that he didn't want to waste. He needed to get his crew moving before it cleared.

"First Team, go!"

Thomas swung out from behind the truck with a set of bolt cutters he kept on the floorboard. He ran to the gate and cut the chain. Mingo laid down cover fire over their heads. They didn't know if there was anyone else alive in there but they had to assume there was and that they were ready to fire back.

When the chain was cut, Thomas leaned his shoulder into the

heavy steel gate and pushed it along the rollers. First Team, his breaching team, rushed through the opening he created. Someone inside the main building broke out a window and fired a few wild shots at them. Mingo, in concert with some of First Team, opened up on the window and the shooting soon stopped. They'd neutralized the threat.

There was a crash and the sound of splintering wood as First Team laid a boot to the storefront and smashed the antique door into kindling.

"Go! Go! Go!" the team leader yelled, rushing his stacked team inside. He fell smoothly into line behind them and they began clearing the main building.

"Second Team, go!" Thomas said into his microphone. There was no sign of stress in his voice. No rush. This was everyday business for them. Routine.

A second fire team sprinted through the gate, weapons raised. They rushed around the back of the building and into the yard where farm supplies were stored. There were stacks of gates, cattle feeders, water tanks, and every manner of livestock fencing. The team split up and set about securing the various other structures on the property. More shots came from inside the store building. They were single, precise, kill shots. Indications the team had found folks hiding and dealt with them.

They were executions.

Thomas removed a fire extinguisher from a bracket on the side of his truck. He walked casually to the smoldering remains of the hay bale and blasted it with a prolonged, powdery burst from the extinguisher. When the device ran dry, he tossed it to the side. The densely-packed hay had shaped the grenade's blast in a peculiar manner and he spotted the remains of the man he'd been talking with through the gate. He looked like a giant ice cream scoop had come down from the sky and taken a scoop from his top half. He was all hay, blood, and powdered fire retardant, like some psycho's version of a powdered jelly donut.

"Damn, bro," Thomas muttered, shaking his head at the corpse. "You should have run."

"Inside clear," came the transmission from First Team's leader.

"Second Team?" Thomas asked.

"Perimeter secure."

Thomas turned away from the wrecked body and beckoned toward the men remaining in the trucks. The passenger in his truck scooted to the driver's seat, started the engine, and eased through the gate, heading behind the building. The rest of the caravan was made up of similar vehicles, though some pulled trailers. The final vehicle was an M49A2C fuel tanker and perhaps their most important piece of gear.

When the last truck passed by him, Thomas dragged the gate closed and set the chain back in place. With the vehicles concealed around back and the gate chained, the place would appear unchanged from the road. While they didn't exactly depend on stealth, why invite trouble? Yet if trouble did come they were more than equipped to handle it.

Thomas stalked around the building, headed for the yard area and taking in the remaining inventory around him. Most of this farming shit meant nothing to him. As far as he was concerned, cows were for eating, not for babysitting. He didn't give a damn how you kept, fenced, or medicated one. All he cared about was how you cooked them. Preferably with a slight char to the outside and medium rare on the inside.

He spoke into his radio. "Second Team, gate is closed. Get a couple of concealed sentries on the front and make sure the perimeter is tight. Lawdog? Mundo? You with me?"

"Yeah, T?" Lawdog replied.

"You got someone checking tanks?"

"Roger that, T. Already on it."

"Then you and Mundo get inside and start hitting the books. Get me a list of those bulk fuel customers and where the fuck they live. We don't roll again until the trucks and tanker are full."

"On it," Lawdog replied.

Lawdog and Mundo were his most computer literate men. They had a little Honda generator and a long extension cord. If the records were computerized, they'd boot the machines and find a way in. If there was anything petroleum-based and combustible in the area, they'd find it.

"Where's my taco truck?" Thomas called.

A man carrying a three-foot long pipe wrench gestured to a particular truck in the sea of similar vehicles. Thomas didn't acknowledge the gesture but jogged off in that direction. Shootah and Buddha Boy were in charge of the food and they were searching for a good spot to set up the camp kitchen.

"Y'all find something good to throw on that fire," Thomas said. "I could eat the tires off one of these trucks."

"We saw a couple of cows while we were sitting there at the gate," Buddha Boy said. "They kept turning into steaks and burgers right before my eyes, like in one of those old cartoons."

"Then make it happen," Thomas said. "We're burning daylight."

Someone had opened a back door to the main building and Thomas headed in that direction. There was a covered back porch and loading dock area piled with more farming shit. While Thomas stood there studying the various shrink-wrapped pallets, a roll-up door rattled open on the dock. Men from First Team began slinging bodies off the dock and onto the ground.

Thomas watched with detached interest. He didn't really care who they killed or how many. What interested him was their appearance. He was trying to figure out if the men they'd killed were owners and employees of the company or if they were men who'd just been occupying the place. From the bibbed overalls and goofy trucker hats, he figured these men owned the joint. They were at least locals.

"Hey, Jawbone," Thomas called, speaking to a short, muscular man. He was dressed the same as Thomas, in the uniforms they'd all been issued by the Army.

"Wassup?"

"There's got to be some wheelbarrows or carts around this place. Get a couple of guys and haul these dead fuckers out of here."

"Where to, T?"

"I don't give a damn as long as I don't have to see or smell them."

Jawbone scratched his head and scanned the yard.

Thomas spotted a nested stack of wheelbarrows beneath an open shed. "There," he said.

Jawbone looked but didn't immediately see them.

"There," Thomas repeated. "Right. Fucking. There." He jabbed with his finger.

"Oh yeah," Jawbone said, heading off in that direction.

"Dense motherfucker," Thomas mumbled. He heard men approaching and saw it was Lawdog and Mundo with their tiny red generator.

Lawdog stopped at the pallet of stacked plastic sacks. He tore open a section of the plastic wrap and scanned the label, tracing it with his finger until a smile split his face.

"What?" Thomas asked.

"This is the good stuff," Lawdog said. "The kind of fertilizer you can blow things up with. Oklahoma City bombing level stuff."

Thomas stared at it. "That right?"

Lawdog nodded.

"You know how to do it?"

"Oh, hell yeah."

"Good to know," Thomas replied. "But right now we need fuel more so get your ass in that building and find us some."

"You got it, T," Lawdog said, following Mundo inside.

Thomas brought up the rear and entered the dark expanse of the farm supply. While old country stores had faded into obscurity, replaced by convenience stores with their bright lights and relative uniformity, farm supply stores carried that atmosphere of bygone days. Inside, the narrow planks of the oak floor creaked as Thomas walked. The ceiling was tinplate, with the fine detail obscured by multiple layers of dingy paint. There was a smell that was somewhere between a barn and a hardware store, consisting of oil, wood, smoke, and grains.

"This place is big," Thomas said to no one in particular. Besides

Lawdog and Mundo, several other men with specific areas of expertise were moving through the aisles, searching for supplies. "We push some of this shit out of the way, we can sleep in here."

"There's a woodstove too," Flaco called from the far side of the room. "Already got a fire going and everything."

"Let's keep it going," Thomas said. "Gonna cool off fast in here with all these doors open. It would be nice to sleep someplace warm for a change." He wandered to the front window. The single-layer glass provided no insulation and was as cool as the outside air. Thomas could feel the cold on his face.

"We *entertaining* tonight?" Flaco asked, his tone implying he was definitely hoping for it.

"Naw," Thomas replied. He enjoyed entertaining as much as the next guy but they had work to do. "We learn the lay of the land first. These farmers might have neighbors who wanna pay us a visit for punching their buddies' tickets. Possibly tomorrow."

"Roger that, T." Flaco picked up a green can from one of the merchandise displays and held it up for Thomas to see. "Look at this shit. Bag Balm. Who the hell would buy something like this?"

"No idea. What's it for?"

Flaco studied the label. "Dude, I think it's for your udders."

Thomas shook his head. "Fucking farmers."

2

Thomas woke to the smell of frying ham and pork bellies, the remnants of a pig Buddha Boy killed two days ago. The farmer who owned the pig complained and Buddha Boy dispatched him the same way he took the pig. A single round between the eyes. Thomas hoped they made biscuits and gravy. Nothing said good morning like biscuits and gravy. Eggs would be nice too. The only eggs they had were powdered but it sure beat the hell of out of no eggs at all.

He was a latecomer to the magic of a good breakfast. He didn't realize until he got older what he'd been missing all his life. He couldn't recall ever having had a homemade breakfast during his childhood. Usually in his house it was the "find it your own damn self" system. Kind of like a buffet except without the food. Most days he got his breakfast at school. Later, when he started earning on the street, he could buy his breakfast. That was when he got introduced to the Waffle House and learned what breakfast was all about.

The previous night he'd made his bed out of a half-dozen bags of goat feed. His men had laughed at him as he'd tested sacks of grass seed, chicken feed, and Purina Catfish Chow for their relative comfort. He found that goat food was his preference. It was firm without shifting too much when he moved. It also had a sweet molasses scent that reminded him of cookies.

They'd run perimeter security all night, four men with night vision, body armor, and select-fire M4s. Things had been quiet. Sometimes gunfire of the type they'd unleashed when evicting the previous tenants brought visitors either searching for vengeance or to scavenge from the dead. Thomas had fully expected a few shots in the night, either warning or lethal, but there had been none.

He crawled out of his sleeping bag and sat up, yawned, and reached for his boots. The military had taught him to be a creature of habit, to develop personal *systems* that allowed him to function at optimal efficiency. He always slept with his rifle to the left side of his body. The boots were also at the left, at chest level. One boot held his Beretta M9 and the other held an unsheathed Cold Steel combat knife. Both the pistol and the knife were ready to grab and fight if it came to that.

It was a gray day outside and dim light filtered into the room. Some men were sleeping. Others, like him, were stirred to wakefulness by the daylight or force of habit. There was no hurry. They had nowhere to be other than where they wanted to be. Nothing to do other than that which they wanted to do. No orders, no training, and no bullshit.

One of the men added a log to the fire. The room was cool but a good bit warmer than a tent. Certainly warmer than sleeping up under the truck, which they had to do sometimes. Thomas emptied his boots of weapons and slid them on. They zipped up the side which saved a lot of time lacing. He stood and made his way to the stove, drawn to it like a cat to a sunbeam. Moments like this made settling down look like an attractive prospect. There was nothing comfortable about life on the road. You always had to be on edge, always waiting for the next challenge, the next attack.

He'd grown up that way, though, and knew no other life. He'd never been comfortable, never seen home as a warm, safe place where you could back up to a fire and hang out with people you cared about. That was a fairytale for soft people and the sheep they preyed on. He had no intention of getting soft. No intention of giving into the temptation of having a comfortable bed to settle into each night. He'd stay hard, stay sharp, and stay free. That was his life.

Thomas had found his family, his brotherhood, on the streets. When he'd become an adult, that same family had asked him to join the military. The gang wanted their soldiers to be trained like real soldiers. They wanted shooters who could really shoot. They wanted fighters who could bring warfighter skills to the street. Thomas had done what was asked of him.

At first, he hated the Army. He didn't like being told what to do. There were rules for everything and punishments if you fucked up. Many times he was tempted to kill men for the way they talked to him. He could catch them off base or have a training accident. He'd killed men for that very reason on the streets and held no fear of doing it again. If he got arrested though, or got his ass thrown out, he wouldn't be able to return to his street family. He'd have failed them. They had big plans. Big plans for him and the others like him who hid among the ranks of the military. He'd bitten his tongue, learned discipline, and at some point realized his newfound discipline made him way more dangerous than he'd ever been before.

None of the gang's larger plans were going to happen. After the collapse, his gang had been wiped out by a rival. Now all he had was the others like himself. Men he'd identified in the ranks through their tattoos and the way they greeted each other. Before the shit hit the fan, he'd found over a hundred others like himself. They shared a history and a common upbringing. They shared a bond even beyond that the military instilled in them. Thomas built on that to establish the name by which they identified themselves. *The Bond.*

The name didn't immediately identify them as gang members. Anyone who overheard them using it might have assumed that, due to their uniforms, it was simply referring to their bond as servicemen. Though some of them had come from different gangs, none of them had been direct rivals, otherwise Thomas's effort to build these men into a team probably wouldn't have worked. But it had. They all had similar backgrounds, they all knew the same world, and they shared the same values.

When the world crapped out on them the military was in shambles. There was no longer a cohesive mission, and desertion rates skyrocketed. For those who remained behind, commanders followed along party affiliations or other, less obvious, allegiances. Bases became entities unto themselves. There had been such a division in Washington that it seemed like commanders had been waiting for an opportunity like this.

The men of The Bond stayed in touch with each other through an encrypted chat app up until that quit working. When it did, they fell back on the plan they'd been working out over the past weeks. They stole a fleet of surplus multi-fuel trucks from their base, then stole weapons and supplies that members of The Bond had access to. Funny thing was, their base was in such disarray that no one cared. People were looting gear and selling it to civilians or smuggling it to family. People were disappearing from the ranks every night. Before long, there would be no one left but those who only knew military life.

Thomas held a meeting each morning. The only men excused were those who had just come off sentry duty and needed sleep. Everyone else had to be there. Today, the men gathered in the main room of the farm supply with paper plates heaped with steaming food. Thomas didn't believe in being stingy with food. Feed the men well and they'd follow you. They had bacon, fried ham, powdered eggs, and biscuits with little jelly packs they'd found in a fast food restaurant. There was some grumbling about the lack of gravy.

"Done spoiled you assholes," Buddha Boy said. "You miss one day of gravy and you think it's the end of the world."

"Yeah, pretty much," Lawdog agreed.

"You eating good, aren't you?" Buddha Boy asked. "Ain't no need to grumble."

"He's right," Thomas pitched in. "Probably ain't nobody for miles got this good a breakfast in front of them right now so y'all shut the hell up and listen."

The men fell silent. The meetings were good-natured and casual but when Thomas told them to get quiet he meant it. Men had died to get that point across and it was embedded in everyone's mind with a crystal clarity. He was the boss and his word was law.

Thomas took up a piece of ham in his hand and tore at it with his teeth. "What's the fuel situation?"

"Between kerosene, home heating oil, and off-road diesel there was enough to top off the trucks but none for the tanker," Mundo said.

"You find anything in the bulk fuel records?"

"Didn't even have to use the computer. They had a detailed paper log with receipts, gallons delivered, and the account information. There's some big farm accounts taking a thousand gallons at a clip. Running them big tractors and combines, I guess. If those people ain't farming and they're sticking close to home, they can't be burning fuel that fast. My guess is we could hit one or two of those bigger accounts and fill the tanker."

Thomas chewed and processed. "Filling that tanker is priority number one. The next stop is Chillicothe, and I bet there ain't shit left there. Too many people. Not enough food and fuel to go around. They gonna be some desperate assholes."

"I like desperate," Shootah said. "Desperate women do about anything a man wants."

"Desperate women are about the only kind that will hook up with the likes of you," Thomas cracked. "But forget women. We talking business now. Lawdog, you and Mundo figure out which of those big fuel accounts are the closest. Pick three of them and send a two man team to scout out each of them. You'll go on foot and report back with what you find. Physically verify they got fuel left and how much. Try to avoid conflict. You know we're all about peace and shit."

He couldn't even say it without a smile. His men agreed, cracking up and laughing.

"Yeah, I been thinking about trading my cammies for tie dyes," Mundo said. "Start listening to Phish."

"Fish?" Buddha Boy asked. "Like bass and trout kind of fish?"

"It's a band, fool," Mundo said. "Hippie shit. Like the Grateful Dead. Woodstock. All that business."

"What the fuck I know about that?" Buddha Boy asked. "I'm a soldier. I ain't no fucking hippie expert."

"You a soldier of The Bond, not the United States," Thomas reminded him. "Don't forget that. None of us work for the government anymore. We work for ourselves. We work for each other."

Lawdog shoved the last of his bacon, ham, and jelly biscuit in his mouth and tossed his plate off to the side. "Speaking of work, what you want the rest of us to do?"

"Toss this place," Thomas said. "I ain't sure what farmers use that we might need but I think I saw propane tanks outside. Buddha Boy needs that for the stove, so make sure we got plenty. Otherwise you'll be eating cold pop-tarts instead of biscuits. Check for tools, hardware, ropes, chains, vehicle maintenance supplies, anything you think we might need. If you find something better than what we're carrying, toss the old shit and take the new. There's also more people moving around in the day, so we'll need perimeter security."

"When we track down those fuel accounts, we going to go collect it as a team?" Mundo asked.

Thomas nodded. "Once we find enough fuel for the tanker, we'll secure the fuel. We keep going until the tanker is full."

"Got it," Mundo replied.

"Any questions?" Thomas asked.

There were none.

"Everyone clear on what they're doing?" he asked.

There were nods around the room.

"Then get on with it. Let's make shit happen."

3

The Ashford family was getting ready to sit down to a dinner of venison stew made from a deer Mr. Ashford had hanging in the barn. The stew had been simmering on the woodstove all day, torturing the family of six with the aroma. Mrs. Ashford was frying cornbread in a skillet over the same stove. She called it Johnny Cakes and her children were intrigued by the idea. They thought the little round cakes resembled pancakes that should be eaten with syrup, not stew, and they were eating them nearly as fast as she made them. They'd had a good day, considering the state of things. The family was warm and they had food. They were confident they would survive whatever was going on with the country. Then they heard a horn.

Mr. Ashford was sitting in his recliner by the woodstove, reading an old farming magazine. He bolted from his chair and ran to the window. He carefully pulled the curtains aside and peered out. He turned back to his family and found them staring at him, eyes wide. "There's someone at the gate. It looks like an Army truck. Everyone in the basement *now!*"

The family knew not to argue. They'd done this same thing, both as a drill and because of unexpected visitors, many times. Mrs.

Ashford ran to the kitchen and threw open the basement door. She grabbed a shotgun from where it stood beside the broom in a corner. The children were already filing down the dark stairs, one of them carrying a flashlight. She gave her husband a nervous glance and he smiled at her.

"It'll be okay," he said.

She tried to smile back and failed, then fell in behind her children, locking the basement door behind them.

Mr. Ashford picked up his deer rifle and tugged on his farm boots. He was preparing to go onto the porch and address the visitors when the back door was kicked open. The jamb splintered and the door swung hard, banging off the wall. A man in camouflage fatigues and web gear stepped through the door. He was moving with practiced fluidity, a rifle raised and following his eyes as he scanned the room.

Mr. Ashford awkwardly threw his rifle up but was too slow, too awkward. A short burst of gunfire exploded in the tight quarters of the home, the rounds stitching up Mr. Ashford's chest. He fell backward into the window, shattering it outward with a flailing arm before sagging into the floor.

The shooter advanced into the living room, a second man following immediately behind him. It was Mundo in the lead with Body Bag behind him.

"The basement!" Mundo barked. "I saw the door closing when I looked through the window!"

Body Bag advanced on the closed basement door and tried the handle. Locked. Instead of standing off the side of the door like he was trained to do, Body Bag stood directly in front of it. In the basement, Mrs. Ashford knew what those gunshots and what that rattling knob meant. It was up to her. She fired her shotgun and a cluster of buckshot pellets punched a fist-sized hole through the door. Those same pellets ripped a chunk from Body Bag's face and neck. He staggered backward, holding his neck, falling into the kitchen table, blood spraying. The table tipped, dumping him into the floor.

"Shit!" Mundo yelled, flattening himself against the living room wall.

There was a second blast from the shotgun, lower this time. Whoever was down there wasn't taking any chances. The round punched out more of the door but didn't hit anyone.

"You with me, Body?" Mundo yelled. When there was no answer, he peered around the corner and saw his friend dead on the kitchen floor. One eye was missing, along with a good part of the right side of his face.

"Assholes!" Mundo screamed. "Fucking assholes!" He yanked a grenade from a pouch on his gear, pulled the pin. He ran toward the basement door and shoved the grenade through the splintered hole like he was throwing garbage in a garbage can.

In the basement, the Ashfords had no idea what was about to happen. Mrs. Ashford was trying to wield the shotgun while one of her children held the flashlight from a safe vantage point. All she heard was something heavy clattering down the steps. It sounded like a can of soup. She never had the chance to figure out what it was.

Mundo flew out the back door at full-tilt and leapt off the porch. The grenade exploded and the basement level windows blew out in a spray of glass. It was too much pressure in too small a space. Trying to run while keeping an eye on the house, Mundo ran straight into a swingset. At the last minute he tried to jump one of the dangling swings but the seat hooked both feet and he face-planted in the mulch.

There was a loud crash from a different direction and Mundo pushed himself up, trying to figure out what was going on, but it was his people. The tanker had crashed through the gate and was charging up the driveway. Somehow the gate had become hooked on the undercarriage of the truck and was dragging along behind it, rattling like a loose tailpipe dragged behind a car.

"*Mundo! What the fuck?*" came a burst across his radio. "*What's going on?*"

Mundo heard a whooshing sound, followed by a single, high-pitched scream. He glanced back toward the house and saw smoke pouring from the windows. The grenade must have ignited something, perhaps an oil tank in the basement. The house was on fire, smoke and flames pouring from the basement windows.

"They got Body Bag!" Mundo shouted into his radio. "They were holed up in the basement and I had to frag'em."

"Good job," Lawdog said sarcastically. *"People will see that smoke for miles and want to know what the hell is going on. You might as well have sent up a flare."*

Mundo got to his feet and waved toward the tanker. He jogged toward a nearby tree, wanting to keep something between him and the house in case there was anybody alive in the upstairs. He'd not had a chance to clear the house before things went south but they'd be dead soon enough. The house was fully engulfed.

The tanker swerved in his direction, cutting across the lawn, then slowing as it approached him. Lawdog rolled down the window and killed the engine. It was hard to talk over the noise of it. "Where to?"

Mundo and Body Bag had done the recon on this place earlier. They were the team that found it and located the bulk fuel tank with the remaining fuel. He pointed to a small barn-like structure made of corrugated steel situated away from the larger equipment barn. "Fuel shed. There's a solar panel powering a twelve-volt pump setup. We can pull right up to it and start pumping into the tanker. Their pump might be too slow, though."

"We'll figure it out. Hop on. We better get moving. That fire is sending up smoke signals and neighbors might start showing up."

Mundo knew he was right but he'd done what he had to do. He climbed onto the running board and hooked his arm through the open window, switching his rifle to his offhand. Lawdog restarted the engine. Just as he began to ease forward there was the sound of gunfire coming from the house.

"Shit!" Lawdog yelled, stomping on the accelerator pedal. They needed this truck and the last thing he wanted was the engine getting shot up.

Feeling exposed on the side of the truck, Mundo jumped clear. He rolled several times and took cover behind the base of a tree. He leveled his rifle and dumped rounds at the house, moving from window to window, assuming that was where the fire had to be coming from. He shot out his mag, ejected it, and was well into his second when someone kicked him in the leg.

He rolled onto his back and started to raise his rifle to the threat but a hand caught it. It was Lawdog.

"Your crazy ass is going to get shot!" Mundo yelled. "Get down!"

"It's rounds cooking off, dumb shit," Lawdog said. "Ain't nobody shooting at you."

"What?"

"Ammunition. The fire. Rounds are exploding," Lawdog repeated slowly, as if he were trying to explain something complex to a very young child.

Mundo flicked his safety on and extended a hand toward Lawdog. "Help me the fuck up. Here I am trying to save your ass, trying to provide cover fire, and you call me a dumbass."

"I call 'em like I see 'em."

The tank was round, mounted on a raised stand, and held five hundred gallons. There was a stained rod hanging on hooks that was used for measuring the depth of the fuel in the tank. While Lawdog readied the tanker for receiving fuel, Mundo flipped open the inlet on the round tank and lowered the rod into it. He pulled it out, then held it against the outside of the tank to see how much fuel was in there.

"A little more than half," Mundo said.

"Better than nothing," Lawdog replied.

"You want to use their nozzle?"

"Too slow. I told you, people will probably start showing up soon. We gonna end up having to shoot our way out of here."

Lawdog uncoiled a heavy hose from the tanker and they dropped one end of that into the inlet on the bulk tank. Lawdog restarted the truck and activated a transfer pump that began quickly moving the fuel. They could hear it splashing inside the tanker but there was nothing quick about the process, especially when they were expecting company at any moment.

The pump on their truck moved fuel at twenty-five gallons per minute. They were around fifteen minutes into the process when it started sucking in air and the transfer rate slowed. Mundo moved the intake hose around, making sure it was catching all the fuel.

"Don't shove it to the bottom," Lawdog warned. "That's where all the shit settles. It will clog things up."

"I know that," Mundo grumbled.

Lawdog killed the pump. "Roll up the gear. I'm getting a weird feeling. I'm going to grab some binoculars and check our six before we move out."

Mundo hated taking orders – they all did – but Lawdog was a senior guy, a lieutenant in their organization. Lawdog took some binoculars from the cab of the truck and climbed up on the bumper, scanning the area.

Mundo finished with the hose and secured everything for the road. "We going to go through these barns or anything?"

"Uh, no. We got company."

Mundo moved around to the front of the truck. He squinted into the distance but couldn't see anything without optics. "What is it?"

"Men with guns walking down the road. I told you that fire would draw people." Lawdog hopped down from the bumper.

"I told you I didn't have a choice. They were holed up in the basement. Besides, we got men. We can take them."

"We got business to attend to. We need to get on with it," Lawdog said. He went around to the driver's side of the tanker and stashed the binoculars. "Get in."

Mundo climbed in the passenger side. "What's the plan?"

"I only see folks coming from the east. We're going to go west, following the farm road through the field. Once we put some distance between us, we'll get back on the road."

"What do you need me to do?" Mundo asked.

"Shoot people if they get close."

Mundo smiled. "Roger that."

❧

TWO FUEL RUNS that day left The Bond with topped-off trucks and a full tanker. The second run went similarly to the first, with the exception that there was no grenade and no fire. Still, a rural family was left dead and the bulk fuel intended for their farming operations was stolen. That was of no concern to the members of The Bond. A trail of bodies was nothing new to them. It was business as usual.

Was a tornado concerned about the homes it flattened? Did the locust care about the crops it decimated? Did the coyote worry about the calves it ate? The Bond saw themselves similarly. Predators were a natural outgrowth of the circumstance. They were as inevitable as rain. A force of nature as inevitable as death itself.

"Y'all done good," Thomas said. "We got food, fuel, and a warm place to sleep for a few nights. You earned yourself a little fun."

A cheer went up from the men. Their efforts were always rewarded and they appreciated that about their leader. It was how Thomas maintained loyalty, how he kept The Bond in line.

"We send a team out in the morning. They'll go hunting in Chillicothe and bring back party favors. Three trucks. Just like before, we draw straws. Short straws stay here and keep watch."

"Why can't we all go?" Mundo asked. "We should just move on and set up camp in Chillicothe. We can do what the hell we want until we get tired of the place. We pick it clean, then move on. Why we got to stay out here in the boonies?"

"You ain't thinking with your brain," Thomas pointed out. "Cities have resources but what else they got?"

"People," Lawdog said, giving Mundo a smug look.

Thomas pointed at Lawdog like a teacher acknowledging a smart student. "That's right. They'll be nipping at our heels like starving dogs, trying to take our shit. We'll have to worry constantly about being ambushed or snipers shooting us from windows. There's probably other gangs there too – cops, bikers, and bangers."

"Ain't no gangs worse than us," a man said. "The Bond is the ultimate."

Thomas smiled. "I agree with you there, Noodles, but if they catch us off-guard we could lose people. Ain't nobody wants that. The Bond is smarter than everyone else. That's why we're going to last and they're going to fade out."

"What are the mission priorities?" Lawdog asked. "Anything particular we need, besides the party favors?"

"We were able to stock up on medical supplies here," Thomas said. "I'd never thought of a farm supply as being a pharmacy before but they are, just for animals. A horse bandage works on a man just as well. Some of the antibiotics are the same. The topical stuff is the same. So we're good on that. Ammo is always a need. Long-term food. Hygiene items. Spare tires for these trucks."

A man who went by the name Cold Case spoke up. He was one of the two mechanics in the group. "These trucks are getting heavy. Weight is a concern. Anything we can do to keep the weight down would be helpful."

"You got any suggestions?" Thomas asked.

"Keep an eye out for lightweight gear like aluminum jacks and aluminum wrenches. Think twice before dragging back some heavy crap you don't really need. It might also be a good idea to pick up a few more trailers. We can pull weight easier than we can haul weight at this point."

"You heard the man," Thomas said. "Keep an eye out for trailers. A couple of those box trailers like contractors use would be ideal."

"Or those boxed-in car trailers like people use for race cars," Lawdog suggested. "I'll add that to our list."

Mundo grinned. "That would be ideal for bringing back the party favors."

"But you're definitely good with us bringing back party favors?" Lawdog asked. He didn't make any assumptions without a clear okay from the boss.

"You've earned it," Thomas said. "No more than one woman per man. We don't want a riot on our hands."

"And no sheep, Mundo," Lawdog said with a grin.

Mundo grabbed a sack of grass seed from a pallet and heaved it toward Lawdog. He caught it but the weight bowled him over. The other men cracked up. Those two were always jabbing at each other but it wasn't serious.

"Easy now," Thomas said. "You'll need your strength for tomorrow. Save the fight for the enemy."

Lawdog rolled the sack off himself and took his seat. He flipped Mundo the finger.

"Take three trucks and empty them of all but the essentials. I want that done before dinner because the away team needs to leave before dawn. It gets dark early and I want you out of that city before dark."

"What about alcohol, T?" Mundo asked.

"What about it?"

"If we score some, can we bring it back?"

Thomas responded patiently. "We been through this shit, man, and I thought I was clear. You guys can smoke all the weed you want. I don't give a shit. Stay high all day long if you want, but there will *not* be booze in my camp."

"A man can drink without getting drunk," Mundo pointed out.

"Yeah, but how many times does a drinking man say, 'Oh, one more ain't gonna hurt?'" Thomas said. "Then he has another and another until he's falling down drunk. A man don't want to drink alone either, so he's always got buddies drinking with him. Then you got a whole camp full of drunk-ass men who can't defend themselves. I got your back and you damn well better have mine. You can't do that when you're drunk. If booze is that important to you then I got no place for you."

Mundo sighed loudly and looked down, chastised. It was always him bringing the topic up because he missed drinking more than he missed a lot of things about the old world. Some of the guys would bitch about missing a particular food, video games, or going out to the club. Mundo didn't care. Mundo missed drinking and Thomas didn't show any sign of weakening on that point.

Noticing that Mundo had quit arguing but had not clearly conceded, Thomas addressed him. "We good, Mundo? You understand the rules, right?"

"Yeah, T."

"I hope so. What's the penalty for being drunk?" Thomas was aware they all knew the answer but he wanted them to say it. He wanted Mundo to hear it again.

"You get beat to death," several men said.

"By who?" Thomas asked.

"By everyone," Lawdog said. "Cause you put everyone at risk."

Thomas smiled. "That's right. And I don't have to point out that there's some strong dudes in this room. Getting beat to death by this group is gonna hurt. You got me?"

Thomas was pleased to notice that even Mundo was with the program now, nodding along with the rest. "That's good. Now what's for dinner?"

"Shish kebabs, baked potatoes, some grilled vegetables, and macaroni and cheese," Buddha Boy announced.

"Damnation." Thomas grinned. "That sounds pretty damn good. Y'all best be getting to work on that. Sooner you're done, sooner we can all eat."

Thomas's strategy of announcing what they were having for dinner achieved its desired effect. Hunger motivated the men and they rushed into their work. If he'd allowed them to put their chores off until after dinner it would have taken twice as long. He was also amused to find that this tactic worked on himself. Hearing what awaited them when the trucks were emptied, Thomas pitched in to help alongside his men.

4

The strategy they used in Chillicothe was the same they'd used in Columbus, and in several smaller cities along their route. The three trucks ran in a tight convoy, sticking to around thirty-five miles per hour once they entered the populated parts of the city. There were six men per truck; a driver and a navigator rode in the cab with four gunmen riding in the bed. The olive drab covers that normally protected the truck bed had been removed to allow the gunmen to see their surroundings. One of the trucks pulled a livestock trailer, a new addition picked up on the way into the city.

They'd used a different strategy in Toledo and had learned since that experience. There they'd chosen to not alarm people with their presence. They drove along, searching for the supplies they needed. They didn't appear threatening and made an effort not to fire their weapons. That "kinder and gentler" approach nearly got them killed. Organized elements within the city had seen their trucks and correctly assumed they held all kinds of goodies. They could have even assumed that The Bond soldiers were an aid convoy there to help folks. Either way, the locals boxed the convoy in and forced them to fight their way out of the city.

They'd lost two trucks, which they'd since replaced. They lost three men, which they'd not been able to replace. The Bond couldn't just allow anyone off the street to join. You had to have the right credentials -- military with a gang background – and they weren't exactly accepting resumes.

A lesson had been learned there. They understood that it was better to send in a small, agile force of fighters rather than to commit their entire convoy to the mission. Those small groups scavenged, looted, and occasionally brought back women for entertainment. The bulk of the convoy never passed through the center of a city now. They camped on the outskirts and launched raids into towns. When they moved on, they stayed on outer beltways or took side roads to skirt the city.

The other thing they'd learned was that there was no benefit in trying to present a peaceful presence. They found no advantage in trying to appear non-threatening. When they went in, they cranked their menace to full volume. They didn't waste ammo blasting away at windows, cars, and signs. They did expend it on people, though. If you were unfortunate enough to be out walking around when The Bond hit town, you were probably going to die just to set an example.

The one exception to that was if you were an attractive woman worthy of an invitation to the after-party. That invitation came in the form of being zip-tied and hooded until the mission was over. Anyone else wandering the street, tending a garden, scavenging, or otherwise minding their own business was likely to be shot.

The couple of times they'd tried it since Toledo had established this as a sound approach. When they hit town, they were the baddest of the bad. They were not people you wanted to fuck with. They were not travelers whom you should attempt to rob, you shouldn't try to steal their vehicles, nor should you try to engage them in a firefight. The safest thing for you to do was run. If you couldn't run, you had better burrow into a deep hole and stay there until they were gone.

In Chillicothe they hit a suburban shopping center first. While the conditions from town to town varied, they'd found these shopping centers located away from residential districts to be less ravaged than those closer to the population centers. This one didn't have a grocery store or a gas station, the two things that interested most people right now. They pulled their trucks into a central lot and parked them alongside each other. A single man was designated to watch the trucks.

"You know the routine," Lawdog said. "You need us, you fire a shot. Do *not* leave the vehicles for any reason."

"Ahh, why I got to stay here and watch the trucks?" Joker complained.

"Because you ain't good for nothing else," Mundo jabbed.

"Yeah, fuck you," Joker said.

"Knock it off and listen," Lawdog growled. "We'll split up by truck teams. Stay close to your team. My team is going to hit the restaurants and see if we can scrape up any food. Skitzo is running second team. You guys will be hitting the sporting goods store and the department store next to it. Third team is under Droopy. You guys are going to hit the drug store. If that place is cleaned out, head down to the building supply store. We're needing some big waterproof lockers for storing stuff. Can't just keep throwing shit in the truck like it's a closet. We need some organization. Any questions?"

"We supposed to haul all that back here to the trucks?" Droopy asked. "Why can't we just take our truck with us?"

"'Cause that ain't how we doing it," Lawdog said. "We leave the damn trucks here. If you find a bunch of stuff we need, put it out front with a guard on it. We'll go around and collect it when we're all done."

"He's just too sorry to walk down there," Mundo said. "His ass is getting lazy in his old age."

"I'll show you some old age when I kick your ass around this parking lot like a soccer ball," Droopy warned.

Mundo laughed and Droopy lunged at him. Mundo twisted and slipped away.

"Get moving," Lawdog said. "You fools are wasting time."

The teams moved off, the men adjusting gear and clothing that had shifted during the truck ride. Lawdog and Mundo were on the same team. Mundo walked with an energy none of the other men felt, like he was walking a foot off the ground. He always acted like he was jacked up on something but that was simply the way he was wired.

"Better watch fucking with Droopy," Lawdog cautioned. "He'll catch your ass one day and mess you up good. He'll squeeze you like a tube of toothpaste and wring all your insides out."

"Ah, we just playing," Mundo said.

"*You* just playing. Cat like Droopy don't ever play. Shit is always serious for him. He get a hand on you, you might be a dead man."

"He get a hand on me he better hope I'm a dead man."

Lawdog laughed. Mundo would never learn. He was going to pick on the wrong man one day and that was going to be the end of him. Since Joker, back guarding the trucks, was from their team, Lawdog had five men total, compared to the six the rest of the teams had. They were going to hit some of the chain restaurants and see what they could find. They had no expectation they'd find a working freezer full of steaks or a steaming plate of mozzarella sticks but there might be other things they could use.

Most people who hit these places were after canned foods but there were other things a group the size of The Bond could use. They found bags of tortilla and potato chips, condiments, jars of olives, pickles, and sun dried tomatoes. Sometimes there were cases of pasta and noodles stashed away in storerooms. If the restaurant had a bar they often found items that people seeking beer and liquor overlooked, such as those tiny cans of juices used to make mixed drinks. These items weren't staples the men could live off of but they could certainly spice up a bland meal.

They headed for the front door of a chain restaurant of the upscale casual variety. The men had been on guard initially but the place was dead. They hadn't seen a soul or heard anything. The parking lot was relatively clear of trash, and there weren't many broken windows. It was like an early Sunday morning in the old world, the quiet hours before the stores opened and the customers flooded in.

"You ever eat at one of these joints?" Mundo asked.

"On military pay?" Lawdog snorted. "You gotta be kidding."

"No shit," Mundo said. He reached the door first and extended his hand. He tugged on the handle of the front door, not surprised to find it locked. Mundo missed the one thing, the subtle rattle that caught Lawdog's attention.

Lawdog flattened his face against the glass door and looked down. He took a hard step back, then shoved Mundo to the side, out of the way of the door. He swung toward his men, waving an arm at them. "Take cover," he hissed.

He-Man, Wolfie, and Jawbone got the message and flattened themselves against the wide stone columns that supported the awning along the sidewalk.

"What is it?" Mundo demanded.

Lawdog gave him a shitty expression and gestured with his hand for Mundo to drop the volume.

"What is it?" Mundo repeated at a slightly lower volume.

"The door is chained from the inside. There could be people in there."

"Wolfie, He-Man—you guys circle around. Find the back door and keep an eye on it. I'm going to see if I can flush 'em out," Mundo said.

The pair took off running, the sound of their boots echoing off the hard planes of the buildings.

"So you apparently got a plan?" Lawdog asked.

"I do," Mundo replied.

"And you are confident enough of this plan that you don't feel a need to at least run it by me?"

"I got this."

Lawdog glanced at him doubtfully. "There's no 'I' in team."

The snide comment made Mundo snicker.

"*In position, Mundo,*" came a voice from the radio.

"What's your plan?" Lawdog asked.

"Watch and learn, Junior," Mundo replied. "Watch and learn." Mundo let his rifle dangle from the sling and took a few steps to where a heavy steel garbage can sat. He rocked it to the side, got a hand under it, and picked it up over his head, rushed toward the storefront, and launched the can through the plate glass window with a grunt of effort.

Lawdog shielded his face with a forearm but it was unnecessary. The tempered glass shattered into a rain of tiny glass pellets and the garbage can rolled noisily across the restaurant's tile floor.

Mundo grinned at his buddy. "Impressed?"

Lawdog rolled his eyes. "You call that a plan? Any idiot could have done that."

Mundo tapped his forehead. "Strategy, my man. Notice all that noise it made?"

"Yeah, how could I miss it?"

There was a gunshot, then another, from the back of the restaurant. It had to be their guys. They could hear it both through the broken out window and echoing off the various buildings in the complex.

Droopy's deep voice came across the radio. "*You all good?*" His team must have heard the shots.

Mundo raised his radio with a grin. "I think we're good, Droopy. Wolfie? He-Man? You guys good?"

"*We good,*" He-Man replied. "*We've detained three females. One male down. They came out the back door of the restaurant.*"

"*Damn, you ahead of us. We ain't found nobody yet. Droopy out.*"

Mundo nodded at Lawdog. "You hear that! Told you I had a plan. Drove those assholes out the back door and into our trap. Flushed them right out."

"Whatever," Lawdog said. He stepped through the window, the shards of glass grinding beneath his boots.

Mundo followed behind him. Jawbone brought up the rear, facing backward and watching for any signs of movement. Lawdog headed straight for the back door. They could hear shouted commands and sobbing in the distance.

"Jawbone, make sure the rest of this place is clear," Mundo said. "Check everywhere." He jogged toward the back door, trying to catch up with Lawdog, while Jawbone raised his rifle and started a methodical search of the interior of the dim restaurant.

Mundo reached the back door, paused, then eased out with his rifle high. Three young women were on the ground, sobbing and hugging each other. A dead man of about the same age lay sprawled in the grass, the back of his white shirt saturated with blood. His eyes were open and his scalp bleeding, the second round apparently having caught him in the head.

"Y'all did good," Lawdog said to the men who'd captured the prisoners.

One of the women, more angry and in control than the other two, lit into Wolfie. "Why the *fuck* did you have to do that? We don't have guns. We weren't going to hurt anyone. We were trying to get away!"

"If we wanted to let you get away, we would have," Mundo said. "We needed to speak to you a moment."

"Really?" the woman challenged. "About *what*?"

"You'll find out soon enough," Lawdog said. "Now shut the hell up. We ain't here to answer your questions."

The woman launched into a string of obscenities and insults. She cursed Lawdog and his companions back to their earliest ancestors.

"Get me some fucking lightbulbs," Mundo said, gesturing at He-Man.

Apparently, knowing just what kind of bulbs Mundo wanted, He-Man slipped in the back door and went inside the restaurant.

Mundo raised his radio. "Jawbone? I sent He-Man in there after something. Please don't shoot him."

"*Roger that*," Jawbone replied.

He-Man jogged back out the door in a few minutes with two packs of regular incandescent bulbs in his hand. The entire time he'd been gone, the woman continued her diatribe, vacillating between a demand for answers and berating the men. Mundo and Lawdog let her go on, giving each other a weary glance. They'd been down this road before. They'd been called a lot of things in a lot of different languages and they didn't care anymore. It didn't bother them in the least.

Mundo took the bulbs and handed his rifle off to Lawdog. He approached the vocal woman and stood in front of her until she quit yelling, her curiosity getting the best of her.

"What?" she hissed.

Mundo lunged at her, shoving her over backward on the ground. Despite her best efforts to prevent it, he was soon sitting on her chest, pinning her to the ground. She heaved and tossed but couldn't get him off of her.

"Get! Off!" she demanded.

Mundo removed a delicate glass bulb from the package. He held it up over his head and mugged to his men. "I just had an idea."

They laughed.

"Dumbass," Lawdog chuckled.

Mundo gave the woman a cold stare. "Open up."

"What?" she growled. "What are you going to do?"

Mundo pressed the bulb against her lips. She tried to twist her face away but he laid a gloved hand on her forehead and held her steady. "You better open the fuck up."

Her anger was replaced by fear as he pushed the bulb harder. She felt the smooth surface grind against her teeth "It's gonna break," she hissed.

"Damn right it is. You better open up."

She relented, seeing that she had no choice here, that the bulb was ready to shatter under the pressure of his insistent pushing. If it did break, her mouth would be sliced to shreds, her lips and gums mangled forever. Her eyes filled with tears and she opened her mouth wide. Mundo shoved the bulb inside. She gagged and choked, her neck spasming as she fought to breathe around it.

"Breathe through your nose," he told her. "Don't try to spit it out. We gonna leave it right there."

Mundo yanked a roll of duct tape from a dump pouch on the back of his web gear. He made two passes around the woman's head, taping the bulb firmly inside her mouth. He enjoyed the terror in her eyes. There was not a flicker of compassion, of sympathy, anywhere within the soulless shell of his body. He was an animal with his prey pinned beneath him.

"I'm going to cuff you," he warned. Her terrified eyes were glued to his. He had her full attention. "You better not try nothing. That bulb is pressing down on your tongue so you're not going to be able to scream or yell, but you better not try to get away either. If you show any signs of not sticking to the program, you know what happens?"

Petrified now, she had no reaction.

"That's a question. I asked you if you know what happens?" he repeated.

She shook her head.

In a lightning fast gesture, Mundo punched his fist into the cupped palm of the other hand. The sudden, violent gesture startled all three women. The two who were not gagged cried out in fear, uncertain of what was about to take place. Mundo leaned close to the woman beneath him. He hovered over her face with a predatory indifference. He blew his vile breath in her face. He was a cat with a mouse, a chicken with a bug. She was an object devoid of humanity and personhood to him.

"You do anything to piss me off," he warned, "and I'll punch you right in the face. What you think that's going to do to that bulb? What you think that bulb gonna do to your face? I'll tell you what because I've seen it before. It's gonna shatter into several large chunks of razor-sharp glass. It's going to slice up your tongue and those pretty pink cheeks. Your mouth is going to fill with blood and, I ain't gonna lie, you're probably going to swallow some of that glass. The rest you can probably figure out. They ain't no surgery to fix shit like that anymore. You're probably going to die a slow and miserable death."

"Isn't that what's going to happen anyway?" one of the other women asked. "What difference does it make?"

Mundo turned to the speaker but it was Lawdog who answered her. "No. You cooperate and you might live to see another day. We'll decide when we're done."

"Done with what?" the other woman asked.

Lawdog shrugged. "With *whatever*."

"Whatever?" the same woman repeated.

"Whatever the fuck we want," Mundo said loudly.

He got to his feet and flipped the startled woman over onto her stomach. He wrestled her hands behind her and used flexcuffs to secure her. She started to offer mute protest, to resist, but her friends warned her to settle down, reminding her of the punishment. When Mundo was done, he stood up and regarded the other two women.

"Glad to see y'all got a little common sense. Now, am I going to have to fight you two the same way or y'all gonna cooperate?"

The women looked at each other, began sobbing anew, and conceded. Mundo held two bulbs over his head and grinned maniacally. "Boys, I got two ideas now!"

The men chuckled, not at the joke because they'd heard it before, but at Mundo's enthusiasm. The dude needed Ritalin or something. He never wound down. He was always running full volume.

Mundo extended the bulbs before him, one in each hand. He nodded at the women, encouraging them, and they each reached toward him. He placed a bulb in each of their outstretched hands, then watched as the women opened their mouths, slipping the bulbs inside. Their reactions were the same as the first ladies. They choked and gagged as their bodies fought to accept the condition.

Mundo grinned with satisfaction and got out his tape. "I thank you ladies for your cooperation."

5

They were out of Chillicothe by dark, just as they'd been directed, their loud green trucks pulling two new enclosed trailers. One was packed full of salvage and the other, a live-stock trailer, was packed with human cargo. With the shorter days of winter it was full dark by the time they rolled up to the farm supply.

"Three little pigs knocking at your door," Mundo said into his radio as they neared the fenced lot.

"*Acknowledged,*" Thomas replied. "*Welcome home.*"

One of the sentry team rolled the chain-link gate open and the three trucks eased through, the trailers clattering behind them. They drove around back and parked. As soon as Lawdog popped open the door of his truck they were hit with the mouth-watering aroma of grilling meat.

"Daaaammmmmmnnnnn!" Mundo sang. "Didn't know how hungry I was until I smelled that."

Hearing the comment, Buddha Boy grinned. "Oh, I might have outdone myself tonight. I set up a smoker this morning and we've got ribs, pulled pork, and brisket. We've got potatoes, canned corn, macaroni and cheese, and even dessert."

"Dessert?" Droopy echoed, dropping out of the bed of one of the trucks. "What kind of dessert?" He was a big man, fond of his food.

Buddha Boy gestured at an array of Dutch ovens sitting on a row of cinderblocks. "I've got a dump cake, brownies, and a blackberry cobbler."

"I'd kill a man for a brownie," Droopy muttered.

"Ain't necessary," Thomas said, emerging out of the dark. "You get one with no strings attached."

"Well, if it buys me any points, I did kill a few men today." Droopy grinned.

Thomas smiled. "Cost of doing business."

"Not this time. I just wanted to see if I could hit them. They was a long way off but by God, I did it."

Thomas patted him on the shoulder. "Then we'll consider it public relations. Part of the fear campaign. Shit like that makes people want to hide instead of fight back. They get afraid to show themselves on the street."

"When we eating?" Droopy asked, unable to peel his eyes off the heaping, foil-covered bounty piled atop a stainless steel grate.

"We was just waiting on you," Buddha Boy said. "We can eat anytime."

"That all you think about, Droopy?" Mundo asked, patting Droopy on the belly.

Droopy lashed out at Mundo, trying to trap his arm, but the whip-thin Mundo was too fast. "Fat and sluggish," Mundo said. "Too slow."

"I ain't fat. That's my body armor," Droopy said. "You don't cut that shit out, I'm going to hurt you."

"Save it for outsiders," Thomas said, the venom in his voice making the men fall silent. His word was law and the men knew not to challenge it. They could pose questions as part of strategizing and mission planning but they had better do it in a manner that was not accusing or confrontational. If Thomas grew offended, someone died an ugly, screaming death. "Now tell me how the mission went."

The men deferred to Lawdog.

"Good run, T. Got those two trailers like we talked about. Found lots of shit we needed but no big haul of any one thing. Scored some flour and sugar, a few canned things, and some medical supplies. Found some good sleeping bags for anyone who needs to trade up and some expensive long underwear. Cases of it."

"Any party favors?" Thomas asked.

Lawdog gestured at the livestock trailer. "Found seven women over a few different stops. Killed their men and took their shit. What's not to like about that? Check them out."

Thomas approached the trailer and pulled a light from his pocket. He was wearing a headlamp already but the flashlight had a more powerful directional beam. He played the light between the slats of the trailer and saw terrified faces twisting away from the blinding light.

"That's a good haul." In truth, Thomas cared nothing about the women. He was old school leadership and would have preferred the men be more disciplined about their vices. He'd managed to keep them from drinking by allowing them to get high whenever they wanted, but he expected there'd be major dissent if he tried to take women off the menu. Experience had shown him that this was the only thing that kept the men from fighting between themselves.

"You want us to untie them?" Droopy asked. "Take those bulbs out of their mouths?"

Thomas smiled at Mundo. "That's your handiwork, isn't it? You bulb these women?"

Mundo nodded.

Thomas shook his head. "Nah, let's leave them like that. I don't want them moaning and carrying on while I'm trying to eat."

6

For nearly two weeks The Bond picked at the outskirts of Chillicothe like a pack of hyenas terrorizing gazelles. They killed for entertainment and kidnapped for sport. They plundered and looted, bringing everything they found back to the farm supply. It was like living on a remote outpost in a war zone, with daily patrols and relaxation behind fences at night. Experience told them that staying outside the town would prevent them from being pursued by the residents of Chillicothe. No one would venture out this far to find them. Despite the toll that The Bond was taking on the locals, they'd had surprisingly little trouble with them, other than taking some fire when raiding farms for fuel. They fully understood there would be a point where they would have to move on. People could only take so much. Word would spread and people would organize against them. They wanted to be gone by the time it reached that point.

They ate well during their stay, killing what livestock they found and removing prime cuts with no worry about what they wasted. Over those two weeks they left thousands of pounds of unwanted beef and pork for crows, coyotes, and rats. In the farm supply they found a scoped .22 rifle and a large supply of ammunition. It became a sport for the men to pick away at the carrion-eaters who appeared at the fragrant garbage pile downwind of camp. It was there they disposed of the livestock carcasses and the unfortunate people who died as their guests.

They kept the trucks topped off with fuel as they dug deeper into the bulk fuel receipts. With each new source of fuel, a rural family was decimated, their home looted and burned. On one of their raids, they brought back a flat screen television and a DVD player. They started having a movie each night, complete with popcorn topped with powdered butter. They ran the TV off the quiet little Honda generator and everyone, with the exception of those on duty, piled into the main room. They watched whatever stupid movies they scraped up in their looting runs, cheering, cursing, and making fun of the selections.

They put a basketball goal in the back and that provided some distraction until the games got too heated and Thomas shut it down. As usual, it was the loudmouthed Mundo instigating it. He was a good player who couldn't restrain the trash-talking. If he was playing, the games always ended in a fight.

"You gonna get your ass killed one day," Lawdog warned him. "You don't know when to stop. Somebody is gonna blow your damn head off cause that mouth won't quit flapping."

"They can bring it if they think they're bad enough," Mundo said. "I'm invincible."

"You ain't bulletproof, dumbass. You gonna get shot full of holes." Lawdog knew he couldn't rein it in, though. Mundo couldn't stop being an asshole any more than he could stop his heart from beating. "Don't say I didn't warn you."

"Duly noted."

Lawdog understood that Thomas had a hard time keeping the men in check. These were all men who had been used to getting what they wanted on the street. Military life had instilled discipline in them to the point that they learned patience. They learned how to gradually work toward a goal instead of requiring immediate gratification, which was the way of the street. They were all cut from the same mold, basically. Even Thomas. He had vision, though, and that was what kept these men together.

Later that day, Thomas came searching for Lawdog.

"I figure we're going to need to move in the next day or two. The men are getting bored and restless. If life gets too easy they get soft and start fighting among each other. Can't have that."

"Where we headed?" Lawdog asked.

"South."

"Any destination in mind?"

"I'm thinking Portsmouth, Kentucky. Then Ashland after that," Thomas replied.

"What about long-term? Any idea where we're headed?"

Thomas shook his head. "I don't see us settling down, wearing bibbed overalls, and turning into farmers if that's what you mean. I don't think people like us could survive like that. We'd eventually pick a town clean. We'll do best staying on the move. Besides, in one place, we'd get bored. The men would fight all the time and probably kill each other. I see it now when we sit still too long. It's only those parties once a week that keep the men grounded, allowing them to purge that fire inside them."

The thing left unsaid was that those parties always resulted in dead girls. If someone had to die, though, better it be one of them than a soldier they couldn't replace.

"So we sticking to Route 23?" Lawdog asked.

"It's treated us well. I don't have any destination in mind beyond that but it's already cold. We should head south to warmer country. I like a challenge but that don't mean we have to suffer in this damn cold like a bunch of Eskimos. I'm sure there's good pickings down there. We could find another old highway like Route 11 or Route 1 and keep moving along it." Sensing that this might not have been the answer Lawdog was seeking, Thomas continued. "You not cool with the moving around? You don't like my plan?"

Lawdog knew better than to give any indication he wasn't with the program. "Nah, T, I'm good. Just thinking ahead is all. Trying to pull my weight as your lieutenant."

He was telling the truth. He didn't care where they went or even if they went south to take advantage of the warmer climate. He'd grown up hard. He'd seen and done bad stuff, but had surprisingly been able to keep his nose clean enough that his record didn't keep him out of the military. His service there had been a piece of cake compared to life on the street, even when he'd been deployed to Afghanistan. He was as content now as he'd ever been. The Bond was the best of both worlds. He had the brotherhood of military service and the lawlessness of gang life. What wasn't to love about that?

7

The following morning they began tearing down their camp. It would take all day and they probably wouldn't pull out until the following morning. They might have been there one week or they might have been there two. No one counted. No one cared. They would leave with only the essentials, abandoning any useless crap they'd accumulated during their stay. The DVD collection, the ridiculously large television, the basketball goal, and even the basketball itself would be left behind. All of it could be replaced, looted or stolen anew, in the next town. Wasn't that the fun of it anyway? Wasn't that the adventure of the life they'd chosen, living like pirates sailing across the landscape of a battered America in their vintage trucks, taking what they wanted and killing anyone who dared stand in their way?

Since their first stop beyond the military base they originated from, Thomas had established a tradition that one man would be chosen to leave the signature of The Bond when the occasion warranted. They weren't like the Freemasons or other entities who had established signs that would be recognized by anyone who saw it. Their mark was the result of improvisation, something new each time, with the only requirement being that it made clear the name of their organization. Somewhere within what they left behind, the name "The Bond" had to be specifically spelled out. The purpose was to acquaint people with the name. To give them someone to fear. They did it everywhere they took a notion. Every place they felt fear needed to be reinforced. Sometimes it marked a particularly grisly deed, the site of something nasty that The Bond wanted credit for.

Thomas delegated the assignment of leaving a signature at the farm supply to Mundo. Thomas appreciated that Mundo never took a half-assed approach to the task no matter how many times it was presented to him. He could always be counted on for something dramatic, for disturbed visual statements that grabbed your attention almost immediately. He was a little twisted, a little crazy, and he took the job seriously. Despite his shortcomings, Mundo's enthusiasm endeared him to Thomas.

"I'll try to make a good impression, T," he assured Thomas. Mundo had once heard that it was important to make a good impression, though he couldn't recall where. It certainly hadn't been from his dad, his family, or his own circle of friends. None of them ever gave a shit about making a good impression. Maybe it was something he'd heard on television.

Acting with that single-minded determination, Mundo rooted around in one of the trucks and soon appeared before Thomas, Lawdog, and the rest of the gang in a hazmat suit. To an outsider the suit may have seemed something frivolous to retain on the trucks. It wasn't, though. Sometimes they'd chosen to enter buildings rank with the smell of the dead when they were searching for a particular item. The suits made that a little easier to tolerate.

"What the fuck, dude?" Lawdog asked. "What kinda shit are you planning?"

Mundo stood there intentionally breathing like Darth Vader, playing it up for his audience. "I need a volunteer," came a muffled voice from the suit. It was only then that the men noticed he had another suit in his hands.

Lawdog chuckled. "Good luck with that."

"Who's going to help me? I got something good in mind and I can't do it alone. Somebody gotta man up around here."

The men who had been standing around waiting to see what Mundo had in mind suddenly found other things to do, wandering off and appearing busy. No one wanted a part of this. They'd seen what came out of his head before and it wasn't pretty.

"Hey, wait," Mundo called. "Don't y'all be going nowhere."

The men didn't slow, suddenly busying themselves with truck maintenance or loading boxes.

Thomas was enjoying the men's discomfort. "Wait a minute now," he said. "This is kind of like Cinderella. We gotta figure out whose foot fits the glass slipper. In this case, the glass slipper is a hazmat suit. What size suit is that?"

Mundo searched for a label and read it. "Large."

"Ain't gonna fit my big ass then," Droopy said with undisguised relief. "I'm a 2XL. Another one of y'all gonna have to help this freak with his little project."

"He-Man!" Thomas yelled. "Get your ass over here and help this soldier out."

He-Man groaned, but this wasn't the kind of assignment he could gracefully turn down. He'd been called out by name. It was supposed to be an honor to play a role in leaving the mark, no matter how it was done. Besides, Thomas didn't make *suggestions*. Calling He-Man on deck was basically as good as an order. Rejecting the order meant rejecting The Bond, and it was seen as a personal insult by Thomas. It meant someone was going to die. That in mind, He-Man dejectedly pulled on the suit and gestured at Mundo that it was his show.

"Okay, you got me, man. Let's get on with this and get it over with," He-Man said from behind the shield.

Mundo wandered off, He-Man dragging along behind him. The men could hear Mundo laughing behind his mask and it made them laugh too. It was a nervous laughter, all of them glad that they were not in He-Man's shoes. If Mundo was that excited, there was some weirdness about to go down.

That weirdness took them a little over two hours, during which time the rest of the men carried on with their tasks. It was nearly sundown when Mundo announced to the group that they were done. He waited near the front gate while the men assembled there. He was like a tour guide or a proud child ready to show his mother what he'd been up to.

He-Man stood off to the side, a little green around the gills. While he was normally pretty boisterous and loud, at the moment he looked like he wanted to wander off and purge his stomach into the bushes. His appearance stirred no sympathy among the men. They took jabs at him for his weakness, which was an intolerable state among these hard men.

The sun was setting over the flat landscape of Ohio, laying an orange pallor over the dying fall grass. The air was cold and crisp. It would have been a beautiful evening for men prone to noticing such things. This group would enjoy a last fire in the farm supply that night, eating a simple dinner that would require no elaborate cooking and no cleanup. They had to be up early.

When everyone was present, Mundo marched them to the site of his handiwork, the public roadway just north of the farm supply. The men stared in silence at Mundo and He-Man's handiwork.

"It says, 'The Bond'," Mundo said. "You see it, don't you?" He was concerned for a moment that all his work might be for nothing, that his message was indecipherable.

"I see it," Thomas said. "You a sick bastard, man. One sick puppy."

"Got dropped on his head when he was a baby," Jawbone suggested.

Mundo cackled. "You think it will make a good impression?"

"It'll give them people nightmares," Droopy stated. "That shit might even give *me* nightmares."

The men continued to study the scene before them in silence, trying to figure it all out.

"How did you get them bodies to bend that way?" Thomas asked. "It ain't natural."

"It wasn't easy," Mundo said. "Some of them were all stiff and shit. We had to snap them loose and bend them different ways. That's when He-Man lost his shit. The sound of breaking bones didn't sit well with him."

"Going to have to change that name if you don't toughen up," Jawbone called to He-Man. "He-Man supposed to be tough."

Normally a comment like that would have had He-Man charging Jawbone, ready to fight, but in a testament to his state He-Man simply turned away from the scene in disgust. He'd seen all of it he wanted to see.

"What's the matter, He-Man?" Thomas chided. "You don't approve of this message?"

"Ain't that," He-Man said. "That sound, man. Them bones snapping. Joints coming out of place like you was tearing a leg off a turkey. Shit was nasty. Too much for my stomach."

In the scene before them, Mundo and his reluctant partner He-Man had used the bodies of the dead to spell out "The Bond" in the roadway in front of the farm supply. They used the people they'd shot when they took the farm supply as well as the bodies of women who died at their hands after they moved in. The straight letters had been no issue but the letters containing curves had required the significant manipulations that He-Man had described. That was perhaps the most disturbing aspect of it – spines bent counter to their natural range of movement, arms disjointed and twisted, legs splayed at disturbing angles.

Thomas started clapping and out of a sense of obligation the other men jumped in to join him. "Bravo!" As his clapping faded away like the hooves of a departing horse, he headed back toward the camp. They'd had a long day and these men had earned their dinner.

8

When Conor Maguire approached the roadblock he kept both hands in plain sight, resting them on the saddle horn and not making any sudden movements. The two sentries did not raise their guns at him, perhaps afraid he'd take offense and kill them for the insult. They knew this Irishman. Conor noted the way their grips tightened on their weapons and the manner in which they subtly shifted their bodies to better fighting stances. He imagined their thumbs stretching toward the safety levers of their respective rifles, ready to flip them off and open fire if he behaved in a less than civil manner.

The men's wariness came from recognizing this rider. He wasn't intimidating in his size. He wasn't musclebound or particularly tall. He wasn't scarred and snarling like some bad guy from the movies. He wasn't even wearing black, just some dirty European camouflage. The sentries were wary of him because they'd seen him in action. He was skilled in all manner of weapons, both common and unfamiliar. He was devious and possessed of an evil cunning. His tactics were brutal and delivered with no compunction for how many of the enemy he might kill. After all, they were the enemy and their lives were of no consequence to him.

The men were glad he was alone. For all the fear and unease he instilled in them, they found him to be significantly less intimidating than his daughter. She was dangerous and half-crazy, depending on who you believed. She was ready to kill enemy and friend alike if she took offense at something you did. No one wanted to be around her. No one knew what to do with that.

Conor brought his horse to a stop a safe speaking distance from the men. "Wayne sent for me," he announced, the remnants of his Irish childhood present in the lilt of his voice. Despite the years it lingered there like the taste of liquor in a glass of melted ice.

Both men gave slow nods of acknowledgement, not taking their eyes from Conor. One of them gestured that he should ride on by. So much for friendly conversation between strangers. Conor tipped his cap, nudged his horse, and got moving. About twenty feet beyond the sentries, he craned his neck back around to peer at the two men. He needed to satisfy his curiosity. Just as expected, he found them watching him, afraid to take their eyes off him. Afraid to turn their backs to him.

Conor smiled. "Why is everyone so scared of the little ole Mad Mick?" he wondered aloud.

He understood why they were afraid, though. It was for the same damn reason that everyone he'd ever fought with carried a sliver of fear at being in his presence. It was because they knew he had no limits. If all was fair in love and war, he took it to a new level. The things he did to those who crossed him were the stuff of legend.

Around the next bend in the road the land opened up. For the past eight miles he'd followed a narrow river valley. Mountains rose on both sides, their slopes so steep that some trees jutted straight out of the mountain, growing horizontally rather than upward. The road was set into the base of one slope while the broad churning river spanned the bottomland between the mountains. There was room for nothing else in the tight space, other than the occasional roadside turnout where men stopped to fish, relieve themselves, or toss out their empties.

Conor didn't mind the terrain but some found it to be claustrophobic. Being in these Appalachian valleys, having to stare up to see the sun, was like standing in the bottom of a hole. Strangers sometimes found it difficult to breathe here. Others couldn't tolerate that valley-dwellers might only get two or three hours of direct sunlight a day.

Conor's destination was a wide spot where the mountains temporarily splayed apart like the legs of a staggering and bandy-legged drunk. To the right of the road was the fire hall where Wayne and the rest of his Michigan band were living. Originally just passing through on their way to a more hospitable climate, Wayne had decided to winter over with his people after they hit hard times. They were tired and the weather was turning on them. Stopping early allowed them to lay in supplies and prepare the firehouse to be a winter home. It wasn't comfortable and there was no privacy but they were better off than some.

Since Conor last visited the firehouse they'd moved more vehicles around the perimeter of the parking lot. The cars served both as fencing and as cover for shooting positions. A couple of charred and blackened sections of asphalt reminded Conor that he and Wayne had gotten off to a difficult start. There had been some explosions, the odd bomb or two. That happened around Conor sometimes. Besides, what relationship didn't benefit from a few fireworks at the beginning?

Since that time, Conor and Wayne had come to an understanding. They'd become allies. Both wanted the same thing—to protect their people and maintain peace within their larger community. Wayne and some of his men had helped in the battle against Bryan, the man responsible for Barb's kidnapping. They'd proven themselves to be capable and reliable.

There were additional sentries posted around the barricade of vehicles and Conor spotted Wayne among them. The men were using the radios they found among the gear at the fire hall so the first sentries had probably alerted him that the crazy Irishman was on his way. There were openings in the car barrier for taking the horses into the inner sanctum, little mazes too small for a vehicle to enter, but

Conor chose to dismount. He tied his horse off to the shattered side mirror of a black Jeep Cherokee with rusty wheels and flat tires.

Wayne wove his way through the maze of cars and extended his hand to Conor. "Good to see you, my friend."

"Good to see you upright and on this side of the dirt. I heard you were looking for me."

Wayne nodded. "I saw Johnny Jacks' son and daughter-in-law the other day. I asked them to relay that message if they saw you."

"They did. We've dropped in on them every couple of days to make sure they're recovering from their injuries. They had a rough go of it."

"They may recover from the physical injuries but the mental effects may take a while longer. You don't experience a home invasion, take a beating like that, and not be changed by it."

"They also lost someone dear to them," Conor said. "I hate to be practical about it but if the whole mess makes them a little meaner and a little quicker on the trigger, it'll improve their odds of survival."

"That's one way of looking at it."

"So what did you need of me? Johnny and his folks didn't know. Just said to catch up with you at my first opportunity. We best get on with it. I can't be lollygagging about the countryside when I've got knitting and shit to attend to."

Wayne smiled at that, the thought of the most dangerous man he'd ever met sitting around a circle of old ladies knitting. Conor had this way of talking that made it hard to tell when he was joking and when he was being sincere. It made him hard to read. One thing was certain, though. If he ever saw Conor coming at him with a pair of knitting needles he was running like hell because it meant someone was about to die a silent and painful death.

"I've got a little mystery on my hands," Wayne said, "and I need some backup from someone who knows the country and knows how to handle himself."

"Oh, I love a good mystery," Conor said, intrigued. "Especially if it involves aliens."

Wayne considered this. "There could be aliens, but I don't think so. Pastor White's folks found a body in the river by their church. It was snagged on a tree and had a couple of bullet holes in it."

"Ah, but uncovering strange bodies is nothing new," Conor said dismissively. "In times like these, people settle old scores or they shoot people while trying to rob them. They dispose of the bodies without telling a soul. It could even be a body left over from our recent battle. Could have been snagged upstream and just broke loose."

"Not with the turtles in that river. If my people leave a stringer of fish in there overnight, we have nothing but fish heads by morning. Turtles would hit a human body like a buffet and leave nothing but a skeleton."

"Sounds like you have a firm grasp on the facts," Conor said with a grin, "being that you're an amateur medical examiner and all."

Wayne chuckled. "No. The pastor said his folks know the man. They said he was by their camp a few days earlier asking after his mother."

"Okay, that gives us a little more to go on. Guy shows up looking for his mother and two days later he turns up in the river poked full of holes. How did this get dumped in your lap?"

"Some of the pastor's folks asked me about it. They're concerned there may be a murderer in their community."

"Hell, I can speak to that," Conor said. "It's likely there're dozens of murderers in their community. It's what people do when the rules go by the wayside and Johnny Law ain't on the job. Did the pastor himself speak to you about this?"

"No. I'm not sure he can speak at all after Barb broke his jaw. Her actions made my presence in this neighborhood a little difficult, as you might imagine. The pastor sees me as being aligned with that crazy Irishman and his daughter. His feelings are still a little hurt."

"I imagine so. He got his ass handed to him by a little girl. That doesn't sit well with some people."

"Yeah, well she's not a little girl anymore, Conor, and the only reason I'm considering getting involved here is because I need to mend some fences. This might allow you to mend some fences too.

People respect the pastor in this community. We need to acknowledge that."

Conor nodded. "I get that and you're right, but a wise man learns who he's messing with before he runs his mouth. She warned him."

Wayne held a hand up. "I'm not here to argue that point. I know why she did what she did. But back to this dead body, the pastor's people are scared because they thought they knew their community. They're genuinely concerned that there might be a kidnapper out there who might kill to keep his secret. If it buys me some brownie points with the locals, I'm at least willing to give this matter a little of my time."

"Then I'm with you," Conor said. "Winning local hearts and minds is a worthwhile effort. Do you have anything to go on?"

"The pastor's people said the dead man was from this valley but hadn't lived here in years. His mother did, and he walked several days from a neighboring town to check on her but the house was empty. There were indications that people had been in there recently so it made him think she wasn't dead. They all say she was a hard country woman who grew up without power and would have been fine in these conditions. She had a woodstove, canning, and a few chickens."

"And the pastor's people had no idea of her whereabouts?"

"No one recalled seeing her since the early days of the collapse. When they passed that information to the son, he said he had a few folks he wanted to talk with before he gave up and went home. The next thing they knew, he showed up dead in the river."

"And they suckered you into helping?"

Wayne smiled. "They asked and it'll be a long winter with no friends close by. I'd rather have Pastor White's folks waving at me than shooting at me."

"When do you want to start?" Conor asked.

"No time like the present."

9

Two miles up from the firehouse, Conor and Wayne approached a decrepit mobile home rising from a pile of wrecked vehicles, broken appliances, old lawnmowers, and assorted other junk. Wood smoke rolled from a stovepipe jutting through a wall, pointing crookedly toward the gray sky like a beckoning finger. Wayne called out and a scrawny young man poked his head out the door. He waved, told them he'd be right with them, and ducked back inside. When he reappeared a moment later he was wearing a brown canvas work coat with a Red Man Chewing Tobacco toboggan pulled down to his bushy eyebrows.

"That's Bernard," Wayne said as the boy walked toward them. "His family said he'd guide us to the old lady's house."

Conor studied the young man. Beneath the open zipper of his coat he wore jeans with a camouflage shirt tucked neatly into them. "He appears to be about twelve years old."

"He's twenty-two, according to his parents. I asked because I didn't want to be responsible for someone's kid."

Conor cast an eye to the steep mountains to either side of them. "They ripen late in here. Grow tall and stringy like weeds. I guess they don't get enough light."

Wayne smirked. "Apparently, the girls get plenty of light. Most are married and have several kids by his age."

"Whereabouts am I riding?" Bernard asked when he reached them.

"You'll be behind me," Wayne said. He extended a forearm to help the boy swing up but Bernard stepped nimbly onto the rotting trunk of a Pontiac Fierro. From there he flung himself across the back of the horse and awkwardly wiggled into position.

"Where we headed to, boy?" Conor asked.

"I ain't no boy," Bernard snapped, offended by Conor's tone.

"I'd recommend you not get off on the wrong foot with Conor," Wayne said. "If he tells you a chicken can plow the cornfield then you best be getting the harness."

The boy continued to glare at Conor, who gave him a bemused smile. While Bernard must think he was menacing with his hateful squint, Conor found him to be more comical. With the toboggan pulled down to his eyebrows and his large red ears sticking out like jug handles to each side, he almost appeared cartoonish, like a Norman Rockwell caricature of a gangly teenager.

Wayne clucked his horse into motion. "I reckon there are folks who hold a grudge over your daughter breaking the preacher's jaw."

"Reckon they is," Bernard agreed.

"This could be a long ride," Wayne muttered.

Conor emitted a loud, musical laugh. He loved an adventure and he'd be seeing new country today. Let the lad sit there like soured milk. It wouldn't ruin his day.

The clop of their shod horses on the dirty asphalt was the only sound beyond the churning of the dark river. It had rained the night before and the road was damp, carpeted with rotting leaves in yellow, brown, red, and orange. Conor found it beautiful despite the state of things. He'd learned a long time ago to take beauty where he found it because he might not find it again. It was a lesson learned from his mother when he asked why she spent so much time tending flowers that were only going to die when the weather got cold.

After nearly thirty minutes of riding Bernard pointed a bony finger with a grimy nail toward an overgrown driveway. "That there takes you to Fannie Bell's house."

Conor assumed Fannie Bell must be the missing lady, though he'd not heard her name before. It was the kind of antiquated name that no one used anymore. Her tiny frame house hung on the hillside like God had kicked the toe of a boot into the steep slope then shoved the house into the pocket he'd created. It was all hill in the front and hill in the back with no yard to speak of. If a drunk fell over in the yard, he'd roll for a good distance before stopping. Same with snow and ice. One slip and you'd not stop until you hit the main road or collided with a tree. Conor wondered how many guests Fannie Bell had lost in that manner.

They turned up the faint gravel path that led to the house. It was the kind of driveway that belonged to people who didn't own a vehicle. Conor figured it was a bear to negotiate even in ideal conditions due to its narrow footprint and deadly steep shoulder. Kudzu was well on its way to overtaking the house and the dead brown vine enclosed it like a cargo net trying to snatch the house into the depths of the Earth. It was built of Masonite siding covered in three colors of peeling paint. It had a metal roof with rust showing through multiple applications of silver roof coating. There was a chimney of square gray flue block that climbed one wall and jutted through the eave. There was no smoke coming from it on this cold day.

Conor knew that in a little old house like this a rough-spun country woman could survive indefinitely if she had a good supply of preserved food. If the house didn't already have gravity-fed spring water, the cheapest means of running water available, it was likely there was a spring within a short walk of the house. There was plenty of deadfall and scrap wood for Fannie Bell to burn in her stove. She'd have been fine.

Just because you had the tools to keep you alive didn't mean you'd live, though. Besides natural causes there were plenty of unnatural ways to die. The simplest was that somebody meaner than you decided they wanted your stuff and were willing to kill you to get it. You could be the most prepared individual in the world and die of simple bad luck. Skills and supplies were not a magic elixir that guaranteed survival.

They stopped at a porch that spanned the entire front of the house and tied their horses off near a bottle tree. The base of the tree trunk was painted white in an old country tradition of painting yard trees to match the house. The branches had been pruned back in a harsh and unflattering manner, the stubs that remained decorated with an assortment of multicolored glass bottles.

Bottle trees were a southern tradition thought to have come from Africa. Superstitious folks thought that spirits wandering in the night would get trapped inside the bottles and not be able to find their way out. In the morning, the sunlight would destroy them. Conor didn't worry much about spirits. He worried more about things that required a bullet to stop. Many of the ghost stories, songs, and superstitions of these Appalachian people had come over from Ireland. Those same Irish immigrants had contributed to the complex accent of the region.

The lanky Bernard went to the concrete steps and latched onto a handrail made of galvanized water pipe. The rise and run, two critical measurements of making steps, were inconsistent and awkward. It didn't stop Bernard from taking them two at a time and launching himself onto the creaky porch. "Miss Fannie Bell!" he barked, rapping on the door with his knuckles.

He turned around and shrugged at Conor and Wayne. "She's a bit hard of hearing. That's how we always call to her when we come to visit."

When there was no response, Conor climbed the awkward steps and twisted the doorknob. It was unlocked and he shoved it, allowing the door to swing fully open. There was no reaction from inside.

"A gentleman don't go barging into other folks' houses uninvited," Bernard said. "Ain't proper."

Conor paid the lad no attention, drawing his handgun, and powering up the weapon-mounted light. "Stay here."

The boy huffed, offended that the rude foreigner with the evil preacher-beating daughter would dare to give him orders. He started to follow Conor inside despite his instructions but Wayne latched onto the back of his jacket and held him in place.

"When he gives an order, you best listen," Wayne said. "You'll live longer."

While Conor cleared the house, Wayne and Bernard stayed on the porch. Wayne stood at the ready, rifle raised, in case Conor found trouble. Bernard stalked around, fuming.

"You're supposed to be helping us," Wayne said. "You turn into too much of a pain in the ass we'll haul you back home. We'll let the pastor know that you were uncooperative and you can answer to him."

"I'm a helping," Bernard muttered.

"Clear!" Conor called from inside.

Certain the house was empty, the three men began a more detailed search, scanning for anything that might provide a clue to what happened to the lady. Conor went to her bedroom and played the light around. Every step he made was telegraphed by the creaking of the old oak floors, stained dark but worn from traffic.

The bed was neatly made, covered in a homemade antique quilt. Conor went to the closet and opened the door. He found a lot of empty hangers directly in front of the door which made him think that commonly worn items might be missing but that was purely a guess. He went to the chest of drawers. It was an antique as well, with the veneer cracked and peeling. He tugged on a drawer. It took a good bit of effort to get it started, the drawer ill-fitting and uncooperative. Conor peered into several drawers, trying to get an idea if the woman had packed a bag or not.

The nature of Conor's investigation didn't sit well with Bernard, who was ready for any excuse to tear into him. "So you're the type of feller that would paw around in a granny woman's unmentionables?"

Wayne clouted Bernard on the back of the head with his knuckles. It wasn't a punch but a solid "educational" blow and it damn sure hurt.

"Ouch!" Bernard cried, flinching away from Wayne. "What did you do that for?"

"To save your life, you ignoramus. Apparently, you're too dumb to make any effort to do it yourself. You keep running that mouth you'll learn a hard lesson. Didn't you learn anything from the pastor getting clobbered?"

"I. Ain't. Dumb," Bernard said, emphasizing each word.

"Then quit acting like it."

Conor was ignoring both of them. "I don't know what all this looked like before, but I'd guess someone packed a bag or two before they left. I'd be inclined to think Fannie Bell went to stay with someone."

Conor moved back through the living room, playing his light around. In the kitchen, he saw a stack of mail in the center the table. He flipped through the envelopes and stopped at a power bill. "Charles Lampkins," Conor read. "That Fannie Bell's late husband?"

Bernard shook his head. "Her name ain't Lampkins. It's Richardson."

"That name ring a bell?" Wayne asked Bernard.

"No. Plenty of Lampkins around these parts but I don't recollect a Charles Lampkins."

Conor continued around kitchen, hitting the surfaces with his light. There was a porcelain pig cookie jar and a 1950s aluminum canister set was on the countertop. A pristine white coffee maker with a sparkling glass carafe sat plugged into a useless outlet. Conor wanted to know if there was food inside the refrigerator or if it had been emptied out but was hesitant to check. It could be a disgusting spectacle. He took a deep breath and held it in preparation for the onslaught of rotting food smell, then paused when he noticed a picture stuck to the door with an apple-shaped magnet.

It was a woman in her mid to late sixties standing beside a man. It appeared to have been taken in the yard of this very house. They were both neatly dressed in older, unfashionable clothing, like they'd come from church or a funeral. The man had his bulky arm thrown around the woman's shoulders. She appeared to be a little uncomfortable with the gesture, as if she felt the man's display of affection was too forward or perhaps implied an inappropriate familiarity.

"That Fannie Bell?" Conor asked.

Bernard came closer, crouched, and gawked at the snapshot. "That's her."

"Who's the man?"

"That's Shuck."

"Shuck?" Conor asked.

Bernard bobbed his head in a rapid nod, his eyes blinking as he did so. It was as if the action of his eyes were somehow interconnected to the movement of his head like those baby dolls that closed their eyes in sleep when you laid them on their back. "Shuck Lampkins."

Conor raised an eyebrow at Bernard. "You think that perhaps this Shuck Lampkins could be the same person as Charles Lampkins?"

"Could be. Like I said, there's a lot of Lampkins around here. I don't know a Charles, but I know a Shuck and that there is him." Bernard jabbed the photograph for emphasis.

"A picture like this makes me think that Shuck and Miss Fannie Bell may have been soft on each other," Conor said.

"Why, they're old," Bernard said, his face a mixture of dismissal and revulsion. "Surely not."

"That raises two questions," Wayne said. "Is Fannie Bell staying with her boyfriend and does that affect how her son ended up dead? I can't imagine that Miss Fannie Bell would let this Shuck fellow kill her son and then continue to stay with him."

"It could have been an accident," Conor said. "Shuck might have fired on him before they recognized him."

"Shuck is a mean one," Bernard said. "Sometimes he's right with the Lord and attends church regular. Other times Satan holds sway over him and he don't abide the teachings. Times like those he's liable to do about anything."

"Even killing a man?" Wayne asked.

Bernard became serious. "There's those that say he's done it before."

"Bloody hell," Conor muttered.

Bernard stiffened. "I'll thank you not to use foul language in Miss

Fannie Bell's house. She don't appreciate the dirty talk and I don't either."

Wayne groaned. "I give up, Conor. If you want to beat his ass go ahead. The boy is obviously too dumb to take a hint."

"I'll not do it myself," Conor said. "If the boy needs correction I think I'll let Barb do it. The lad already appears to have a soft spot for her."

Bernard huffed. "That little girl of yours might be able to whoop up on an old man like Preacher White but I won't sit and take it. I'm liable to throw her across my knee and show her who's boss."

Conor and Wayne glared at him. Bernard swallowed, wondering if he'd stepped in a hole he was going to have to fight his way out of. Had he taken it too far? Had he finally pushed the Irishman over the edge? The tension grew so thick that Bernard broke into a sweat. Conor and Wayne broke into hysterical laughter.

Bernard was offended. He sputtered, assuring them he was fully capable of the threats he made. The more he said, the more they laughed. "I'll do it," he swore. "I don't care how much of that Chinese karate crap she knows."

Conor patted Bernard on the back. "You better take us to Shuck's house. On the way you can tell us more about how tough you are."

"I bet he's a regular Shuck Norris," Wayne offered.

That cracked Conor up again and he laughed until his side hurt. Bernard stormed out of the house, his jug handle ears bright red with embarrassment.

10

Shuck's house was about eight miles from Fannie Bell's. It took them nearly two hours to get there because Bernard wasn't a hundred percent certain where Shuck lived, though he swore he'd been there before. Conor had shoved the bill addressed to Charles Lampkins into his pocket because it had a street address on it but that proved to be of little help. There was nothing consistent about street numbers and 911 addresses in this part of the Appalachian Mountains.

Use of the word *street* was generous for some of the named roads in the area. They were more like hiking trails or unmaintained National Forest roads. In an area with high unemployment and widespread poverty, maintaining a driveway was a frivolous expense. Most people couldn't afford gravel and asphalt. They couldn't afford fancy contractors with heavy equipment. Sometimes the best they could hope for was to keep the road passable by filling the deepest ruts with rocks and crumbling shale.

When they finally found Shuck's place they faced an altogether different issue than they expected. Shuck didn't have a driveway at all because he lived on the far side of the river. Instead of a driveway there was a wide spot on the public road where he could pull over and park. Groceries had to be carried across an ancient swinging bridge. The original building materials to construct the house must have been dragged through the river or driven across someone else's bridge and hauled overland.

Shuck's house number was hand-painted and nailed to one of the support poles for the swinging bridge. Another hand-painted sign below it said trespassers would be shot and survivors would be shot twice. Conor couldn't help but wonder if Fannie Bell's dead son had failed to properly heed that warning.

Conor had them continue on by the bridge and out of sight of Shuck's house. He didn't want to draw the man's attention by lingering there, just in case he was home and apt to carry out the warnings posted on his signs. He swung his horse around and faced Wayne.

"I want you to find a position where you can keep an eye on the front of the house. I'm going to go to find a way across the river and do a little recon," Conor said. "I'd like to get a handle on this character before we go knocking on the door and asking him questions."

"Why that's a bunch of bull hockey," Bernard spat. "I've knowed Shuck all my life and I ain't a bit scared to go calling on him."

Before Conor could try to talk some sense into Bernard, he shoved himself off Wayne's horse and stomped back up the road toward the swinging bridge.

"Wait!" Conor hissed. "Get back here!"

Bernard waved him off, muttering as he continued up the road.

"Dammit, hold my horse," Conor said, slipping off his own horse and handing the reins over to Wayne.

Conor jogged off after the boy but didn't reach him before he broke cover and started up the wooden ramp to the swinging bridge. Conor called to him several more times but Bernard continued to ignore him. Conor didn't follow the boy out into the open. He wasn't going to blow this whole trip because of Bernard's ignorance. He crouched behind a cluster of dead, leafless briars and watched the house through tiny binoculars. Though the lad clomped loudly across the bridge planks, Conor saw no reaction from the house.

A loud crack split the air and Conor snapped his attention back toward Bernard. A board had broken beneath the boy's feet and he'd dropped like falling through a trap door. He attempted to catch himself, temporarily halting his fall by latching onto the next board in front of him. Then it cracked too, and his body slipped below the level of the bridge, hanging from it as if he were doing a pull-up.

While Conor was searching for some way to salvage the situation, to rescue Bernard, there was another loud crack. Bernard screamed at the top of his lungs as the board he clung to broke in half and he dropped. Conor grimaced as the boy fell. He listened for a splash, the blessing of a soft landing, but none came. There was a wet thud, then nothing. No pleas for help. No sobs of pain.

As stealthily as he could, Conor slithered forward to peer down the riverbank toward the bridge. He spotted Bernard's body broken and splayed awkwardly on a rock the size of a car hood. It was submerged about an inch below the surface of the water. Bernard's misshapen head was covered in blood and dark water lapped at it, creating a trace of red in the river. There was no way he was alive.

"Shit," Conor whispered. He'd been trying to think of a way to rescue the boy but he didn't have rope and it was clear the bridge wasn't an option. Had he run out onto it there might be two broken bodies in the river.

He examined the swinging bridge with his binoculars and found that some of the boards didn't match the others. In fact, all of the broken boards were newer, which made little sense at all until he examined it closer. He noticed that one of the broken boards, still dangling from the support cable, had been sawn mostly in two.

From the top it would have appeared normal but there was barely a hint of wood holding the board intact as it spanned the cables. When Bernard stepped on it, he would have had just enough time to realize his error before it gave way. Who knew how many boards were booby-trapped like that? The bridge definitely wasn't a viable option for getting to the house.

There was a flicker of movement from the direction of the house and Conor swung his binoculars in that direction. A man, presumably Shuck Lampkins, had come out from the house and was standing on the porch with a rifle. It hung at his side, which led Conor to believe that the man hadn't seen him or Wayne. He clomped down the steps in unlaced boots and headed across the yard toward the swinging bridge.

Conor studied Shuck's face for a trace of concern or remorse but found none of that. If anything, Conor detected a grim satisfaction in the man's expression, a smirk of satisfaction that his booby trap had worked as intended. Shuck set his rifle down, leaning it against the aluminum frame of an old lawn chair with no seat in it. He picked up a homemade grappling hook made of welded rebar and cast it toward Bernard's body. It took a few attempts before he snagged the hem of the young man's coat. With some tugging, he dragged the body from the rocks and let the current take it, carrying away the evidence of what had taken place. Having seen this, Conor could easily imagine how the body of Fannie Bell's son might've ended up downriver. Shuck had done this before. He knew just how to get rid of the body.

Shuck must have heard a noise because he spun and glared toward the house. Conor swung the binoculars in that direction and was shocked by what he saw. An elderly woman stood naked on the porch, her hands clutched around her shaking body. The temperature was in the forties, cold enough that a person could die of hypothermia if they went prancing around the yard in their altogether. The chimney told him they had a fire inside. What made her come outside in that state? Had Bernard interrupted a romantic moment?

Conor felt guilty about seeing her this way, so exposed and vulnerable. He was trying to get a good look at her face so he could see if this was Fannie Bell, the same woman he'd seen in the picture on the refrigerator, but he couldn't tell yet. She kept moving, shivering and twisting in the cold. She took a step, almost a stagger, and there was something off about it. Was her foot injured?

He glanced down and immediately spotted it. There was something around her ankle. It was a lightweight chain like one used to tether out a dog. It was fastened tightly around her ankle and he thought he could make out a padlock securing it. Had Conor not seen this chain, he would have assumed the woman had taken shelter here of her own accord. It made sense that a woman of her age might seek safety with other folks. That she would go to a man she appeared to have a relationship with was logical. If not for that chain, Conor would have returned to tell Pastor White's people that Fannie Bell was fine and living safely with Shuck Lampkins in his house on the river.

But this was clearly not consensual.

Fannie Bell appeared to be a prisoner, and an ill-treated one at that. Ugly red streaks of infection started at the chained ankle and rose up her pale and venous legs. Purple blotches and black bruises wrapped her thin body. When she turned and he had a better view her face, Conor found it to be sallow and hopeless. One of her eyes was black and nearly swollen shut. Conor's blood boiled.

Shuck only returned to the porch when he was certain the body had washed out of sight. He stepped right by Fannie Bell and barged through the open door. He must have said something to her, though, because the elderly woman followed quickly behind him, her posture submissive. Broken.

When Shuck was gone, Conor retreated, working his way back to where Wayne waited with the horses. The man was solid. Despite his curiosity at what must have been taking place with Bernard, he stood his ground and remained with the horses.

"Where's that dumbass Bernard?" Wayne asked.

"Dead. He wouldn't listen to me and took off across the bridge. Some of the boards were booby trapped. He fell through into the river."

"And you're sure he's dead?"

Conor nodded. "His head broke open like a melon. Then Shuck tugged him into the river and let the evidence float away."

"It's hard to fault a guy for protecting his place," Wayne said. "We've all done it."

"I've never killed innocent people for approaching my house. I at least attempt to find out who they are first. The one exception is if they're in the company of a known bad guy. Then they're fair game because of their poor life choices."

"What am I going to tell that kid's parents?"

"That ain't all of it. I think Fannie Bell is here. She's being held prisoner by this sadistic prick. She's chained like a dog and beaten all to hell."

Wayne's immediate reaction was disbelief. "Chained? That tiny old lady from the picture?"

Conor nodded. "It was padlocked around her leg and the leg was all infected. There were bruises all over her."

"How could you tell they were all over her?"

"She was naked as the day she was born."

Wayne was silent, processing this information, but his feelings were evident. Any man who would treat anyone, especially an old lady, like that deserved a good dose of the same. Perhaps a fatal over-dose of the same treatment. There would be no mercy.

"I'm assuming the bridge is not the best option to get to him?" Wayne asked.

"Besides the sabotaged bridge, it's way too exposed. He'd see us coming and we'd be sitting ducks. We need to find another way across and work our way back here. I wonder where the nearest bridge is. I can't remember the last one we passed."

"Ahead," Wayne said. "There's a coal mine. I went there once to scavenge some scrap metal for a project at the firehouse. One of the locals told me about it."

"How far?"

"A couple of miles as I recall."

11

Conor was always impressed by the infrastructure of the mining industry. As a welder, fabricator, and machinist he had a love for the big machines. Some mines were small operations, cut into the face of a hill to chase small seams. Those had little permanent infrastructure and would be abandoned when the coal was mined out.

Other operations were more permanent, running continuously for over a hundred years and covering hundreds of square miles underground. They had massive multi-story green buildings on the top side connected by conveyors. Crude steel elevators with large pulleys hoisted men and machines underground. Once down in the mines, some of the larger operations had nearly as much infrastructure underground, including repair shops, break rooms, and offices.

Had Conor not already had a location that he loved, one of these mines would have been a second choice. They were surrounded by open yard so anyone in the house could see someone coming for a long distance. The tall buildings created the perfect vantage point for observing or sniping. The covered conveyors provided a concealed means for moving between buildings unobserved. Then there were the shops, and Conor was a sucker for a good shop.

"This place is huge," Wayne said, stating the obvious as they rode across the bridge.

There was no concern that this bridge might be sabotaged in a similar manner. It was designed to carry semi-trucks hauling coal or lowboy trailers carrying in mining equipment, some of it so large it had to arrive in pieces. The steel I-beams supporting the bridge were at least three feet tall and would require a serious blast to compromise.

Conor sniffed the air. "Coal smoke." It had a distinctive odor to it that smelled like nothing else.

"There," Wayne said, pointing at a low green building with thick smoke spewing from a metal chimney.

"Let's give them a wide berth," Conor said. "They may consider us trespassers and we've already got enough on our plate for the day."

Once they'd crossed the bridge, they swung hard to the right, sticking close to the river. It put their backs to the occupied building so the men had their heads on a constant swivel, checking to make sure no one was coming for them. They cringed at the sound of their horses' hooves on the hard pavement and couldn't wait until they had dirt beneath them.

The facility was huge. The vast complex appeared almost alien in the remote hollows of Appalachia but they were found everywhere there was coal. It was almost like an airport with its long stretches of asphalt and concrete, though these facilities were significantly more cluttered than an airport would ever be. Broken machinery sat scattered around the plant, along with rusting shipping containers and piles of steel beams. Conor couldn't help but be distracted by it all. Where most saw junk, he saw potential.

Eventually the pavement turned to gravel and, a short distance past that, to an artificially flat expanse of weeds. When they finally moved beyond the reach of the coal company's dozers, the land returned to its natural contours again. Close to the river they found a clear trail, just as they expected. Fishermen, deer, and bear kept the trail beaten down but they soon found it wasn't tall enough for a man riding a horse. After they dismounted and walked their horses a little further, the path became too rough for a horse to traverse at all. There were downed trees that required ducking beneath or climbing over. There were boulders sitting at odd angles that were simply too dangerous to take a horse over.

"Do we leave the horses here?" Wayne asked.

"I hate to leave horses behind," Conor said. "They're too valuable. They'd tempt even an honest man if he saw them sitting here unattended."

"I don't like the idea of you going on alone either."

Conor grinned. "Maybe I was going to send you on alone while I had a nap."

"Yeah, I bet you were."

"The other side of the coin is that I'm not sure I can bring Fannie Bell back by this route. Poor thing appears too frail to be bushwhacking the riverbank like a fur trapper. I'd have to carry her and I'm not exactly in my prime. I'd probably fall and kill both of us."

"Well, you can't take her across that swinging bridge at Shuck's house either, can you? Not with those damaged boards."

"If I don't have to worry about Shuck shooting at me, I could take my time and lay down long planks to span the length of the bridge. Then we could probably walk across it with no worries."

"So you want me to be waiting there at the bridge with the horses?" Wayne asked.

Conor nodded.

"That means you're going to have to kill Shuck. That's the only way you'll buy yourself enough time to safely cross the swinging bridge."

"That's a given. I made my mind up about that when I saw the condition of that old lady," Conor said. "We don't need people like that in our community. Hell, we don't need them in our world."

"You comfortable with being judge, jury, and executioner?" There was no malice or accusation in the question.

Conor didn't hesitate. "Yes, I am."

Wayne acknowledged the response with a nod. "Then let's get on with it."

Conor removed any gear he needed from his horse. When he was done, he was wearing his Go Bag and carrying his rifle. He had the binoculars hanging around his neck for easy accessibility. "I don't know how long this is going to take."

"I don't have anywhere else to be," Wayne said. "I'll wait over there until this is over. Maybe I'll be the one taking a nap."

Conor checked his watch. "It's already getting late. It'll be dark in a few hours. If I see that darkness will improve my odds, I might wait until then. I can't put the old lady at further risk. She's suffered enough."

"Like I said, I won't leave until you're back. Do what you need to do."

The men shook hands and wished each other luck. Conor forged ahead on the rough trail. Wayne watched him until he disappeared from sight and then faced the horses.

"Time to go, boys. Let's backtrack."

Wayne walked carefully, visually checking each foot placement. Riverbanks were an obstacle course and this would be a lousy time to get injured in a spill. There were slick rocks and exposed roots as well as plain old slippery mud. There were damp leaves that, while slick in their own right, also hid other hazards, including deep holes where Wayne could break a leg or wrench an ankle.

He tried to encourage the horses to be careful but they paid him no mind. They had their own way of doing things. The best he could offer was to walk them slowly and cross his fingers that neither took a fall they couldn't get up from. After about a hundred yards he reached the point he could mount his horse again. The branches were higher here and the trail wider, the surface sandy and smooth. He tied Conor's horse to a long lead and let it trail behind him.

Eventually he reached the edge of the mine site and the trail swung up onto the artificially flat plane of the equipment boneyard. The only sound was the constant, almost hypnotic, murmur of the river and of dry brush swept by the horses' legs. Wayne kept his eyes moving. He could smell the coal smoke again and knew there were people about. In general he was fine with meeting the locals but this didn't feel like the best time. The two horses might make him a tempting target for robbery and he couldn't afford the delay. He had a cantankerous Irishman waiting on him.

He wound his way through the boneyard, where the company set out old equipment that was no longer in service. There were complex Bucyrus draglines and power shovels, predecessors of the modern hydraulic excavator that ran off a complex maze of rusting cables laced through banks of pulleys. There were absurdly long D9 Caterpillars with open cockpits and blades that stood as tall as a man. There was a hulking Fiat-Allis HD-31 that was bigger than Wayne's first house.

With his construction background, Wayne was easily distracted by these gigantic machines. He would love to get the opportunity to operate one. Some of the equipment was mining specific and he didn't recognize it. He could only ascertain its likely purpose from the fact that it was all built low to the ground so it could operate within a coal seam deep in the mountain.

Wayne hoped the long line of machinery would shield him from whoever lived on the property. He wasn't far from the bridge and would be back on the road soon, headed toward Shuck's house. He was staring in that direction, trying to gauge how much distance he had left to cover, when one of the mining machines shot forward, blocking his path. Wayne was trapped in a narrow lane with the river on one side and a wall of rusting equipment on the other. He saw a grinning face behind the wheel of the low, dirty machine.

He spun his horse and moved back the way he'd come, trying to get Conor's horse turned without wrenching his head around. When the horse was finally pointed in the right direction, he nudged his own, kicking him into gear. The horse shot forward. If Wayne could make it back to the trail...what then? It was a dead end, at least as far as the horses were concerned.

That decision was taken out of his hands. Before he got that far, a second mining machine shot across the path ahead of him. His route now plugged at both ends, Wayne turned to the left to negotiate a path between the massive pieces of equipment. It was the last thing he wanted to do. Wading a horse through that tangle of metal was a sure way to injure one.

Whoever these people were, they had the advantage. Somehow, they had working vehicles. They could run him down before he ever got out of here on horseback. As sour a pill as it was to swallow, he might have to leave the horses behind and make a run for it on foot. Either that or shoot his way out of here.

He walked his horses beneath the boom of a dragline, his mind racing and searching for the next opening in the boneyard. What he found was a man standing on the tracks of an old front end loader with a rifle leveled at him. There was nowhere he could go and not take a bullet in the process. He reluctantly reined his horse to a stop.

"Get them hands up!" a dirty man in navy coveralls ordered.

Wayne did as he was told, holding the lead tethering him to Conor's horse. To either side of him, the low mining vehicles coasted silently toward him, closing the distance. The drivers stopped their vehicles and got out, weapons pointed toward Wayne.

"What the hell are you doing here?" asked one of the drivers, an older man with a white beard and a camouflage cap.

Wayne saw no reason to lie. "I came through here with a buddy. We needed access to get down the river. We thought we could make it through with our horses but the trail ran out. My buddy went ahead on foot and I'm headed back downriver to meet up with him."

"What's so danged important that you had to get on this side of the river?" White Beard asked. "*My* side of the river."

Again, Wayne went with honesty. "Your nearest neighbor downriver, Shuck Lampkins, is holding an old woman named Fannie Bell as a prisoner. She's naked, injured, and chained up like a dog. Some folks that know her asked my buddy and me to check in on her. That's what we found. We figured the decent thing to do was pay Shuck a visit and see if we could come to an understanding."

"Shuck got his own bridge down yonder," the man standing on the machine pointed out. "Why didn't you use it?"

"First man that tried to talk to Shuck about this woman got shot dead and thrown in the river. That was her son. Second man that tried to talk to him got killed because Shuck's bridge is booby-trapped. We decided that the direct approach is clearly not working."

"You intend to kill Shuck Lampkins?" White Beard asked.

Wayne shrugged noncommittally. "If the situation calls for it, I got no doubt that my friend will deal with it properly. I wouldn't say he's fond of killing but he certainly doesn't shy away from it."

"Why don't you get down off that horse so we can talk," White Beard said. "Staring up at you is making my neck hurt."

"I'll get down if you lower your guns," Wayne said. "Otherwise I want to keep my options open."

The older man nodded, lowered his gun, and then gestured at the others to lower theirs. It was only then that Wayne noted there was a similar appearance to all the men, as if they were related.

"Well if you don't show me yours, I won't show you mine again," White Beard said. "How's that?"

Wayne nodded. "I'm good with that." He climbed off his horse and tethered the animals to a rusty railing. He extended a hand and slowly approached the older of the men. "My name is Wayne. I was passing through from Michigan. I have a group living down at the fire hall."

The old man took Wayne's hand and shook it. "I'm Bud Lester. These two yahoos are my sons. The one on the machine is Tivis. Far one over yonder is Chester."

Wayne raised an eyebrow. "Chester Lester?"

"What of it?" Chester demanded, raising his voice in anger.

"Nothing at all," Wayne replied. "Just making sure I heard you correctly."

Chester launched into a tirade of mumbled curses that Wayne couldn't make out, but assumed were about the nerve of his parents sticking him with a name that made him the constant butt of jokes.

"You know it's a family name, Chester," Bud said. "Now hesh up. This ain't the time to be rehashing family business."

Chester did as he was told but was still angry. Wayne thought he had a legitimate beef with his parents.

"I apologize for cutting through your place here," Wayne said. "We didn't realize it was a problem."

"We all worked at this mine," Bud said. "We decided to move in before winter hits. Wasn't no one else here and there was a good supply of coal for heating."

"You must have fuel for those little buggies," Wayne posed.

"Ain't a buggy," Chester said. "It's a mantrip. This here was a long-wall mine and the mantrip carried the miners back and forth to the face each day. They run on big old batteries." He left a few letters out of the word, referring to them as *batt-rees*.

"They're still charged?" Wayne asked.

"We charge them," Bud said. "My boys worked underground but I worked in the shop, making and repairing equipment. I took a steam boiler and made up a turbine to crank one of our big Cat generators. Ain't nothing fancy but we get a little power out of it. Hot water and lights. Basically it's like a little coal-fired power plant, 'cept a personal-sized one."

"I might have to bring my buddy back around to meet you some-time. He runs a welding and fabrication shop somewhere near here. He'd love to hear what you're doing. It might be something he could duplicate over in his neighborhood."

"Plenty of spare parts around," Bud said. "Hard part is finding a boiler ready to go."

"Well, I hate to be rude, but if I'm free to go, I really need to meet up with my buddy. He might need my help."

"What's your friend's name?" Bud asked. "I might know him."

"Irish guy named Conor Maguire. Some folks call him the Mad Mick."

"That was the Mad Mick that came through here with you?" Chester asked.

Wayne nodded.

"We seen the signs people been putting up about him, warning troublemakers to keep out," Bud said. "And we've heard stories. Didn't know if they was any truth to them or not."

"Oh he's the real deal. Like I said, I'll bring him by one day to meet you if that's okay. You guys would probably get along."

"I hope we do," Bud said. "I've heard what happens to those he don't get along with."

12

The trail between Conor and Shuck Lampkin's house grew worse with every step he took. Downed trees appeared more frequently. Briars became more vicious, lashing him and embedding their curved claws. Eventually even the faintest remnant of a trail faded away entirely and, had it not been for the river at his side, Conor would have been uncertain if he was even heading in the right direction. Just as he was beginning to wonder if he should go back and find an alternative route, the forest opened into a narrow, overgrown farm.

At the edge of cleared land, the grass grew with a lush thickness only found in river bottoms. A few ancient and gnarled trees were draped in vines like ghosts dripping with chains. A vibrant green moss, soft as a baby's hair, grew on the rough bark. Young poplars, willow oaks, and sycamores stood ten feet tall in previously mowed fields, a sign that some tired and frustrated servant of the land was relinquishing his claim to it. The place had once been carved from this unforgiving landscape by a family dependent on an annual hog, a milk cow, and a few chickens. Such families died out, replaced by superstore shoppers and eaters of fast food.

A skeleton of a barn slouched scoliotic and decaying, fighting the forces that tried to pull it into the Earth. The crumbling metal roof held rust holes the size of washtubs that let soft light filter to the weed-filled floor of the structure. Poplar siding sprung loose from rusted nails. Some boards had fallen away entirely and left more gap than wall, revealing an RC Cola can, a brown glass Clorox bottle, and an old headlight that lay discarded like a glass eye that survived the decomposition of its owner.

Beyond the barn was a log corn crib. The chestnut logs had been carefully hewn with a broad axe from what remained dead and standing after the American chestnut blight moved through in the last century. Between the gaps in the logs, Conor spotted a rusty woodstove, a set of metal box springs, and an antique wheelbarrow with a steel wheel on the front. Everything told a story and Conor could read every word of it. He came from people like those who'd lived on this farm. Generations of them, an ocean and a lifetime away.

Even at this time of the year, with the leaves mostly gone and the foliage dying, this area by the river was almost like another planet. The constant backdrop of river noise drowned out most of the other sounds. The thick carpet of moss possessed an insular, sound-dampening quality that absorbed any echo. It also made it hard to hear what might be happening at the house. Had anyone been sneaking up on Conor, he probably wouldn't have detected them. That gave him something to think about as he crept along the narrow strip of land, closing in on the house.

He caught the smell of wood smoke before he saw the place. He hid behind a fat sycamore, the peeling gray base as round as a steel drum. When he was certain it was clear, he sprinted for a rusty blue Ford tractor. The tires were flat and it was settled on its haunches like an ancient beast gone to die. Conor dropped onto his knees and peered carefully through the gap between the seat and steering wheel.

The light hadn't shined directly into this valley in hours but now any ambient light was fading quickly. The curtains were pulled back on every window. Privacy had been sacrificed to take advantage of what little natural light made it into this river bottom. Inside the house, someone had lit a Coleman lantern and a harsh white light filled the kitchen. Conor's stomach knotted as he spotted the naked woman tending a pot on a wood cookstove.

A blurry shape moved past the window and the back door opened. Conor raised his binoculars and struggled to pick out Shuck with a large butcher knife in his hand. A skinned and gutted doe hung from a hook that had once held a porch swing. Shuck carved off a thick roast and carried it inside.

As he moved, Conor followed him with the binoculars. Shuck set the deer meat on the counter and took a seat at the table. He carefully unscrewed the lid from a clear jar and helped himself to a long drink. Conor suspected what the jar contained but the manner in which Shuck pursed his lips confirmed it. This wasn't branch water. It was homemade liquor.

Conor returned his focus to Fannie Bell, noticing for the first time how slow her movements were. Her hands trembled but that could have come from a number of factors – fear, old age, or cold. Shuck was gesturing at her, his mouth moving. He was giving orders. Fannie Bell grabbed a cutting board and set it in front of Shuck. He pulled out the same knife he'd used to cut the roast off the doe. Fannie Bell reached for the deer meat on the counter and was passing it to Shuck when it slipped from her fingers.

She froze and stared down at it. Conor could sense her panic. Shuck stabbed the knife into the kitchen table and it stood upright. He rose from the table and lashed out with a fist nearly the size of the roast. Fannie Bell dropped like a rock when it connected with the side of her head. Shuck lifted a foot. His knee rose above the table height as he aimed a stomping blow toward Fannie Bell's head.

The window shattered from Conor's two rapid shots. Shuck slumped against the kitchen counter, a thick red bloom growing on his shirt. He appeared stunned, trying to figure out what was happening. When he didn't fall fast enough to suit Conor, his rifle still on the bastard, he touched off a third shot. This one, more carefully placed, caught Shuck just below the ear and finished the job.

Before breaking cover Conor yanked his radio from its pouch and keyed the mic. "Conor for Wayne, Conor for Wayne."

Without waiting for an answer, he bolted from cover to charge the house. He was pretty certain he dropped his target but he didn't know if there might be other folks in the house. Shuck might have kids or buddies staying with him. It could be that Miss Fannie Bell's capture was a family project.

Conor kept a constant eye on the house, his weapon raised and moving from window to window, keeping alert for movement. He took cover behind a rusty black Blazer with a garbage bag duct taped over the window. He did a more careful examination of the house from this position, checking each window and both porches. He saw nothing out of the ordinary. He heard nothing but the constant murmur of the river.

Before moving, he tried his radio again. "Conor for Wayne, Conor for Wayne. Come in, Wayne."

Nothing.

He sprinted from behind the Blazer and ran for the back porch. He shoved past the hanging deer carcass and flattened himself against the wall by the door. He peered through the half-glass and saw straight into the kitchen. Fannie Bell was unconscious on the floor, perhaps even dead. Shuck was lying beside her and he was definitely dead, his blood slowly spreading to encircle the two of them.

Conor put a hand on the knob and twisted. It turned in his hand and he shoved it inward, then stood there for a moment, listening. When he heard no footsteps, no voices, he flipped the safety on his rifle and let it hang from its sling. He drew his handgun and hit the weapon light. The only light was the Coleman lantern going in the kitchen and it left dark corners everywhere. Corners that could hold an armed attacker.

He stepped from the back porch into a mud room with a peeling linoleum floor. There was a washer and dryer sitting beside a big stack of firewood. Conor played his light around the room and found no surprises. He eased into the kitchen, passing a coat hook holding a frayed and dirty farmer's jacket. It reeked of body odor.

Conor crouched by the downed woman, touching two fingers to Ms. Fannie Bell's neck. She was startled by the contact but did not open her eyes. Her pulse was strong and steady. He stood up, went to the window, and yanked on the curtain. It was simply an old bedsheet tacked up with two nails and gathered to one side to let light in. Conor spread the sheet over Fannie Bell to allow her a little dignity when she awoke.

He gave the pool of blood a wide berth, not wanting to track it through the house. Not because he was squeamish but because it would compromise his traction if he found himself in a fight. He needed to check for a pulse but there was no part of Shuck's neck that didn't glisten with bright arterial blood. He did manage to reach a grubby arm that had flopped free of the blood puddle. Conor was pleased to find no indication of a heartbeat.

"You deserved much worse, you bloody bastard."

13

Conor rose from the body and pointed his weapon light toward the dark living room. He tried his radio again. "Conor for Wayne, Conor for Wayne."

When there was no response, Conor moved on. The living room was cozy and overheated, the result of a Warm Morning brand wood stove with a brown steel jacket. A tiny glass window allowed Conor to see the red glow of coals inside it. He played his light around the room. It was done in 1950s drywall painted a dingy mint green. There was a deer head mounted over a bulky old television. There was no satellite outside and antennas didn't work in this area, so it was tethered to an old VCR stacked high with cartoons and Westerns.

The door to Conor's left led to a bedroom. His hasty examination revealed a few rifles and shotguns propped against the wall and hanging from a homemade gun rack on the wall. There was a shallow closet with a few changes of clothes and an old dresser missing two drawers. The floor was bare wood carpeted with dirty clothes.

Another door in the corner of the living room door led Conor to dark, narrow steps. They creaked beneath his feet, doing away with any sense of stealth. It was a vulnerable position climbing those noisy stairs and he had to hope he was faster on the gun than his opponent, if there was anyone waiting on him. He moved step-by-step until he found himself in a two room attic. One room held crumbling boxes and odd piles of cast off family possessions. The other room had once been a bedroom but now smelled of mildew and disuse.

Reasonably confident that the house was empty, Conor tried his radio again. "Conor for Wayne, Conor for Wayne."

"This is Wayne. Go ahead."

"Shuck is down. I repeat, Shuck is down. I've taken the house. I need to get this little old lady squared away and then we can see about getting out of here."

"Is Fannie Bell okay?"

"The bastard coldcocked her. He was getting ready to stomp her brains out in the kitchen floor when I dropped him. He forced my hand."

"Good for you, Conor. I'll be on the other side of the bridge waiting on you if you need help."

Conor returned to the downed woman and laid his hand across her forehead. Her papery skin felt a little too warm, perhaps feverish. "Are you Miss Fannie Bell?"

The muscles of her eyes twitched and the lids opened with a reptilian slowness. Her brow furrowed when she realized this was not the man she expected to find in front of her. She surely expected Shuck, the miscreant who'd left her in this condition. While Shuck was responsible for her current state, and a lot more, he was at least familiar to her. She didn't have a clue who Conor was except that he was a stranger, crouched over her naked body, with his hand to her face.

She tugged the sheet higher around her neck and tried to recoil from him but the blow to her head had addled her. She wasn't firing on all cylinders.

Conor pulled back and held up both hands up in a soothing gesture. "Easy now. My name is Conor. I was sent to find you by some folks from Pastor White's church. They were concerned about you. With good reason apparently," he added, glancing toward the dead body just feet away from them.

Fannie Bell followed his gaze and found herself peering into the open, lifeless eyes of Shuck Lampkin's. She had no reaction.

"You are Miss Fannie Bell, correct?"

She nodded, struggling to put the pieces together. She attempted to sit up and it took more strength than she could bring to bear. She settled back onto the dirty kitchen floor.

"Don't rush it," Conor warned her. "We're here to help you."

At the use of the plural, Fannie Bell searched about for whom he might be referring to but didn't see anyone.

Noting her concern, Conor explained. "I have a friend outside. We have horses. We can take you home or to the church to be cared for."

"Home," she croaked. When the words hung up, she tried clearing her throat, but had difficulty speaking.

Conor thought she might be dehydrated. It was likely, considering her condition. "Is there any water in the house?"

She pointed to a plastic cooler sitting at the end of the counter. It was round, orange, and had a tap on the side. It was the same kind of cooler seen on work trucks all around the country. Conor got to his feet and searched the cabinets until he found a clean glass. He filled it from the cooler and then returned to Fannie Bell. He crouched at her side and helped her sit up to drink. He felt a little uncomfortable at having his hand on the dry thin skin of her bare back but she needed his assistance. He could tell that he was supporting her weight. Were he to remove his hand, she'd flop over backwards and smack her head on the floor. It was the last thing this poor lady needed after all she'd obviously been through.

She drank half the glass in one long pull and smacked her lips when she stopped. "Thank you." There was little more life in her voice.

"We need to get you dressed and out of here. What can I do to help you?"

She gestured toward her leg concealed beneath the sheet. "That nasty man has me tied like a dog. There's a chain locked around my leg."

"Do you know the whereabouts of the key?"

She gestured at the dead body with contempt. "His pocket."

Conor stood and circled the dead body. He grabbed Shuck by a sleeve and dragged him free of his own mess. He carefully slid a hand into the man's pocket where he found a pocketknife, a zippo lighter, a nickel, and a small brass padlock key. He returned to Miss Fannie Bell's side and carefully lifted the bottom of the sheet to expose her thin ankles. When he'd first barged into the house he'd been so distracted by the turn of events that he had not paid much attention to the condition of her leg. He'd spotted it earlier when he'd seen her on the front porch but it was much worse up close.

The oozing wound on her leg was likely responsible for her fever he'd detected. The rusty chain had abraded a deep circle around her leg. The wound had scabbed, reopened, and scabbed again so many times that thick encrustations surrounded it. Red streaks, vivid on her pale skin, shot up toward her knee. It had to be incredibly painful with each movement she made. She'd be lucky if the infection hadn't spread to her blood. He'd have to send Doc Marty around to see her because he was fairly certain there were no antibiotics in this community to keep this old lady alive.

As delicately as possible, he lifted the stained padlock from her flesh and used the key to unlock it. The grimy shackle unfastened with a click. Conor unhooked it from the heavy chain and carefully unwrapped the entire assembly, trying not to inflict any more discomfort on Fannie Bell than she'd already experienced.

"Where are your clothes, dear?"

She raised a trembling finger and pointed toward the dark living room. "There's a bedroom yonder. I came with a grip full of clothes but ain't been allowed to wear them. That Shuck had the devil in him. I don't know if it was the drink or what but his soul needed the Lord something bad."

Conor knew to what she referred but he hadn't heard anyone use the word "grip" since he was a kid. It was an old term for a traveling bag, a satchel, and it probably dated from the nineteenth century. It was one of the neat things about living in the area. You found little pockets of people who were relatively unaffected by modern conventions. They had the words, the speech pattern, and the dialect of the people who had come generations before them. Ladies like Fannie Bell, who didn't have television and had probably only seen a handful of movies in her entire life, had more in common with the early settlers of this region than with the current residents. Conor loved that.

He returned with the lady's grip, a fifty year old Samsonite in a dull blue color. "Can I help you to the fire, Miss Fannie Bell? You might be a touch more comfortable changing clothes by the fire, outside the presence of this cursed man."

She nodded. Conor stepped over her body and planted a foot to either side of the woman's chest. He slid his hands beneath her armpits. "If you just hold onto the sheet, I'll do the work. I'm going to swing you up on your feet. I'll go easy with you so don't be scared."

She clutched the sheet tightly around her. In a swift, fluid motion, Conor swung the old lady up like a kettlebell and planted her on her feet. She uttered a sound somewhere in between pain and surprise but Conor held her until he was sure she was steady. In her state he was sure the sudden movement left her head spinning. Once he was certain she wasn't going to tumble over, he moved to her side and escorted her to the living room. He sat her down on a recliner with a human-shaped stain on its light fabric and returned to the kitchen for her bag.

"I apologize for asking this, ma'am, but do you require my assistance? If you do, I promise to avert my eyes."

She considered it for a moment and shook her head. "I think I can manage but I thank you kindly. I'll do as much as I can. Lord, I feel weak as a kitten."

"I'll be in the kitchen and I'll listen for you. You call out if you need anything. Just don't make any quick movements or you might pass out."

She nodded warily. "I figured that out when you snatched me up out of the floor like a sack of potatoes."

While he waited for Fannie Bell to dress, he gave the kitchen a cursory search. He didn't believe in survival by theft but anything left here would just go bad or be stolen by the neighbors. There was no point in that. If there were things in the house that would benefit Wayne's people while they wintered at the firehouse, it was best to take them. Once they returned Fannie Bell to safety and word of what happened to Shuck spread, there would probably be other folks with the same idea. There would be more competition for what paltry belongings Shuck had owned. Conor was reaching for the pantry door when there was a voice on his radio.

"Wayne for Conor, come in."

Conor keyed his mic. "Go for Conor."

"Since I was just sitting out here with my thumb up my ass, I thought I might make myself useful. I came across this bridge one board at a time and I think I tossed all the bad ones. I'm across but wanted to let you know so you wouldn't drop me if you saw movement outside."

"Got it. Can we get back across the bridge as it is or will it need more work?"

"I'll need a couple of more planks. A couple of 2x8s or 2x10s would be perfect. I'm going to poke around the property with my light and see if I can find anything."

"Sounds good. Be careful. I cleared the house but haven't searched the other buildings. I'm going to give the house a once over for anything your folks might be able to use. Miss Fannie Bell is dressing. When she's ready, we'll bolt."

Conor replaced the radio in his pouch and called out to Fannie Bell. "Everything going okay in there?"

"I'm dressed. I'm just sitting here a moment gathering my strength and warming up. I'm sorry."

Conor refilled the glass of water in the kitchen and delivered it to Miss Fannie Bell. "Don't you be sorry. You've been through an ordeal and survived. Now drink up. I think you're dehydrated and will feel a lot better when you've replenished your fluids. Are you hungry at all?"

She shook her head. "He fed me decent but you're probably right that I've not drank enough. Honestly, the heat is doing more for me than anything else. I can't remember the last time I was warm."

"Then you just stay put. You sip on that water while I make a pass through the house. With Shuck dead, I'm gonna see if he has anything that might help folks in need this winter. Do you have anything else you need to take with you besides your grip?"

"No. You need to check the dairy. There's a good bit of canning out there. Shuck's mother canned a little bit of everything. She just passed away a few months before this all happened. I don't think he ever had to take care of himself. That's probably why he kept me here the way he did."

Conor patted her on the arm. "Don't you trouble yourself any more over it. He's dead and can't bother you again. You sit there and warm up. We've got a long ride through the dark tonight and it's a wee bit chilly out there."

In the bedroom, Conor went to the bed and shook the top quilt out flat. He cleared the guns and piled them in the center of it. He tossed the ammo, both boxed and loose, into the same pile. Shuck didn't have much but Conor found a decent skinning knife, a sharpening stone, and two decent pocketknives. He threw those on top of the pile. That reminded him of something and he went to the kitchen.

There he retrieved a handful of Old Hickory skinning and butcher knives. No country home would been complete without them. From the stone-worn blades he could tell they'd processed a lot of meat. He took them back to the bedroom and tossed them in the middle of the pile. He wrapped the blanket securely around the loot like a burglar's burrito and tied it shut so that nothing fell out. He lifted the awkward bundle and carried it out to the front porch.

He spotted Wayne dragging two long boards across the yard. "You have any luck?"

"These should do it."

What folks in this part of the country called a dairy was often known as a root cellar in other parts of the country. It was a cinderblock and concrete structure set back in the hillside so that it was insulated by the soil around it. Items stored in there wouldn't freeze. Despite the occasional rodent and black snake, it was where

Appalachian folk traditionally stored their canned goods, their dairy products, and their root crops.

Inside the dairy Conor found a larger collection of the sampling he'd already spotted in the kitchen. It was a storehouse of sustenance that would have been more common in this area fifty or even one hundred years ago. In old rural America, buildings such as this kept families alive. It would have been their grocery store. It was the fruit of their labor.

Thick pork bellies crusted with coarse salt hung from the rafters by baling twine looped through holes punched in the meat itself. The ropes passed through greasy paper bags that acted as a shield against rodents. Bushel baskets, five-gallon buckets, and dusty cardboard boxes sat filled with potatoes, carrots, sweet potatoes, and apples. Braided bundles of onions and garlic hung from the rafters. Neat rows of glass jars lined deep shelving. There was canned sausage, canned deer meat, canned beef, and every type of vegetable Conor could imagine. There were soups and relishes and fruits. Conor could have filled the bed of a pickup with this bounty.

Wayne joined Conor in the dairy building, shining his own light at the rows of jars. "Jesus!"

"This is more than we can carry tonight," Conor said. "It's gold, though. This would be a big help to you folks."

Stunned, Wayne was slow to answer. "It's a lot of food."

"Of course, I might fight you for one of those pork bellies. There's nothing like homemade bacon."

"It's yours, my friend."

They backed out of the building and Conor shut the door behind them.

"You should let me take Miss Fannie Bell back by myself," Conor said. "You start working on getting this stuff packed. Wrap these jars in shirts, socks, towels, whatever you can find, so they won't break in transit. Stow them in pillowcases, suitcases, gunny sacks, anything that we can hang on a pack horse. When I get Fannie Bell to safety I'll come back with a couple of your men and some of your horses. I think we need to get this stuff out of here tonight. That's the only way you're guaranteed first shot at it. Once I tell Pastor White's folks what happened, some of them may want to take a gander at Shuck's place. There's already enough bad blood between us. I don't want this to become a sore spot. We take it and we don't say anything about it."

"I'm good with that," Wayne said. "You sure you're okay with taking her home yourself?"

Conor chuckled. "You need to be more concerned about the folks I run into."

14

Miss Fannie Bell wore the long skirt of the Appalachian Pentecostal, which was ill-suited for horseback with a traditional western saddle. Once they had her across the swinging bridge, it took them a few moments to get her onto a horse and settled. She wore a coat but the bitter night air was harsh against her fevered skin. Conor rushed back to the house to find another quilt and they wrapped her against the night.

"You hold onto that saddle horn," Conor told her. "Don't worry about the reins. I'll lead your horse."

"It's dark," she said. "How do we know they won't step off into the river?"

"Horses have more sense than that," Wayne assured her. "They know what they're doing. The key is to trust the horse and not fight against it."

"If you say so," Fannie Bell replied, sounding wholly unconvinced.

Conor swung up onto his own horse. It was awkward to mount with the burglar burrito strapped behind the saddle but he eventually got there. He took up the reins, readied his rifle, and turned off his headlamp. He wished he'd brought his night vision gear but he hadn't expected to be out this late. The day had taken him on an entirely different course than he'd planned. Although he should have been at home by the fire already he had no complaints. This was an adventure, and he'd always chosen adventure over comfort. The folks at home knew this of him and wouldn't be too concerned.

"I'll be back with your men as soon as I can," Conor told Wayne. "I'll try to reach you on the radio before we cross the bridge."

"No problem," Wayne replied. "Take your time. I have plenty to do. If all goes well we can load up and head home when you get back. I hope to have everything ready."

"Stay safe," Conor warned. "Miss Fannie Bell, you ready?"

"I reckon," she said, her voice faint in the darkness. "It's in the Lord's hands now. Him and this horse."

Conor nudged his horse into motion and tugged on the reins of Fannie Bell's mount. He wasn't going to push the horses in the darkness. He'd let them find their own pace and the trip would take however long it took. He didn't even remember how many miles they'd come, the trip broken up as it was because of the run to pick up poor Bernard from his parents' home.

The sound of the river was hypnotic. In the darkness it tugged at their senses and filled their heads. There was a moon tonight but it had no more impact in these deep valleys than the sunlight did during the day. Clouds high above them were illuminated by the pale moonlight and those occasionally reflected off the dark water. Otherwise they were back to the sensation of looking up at the sky from the bottom of a well.

"Are you an Irishman?" Miss Fannie Bell asked after they'd been riding in silence for some time.

Her voice surprised him. He'd been lost in thought and assumed she'd probably fallen asleep in the saddle. "Yes, I am, though I've been in America since I was a child. You recognize the tongue?"

"Oh yes. My grandfather was an Irishman."

"Really?"

"Yes, indeed. He came over because he heard there were was work in the coal mines. He originally settled in West Virginia but that was about the time of the mine wars. They were trying to unionize and the company wanted no part of it. The government turned on them too."

"I don't know anything of the mine wars," Conor said. "I know that strikes in coal country can be ugly business. I've only seen one of them in my time here, but I've heard a lot of stories. I take it there was a lot of violence."

"I doubt the stories you've heard can touch what happened to folks back in those early days," Fannie Bell said. "The company put everybody out of the mining towns and forced them to winter in tents. They claimed to own the roads, so the miners weren't allowed to use them. My grandfather had just married my grandmother and she was pregnant. He was worried she'd freeze to death. There wasn't enough food and conditions were just awful. My grandmother said she couldn't feel her fingers and toes for weeks. They didn't have the good winter clothes we have now. They didn't hardly have nothing."

"That sounds awful," Conor said.

"It got a lot worse. You should check it out sometime. Battle of Blair Mountain, they called it. The company convinced the government that the miners were nothing more than terrorists. At one point the company even bombed them from planes."

"You're kidding me? I've never heard of such a thing."

"It's the God's honest truth, Mr. Conor. It's hard to imagine in this day and time but the company had a private army and they were determined to kill everyone who stood in their way. It was a dark time. The government took the company's side and the folks in West Virginia always remembered that."

Conor chuckled. "Miss Fannie Bell, I know a lot about the government and the things they do to people. Nothing you can tell me in that department would surprise me. I fully understand what they're capable of."

"My grandparents moved after that. My grandfather had a bad

temper and he didn't want any part of working for a company that had treated them that way. He wanted to kill those Baldwin-Felts agents every time he saw one of them. My grandmother was afraid he'd actually do it."

"We Irish can be stubborn. We can hold a grudge a good long time," Conor said. "So you knew your grandfather, did you? You had the opportunity to spend time with him?"

"Oh yes. He was a nice man and good to me. Of course, he was already an old man when I was a child and people didn't live so long as they do these days. I remember his stories. The songs. But then there was music in his voice even when he wasn't singing. That's why I remember the accent so fondly."

"We Irish love our songs. Singing connects us to our heritage."

"There was one he used to sing that I can almost remember. *Red Is The Rose*, it was called."

"Oh, I know that one," Conor said. "It's a beautiful song."

"You remember the words, Mr. Conor?"

Conor searched his brain. "I might be able to recall them."

"If you could see it in your heart to sing it with me, it would do my soul good. I can't recall the last time I thought of my grandfather and that song. Amazing how time gets away from you. You get so many memories in your heart that even the precious ones can get lost in there."

Conor was a tough bastard. He'd lived a hard life and done many things, including some he wasn't proud of. He'd killed men who deserved it and men whose only crime was being in the wrong place at the wrong time. He'd loved his mother and his grandmother though, and he'd have chopped off a finger without hesitation to have the opportunity to sing a ballad with one of them again. This might be the closest he'd ever come. It might even be the only chance he ever got to sing one of the old songs again.

He started into it, barely raising his voice above a whisper. He didn't sing much in the company of other folks but this wasn't a performance. He barely got through the opening line before Miss

Fannie Bell's stark high-pitched voice joined him. The words were coming back to her, just as they were to him. Funny how the mind works that way. His voice was low and gruff, the earthy roots of the tune. Her voice was bold and honest, her accent clearly not Irish but her rendering of the song just as authentic as his own. He could tell she'd heard it sung right, straight from the mouth of someone who knew and loved it.

The longer they sang, the louder they became. Conor wondered how far the song carried in the night. Were there people standing in their dark yards wondering what sort of madness this was? Did they assume it was something supernatural? He didn't care. There was only the moment.

When they reached the last note, they both held it, like neither was ready to release the song back into the night, back into memory. Once it was gone, it was gone. Once the moment had passed, there was no reclaiming it. They fell into deep silence and the sound of the river gradually overtook them again.

"Thank you, Mr. Conor. Thanks for singing that with me."

"It was my privilege, Miss Fannie Bell. For a moment, that took me back to my childhood."

"It did the same for me. I saw things I hadn't seen in years. I could smell my grandfather's pipe and the bay rum he used to wear. Funny how those things can still be there in your head after all these years."

"Memory is a strange thing," Conor said.

The song, the oddness of the night, and the hypnotic sound of the river carried them to their own places. Conor thought about the people and events in the past who'd contributed to making him who he was. Starting down that road, the twisting tendrils of memory, was like boarding a train without knowing the destination. You never knew where you might end up. Lost in their own rides, Conor and Fannie Bell didn't exchange another word until they reached the camp at Pastor White's church.

"I wanted to go home," Fannie Bell said when the fires of the camp came into sight.

"I'll stop by here tomorrow. If you want to go home then, I'll carry you there myself. For tonight, I think you should be around other people. Let them get some food into you and tend to that fever. You've survived too much to die of infection."

Fannie Bell fell silent but Conor knew she wasn't happy about this turn of events. On top of her displeasure, Conor received exactly the welcome he anticipated at Pastor White's camp. He announced himself to the sentries and sat his horse patiently while they lit him up with flashlights and confirmed that he was who he said he was. That he was in the company of Miss Fannie Bell, a person known to them, most likely helped things. When they were done, he clicked on his headlamp and could finally see the men in front of him.

A suspicious and disagreeable man with long sideburns and a craggy face immediately started badgering Conor. "Where's the rest of your people? You get them all killed or did you kill them yourself?"

"Probably that daughter of his killed them," observed the other sentry. He was overweight in a manner that made him appear babyish and effectively hid his age. He could have been anywhere from sixteen to thirty.

"Neither of you boys knows me well enough for this to be jest," Conor said. "So if it's not jest, I'm liable to take offense. Are you boys prepared for the consequences of that?"

"What does that even mean?" asked the baby-faced sentry.

"Means I could kill both of you without alerting the rest of your camp. Then I could just turn around and take Miss Fannie Bell home, as she'd prefer to do anyway. You men want to die tonight?"

"Ain't no need for spilling more blood tonight," Miss Fannie Bell said. "This man brought me home safe. Y'all best leave him alone and quit poking at him. I have a feeling you ain't gonna like it when he pokes back."

The men scowled. "Whose blood you spill tonight?" Sideburns asked.

"Shuck is dead. He booby-trapped the bridge to his house and Bernard was killed when he fell through it. We tried to stop him from crossing but Bernard refused to listen to us. Hard heads are apparently a regional specialty."

Baby-face scowled, certain there was an insult buried in there somewhere but unable to extract it. "How you so sure Bernard is dead?"

"His head smashed wide open like a dropped pumpkin. Shuck dragged his body into the river and let it wash away. I have no idea if it will ever be found or not."

Tired of answering questions, Conor threw a leg forward over his horse's neck and slid off the side of the saddle. He helped Fannie Bell to the ground. She was light as a bird and everywhere he laid a helping hand he felt the protrusion of bone. Poor thing needed fattening up.

"You take care of yourself, Miss Fannie Bell. It was a pleasure meeting you and having your delightful company on the ride back."

In the manner of her people, her faith, she was reserved in her public communication with this outsider. She didn't offer a grateful hug or even a handshake. She simply nodded and smiled tiredly. To his farewell, she responded with, "Well."

When the obstinate sentries made no move to help her, Conor lit in on them. "She'll require help, lads. This poor soul has undergone a horrible ordeal. She was chained as a prisoner and has an awful leg wound. She'll be requiring immediate attention. If you got a nurse among you, you best be waking her up. This can't wait until morning."

The men slung their rifles over their shoulders and glared at Conor but did as he asked. Each took one of Miss Fannie Bell's thin arms and helped support her.

"Pastor White's going to have questions for you," Sideburns said.

"You tell the pastor I'll stop in over the next day or so. I've got business to attend to. Reckon I'm going to go back and help bury Shuck unless you fellows want in on that."

The two hurried off and Conor laughed at their predictable reaction. He remounted his horse, settled into the creaking saddle, and turned onto the road. He left his headlamp on, feeling safe to ride to the firehouse with the glowing target mounted to his head. These two groups of men, Wayne's and Pastor White's, kept this area relatively safe and he'd make better time if he could see ahead of him. He set his headlamp to its brightest setting and nudged the horse into a trot. He checked his watch and was surprised to see the hour. With all they'd been through over the day and evening he'd assumed it was later than it actually was. They hadn't hit midnight yet. The night was young.

15

Conor rode faster without having to be concerned with Fannie Bell and the ride to the firehouse took no time at all. As soon as he thought the radio waves might be able to navigate the convolutions of the hills and river bottom, he began trying to reach Wayne's group on his radio. The response was nearly indecipherable, staticky bursts that didn't improve significantly even when he was nearly within shouting distance.

It was something anyone who relied on radio communications in these Appalachian Mountains could tell you. Whether it was law enforcement, EMTs, game wardens, or even the blasted forestry service, they all knew you couldn't trust the damn things. Even with repeaters on the ridge tops the terrain was just too rough. There were too many bumps and recesses, too many hills and hollers.

Conor slowed as he approached the first of Wayne's roadblocks. Fortunately the sentries there had ascertained from his garbled transmissions that he was on his way and were watching for him. What he failed to anticipate was that their initial reaction to Wayne's absence would be to assume that their de facto leader had been killed or mortally wounded. The agitated men bombarded him with questions, speaking over top of each other until he could barely understand a word they were saying.

Finally catching the drift of this barrage, Conor held up a hand. "Easy now! Hold up! Wayne's okay. Quit your yammering and listen to me."

Surprisingly, the men did as he asked. There was none of the defiance and the barely concealed revulsion that seethed beneath the questioning from Pastor White's men. When they stopped, he continued.

"We found Fannie Bell and I just delivered her back to Pastor White. Wayne stayed behind at the home where we found her. There's a ton of food there and if we don't take it, we'll lose it. It's enough to help you guys make it through the winter. The man who owned the food won't be needing it anymore."

"Are you headed back there?" one of the men asked.

"I promised I'd get back to him with several men and some pack horses."

The men didn't question Conor's message. One of them got on the radio and immediately relayed his message back to the firehouse. "Why don't you go inside and warm up?" he said when he had done so. "They're scrambling a team. You might even find some food to chew on while they get the horses ready."

"Thanks," Conor muttered, and prodded his horse toward the firehouse. Just as he had earlier, he tied his mount off to the mirror of one of the cars being used as a fence. He untied the paracord that held his burglar burrito to the saddle and heaved the bundle onto his shoulder.

"What's that?" a man asked, weaving through the barricade to join Conor at his horse.

In the glow of his headlamp, Conor noticed the man had a crow tattooed on his neck. "Guns, some ammo, knives. It's for you guys. Got a place to stash it?"

"I'll take it," the man replied, transferring the bundle to his own shoulder. "Follow me. Got a fire inside to knock the chill off."

Crow Tattoo led Conor inside the pleasantly warm place. They'd installed several woodstoves in the building and the area had no shortage of firewood. One of the additional benefits of having sentries on duty all night was that they could tend the fire. Crow Tattoo set the bundle of rifles onto a folding table and pointed Conor toward one of the woodstoves. "There's a kettle beside that stove with leftover biscuits inside it. Help yourself."

Conor didn't realize he was hungry until biscuits were mentioned, then his stomach began clanging like a fire alarm. He'd turned his headlamp off when he came inside out of respect for all the sleeping people. There were numerous Lucie lights around the room, self-contained, inflatable solar lights that had an internal battery and provided a low light that would last for most of the night. It was enough light to allow the ravenous Conor to negotiate his way to a biscuit. He honed in on the warm biscuits like a bull just turned into a pasture of cute young lady cows.

Most of the people in the firehouse were asleep, stretched out on cots or homemade beds on the floor. Others lay awake reading or listening to music on headphones. Sheets were hung as curtains to offer some degree of privacy but the firehouse was definitely tight quarters. It reminded Conor of those hurricane evacuation shelters he'd seen on the news, grim people stuck in high school gyms waiting to find out if their homes were destroyed.

Conor stepped outside and enjoyed the warm biscuit on the cold night, then moved on to the second biscuit he'd stuck in his shirt pocket. He enjoyed it more knowing how much Barb would have frowned at the idea of him carrying a biscuit around in his pocket.

In short order, Wayne's men were ready and they moved out. The trip from the firehouse to Shuck's house was relatively quiet. Most everyone in the community was settled in for the night and they saw not a soul outside of their own party. Had Conor been alone, he'd have turned his headlamp off once he was out of familiar territory and rode in darkness, as he and Miss Fannie Bell had earlier. These men were not comfortable with that. Conor relented and they made the whole journey by the glow of their collective headlamps.

He halted the column of riders at Shuck's bridge. The men were on edge from being pulled from their sleep to ride through strange territory in the cold and dark. However, they did not complain, aware that their mission was important for the well-being of their group. It was a task of necessity.

"Conor for Wayne, Conor for Wayne. In case you haven't seen the glowing inferno across the river, we're here."

"I was inside but I see you now. Lit up like a football field over there."

"I'm going to tie the horses off on this side and leave one man with them. The rest of us are coming across the bridge to carry what needs carrying."

"That'll work. There's a stack ready to go. It's laid out on a tarp in the front yard, close to the bridge."

Conor had the men tie off their horses and left a man named Luke to watch over them. There were no houses anywhere close to Shuck's and they hadn't seen any signs of life in the community on the way over but you never knew. Conor led the way across the bridge, pointing out the places where a single narrow plank spanned gaps in the boards. "Step carefully. Last man to slip off this bridge didn't fare so well."

Once they were across Conor saw that Wayne had done an excellent job of staging the loads. A tattered blue tarp was stretched out on the frosty grass. Burlap feed sacks were packed with carefully wrapped canning jars and tied closed at the top with baling twine. Two sleeping bags were packed in the same fashion, creating long, quilted sacks packed with food. A couple of battered suitcases were filled solid with glass jars, judging by the weight of them.

Numerous lengths of rope, electrical power cords, and fence wire were piled onto the tarp for use in securing the loads onto the horses. The thought crossed Conor's mind that at some point he may actually want to design a cargo buggy that could be pulled by a team of horses. He was surprised he hadn't thought of it earlier but things had been a little busy since the shit hit the fan. A buggy like that would have been ideal for transporting this burden back to the firehouse. Surely there had to be an old hay wagon somewhere in the community he could easily convert.

Wayne showed the men where he was in his tasks. He had most of the food staged in the yard and was doing a more thorough search of the house. He was searching for items they'd passed over earlier such as towels, toiletries, blankets, and cookware. His folks had to leave a lot behind on their trek southward and there were a lot of things they needed if they were going to winter over in the community. Come spring, they would be choosing to continue their journey or considering whether to stay in this community a little longer. If they stayed, these items would be of use. If they decided to move on, the gear could be left behind for the next resident of the firehouse.

"Have you found any tools?" Conor asked.

"There's a tool shed behind the house," Wayne said. "I haven't had the opportunity to go through it. I did stick my head in there just to see what the outbuilding was being used for. A lot of the stuff inside there was really old, like the rest of the farm. I think this place was at least two generations past having been an active working farm. It's pretty neglected."

"I'm going to take a look in that toolshed. If you have food and weapons covered, I want to see what other kind of kit the Lampkins family might have."

"While you're doing that, I'll have my guys load the horses. I'll continue searching the house. There's places I haven't got to yet."

Conor stalked through the tall, dew-soaked weeds to reach the toolshed behind the house. It was a crude building about twelve feet long and sixteen feet wide. The walls were plywood that had been painted white to match the house. The windows were repurposed from other structures, each a different size. The door was an antique house door, painted blue and held shut by a rusty hasp with an old bolt securing it.

Conor extracted the bolt, flipped the hasp back, and swung the door open. He played his light inside and saw immediately what Wayne meant about the age of the contents. This was the kind of shop put together by a man in the 1950s rather than a man of more recent decades. It was neatly organized with mostly older tools. Sadly, many had a thin veneer of rust from disuse and neglect, though they could be cleaned up with a little work.

There were several metal cabinets with tiny plastic drawers full of odd screws and hardware. Lines of Maxwell House coffee cans held larger bolts, nails, and screws. There were hand planes and Yankee twist drills. There was a large assortment of hammers of all shapes and sizes. Not just the more common sledgehammers and carpentry hammers but tiny tack hammers. There were ball peen hammers in a dozen sizes. There were cobblers' hammers, brick hammers, and a variety of blacksmith hammers. This was the kind of workshop assembled by a man who had known the hard days of the Great Depression. A man who had known the deprivations of poverty. Someone who had learned a long time ago that sometimes a piece of repurposed trash could be useful when there was no money to spend.

One of the things that fascinated Conor about these old-timers wasn't just the tools they owned but the tools they purpose-made to do a particular job. Most couldn't run out to the store to find what they needed and they certainly couldn't go online to order specialty tools. They analyzed problems and made the appropriate tool if they were industrious enough. Over the years he'd seen many homemade tools designed for shucking corn, processing livestock, harvesting crops, and doing repetitive farm tasks like fencing.

People didn't think the same way these days. They preferred to buy rather than to build. They saw "homemade" as equating to poverty instead of indicating initiative. Conor was the opposite. Even the things he did buy from the store were not so sacred that he wouldn't tear into them if he thought he could improve on them.

Seeing nothing he wanted or needed he made note of several items that might benefit Wayne's people if they were short of tools. He backed out of the building and secured the door. When he returned to the front of the house he found Wayne and two of his men standing by Shuck's body with picks and shovels, starting to dig a grave.

The waste of time irritated Conor. Without a word, he walked up to the body, grabbed Shuck by the pants leg, and dragged him out onto the swinging bridge. He cast a glance back to the men in the yard, their digging halted, their headlamps pointed at him. In the glare of their lights, he shoved Shuck's body with his foot and unceremoniously dumped the bloody corpse off into the river.

"We figured we needed to bury him," Wayne said when Conor rejoined them.

"Why?" Conor asked.

Wayne shrugged. "It's what you do, I guess."

"Not that fucker. He didn't deserve a proper burial. You didn't get a good look at that old lady. Thin as a pencil, one half of her face black from his fists. Hell, she still might die from the infection in her leg where he kept her chained up like an animal. I don't think Shuck Lampkins is worth the expenditure of a single calorie. He certainly didn't hesitate to drag Bernard's body into the river and let him wash away. Let the turtles eat Shuck if they can tolerate the stench."

There was no protest. If anyone intended to voice one, they choked it down after bearing witness to the intensity with which Conor backed up his actions. He understood that the attempt to bury Shuck had likely arisen because the men didn't know what else to do with him and reverted back to custom. Conor knew exactly what to do with him. His beliefs, as well as his customs, lay somewhere in between karma and the Golden Rule. Shuck had reaped what he had sown.

Noticing that the men were no longer ferrying loads to the horses he asked, "Have you got everything?"

"We took as much as the horses can carry," Wayne replied. "The body was pretty much the last loose end and you took care of that."

Conor smiled at the comment. He was nothing if not decisive. "There's a few things in the toolshed your people might be able to use. Hammers, saws, fasteners. Stuff you can't buy anymore."

"We can't haul another thing tonight. The horses aren't happy with what we put on them already. We can come back for another trip tomorrow."

"Don't bet on it," Conor said. "Once word spreads that Shuck is dead, people will hit this place out of curiosity. They'll clean it out."

Wayne's face crumpled in concentration. He was too tired to think clearly at this point. They all were. It had been a long, physically-demanding day.

"You should send your guys on back," Conor said. "You and I can go through the house again. We can take our time and make certain there's nothing else you all need and we can cache it in the woods beside the road. That way you don't have to cross back over here to get it. Even if someone moves into the house, you can slip in and retrieve the goods without anyone being the wiser."

Wayne nodded. "I should've thought of that."

"It's the lack of sleep, man. Takes twice as many brains to figure out half the shit."

16

Wayne sent his team back home with the horses and the tired men didn't complain about the decision. Their horses bristling with loot, they would ride slowly and patiently back to the firehouse. There they could get help unloading the goods. Tomorrow they could be inventoried and stored once everyone had gotten some sleep. Conor resisted the impulse to give them a dozen warnings on safety before they left. He did that with his own family and they had to tolerate it. These guys did not. Besides, they hopefully knew the score by now. Be vigilant or die. It was that simple.

Wayne and Conor set aside a couple more tarps and a sheet of black plastic they'd found in an outbuilding. Their plan was to use the tarps and plastic to shelter their loot, then use branches and leaves to camouflage it. Wayne would have liked to rescue some of the mattresses and beds for the firehouse since they didn't have enough comfortable accommodations for everyone. However, transporting a mattress on horseback, even on a pack horse with no rider, was too challenging. Even if you could get the bulky, awkward load properly secured, it was unlikely the horse would cooperate with hauling it.

The food had been the priority on the first pass. The second pass would focus more on housewares and comfort items. They would take tools, camping gear, toiletries, and anything that might make their stay more tolerable.

Wayne was going through an end table with drawers, setting aside a half-empty box of light bulbs when he stopped in his tracks. "You know, those light bulbs reminded me of something. In all of the excitement, I forgot to mention that the coal plant we passed through upriver was definitely occupied. The residents ambushed me as I was passing through there."

Conor was sorting through the contents of the hall closet, setting aside blankets and towels for the folks at the firehouse. He stopped and cocked his head at Wayne. "You got in a firefight and somehow forgot to mention that? I didn't even hear the shots."

"It was no firefight. There was no time for a firefight. They totally got the jump on me. If there had been any shots it would've been them blasting my dumb ass into the next life. There wasn't even a place for me to hide."

"And they just let you go?"

"They did," Wayne replied. "They were just wondering who I was and what I was doing in their territory, which was an understandable reaction. That wasn't the interesting part. It's a man and his two sons living there and they're people after your own heart. What is it that you guys in the U.K. call people who can cobble a bunch of stuff together to make useful things?"

"Bodgers." Conor chuckled. "It's not a compliment though. It's basically your equivalent of calling someone a hack or a butcher. It's a term of endearment when made from one bodger to another."

"These guys are definitely bodgers. They came after me on these little mining buggies they called mantrips. They told me they were battery-powered and I asked them how they kept them charged. They said they'd converted an old coal boiler into a steam generator and were able to produce enough power for their own use."

Conor stood there dumbstruck. "That makes complete sense. For someone who knew what they were doing, it would be completely feasible. It's not been a big issue for me because we have the solar power but it could be helpful for other folks. Of course, if you don't know what you're doing it's the same as building a bomb that will scald you to death when it blows up."

Wayne frowned. "That's...concerning."

"The risk would be acceptable if you knew what you were doing. These guys live right there at that coal mine?"

"Yeah," Wayne replied. "The dad said he worked in the shop and his sons were miners there. They moved onto the property to have access to coal for heating over the winter."

"I'd definitely like to meet them and see what they've got going. One of those battery-powered mantrips would be nice right now, wouldn't it? I don't know what the range is but it would make hauling this stuff back to your place a snap."

"I guess we could go catch them tomorrow if you wanted," Wayne offered, shoving blankets and towels into a garbage bag.

Conor considered the idea. "I'd better wait a day or two. I hadn't expected to be away from home this long. I kind of feel like I need to get back there and check on things."

"Everything okay on the home front?"

Conor grinned. "Well, you may have noticed that daughter of mine is a bit temperamental. She's been a real powder keg lately."

"Yeah, I got that impression. Not sure the girl knows her own strength." He said it as an observation, not a judgment. Wayne didn't appear to have any of the overt hostility toward Barb that a lot of people had right now. There may have even been a bit of begrudging respect in there.

"I worry that she *does* know her own strength and has no qualms about using it. It's my own fault, really. I'm afraid my parenting style has backfired on me. I raised her to be tough and to not take shit off anyone. I didn't want her to ever have to be afraid."

"That's good. Raising strong kids, especially daughters, is important."

"I know, but I always assumed her standard of what was insulting and inappropriate would be the same as mine but it's not. I'm real-izing that, despite her age, she might not have the maturity to deal with the skills I've given her. It's like putting nuclear weapons in the hands of some teenage dictator."

Wayne smiled at the comparison. He crammed the loot down in the garbage bag and tied the top shut. He removed another bag from the box and shook it open. The bags had come from the firehouse. They'd figured out earlier that Shuck didn't keep garbage bags. It appeared that he, and perhaps the generations of Lampkins before him, always threw their garbage into the river. Many of the houses along the river were known to discharge even their sewage directly into the river. Local fisherman knew to never stand in front of any pipe jutting from the bank for that very reason.

"I wouldn't worry about her too much. She's not a lost cause, she just has a little growing to do. If you've given her the basic tools, the right values, she'll come out fine on the other end of this."

"That's assuming she doesn't leave a trail of bodies behind her," Conor mused.

Wayne shrugged. "There is that possibility."

Conor hesitated to say anymore. He didn't tend to process things out loud. He'd lost his wife early in their marriage and had gone so long without a partner that discussing the internal workings of his mind and heart was strange territory for him. This matter with Barb concerned him though, and he hadn't arrived at a solution on his own. "I just worry about her. She's turned on nearly everyone in her sphere. She threatens someone nearly every day and a couple of times it's gone beyond threats. I've had to pull her off several folks."

On a whim, Wayne pulled the cushions off the couch and searched beneath them, explaining, "I had a paranoid great uncle who always kept a gun under the couch cushions." Sure enough, he found a .38 revolver that must have been fifty years old and had no bluing left on it. He held it up for Conor to see.

"Maybe you and Shuck are related? A long-lost great-uncle?" Conor suggested.

Wayne cringed at the thought. "Back to Barb, what little bit I know about you makes it clear you didn't have a normal upbringing. You may not understand this, but what Barb is going through is not a whole lot different than what I went through in high school. It's a variation of what a lot of my friends went through. Your body is grown but your mind is still developing, then suddenly you've got all this freedom. You think you're Big Dick Willie from the south side of Philly."

Conor laughed. "I thought it was Big Dick Sammy from south Miami?"

"When I was growing up, that summer after high school, I had no idea what I wanted to do. I got a job on the assembly line at GM making more money than I'd ever seen in my life. I was living at home with my parents and didn't have a lot of expenses. I bought a fancy Mustang and went out drinking with my high school buddies every night. I was fighting, raising hell, and chasing women. On top of it, I didn't have any respect for anybody. I started getting in trouble. One thing led to another and I got locked up. Lost my job, my fancy car, and my dad booted me out. Told me I couldn't live there with them and act the way I was acting."

"So what did you do?"

"Joined the military. That's what you did in my day when you needed straightening out. If you couldn't do it yourself, they would do it for you. And they did."

"So, you think I need to send Barb off to the military?"

It was Wayne's turn to laugh then. "I don't think the U.S. military is ready for Barb. The Israelis possibly, but not ours."

"Now that's a thought. The Israelis." In his weariness, with his filters dropped, Conor almost went on to mention that he had contacts there who could make that happen but he caught himself.

"My point is, this sounds to me like a classic case of someone struggling to find themselves. I think the only way you get over it is to be thrown out into the world to see if you sink or swim. When you're at home, everything in your life follows the same old patterns from when you were a kid growing up. Your interactions with family are following old patterns from your childhood. They always treat you the same way. It's hard to figure out who you are because you're stuck in a mold that was built over the course of your lifetime. The only way you ever escape that mold is to get out on your own and totally change your environment. That's been my experience. With no one to prop you up if you fall, your own strengths and weaknesses become evident. You learn the truth of your character. The fluff burns away and what's left is *you*."

"You sure you're not a therapist in disguise? You have a lot of insight."

"Doctorate from the school of hard knocks and bad decisions."

Conor smiled but what Wayne said made sense to him. The more time he spent with the man, the more he grew to respect him. Conor hadn't gone through what Wayne described because his own childhood and teenage years had been so different. He'd matured early because he'd had to. While he'd been raised under the wing of a strong, stern mother, he'd also been influenced by the steady stream of organized crime figures that passed through their house. His childhood had been far from normal but he wouldn't change a thing. It made him who he was and he was okay with that.

The conversation with Wayne gave him a lot to think about. His job wasn't to fix Barb but to give her the opportunity to fix herself. He didn't need to remind her of who he'd tried to make her into. He didn't need to tell her who she was. What he needed to do was let her discover for herself who she was.

17

It took Conor and Wayne most of the night to construct their cache along the road. The easiest thing would have been to build one in the woods alongside the house, but if someone moved in it might be difficult to sneak over the bridge and ferry the mountain of goods back to the road.

The best spot ended up being across the bridge and down the road about sixty yards. That section of the road was secluded and no one should be able to see whoever was sent to retrieve the items. Even though it wasn't a long walk from the house, it took them a good bit of time to carry the numerous garbage bags, sacks, and buckets into the woods and stack them. In their exhausted state, they were staggering, falling, and dropping things pretty frequently by the time they were done.

Once they had everything they wanted from the house, they stretched a tarp across the pile, then put a sheet of black plastic on top of that. The plastic was weighted down with branches and fallen leaves until it was mostly indistinguishable from the terrain around it. From the road, no one would be able to tell that there was a cache hidden only a dozen yards away from them. When they were done, they sat down on a large boulder near their horses.

"I'm almost too tired to climb on that beast," Conor said. "I'm about ready to just grab his tail and let him drag me home."

"Then let's mount up," Wayne said, getting to his feet. "The longer we sit there, the harder it will get. Then one of us will pass out and we'll be laying there in the morning like a couple of drunks."

"It's almost morning," Conor said, glancing at his watch.

Wayne grabbed Conor by the sleeve and tugged. Conor struggled to his feet and limped to his horse. "I'm feeling too old for this tonight."

"You'll be fine after some sleep."

It took Conor three strong lunges with his foot in the stirrup to finally muster enough momentum to spring onto the back of his horse. Wayne was laughing so hard that he had to wipe tears from his eyes. They carried no bags of goods with them, only their personal gear. The sun would be up before they made it back to the firehouse and they didn't want to draw the attention of anyone moving around at this early hour. With sacks of loot strapped to their horses they would appear to be men who'd been out stealing. That was the last thing they wanted to look like in a day when everyone was armed and there was no law. People were inclined to shoot first and sort through the details later.

They kept their weapons at the ready and rode without headlamps. Though it wasn't light yet, the sky was already changing color. The horses were familiar with this trip by now and needed no guidance. For the first time, Conor understood how cowboys fell asleep in the saddle. Exhausted as he was, riding in the dark, the rocking motion of the horse was both hypnotic and lulling.

Wayne must have been feeling the same way because he started talking. "We should reach the firehouse just in time for breakfast."

Conor rubbed his eyes and yawned. "Can't decide if I'd be more excited about a meal or a bed at this point."

"Well, the quality of the meal depends on who's cooking and how creative they can get with what they have available. I can offer you a spot to stretch out by the fire but it can be a little noisy around the firehouse this time of day. It's cool enough that everyone stays inside.

I can make all the threats I want but once the kids are up it's hard to keep them quiet."

"That's okay. I think I'm just going to head back to my place. If I get too tired on the way, I'll just peel off into the woods and find me a secluded spot to stretch out. I've got a bivy sack with me and I'm no stranger to sleeping on the ground."

"You're going to come back to meet those guys with the steam generator, right?"

Conor nodded, which was complicated by another yawn he could not stifle. "Give me a day or two. I'm old and don't snap back from missing a night's sleep like I used to. As soon as I've recovered, I'll be back."

"That's good enough. No hurry."

They reached an intersection where Wayne was going to head right to the firehouse and Conor was going to head left toward Pastor White's camp and, beyond that, his own place. They paused for a moment.

"I wish there was an alternative route by the pastor's camp," Conor said. "Just getting by that place is going to take more energy than I have. They told me last night the pastor would probably want to talk to me about what happened to Miss Fannie Bell."

"There's no way by their camp without bushwhacking on the far side of the river. You could do it on foot but it's probably too rough for a horse."

Conor chuckled at himself. "If you only knew some of the things I've done in my life, Wayne. Some of the truly evil fuckers I've stared down. Some of the situations I've been in. I reckon I can face one scrawny preacher. I might as well get on with it and take my medicine."

"Say hi for me," Wayne said with a sarcastic smirk, turning his horse away and giving Conor a wave. "Thanks for the help."

<h1 style="text-align:center">18</h1>

Conor was exhausted nearly to the point of hallucinating when he neared Pastor White's camp. He felt disoriented, as if he'd slept through part of the ride. That concerned him. While he might be able to ride in his sleep, he highly doubted he could shoot and otherwise defend himself in that state. The morning sun was warm on his back and increased his desire to crawl off into the underbrush to sleep. Two guards manned the entrance. As his bleary eyes struggled to focus, the two blended into one and he realized it was but a single man. The guard was scrawny, with sharp, hawkish features, a bowl haircut, and a scowl that Conor assumed was triggered by Conor's appearance at his assigned duty station.

"What do *you* want?" the guard demanded, his voice thick with disdain. He obviously knew who Conor was and didn't approve.

It was the same snarky tone Bernard had used earlier but Conor was less patient. He was tired and hangry. "What's your name, son?"

"It's Jackson and I ain't your son, old man. If I was I'd probably throw myself in that river and kill myself."

Conor sighed. "You might not have to, Jackson. I might do it for you. I'm a tired man. When I'm tired my patience wears thin and my judgment slips. I do things I sometimes regret later. If you persist with the attitude, I'm going to snap your spine and shove your head up your own arse. Now you may think that's an idle threat, that such a thing couldn't be done, but let me assure you that it can. In fact I've done it. It requires a little trimming with a sharp knife to make everything fit just right but it's a sight that leaves a strong impression. Now tell me, is that how you want to be remembered by your loved ones? Found in the middle of the road with your head shoved up your own bunghole?"

"No sir," Jackson admitted, his brows crinkling as he imagined his family finding him in such a state.

Conor was impressed at the sudden improvement in the young man's attitude. It was almost magical how quickly people cooperated once you planted a disturbing image of their own death in someone's brain. Jackson was a fast learner. His parents should be proud.

"What I need is to speak with Pastor White. I returned Miss Fannie Bell to you people last night and was told the pastor might have some questions. I'm back to check on her and answer any questions the pastor might have. I'm exhausted, but I had to pass by here anyway, so I decided to stop."

"The pastor might be busy," Jackson said.

Conor's face registered his disappointment. He let out a long exhalation. "Jackson, I thought we were making such progress. Well, you had your chance. Let the pastor know I was by but you turned me away." Conor nudged his horse and started back toward the road.

"No!" Jackson cried. "Hold on for a minute. Don't leave."

Conor stopped.

"I just meant that I ain't seen him in a little bit. I'm not sure what he's doing."

"You find him *now*, boy. I'm growing weary of you."

"I ain't supposed to leave my post."

"I'll watch your post until you get back but make it snappy. I warned you, lad. My patience is slipping."

Not wanting to find out what an impatient Conor was like, Jackson flew from the gate, gangly and bandy-legged in his running. It was perhaps the most inelegant movement Conor had ever seen from a person in possession of all their faculties. Conor's eyes strayed around the camp, which was comprised of the church, a large picnic shelter, and a few tents. There were smoky fires for cooking and warmth. One heated a washtub for laundry or bathing. Women bundled in warm clothing cooked together over another. Around a third, stiff men stood circled and clannish, giving Conor a wary side-eye.

These people had always been distrustful of him. It was their way, both due to the insular nature of the community and their role as protectors. He was an outsider. An unknown. All they knew of him was violence and that he had a daughter who'd assaulted one of their own. They didn't like him and didn't trust him.

"Conor Maguire."

Conor turned toward the voice and found Pastor White closing in on him. The greeting was neither warm nor antagonistic. It did come with a slight hissing sound though. Pastor White still couldn't fully open his jaw thanks to Barb's vicious kick. Conor dismounted and stood with his reins in his hand. The pastor didn't come close and neither man extended a hand to the other in greeting. This was a meeting of tolerance, an exchange of information. A lot of fences would have to be mended before there was anything resembling trust between the two parties.

"Pastor White," Conor replied with a nod. "I wanted to check on Miss Fannie Belle."

Jackson stood behind the pastor, unsure of what to do with himself. He shifted nervously, gripping his gun too tightly.

"You can go stand with the other men, Jackson," the pastor said. "Leave Mr. Maguire and I to talk for a moment."

Jackson did as he was told, casting a wary eye at Conor as he departed. It could have been fear, or a warning not to further injure the spiritual patriarch of this community. Conor paid the lad no mind.

"I have a doctor living at my place," Conor said. "I thought I might send him over to check in on her. The leg wound could kill her if that infection isn't brought under control."

"That would be appreciated. We've cleaned and fed her, prayed and cared for her. As you've said, she'll need medications that we don't have. We'd be obliged to you, as we already are for your role in bringing her home."

"No offense, but we wouldn't be doing it for you. She's a sweet lady and I'd like to see her come back from this. She has to be tough as nails to endure what he put her through."

"She's not told us much about it. She's a proud lady. From what I hear about her wounds, the conditions must have been rough."

"More than rough, they were deplorable. Shuck Lampkins had her chained like a vicious dog. She was naked and cold. I watched him beat her down. He was preparing to stomp on her head when I put a bullet in him."

The pastor flinched at Conor's blunt portrayal of both the scene he found and the manner in which he addressed it. "My people said Bernard was killed too?"

"Shuck booby-trapped his bridge. We tried to keep Bernard from rushing across but he wouldn't listen to us. He fell through the bridge and hit his head on a rock. He died instantly."

"Were you able to retrieve the body for his parents? For a proper burial?"

"Shuck dragged him into the river. He may never be found. For his actions, we offered no Christian burial to Shuck either. I tossed him into the river like the sack of garbage he was."

The pastor nodded, processing this. The bruising on his face was starting to go away, faded to yellow, but not completely gone. Conor would have sworn Barb left the print of her bootlaces on the man's face.

"Well, it's done," Pastor White said with finality, as if it weren't the way he would have done it but there was no fixing it now.

Conor yawned and it caught the pastor's attention.

"You best get on home," he said. "You say you'll return with your doctor?"

Conor nodded. "Tomorrow, I think. I may be able to send him back here today but I won't be with him. I need sleep. Lots of it."

Conor positioned himself to remount his horse. He had to gather himself for it, the act nearly requiring more effort than he had on tap.

"Mr. Maguire?"

Conor paused, one foot in the stirrup, both hands grasping the saddle horn.

"If you can't bring the doctor yourself, I reckon I'd prefer he come alone. I ain't ready to face that daughter of yours yet. No offense to you but it's a sore spot." The pastor gently stroked his jaw. "A very sore spot."

With an awkward motion, Conor launched himself onto the horse's back. He settled himself and adjusted his hands on the reins. "I understand that and I'll make sure they know. At some point you two may have to make peace though. This isn't a very big community."

The pastor shrugged, wincing when the movement caused a sharp pain in his jaw. "I'll be praying on it."

19

As exhausted as he was, Conor could not pass by Johnny Jacks' house without stopping. He may have been a hardened killer, an assassin of men, but he hadn't been raised to be rude and to have passed by the older man's home without stopping would simply have been rude. Besides, he had an idea brewing that he wanted to run by Johnny.

He turned at the driveway, paused to yawn for the millionth time, and unlocked the gate. The creaking hinges would alert the family to his presence as surely as if he were to sound a horn. He awkwardly closed the gate without dismounting and, when he faced the house, found Jason Jacks waving to him from the porch.

Conor allowed his horse to walk the distance at its own pace, letting him cool down from the ride. By the time he reached the house, the rest of the family was also standing on the porch waiting on him. All showed signs of healing injuries. Sam's face was scratched from the treatment she received during her abduction. Johnny had a colorful bruise to the side of his face and looked like the porch rail was all that was holding him upright. That the man was still alive and upright after taking several bullets was a testament to his toughness. Certainly Doc Marty and Shannon had made a valiant effort to keep the man alive, but it was his own grit that pulled him through it.

Jason was the worst of any of them, having fought with all he had in an attempt to stop Sam's abduction. In the process, he'd lost many of his teeth and his mouth looked like he'd been snacking on gravel. His lips were no longer swollen but had been split in three places. His face was a roadmap of cuts and scrapes joined by bruises. He'd given up on shaving because the skin was so damaged. A beard would help conceal what were certain to be permanent scars.

"You look like shit, lad," Conor said.

"You should see the other guy," Jason quipped.

"I did," Conor replied. "Pretty sure I killed him."

Despite the grim nature of their conversation, there were smiles on every face. It was battlefield humor which might appear misplaced in such a pastoral setting, on the porch of a country farmhouse amid rolling pastures, but it was not. That was part of the nature of this apocalypse they were all entrenched in. The calm could be deceptive. The battlefield could be anywhere now, the enemy anyone with a weapon and bad intentions.

"You don't look so good yourself," Sam said. "You look like you're about to fall off that horse. You drunk this early in the morning?"

Conor laughed at that. He rarely drank, preferring to have his wits about him in his line of work. He never wanted to be laying about drunk when someone with a grudge decided to take their revenge. "Drunk with exhaustion, Sam dear. I've not slept since I left here yesterday."

"Why not?" Johnny asked. "Run into trouble?"

Conor sighed. "It's a long story and I'd like to sit down to tell it, but I'm afraid I won't be able to climb back on me horse."

"We'll help you," Jason offered. "Join us in the house. We've got some cold sweet tea. It might give you just the boost you need."

"Sweet tea?" Conor asked, an eyebrow cocked eagerly. He resembled a miser being offered a bag of gold.

Sam winked. "Just like Bojangles makes it." She'd heard of his weakness for Bojangles.

Conor grinned and slid from his horse. "Missy, you surely know the way to a man's heart." He tied his horse off to the porch rail and pulled himself up the steps. He followed the family inside and took a seat on the couch. He noticed it was a new one, brought in to replace the one Johnny's wife had died on.

Sam went to the kitchen and was back in a few minutes with a plastic milk jug of sweet tea and several tall glasses. "This house has a spring box in the basement. I've seen a lot of old houses with spring boxes in a dairy or spring house, but this one is more convenient. We'll have cold tea all next summer."

"My parents built this house just after they got married in the 1920s," Johnny said. "That was a modern convenience at the time. Kind of like us having a refrigerator in the kitchen. By the time I came along it was just a novelty. I liked playing in it when I was a kid."

With his first sip of the sweet tea, Conor felt like an intravenous solution of some magic elixir had been introduced into his body and he groaned. "That's good stuff." He crossed his legs and leaned back on the couch, relishing the moment.

Sam smiled. "Thank you."

"That blood on your shoe?" Jason asked.

"Oh, I'm sorry. Guess I should have taken my boots off before I came in."

"That's okay," Jason said. "I was just wondering how it got there."

Conor launched into the story of Miss Fannie Bell and Shuck. He mentioned how he needed to send Doc Marty back to check on her so they might expect a visit from him when he headed over this way.

"And there's one more thing," Conor added. "A favor if I might be so bold."

"You can ask anything," Johnny said. "This family owes you and we honor our debts."

"You owe me nothing," Conor said. "We're friends, and friends do for friends."

"Then by that same token, ask your favor," Johnny said. "If it's within my power, it's yours."

"I'd like to get Barb out of the house for a while," Conor began.

"She's going through a bit of an adjustment and I think she needs...something. Some new faces. Some new responsibilities. Some new adventures."

"We'd be glad to have her," Johnny said without hesitation.

"She'll bring her own food and weapons. She can help out with security in the area and deal with situations like the one I just dealt with."

Johnny held up a hand, gesturing that no more explanation was necessary. "She'll be fine. It'll be nice to have someone with her skills in the neighborhood. We have a spare room upstairs and she's welcome to it."

Conor sighed deeply, as if this were a burden lifted from him. "I really appreciate this, Johnny."

"No thanks required, my friend," Johnny replied. "We're pretty gimped up around here, so a spare set of hands is welcome."

Conor drained his tea and struggled to his feet. "Well, I better be going. If I sit any longer, I'm going to fall over and start snoring. I need to get home."

"You're welcome to stay," Jason said. "Take you a little nap if you want to. It's safer than travelling in a daze."

"I think I'll be fine."

"You need a boost onto that horse?" Sam teased.

Conor winked at her. "I think I can get on, but I might need you to tie my feet together under his belly so I can stay on."

20

Conor was beat when he reached his beloved compound at the top of Jewell Ridge. He'd learned a lesson on this trip. He had a stash of Modafinil at his compound, an amphetamine-like drug he could take to function without sleep on long operations. He never carried any with him unless he was certain he was going into a mission where he'd need it. That was going to change. From now on he was going to carry two doses in his regular kit. If he'd had some with him the previous night he'd have taken it. As it was, he was so nauseated from exhaustion that he'd certainly have vomited in the bushes if there was anything in his stomach to heave up.

He got on the radio before he rounded the last bend to let them know he was nearby, not wanting to take a chance that an overenthusiastic family member might open fire. After his transmission was acknowledged, he fished a lanyard of keys from around his neck, slid off his horse, and unfastened the rolling gate. He pushed it out of the way, then tried to get back on his horse but couldn't generate enough swing. He was done for.

"Fuck it," he mumbled just as Ragus came running up to help

him. Conor walked his horse through the opening while Ragus rolled the gate shut and locked it. "Where is everybody?"

Ragus fell in step beside him. "Outside the gym. They're doing martial arts training. Well, it's training for me but just practice for them. They're showing each other different moves. I'm just trying to learn enough to stay alive."

Conor experienced a flash of concern. He hoped exchanging martial arts techniques didn't mean that Barb was creating an opportunity to get physical with Shannon and Doc Marty. It was easy to do in martial arts sparring. Forget to pull a punch or a kick and someone could be seriously injured. It happened all the time when opponents had a grudge or something to prove.

Normally he wouldn't have to be concerned with such things but, as he'd explained to Wayne, Barb had taken a dark turn lately. She could be dangerous if the mood hit her. He felt like he had a plan for that, but he had to pitch it to her. If she didn't take it well, he might be the one suffering from her overenthusiastic sparring. He could end up like Pastor White, with his lower jaw spun round to the back of his head.

The gym was located in one of the smaller shop buildings on the property. When he staggered up he was pleased to find everyone enjoying themselves. He saw no bloody faces and no limbs hanging at odd angles. That was a relief. He pulled his gear off his horse and dumped it onto the ground by a wooden bench, sagged onto the bench, and cleared his rifle.

Barb, Shannon, Ragus, and Doc Marty all stopped what they were doing to watch him.

"You look like shit," Barb said in her customary delicate manner. "Like some kind of tactical wino."

Conor gave her a tired smile. "What happened to 'Good to see you, dear old Dad'? What happened to giving your weary father a hug?"

Barb rolled her eyes. "Well, if you're going to get all weird and weepy about it," she said, making a big show of walking over to give him a hug. She threw her arms around him and recoiled almost immediately. "Geez, Dad, you smell like a carcass. What the hell have you been doing?"

"What *haven't* I been doing would be easier to answer. I've ridden a lot of miles, killed a man, watched another die, saved an old granny woman, and toted a houseful of gear. I've sweated through me clothes a half-dozen times and wallowed in the blood of a miscreant that God must have dropped on his head. I watched a smartass kid fall to his death and I heaved a body off a bridge without so much as a word of prayer for his cursed eternal soul. You name it, I've probably done it. Except for sleeping. I haven't done any of that."

Doc Marty shook his head. "I thought you left to make a social call on Johnny Jacks. Twenty-four hours later you come in rambling out of your head."

Barb frowned at Doc Marty like he was an idiot. "I thought you knew my dad," she said. "That's how he rolls. He goes to feed the goats and returns with a necklace of human ears. He goes to the grocery store and a third world nation collapses because their dictator dies under mysterious circumstances."

Conor ignored them. "Ragus, my boy, would you mind tending to my horse? She's had a hard day and needs some attention. As a matter of fact, the same might be said for me."

"Then go to bed, old man," Barb suggested. "Can't have you falling and breaking a hip."

Conor yawned and held up a finger, urging her to hold that thought. "That's on the agenda. Have a few matters to take care of first."

With their training paused for the moment, Barb slid on a jacket. She'd been in a t-shirt but it was too cool for that if they weren't working their asses off. "Ragus has your horse. I'll take care of your gear if you can't totter back to the house with it. Don't worry about it."

"That's not it," Conor said. "Bear with me a second." He launched into a somewhat abbreviated version of what he'd gone through since leaving the house last. Had he not been exhausted, he'd have told the story with his usual flair and they'd have been there for a long time. As it was, he merely hit the highlights. By the time he was done, everyone had taken a seat and was shaking their heads.

"Nice story, Conor," Doc Marty said, "but it probably could have waited until after you'd gotten some sleep."

"There's a point. I need you to go over to Pastor White's camp and see to Miss Fannie Bell. The evil bastard that was keeping her had a chain around her ankle and it left a nasty wound. She had to walk around that house dragging the damn thing behind her. Her leg was already infected. I'm afraid if it's not dealt with she'll develop sepsis."

Doc Marty nodded. "That's a strong possibility, especially if she has poor circulation to her legs."

"Like my father does to his head," Barb jabbed.

"Exactly," Doc Marty agreed.

"I told them you'd be over today. Don't wait until I wake up. As tired as I am, I don't know when I'll wake up. Take Ragus and Shannon with you."

"Not me?" Barb asked.

"No, we need a few minutes. I have something I want to talk to you about."

Barb groaned.

Conor struggled to his feet. Just as had happened at Johnny's, those few minutes of sitting made it infinitely harder to start moving again. His body became stiff and it took a lot of effort to break it free of the effects of gravity. He could easily have laid over on the bench and passed out there for several hours, but he needed to deal with something. Since proposing the idea to Johnny and his family, the matter had bounced around in his tired mind for his entire ride back to his compound.

"Take a stroll with me, Barb. Let's walk the perimeter."

"We can do that," Doc Marty said. "Things are fine here. You just go on to bed."

Shannon put a hand on her father's arm. "Dad, he wants to talk to her alone. Get it?"

For a moment Doc Marty didn't get it, then awareness dawned on him. "Oh, okay. Got it. Shannon and I will go get our medical gear together." They wandered off toward the quarters they'd been staying in.

When Conor's gaze returned to his daughter, he found her staring at him with a raised eyebrow. He might have been able to fool some of the people he dealt with in his life, but he'd never been able to fool her. His attempt to maintain a poker face around her was a wasted effort. It was entirely evident that her father had something on his mind and it made her very suspicious.

Despite her reservations, she was aware if she wanted to hear what was on his mind she had to let him tell it in his own way and on his own schedule. If he wanted to take a walk, she'd take a walk. Her gear was propped against the outside wall of the gym building. She slipped on her gun belt, her chest rig, and her pack. She picked up her rifle and faced her dad. "Well?"

Conor was wearing his chest rig but he left his pack sitting on the ground. He slung his rifle over his shoulder and started walking. Barb fell in alongside him. The sun was warm but the air was cool, possibly in the mid-forties. It had frosted overnight but the sun had melted it, leaving small puddles of moisture in the dead leaves that covered the ground.

"You've got something written all over your face," Barb said. "If that's the same poker face you used in your professional career, it's a wonder you weren't killed years ago. Not sure it would fool anyone."

Her lack of tact was not something she'd inherited from Conor. He was a master at using his Irish charm to waltz into a conversation from the side. Conor wondered if that bluntness might be tempered over time with maturity and experience, or if it would always be part of her. If that was the case, she would have some bumps along the road of her life. Being buried in his thoughts and not responding to her comments did nothing to dispel Barb's concern.

"You going to come out with it or not? Do I need to throw you to the ground and start pounding on you?"

"Barb, as your father there is something I need to tell you."

"Is this about the birds and the bees?" Barb asked without missing a beat. "Because we never had that talk."

Conor became flustered, which was likely Barb's intention. She was paying him back for being obtuse. "No, it's not about the bleeding birds and bees. It's about you being a right pain in the arse to everyone in this house."

He hadn't exactly intended for it to come out like that. He had been trying to find a way to sugarcoat it, but Barb didn't understand sugarcoating. She didn't understand his roundabout way of speaking and skirting around the issue. Barb understood direct and plainspoken. Painful as it was, that was what was required.

He waited for Barb to respond, but she said nothing. Conor could tell, could sense, that his comment had both stunned and insulted her. What he couldn't tell was if it had hurt her feelings or not. Barb was difficult to read. Even he had difficulty with it. She was not the sensitive type, but this was new territory for them. More than anything, he worried about doing damage to their relationship that might never be fixed.

"Barb..." he began, unsure of what he was going to say behind it.

"No," she interrupted, holding up a hand. "I get it. I *have* been on edge lately. I'm not an idiot. I see how people react to me and I know it's my own doing."

"Why? What's going on that my cool and collected daughter is suddenly turning on everyone around her?"

Barb shrugged. She kicked an acorn with the toe of her boot. "It's complicated. I'm not sure I understand it entirely myself."

"Is it...a girl thing?" Conor asked hesitantly.

Barb turned on him, appalled. "Fucking hell? A girl thing? What the hell does that even mean?"

Conor backpedaled furiously. "I wasn't trying to offend you, daughter. I just don't know much about this emotional stuff that women go through. Sometimes I wonder if the two of us even have enough normal emotions to fill a beer can."

She smiled at that image. "You might be right there."

For a moment it looked as if she was going to say more but chose not to. Conor saw that the burden of continuance was upon him. He'd started this. He'd opened the gate. He had to push forward. "I've been thinking that it might do you good to get out of the house for a little while. Get out on your own and be around some new folks. Have some new experiences."

She gazed at him with an incredulous expression on her face. "You're throwing me out of the house?"

Conor's heart sank. Why did she have to rush to the worst possible interpretation of what he'd said? "No, Barb. That's not what I'm doing. I would never do that. I was just talking to Wayne about my concerns and he said some stuff that really made sense."

"So you were talking to Wayne about me?" Barb asked. Her tone made it obvious she didn't care to be the subject of discussion between her dad and some man she barely knew.

"The topic came up. We had a lot of time on our hands. We talked."

Barb nodded in acknowledgement but had an expression that was both knowing and accusatory. He could make this sound as innocent as he wanted but she didn't believe a word of it. "Oh, I get it, alright. A single father singing the woes of raising a daughter. Two men commiserating about the hotheaded nature of women and those damned emotions, those female things they don't understand."

"It was nothing like that," Conor assured her. "The timeline is a little fuzzy, but I recall we were talking about Pastor White and relations in that part of the community."

"Ah, there's another one with a fine understanding of the female sex."

"We were just talking about your little scuffle."

"T'werent a scuffle. I tried to decrapitate him with my boot."

"It's *decapitate*, Barb. Decapitate, not decrapitate."

"Not when it's done to a shithead."

"We were talking about community relations."

"Oh, I get it now. So your daughter is bad for your public image? Maybe you need to hire a publicist to correct the damage she's done?"

Conor started to deny it then realized he couldn't entirely. There was some partial truth there. "Actually, I think only *you* can repair the damage that's been done there."

"The bastard deserved it. He has no respect for women and that's why I did it. He needed to have his jaw kicked loose."

"I'm not suggesting otherwise, Barb. I'm just suggesting that there may have been overreaction on both sides. We might have to work with Pastor White and his people in the future. We might need a little trust there – a little good faith. Hearts and minds, darlin', that's how you win the people."

"I thought you won people over by filling their bellies?"

"No, that's your own troops."

They fell into an awkward silence after that. Conor felt like he'd said all he needed to say. If he continued to explain his position, he felt like he might undermine it. Could be it was best to just let it rest for a little while. He was exhausted and probably not in his best debate form.

"So what was the conclusion of your summit with Wayne on your wayward daughter? Was that where you decided that kicking me out was the solution?"

They passed a pile of plastic reels that had once held mining cable. Conor took a seat on one. He gestured at Barb to pull up another. "To be honest, the way you've been acting has not made me question you, it's made me question some of my parenting decisions. I raised a strong, capable daughter, but sometimes you're a bull in a china shop. I'm not saying this to be critical but to make you aware that you might need more to keep you occupied. You've been raised to be a sheepdog, but if you don't have enough to deal with you'll start nipping at your own sheep."

"Kind of like I am now." It was not a question, but a statement. Perhaps even a revelation.

Conor nodded. "Like you are now."

Barb mulled over her dad's words. She didn't want to issue an immediate blanket denial because she too understood there was something going on inside her. She was too short tempered and frustrated. She became angry over things that weren't worthy of her anger. She lashed out, sometimes violently, at provocations that, in hindsight, were not worthy of reaction. The problem was that she didn't know how to solve this problem on her own. Perhaps if people were offering insight she should listen, even if what they said stung a little bit.

"Seriously, Barb, this is keeping me up at night. Several times I've convinced myself that I failed you. That I've made you into something that would bring you nothing but frustration and unhappiness. I know that's not the case, though. I have confidence that I raised this razor-sharp child with the idea that I could throw you out into the world and you would always bob to the surface. You would always land on your feet and be able to set things right no matter the situation. The problem is I never threw you out into the world. I prepared you for launch but never launched you."

The idea that he might be throwing her out was no longer a joke and genuine worry clouded Barb's face. "Seriously, Dad, if you're throwing me out, where is there for me to go?"

Conor chuckled and patted Barb on the leg. "No way. You always have a home with me. But I do think you do need more responsibility. I talked to Johnny Jacks and his family about you staying with them for a little while."

"My God, you've lent me out as a farmhand?"

Conor laughed. "I know they could use the help around the farm, but the idea was that you could act as kind of a sheriff in that part of the community. You could deal with situations like the one Wayne and I just dealt with. You can keep an eye open for threats. You apply your intelligence, your tactical thinking, to the problems of that community and you help people out. It's only a short ride down the mountain."

"It seems further now."

"You know I would never do anything to hurt you, Barb. I seriously think this would do you good. You may even enjoy it."

"Pastor White's people hate me for adjusting his profile. The folks at the firehouse are scared because they saw the way I wrapped up one of their men. I can't imagine that I'll be met by anything but hostility over there."

"This was partly Wayne's idea. He's fully behind it and I think he's right. You need more room to spread your wings and see what you're made of. There's no point in me giving you all these skills and never letting you use them."

"So this house isn't big enough for the two of us?" she asked. "Just like a line from some cheesy Western?"

Conor laughed. "You know my house is always *our* house. There will never be a time or place in this world where you are not welcome at my side. This won't be easy for me either, Barb. I'll worry about you constantly. I'll never walk through this house that I don't wonder where you are and what you're doing."

Barb glanced away, watching a squirrel trace an ascending spiral path up a poplar. "You know, Dad, my first reaction was to be pissed off. I felt like you were pushing me out of the house to make room for Ragus, Shannon, and Doc Marty. I don't feel that way anymore. I understand you're right. I *do* feel confined and I'm not certain I even understood that until you said it. I'd like to try this. Like you said, I think it would be good for me. If I get over there and I hate it I can always come home, right? You aren't going to change the locks on me, are you?"

Conor's heart was too heavy to laugh. It was the first time he ever felt as if he was sending his baby girl out into the world on her own. It felt like she was going away to college or to get married or something. It was a tiny step but things would never be the same again. She would still be his daughter but she would also be her own woman in a way she'd never been before. He had an idea that she would find excitement and adventure in the world. As for him, he'd immediately feel much older and much more alone than he'd ever felt before.

"So when do I leave?"

"That's entirely up to you, but we could go tomorrow if you want. That will give you time to pack your gear. I'll take a pack horse for your food and gear, then bring it back with me."

"Well, I guess I need to get back to the house so I can get started. You sure you'll be okay without me, old man?"

Conor couldn't answer. Exhaustion made the emotions run close to the surface. He muttered something, aware that anything he said might turn into a sob. He couldn't count the number of men he'd killed, both in the name of business and patriotism. He'd done some nasty things to some nasty people. Yet a heart-to-heart talk with his little girl could floor him like nothing else.

21

The next morning they secured the compound and headed out as a group. They planned on being back that evening -- everyone except Barb, that is -- but plans could change on a dime. They made sure all their animals had food and water for a few days, then locked everything up tight. Doc Marty and Shannon had followed Conor's advice to go check in on Miss Fannie Bell the previous day, just after Conor got home, so today's visit would be a follow-up. Conor led a pack horse with personal gear and provisions for Barb. He was confident Johnny Jacks would treat her like family, that was the kind of man he was, but Conor didn't want to be a drag on anyone else's supplies. She would take her own food and ammo. Ragus was just tagging along for the ride. He'd become so proficient at running the compound lately that he got stuck there taking care of things more often than he cared for.

"That's the price you pay for making yourself useful, lad," Conor teased. "Had you been a laggard I'd have to make other arrangements."

The mood of the group was somewhat subdued. Doc Marty and Conor refrained from jabbing at each other in their normal manner. Barb kept to herself and held back on the typical snide comments that escaped her mouth as easy as an exhalation. She wasn't upset about the turn of events. Her silence was due to thoughtfulness about what lay ahead of her. It would be an entirely new experience in a whole range of ways. She was used to being part of a team with her father and this adventure would be more of a solo experience. In fact, that was the whole point. She felt capable of taking care of anything she might face but her mind couldn't sit still. It kept jumping to scenarios.

Conor intuitively understood that his daughter was lost in thought. It was like the serious state she fell into before a mission. Doc Marty, Shannon, and Ragus were uncertain as to how to read the situation. They took her silence for broodiness or anger, both of which could be concerning in the hands of Barb. From what they knew of her, if Barb wasn't happy, no one was happy.

They reached the entrance to Johnny's place at midmorning. A strong sun followed an overnight frost and a chilly morning. The group took advantage of the pause to shed some layers and stash them in their packs.

"I think Shannon and I will ride on over to Pastor White's camp," Doc Marty said. "Say hello to Johnny for me. Tell him I'll pop in on my way back through if he has any concerns about how he's healing."

Conor nodded. "He's a tough old bird. Appears to be healing well from what I can see. He's moving around and he wants to live. That's important because I've known men to die from what he went through."

"Same here," Doc Marty said. "The whole family is made of tough stuff."

"What about me?" Ragus asked. "You want me with you, Conor, or do you want me to go with Doc Marty and Shannon?"

Conor knew where the lad wanted to go. He and Shannon were nearly inseparable so he thought a little space might do them good. It would force the boy to get his head out of his ass and pay attention to his surroundings. "You stay with me, lad. After we get Barb squared away the three of us will ride over to the firehouse. I want to let Wayne know that Barb's around."

"So you think he needs fair warning?" Barb asked. "Maybe you should just put a warning sign at the end of the gate, like I'm a vicious dog or something."

Conor grinned. "Now there's an idea. But no, that's not the point. The idea is that he might actually be able to use you as a resource. He gets sucked into a lot of these things like hunting for Miss Fannie Bell, but he has a lot on his plate. He's trying to get his people and that firehouse in order for winter. He can't take care of that if people are depending on him to police their community. I'm hoping he'll refer some of those situations in your direction."

"Yeah right," Barb said, unconvinced. "This whole community is more likely to burn me at the stake than depend on me for help."

Johnny's dog had picked up on the sound of their conversation and began barking. Doc Marty and Shannon took this as their cue to leave and departed with a wave. Ragus walked the gate open from the back of his horse. Conor slipped through leading the pack horse, Barb on their heels. Ragus tried to shut the gate in the same way he'd opened it but found it difficult. He couldn't get his horse positioned just right so he ended up jumping off and doing it the old-fashioned way. By the time Ragus caught up with Conor and Barb, Johnny's entire family had filtered out onto the porch to greet their guests. As Conor knew they would, they greeted Barb as if she were a long-lost family member. That made Conor much more comfortable with the situation. Despite all the things Barb was, she was still his baby girl.

Jason took the lead for the pack horse from Conor and tied it off to the porch. He wasn't a man who waited around to be asked before jumping into a task. He began unpacking Barb's gear and stacking it on the porch. "All this go?"

"It does," Conor replied. "I'll take the horse back with me. I figure you have plenty of horses around if she needs a pack animal while she's here."

Jason chuckled. His dad was an infamous trader and rescuer of horses that people couldn't care for. He usually had dozens of animals at a time, though he'd been trading off a lot of them recently.

The lack of fuel brought about a proportional increase in people's desire to have animals that ran off grass instead of gas.

Ragus dismounted and tied off his own horse. Unsure of what else to do, he began carrying Barb's gear into the house. "What do I do with this stuff?"

"I'll show you," Sam said. She grabbed a heavy ammo can and rushed inside the house. "Barb will be upstairs."

"This bag is heavy," Ragus called back out the door. "This your makeup and perfume, Barb?"

She ignored him, sitting on her horse and staring at the house. He wondered for a moment if she had changed her mind. If she did, he couldn't force her to stay. They'd continue on and he'd try to find some new way to deal with what she was going through.

Johnny, perhaps sensing her hesitation, her uncertainty, spoke up. "Barb, we sure are glad to have you. Our house is your house. Besides just having someone new to speak to around here, it's comforting to have someone with your skills around the house. We've done the best we can but we're obviously not covering all bases." To emphasize his point, he gestured toward one of his healing wounds.

Conor wondered if Barb might live up to her name and reply was some smartass retort. Some remark about how she appreciated Johnny taking her in when her own father threw her out of the house to make room for strangers. She didn't though. She smiled warmly -- actually smiled a genuine smile -- and told Johnny, "I appreciate you having me. I'll be glad to help out in any way I can."

Conor couldn't hold back a smile of his own. This was going to work out after all. He just knew it.

"I guess you know where the barn and the paddock are if you want to turn out your horse," Johnny offered.

Barb looked at her father, uncertain about how to reply, and he took over.

"Johnny, I think we're going to run down to Wayne's camp since it's early. I want to let him know Barb is going to be staying with you for a while."

"He wants to *warn* him," Barb told Johnny, rolling her eyes.

Johnny laughed. "That should be good. You should let the pastor know too." Johnny was too old to leave thoughts unsaid. He wasn't an unkind man but saw no reason to hold back. He called them like he saw them.

"I'll keep my feet firmly in the stirrups," Barb said. "No kicking."

Johnny winked at her and grinned.

"I have hopes she and the pastor will eventually shake hands and make nice but that's between them," Conor said. "I'll not press the issue."

Barb finally climbed off her horse and Johnny held the door for her to go inside. She wasn't the homey sort. She cared more about utility and function than comfort. It didn't much matter to her where she slept as long as she could sleep comfortably enough to wake up feeling ready to go. She'd been so young when her mother died that she didn't even recall living in a house decorated with a woman's touch. She stared at the decor, feeling a little out of place.

Sam, perhaps eager to have another female in the house, was excited to show Barb the accommodations that had been made for her. Out of politeness -- *yes, Barb could be polite* -- she followed Sam up the stairs to the neat bedroom that had been set up for her. She reminded Sam that she didn't want them to go to any trouble for her but that she was appreciative of the effort they'd made. She didn't always use her manners. Not all folks were deserving of them but these people were. They were among the good ones and she had nothing to prove to them. No boundaries to establish nor territory to squabble over.

Worried that his daughter might be uncomfortable being the focus of so much attention Conor called to her from downstairs, letting her know he was ready to ride to Wayne's camp at the firehouse. He asked if any of the family wanted to go with them but everyone passed on the offer.

"I'm not fit for the saddle," Johnny said, shaking his head in disappointment. "I tire quickly and there's holes in my middle that ache if I jostle around too much."

Conor patted the man on the back. "Well, I certainly don't want to get you in trouble with Doc Marty. He gets a little bent out of shape when his patients aren't following his instructions."

Johnny nodded, wide-eyed. He did indeed understand the wrath of Doc Marty and Shannon, having suffered it when he tried to get back to his farm chores a little too early.

"What about you, Jason?" Conor asked as they all filed out onto the front porch.

"Nah, fences to check. Four pregnant mares needing attention. The list goes on from there."

Conor understood. Farming had been a family activity up until machinery had allowed one man to do the work of several. Without the machinery there was a huge labor gap revealing itself. Even those with horses lacked the proper horse-drawn equipment to put them to work.

The trio mounted their horses, said their good-byes, and headed down the driveway. They paused at a shallow brook that ran along the road and allowed their horses to drink.

"Those are good people," Conor remarked. It was an offhand statement, merely voicing the thoughts passing through his head.

It was such an obvious statement that no one felt a need to respond to it. They sat in silence, listening to horses lap at the water, until Ragus spoke up. "Yeah, we're hoping some of it rubs off on you, Barb."

Conor snapped his head toward Ragus in surprise, ready to launch himself between them. Barb's face revealed her own shock. Ragus gave them an innocent grin. To Conor's relief, Barb began laughing at his audacity and Conor soon joined in.

Ragus's offhand comment had been uncharacteristically bold. Considering Barb's temperament of late, it had almost been foolhardy, perhaps even dangerous, but it broke the tension that defined the relationship between the three for the last weeks. They were suddenly back to being the family they'd been before Doc Marty and Shannon had arrived.

Barb laughed until there were tears in her eyes. "There will be payback for that, kid. You won't know when and you won't know where there will be payback," Barb said, giving Ragus a wink.

After the horses drank their fill the riders directed them back onto the road and toward the firehouse. Despite the fact that Pastor White's camp lay unavoidably between there and the firehouse, Conor was as happy as he'd been a while. In their laughter, he felt as if order had been restored. You never knew what it would take to set the world right sometimes. It was never what you thought. You could plot and strategize all you wanted but sometimes the stupidest, most random thing worked the miracle that you needed.

22

Conor and his group did not have to pass through Pastor White's security to reach the firehouse. Their guard station didn't block the main road but was off to the side, instead blocking the entrance to the pastor's camp and his roadside church. The guard post was really nothing more than a token gesture because no fences separated the church property from the roadway. Conor could simply ride ten feet past the sentry, turn his horse to the right, and he'd be in the yard of the church. If there was ever a real threat in this community, they'd have to do something a little different. He understood that the church was the center of their lives but the location couldn't have been any worse from a defensive standpoint.

He noticed that the guard was the same lanky, hatchet-faced man he'd dealt with yesterday when passing through. Jackson had been his name, Conor recalled. He didn't know if that familiarity would be a good or bad thing. The sentry completely ignored Conor, having established some boundaries with him on their previous encounter, but Barb got the same squinty-eyed and hawkish expression that Conor had received yesterday. It was a glowering gesture of hostility, an acknowledgement that Jackson knew who Barb was and she wasn't welcome there.

"Should I lunge at him and see if he flinches?" Barb whispered, smirking.

"He'd pee on himself," Ragus said.

"No," Conor said. "I told you we wouldn't stop here unless asked to do so."

"Yeah, like that's going to happen," Barb said.

"Perhaps not today but at some point I expect it will," Conor said. "They're going to need us and we're going to need them."

"You might have mentioned that before I tried to amputate the pastor's face with my foot."

Conor shot her a look. "I recall suggesting you both cool out a little and it did no good."

"Cool out?" Ragus asked.

"He means chill out," Barb said. "He's not as hip as he thinks."

"Oh, don't doubt me, my child. I'm way more hip than you think. Keep badgering me and I'll climb up on a car at the firehouse and do me twerky dance."

"You'll only be embarrassing yourself, old man," Barb replied. "I long ago grew immune to your antics."

"We'll see."

No one from the pastor's camp hailed them. If Pastor White himself was about, he didn't show himself. There were no hurled insults or snide comments, nor were there any threats. The looks they received were not inviting but they also didn't carry the promise of violence. They appeared to be people more disappointed in the actions of another than ready to kill over them. Was it possible that Conor returning Miss Fannie Bell to them had earned some points and broken the ice? Would they be willing to give his group the benefit of the doubt? That remained to be seen.

From the road they could see that the pastor's camp was at full hum. People were moving around and cooking. Others were cleaning clothes in washtubs of steaming water. The men were gathered in tight circles and speaking conspiratorially between themselves.

"Well, that went well," Ragus said when they were out of sight of the camp.

"They must've been petrified with fear," Barb quipped.

"I could swear that I saw a couple holding onto their jaws," Ragus said. "Just in case your feet started flying."

"They also knew you were coming," Conor said. "Doc Marty and Shannon are in there somewhere seeing to Miss Fannie Bell. The pastor may have expected us to stop and instructed his people to behave if you showed up. Do I need to give you that same lecture?"

"You had to say that, didn't you?" Barb asked. "You were *there* when I spun his jaw off his face. You know why it happened and you fucking well know he deserved it. I didn't provoke the man any more than I provoked the folks back at his camp. I didn't tolerate his shit and I won't tolerate theirs. I've killed more men than I've kissed and that should tell you something about Barb Maguire."

Despite her rant, both Ragus and Conor were smiling.

"She's definitely your daughter," Ragus cracked.

"That she is," Conor agreed. "So much fire in her blood that sometimes she burns herself."

"Whatever," Barb muttered.

23

The appearance of riders at Wayne's camp had a more pronounced effect than it had at Pastor White's camp. There was a single guard and, alerted by the sound of approaching hooves, he'd taken cover behind a junk car.

"Mad Mick, party of three," Conor announced. "We'd prefer a booth. Something toward the back if you have it."

The sentry eased out from behind the car, his gun lowered now that he recognized the visitors. Conor had spent some time with the man the other night and recognized him too. He was among the party that Wayne had taken to Shuck's house to bring back items the camp could use. He recalled that the man's name might be Brad.

"Wayne ever recover from our trip or is he still out cold?" Conor asked.

"Nah, he's awake," Brad replied. "It's been a little lively around here this morning. We had some company show up."

That immediately got Conor's attention. "Were you attacked or you mean real company?"

"Real company. As in a social call."

"Who? Someone we know?"

"Wayne can fill you in on the details. They're standing around the fire. It's a guy we knew from Michigan. They must have followed us and just caught up. I don't know all the details because I've been stuck out here."

"Then pardon us, Brad," Conor said. "I'd like to hear what the man has to say."

The firehouse was immediately on the side of the road, much like the pastor's camp. Such situations were hard to avoid in the narrow, mountainous valleys of the central Appalachian Mountains because the only buildable land tended to be at the very bottom or very top of the mountains. What Wayne did differently than the pastor was he that he had guard posts along the road before you got to his camp.

Brad waved them by, a token gesture since Conor had already spurred his horse into a trot. He was anxious to hear news from outside but thought it unwise to run his horse into an armed camp. He found Wayne, some of his folks, and a contingent of newcomers gathered around a smoky fire across the road from the firehouse. It was along the riverbank, where Wayne's people gathered to talk about business away from sensitive ears. When Conor's group appeared, all conversation stopped.

Conor climbed off his horse, searched about for a moment, and then handed the reins off to Ragus. "Water him, please," he said, pointing toward the river.

Ragus stood there frowning, knowing he'd miss any good conversation. While he was lamenting that, Barb tied her reins over his outstretched forearm. "Water it, please."

He frowned at her and was greeted with a smirk. Before he could say anything she'd walked off to join her dad.

Conor shook hands with Wayne and a few of the other men. Wayne went out of his way to shake hands with Barb, making certain she was included. To Barb, who had been a little uncertain of how she'd be received, the gesture helped put her at ease. They were treating her with respect and that went a long way with her.

Wayne stepped back and gestured toward a thick-chested Hispanic man standing behind him. "Conor, this is my old friend,

Pepe. He lived south of Detroit in Taylor, Michigan. We worked together on a lot of construction jobs over the years."

Pepe extended a hand, shaking with both Conor and Barb. He was intense and focused in the manner of people who'd either come from a military background, law enforcement, or life on the streets. It was that hyper-aware, switched-on state that bordered on paranoia but kept you alive when random people might want to kill you.

"Good to meet you, Pepe," Conor said. "How the hell did you ever find their camp back here in the middle of nowhere?"

"Wayne came by my house before he left town, explained where he was going, and how he was going to get there. He told us to get on Route 23 at Toledo because the interstate highways might get gridlocked if cars ran out of fuel. He was right from what we heard. We followed Route 23 all the way here. It wasn't easy, though. We should have left when Wayne did and stuck with his group."

"We had symbols prearranged," Wayne said. "When you're rough framing a house, you have layout marks that indicate studs, jack studs, trimmers, cripples, and all of the other standard cuts of lumber that make up a house. One of the symbols is a circle with a slash through it. I told Pepe that if we had to get off the road for any reason I would leave that mark on the back of an exit sign."

"And we found it," Pepe said.

"Were you able to drive down? You have fuel and working vehicles?" Conor asked.

"No, man. We're hoofing it. If we'd been in our trucks we may not have noticed his mark, even though we were constantly watching for it. Since we were walking, it was easy to spot. We didn't know if we should get off at the exit or keep walking down Route 23 but we decided to take a chance. I wanted to see if Wayne and his folks were close by. Most of our people stayed back at the exit while we came looking."

"We have folks headed there now to bring them in," Wayne explained.

"So you walked all the way here from Detroit?" Conor asked.

"No," Pepe said. "We just walked from the Huntington, West

Virginia area. We got that far before we lost our vehicles. It's a long story."

"And a scary one," Wayne said.

"Really scary," Pepe said. "All I've got is bad news."

"We wouldn't know what to do with good news," Conor said. "It's in short supply these days."

"We stuck around Detroit until it was almost too late. Gangs barricaded the roads and were systematically looting neighborhoods. It turned into a war zone. After they looted a neighborhood they burned it, because that's what they do in Detroit."

"They love their Devil's Night," Wayne agreed.

Pepe nodded. "The chaos made it difficult to get out of the city, even though we'd hoarded away fuel for the trip. Some of us had campers and some had enclosed tool trailers that we used for our construction businesses. We packed them with hunting gear, camping gear, food, and everything we could carry. We treated it like we were fleeing a wildfire and didn't know if we'd even have a home to go back to."

"Sounds like you were prepared," Wayne said.

Pepe shrugged. "I thought we were. We ran into some hassles on the way but we dealt with it. Flat tires, abandoned vehicles blocking the roads, attempted carjacking, that kind of thing. Then around Chillicothe, Ohio, we ran into the remains of some massive firefight. There were bodies everywhere. Neighborhoods had been burned to the ground. A path of total destruction. We saw some folks going through the dead bodies and at first we thought they were looting them but it turned out they were searching for missing loved ones. When we asked locals what happened, they said it was a group called The Bond."

"The Bond?" Conor repeated. "What the hell is The Bond? Some kind of gang?"

Wayne shrugged. "No idea."

"They told us that The Bond hit town a few days ahead of us and set up camp on the outskirts. People thought it was the Army at first because everyone was dressed in Army uniforms, driving old Army vehicles, and using military gear," Pepe said. "But I don't think it was the Army."

"How do you know it wasn't the Army?" Wayne asked.

"Because if this was the Army, things are worse than we ever imagined. People approached the strangers at first because they thought they were there to help. Like they were part of some relief effort or something. They found out pretty quickly that wasn't the case. These guys did whatever they wanted. They took women, food, fuel, and whatever they found. Anyone complained, they died. Anyone stood up to them, they died. Hell, they said The Bond killed people just for target practice. Just to see if they could hit them."

"How many people are you talking about?" Conor asked. "If people confused it with the Army, you must be talking about a lot of people."

"Could have been a hundred or more," Pepe said. "People don't estimate well when you're talking about a group that large."

"You're lucky you didn't cross paths with those guys," Wayne said. "It might not have ended well."

Pepe's face darkened. "Oh, we did cross paths with them eventually."

"You ran into The Bond?" Conor asked.

"Literally," Pepe said. "We were trying to cover as much distance as possible. Several in my group had relatives in the south with farms. We figured the south would be more hospitable even if we had to rough it for a while. Without power, there just aren't enough trees and furniture to keep Detroit residents warm this winter. People are going to freeze if they don't die from the lack of food and clean water first. So anyway, we're driving as fast as we safely can, just stopping to refuel from our cans and take bathroom breaks. Then we hit the outskirts of Huntington, West Virginia, just as it was getting dark one night. We didn't want to stop there because there were too many people. We decided to push through and stop once we got past it. We were driving slow, running on our park lights only, and we ran right smack into them. They'd parked in the middle of the damn road."

"The Bond?" Wayne confirmed. "You're sure?"

Pepe nodded. "Oh, I'm sure. They just stopped in the road and set up camp right there. Next thing you know, we run up against a roadblock and two armed men. We'd talked about how to handle this situation and we had a plan. At least we thought we did. The lead truck had a heavy bumper and was supposed to push through the roadblock. They were supposed to run over anyone who got in the way but they panicked. They stopped and it all went to shit from there."

"What happened?" Conor asked.

"We had radios for communicating between vehicles," Pepe said. "I was in the second vehicle. I immediately told my folks to throw it in reverse and get the hell out of there. Some of the vehicles further back were able to turn around and get away. Some backed into each other in the chaos. Airbags were popping because people were hitting each other. Trailers were jackknifing and getting hung up on the guardrail."

"What did the sentries at the roadblock do?" Wayne asked.

"I figured that the main force must have been occupied somewhere else. Perhaps searching for food or fuel, maybe off looting somewhere, because there wasn't a lot of response when the shooting first started. It had to be the same folks, though, because of all that military gear. I would have thought it was the Army too if we hadn't heard those stories in Chillicothe," Pepe said.

"How did the shooting start?" Conor asked.

"They tried to pull our lead driver out of his truck. He panicked and shot the sentry. He had his family in the truck with him and he got scared. The guy went down but the second sentry opened up on the driver. I had my rifle ready to go. I popped out the door and nailed the second sentry, then ran up to see if my driver was dead. The sentry I hit wasn't dead and he was trying to get to his gun. I ran up on him and shot him again. I had a light on my rifle and I could see the guy had a gang tattoo I recognized on his neck."

"You sure it was a gang tattoo?" Wayne asked.

Pepe raised an eyebrow. "You know my roots, dude. I grew up with that shit. This was ink I recognized. Detroit stuff."

"Got it," Wayne replied.

"So my guy's wife was screaming her head off. I check her husband and he's dead. I run back and tell my wife she's got to drive our rig because I'm going to have to drive his truck with his family. Then I noticed that we were boxed in. The truck behind me tried to bang out a U-turn and got hung up. They were stuck. My family and the dead guy's family were trapped between the roadblock and the stuck vehicle. To make matters worse, I could hear men shouting from the direction of the roadblock. There were more men coming.

"I ran back to the front truck and told my friend's family they had to get out. Just grab what they could grab and follow me. They were all screaming about their stuff but I told them they had to come with me right then or they were going to die. They piled out and we ran back to my truck. I had a bugout bag behind the seat and I grabbed it. I told my family we were going to have to run and they weren't any more excited about it than my dead friend's family. I had to scream at them to get them moving. We just started running. They were all crying and screaming. We ran as hard as we could, trying to find our folks."

"Did you *all* reconnect?" Wayne asked. He gestured at Pepe's companions. "I mean obviously you found some of them but did you find everyone?"

Pepe nodded. "Thank God for the radios. Except for the man who got killed, we didn't lose anyone. What we lost was gear. About half of the vehicles in our caravan were lost at that roadblock. Some folks eventually figured out they had to disconnect their trailers to get turned around. That meant the vehicles we managed to keep lost any fuel and gear they had in the trailers and campers. That devastated us, man. We were pretty sure we'd make it down south before things fell apart. Now we're crippled and in survival mode."

"Did you walk all the way here from Huntington?" Conor asked. "That's a pretty good haul."

"No," Pepe said. "We made room in the vehicles we kept and crammed inside them. Had to throw away a lot of gear, though. We made it to Pikeville, Kentucky, before we burned up the last of our fuel. We've been walking a couple of days."

"I'm sorry, man. I know what that's like," Wayne said, patting his old friend on the shoulder.

Recounting his experience had depressed Pepe. His excitement at finding Wayne's group was replaced with hopelessness as he remembered their situation. "We're pretty much fucked," he said. "We had a plan. We had enough gear to at least get us started. Some of us lost everything except the clothes and gear on our backs. Our friends who managed to keep their vehicles had to dump part of their gear to make room for us. We should have left when you guys did, Wayne. We might have made it then."

Wayne shrugged. "You see how far we got, man. We didn't make it, either."

"What are you going to do? What's your plan?" Conor asked. He did his best to make it not sound challenging, like he was trying to run Pepe and his group off. He'd sounded that way when he'd first encountered Wayne and he was trying to do better, trying to improve his people skills. Like Barb, he was a work in progress.

Pepe didn't take offense at the question. "We have to get off the road. I don't think we have any choice."

"Why?" Wayne asked.

"Because I think The Bond is headed this way."

24

"Wait," Conor said, holding up a hand. "You haven't run into them since Huntington. What makes you think they're headed this way?"

Pepe shook his head as if trying to rid it of a bad memory. "We don't know for certain, but once we literally ran into them, several things we'd seen along the road fell into place for me. There was a lot of devastation on Route 23. Massive campsites with a lot of trash around them."

"That could have been anyone, Pepe," Wayne said. "There are a lot of people on the road and a lot of them are headed south."

"We saw a lot of that, but this was different. There were signs of gunfire everywhere but these people don't just shoot up a place, they devastate it. We found spent 40mm grenade casings along the route. Twice we found discarded rocket launcher tubes near buildings that had been blown all to hell. None of that hit me until we found out about this group. We were apparently following in their tracks on our entire journey."

"And you're certain the things you found are tied to this group you call The Bond?"

"Hell, man, how can I be certain of anything?"

"It's possible they are thinking the same way I thought," Wayne told Conor. "They realize the communities along the interstate will be picked over and they're hitting smaller routes."

"I wonder who they are," Conor said. "What is The Bond? Why that name?"

"I don't know," Pepe said. "They're proud of the name though."

"Why do you say that?" Conor asked.

"They leave their mark."

"Like a sign? Do they write it out with spray paint or something?"

Pepe laughed coldly but there was no mirth in his eyes. "They write it but not in spray paint. A couple of times we found it written in the dead."

"They carved it into the bodies?" Wayne asked, appalled but trying to grasp what Pepe was alluding to.

"Sometimes. Other times they twisted the dead up until they spelled the name out with the bodies. We found that twice."

"That's fucking sick," Barb said.

"That doesn't sound like military men unless they've gone very, very bad," Wayne said. "The people I served with wouldn't do shit like that."

"The people we spoke to in Chillicothe were certain they were military," Pepe said. "They had military weapons and older military trucks. They wore uniforms."

"They might be running those multi-fuel trucks," Conor said.

"Just what I was thinking," Wayne said. "They'll run off anything petroleum-based. Diesel, gas, heating oil, aviation fuel, you name it."

"Man, I hate to ask but do you know of any place we can hole up?" Pepe asked. "I'm not asking for charity. We'll try to fend for ourselves until we can move further south but we need to get off the road for a little while. The children are cold and exhausted. Everyone is terrified of The Bond catching up with us. We need a place to stop for a few weeks and regroup. After that, we'll continue on south and hope we can outrun the winter weather."

Wayne looked at Conor. "You know the area better than I do, man. You got any ideas?"

Conor thought for a moment. "I don't know of any place in the immediate area that would have enough room for you. Wayne's folks have packed the firehouse until it's busting at the seams."

Wayne nodded in agreement to that. "What about Pastor White?"

"I don't think he has the space," Conor said. "His church is packed and Pepe's group would be a lot of fresh mouths to feed. Plus the people of his church can be kind of clannish. They are suspicious of outsiders."

"What about Shuck's house?" Wayne asked.

Conor raised an eyebrow. "You might be onto something. How many people in your group, Pepe?"

"Thirty-two."

"It might be tight but it's better than nothing and it's not too far off," Wayne said. "We'd need to let the pastor know that folks were going to be staying there. Wouldn't want any of his people heading up there with the same thought only to find it occupied already."

"Can you take care of getting them there, Wayne?" Conor asked. "Show them around and how to work the wood stove?"

Wayne thought for a moment, replaying the route in his head. "Definitely."

"Okay, then," Conor said. "Here's the plan. You help Pepe get his people together and then deliver them to Shuck's place. I'll head up to the pastor's camp and let him know that folks are going to be staying at Shuck's place."

"That works," Wayne said.

"Then I'll be back in the morning," Conor said. "We need to go on a little mission."

Wayne groaned. "Don't tell me we're going on a road trip? I'm still wore out from the trip to Shuck's house."

Conor nodded. "We have to. You guys are close to the road. Your camp would be the first thing The Bond found if they got off the road here. Do you want to take that chance?"

Wayne turned it over in his head, weighing the options. "No. We've already spent too much time getting this place set up for the winter. I don't want to move again and I sure as hell don't want to be run out."

"Even if you could move your folks, we couldn't move everyone else in the community," Conor said. "There'd be nowhere to put them. We need to figure out who this group is, what they're doing, and plan accordingly."

"What does plan accordingly mean?" Barb asked. "How do you plan for something like this?"

"Why, you plan to kill them," Conor said, as if it were the most obvious thing in the world.

"How many people are you talking about taking?" Pepe asked.

"Light and fast," Conor replied. "Wayne and me in the lead with a second wave following up behind us."

"A second wave of what exactly?" Pepe asked.

"Fighters, of course," Conor said.

Pepe snorted. "Dude, you can't fight these people. There's at least a hundred of them. They have serious weapons. Belt-fed machine guns, grenades, rocket launchers. Who knows what else?"

"We have some tricks up our sleeves too," Conor said. "I've been around the block a time or two myself."

"I'm willing to help you," Pepe said, "and I have other guys in my group who would probably help. This sounds like a death mission though. It's like cavemen throwing rocks at men from the future with guns."

"Leave the worrying to us," Conor said. "We're resourceful."

"I can attest to that," Wayne said. "There's more to Conor than meets the eye."

"Maybe so, but I see one guy against an army," Pepe countered, staring Conor up and down, his expression doubtful.

"I don't intend to do this by myself," Conor said. "Wayne and I will scout ahead and collect intel. By the time the rest of the team catches up with us, we should know a little more about The Bond."

"So what do I tell my people?" Wayne asked.

"Tell them the truth. Get those fighters together that you brought to our last battle. Tell them they'll be heading north on the highway the day after tomorrow."

"What about my camp?" Wayne asked. "I probably need to leave some folks at the firehall."

"I'll have people check in on them," Conor said. "Don't worry."

Wayne smiled. "You telling me not to worry does nothing to ease my fears."

Conor reached out and shook Pepe's hand. "Good to meet you, my friend, but I sure wish you'd arrived with better news. Let Wayne know how many people you can commit to the fight. If he doesn't have enough horses for you, I may be able to get some from a friend of ours."

"Johnny Jacks?" Wayne asked.

Conor nodded. "I'll be back in the morning. I've got a lot to do before then."

25

For the entire ride to Pastor White's camp, Conor was bombarded with questions from Ragus and Barb. Ragus, who'd missed most of the conversation because he'd been stuck tending to the horses, simply wanted to be brought up to speed on what he'd missed. He was incredulous that they'd been talking about something so important while he'd been performing such a trivial task.

"You should have come and got me, Barb," he said.

"Sorry, waterboy, didn't want to miss anything good myself," she shot back.

Ragus screwed up his mouth in a frown. "For a brown-haired kid, I get treated like a red-headed stepchild an awful lot."

"All jobs are important," Conor assured him.

Barb leaned toward Ragus and said in a loud stage-whisper, "That's what they always tell the incapable to make them feel better."

"That's okay, Barb. I find some consolation in the fact that I'm at least charming and likable. If manners were brains, you'd be simple-minded."

When Barb frowned, Conor intervened before she decided to knock him on his ass.

"I need you two to listen. When we get to the pastor's camp, let me do the talking. We've got too much on our plate right now to get into an argument with these people. We may need them."

"*You* may need them," Barb scoffed. "*I* won't need them."

"If you and Ragus are on the road with me, Wayne's folks might need them. Pepe's folks might need them. Johnny Jacks might need them. For that reason, we need them to act as part of our community. This is *exactly* why you are muzzled until we get past the camp."

"Muzzled," Ragus chuckled, whispering it so only Barb would hear.

She shot Ragus a murderous glance that shut him up. Conor appeared not to notice. No surprise there since he'd long ago shot his ears out on the job. Too many gunshots and explosions without the benefit of ear protection.

When they reached the pastor's camp, Jackson was at the gate. His constant presence there made Conor wonder if the man was being punished for something. When they rode around the corner and into his line of sight, Jackson snapped to attention and scowled at them as he'd done earlier. His eyes widened when the trio swung their horses in his direction and pulled off the road. They stopped in front of his gate and he appeared terrified, torn between calling for help and running.

"What do you want?" he eventually managed to get out. "Your doctor friend left already. Said he was going to see Johnny Jacks."

"Now is this any way to greet an old friend?" Conor frowned. "I kind of thought we'd come to an understanding here. Besides, I'm not here for Doc Marty."

Jackson was holding his rifle but knew better than to point it at them. He tossed his head in Barb's direction. "Any understanding we have don't apply to her. She ain't welcome here."

"That you talking or is that the pastor's word?" Conor asked, an edge in his voice.

Jackson hesitated, wondering if he'd gotten ahead of himself.

Reading between the lines, Conor prompted, "You should go get the pastor."

"Ain't seen him in a little bit," Jackson said, a defiant lilt to his voice. "He might be busy."

"Just go get him, Jackson. There could be trouble headed this way and he needs to know about it. I don't have time to fuck around with the likes of you."

Jackson, used to the insular world of his own people, people who didn't use such language, had never been spoken to in such a way. He frowned at Conor and rushed off.

"I thought you were our spokesman because you were the nice one," Barb said. "There you go cursing at the poor fellow. You clearly discombobulated him."

"I was simply using profanity as an explanation point. I was expressing the emphatic nature of our message for the pastor."

"Got it," Barb said. "I'll remember that line. May need to use it in the future."

Jackson headed back their way. The man was a ball of energy, trying to hurry but not wanting to rush ahead of the pastor, who was trailing along at an unhurried pace. The pastor nodded and spoke to folks he passed, like a politician in the grocery store, aware that each interaction, no matter how small, might carry some significance. Eventually the pastor reached them. He gave them a single nod as a group, electing not to acknowledge each of them individually because that would have required making eye contact with Barb, something he was determined not to do.

"You got this young man all bound up, Conor Maguire," the pastor began. "He ain't used to the devil's talk."

"He was intent on playing games when I urgently needed to speak with you. I had no time for his foolishness."

"Then I reckon you should get on with it." The pastor spoke quietly, as if not trying to move his jaw very much.

"Two things. The first is that a group has shown up at Wayne's camp at the firehouse, folks he knew from Michigan. They ran into some trouble on the road and need a place to stay for a few weeks. We're going to put them up in Shuck's house since it's sitting empty."

"We did plan on making a run up there at some point to check for supplies," the pastor said. "Wanted to see if Shuck had anything we might be able to use."

"You can forget that," Conor said. "These folks are on their way up there now. If your folks are looting and scavenging while the house is occupied it will only lead to trouble. Best to head that off right now, leave the house be until they're gone."

The pastor's right eyebrow flickered for a second, as if he were shocked at the audacity of this outsider coming into his community and announcing such a decision without consulting him. As far as he was concerned, this was *his* territory. "I sure wish you'd spoken to us about this first."

Conor shut that down. There were bigger concerns. "It's done. They're moving in now and they'll stay as long as they like. That a problem?"

The pastor raised a hand in concession. "I guess not. Whatever you say since you're apparently the boss around here." With the stiffness in his jaw there was a lingering, hissing quality to his words that was almost reptilian, but did not mask his sarcasm.

"There's more."

The pastor gave a sweeping gesture that indicated the floor was Conor's. He was clearly trying to avoid speaking, not wanting to give Barb the satisfaction of knowing she'd hurt him.

"The group from the north, Wayne's friends, said they ran into trouble with a large, well-armed force calling themselves The Bond. They had military vehicles, military weapons, and were laying waste to the communities they passed through. The visitors believe they're following Route 23."

At the mention of Route 23 the pastor's eyes widened. "Route 23, you say? Why that goes right by here."

Conor nodded. "Wayne's friends traveled all the way from the Detroit area on Route 23. They passed signs of The Bond's violent activities along the way, but didn't recognize it as being the work of one group. Then in Chillicothe, Ohio, they ran into folks who had experienced the ferocity of this group firsthand. That's where they heard that they called themselves The Bond. When Wayne's friends got into Huntington, West Virginia, they ran headfirst into the group, losing most of their vehicles and supplies. They're heading south toward people they know but are afraid they're going to be overrun by The Bond on the road. That's why they're searching for a place to shelter for a while."

"You think we're in danger?"

"I don't know but we need to find out. A group that large, that well-armed, living by what they can loot and scavenge on the road, could be the end of this community. We need to know what we're dealing with."

"How do you propose we do that?" the pastor asked.

"I'll be leaving tomorrow afternoon with Wayne. We'll try to intercept The Bond on the road and see what we can learn about them. The day after we leave, I'm hoping to have a small force join us on the road so we can engage them."

"Engage them? You said they're heavily armed. They have military weapons and vehicles. What do you expect a handful of men on horseback will be able to do to them?"

"A small force has its advantages," Conor said. "They can move quickly. They're not tied to the highways like men in trucks."

The pastor didn't seem convinced. "Just sounds like a way to lose good men. You'll be lucky to bring any of them back alive."

Conor scrutinized the pastor. "Does that mean you'll not send any of your men along with our force? The men of this community should play a role in defending it. I mean, technically, my family is probably safe on our mountain. We have weapons and defenses that can repel a force like that. If I'm willing to fight for you though, you should probably be willing to fight for yourself."

The pastor rocked onto his heels and shoved his hands into his back pockets. "I didn't exactly say that I wouldn't send anyone. I can ask my men but it's entirely up to them if they want to go. I can't say how many will be anxious to ride off to die."

"If we don't send a force, more will die. Ugly things will be visited upon your community. You may lose everything. Your men dead, your women taken, and your church in ashes."

"I'll counsel them on it. We'll pray about it. That's all I can do. When do you need a decision?"

"Wayne and I are leaving tomorrow. Hopefully the larger group will head out the following day. I expect they'll travel a bit slower. Any men you send will need a horse, a gun, ammo, and sleeping gear. If they have food, that's great. If not, we'll see that everyone is fed."

The pastor nodded absently, lost in thought. "Conor?"

"Yes?"

"You may not be a righteous man, but you're a brave man."

"Not sure I'm a smart man either, but my lot is cast already."

26

After departing the pastor's camp they rode to Johnny's house. They didn't tax their horses with too quick a pace. There was no need for it at this point, despite the possibility that The Bond was headed their way. It remained only a possibility at this point. It could be mere coincidence that The Bond had been traveling the same route as Pepe's group. Conor needed to know, though. Better to be proactive than reactive. He and Wayne could scout for The Bond, determine if the threat was real, and decide on a course of action.

When they reached Johnny's house they found Doc Marty and Shannon sitting on the porch with the family. Despite the time of year, late fall heading into winter, the day had warmed up into the fifties and they were enjoying the sunshine. In another month they probably wouldn't have any more fifty degree days and no one would want to be outside unless they had work to do.

The riders tied their horses off, having caught Doc Marty in the midst of a story about an adventure he and Conor had been on in the old world before things went to shit. Conor didn't hear enough of the story to place it. They'd had quite a few adventures together but Conor didn't usually talk about them. Even getting him to tell the story about Doc Marty stealing his teeth had been like, well, pulling teeth.

"Didn't we sign agreements to not talk about such things?" Conor asked.

Doc Marty waved him off. "I was just talking about the experience of working with you, not the mission. I wouldn't disclose anything top secret."

"He's probably safe right now," Johnny said. "No cell phone overhearing the conversation, no internet-connected refrigerator monitoring us, no digital assistant recording what we say."

Conor conceded that with a nod but he felt differently. The kind of people he'd grown up with – Irish organized crime figures, IRA soldiers – had instilled a code of secrecy in him. It wasn't something he could just brush aside. It was ingrained in him that he didn't talk about work with people who weren't in the life or weren't involved in the job.

"You okay, Conor?" Doc Marty asked. "You appear more sour than usual."

"Was it trouble with Pastor White?" Jason asked, and Ragus smirked.

"No." Conor launched into the story about Wayne's friend Pepe and their experience with The Bond. By the time he was done with that, the visit with Pastor White was a minor footnote in the story.

Sam was visibly upset by the time Conor was done. There were tears in her eyes. She was pacing the porch with her arms wrapped around herself. "What is this? We can't catch a break? Why does it have to be this way? We just went through this with those people who kidnapped Barb. Is this what it's going to be like all the time? Living from threat to threat? Having to fight off strangers? I don't want to live like that!"

Jason caught his wife mid-stride and slipped an arm around her, cradling her head against him. He stroked her hair and spoke to her. "It's okay, baby. This might not be people coming here to hurt us. We could just be in the path of people of who don't even know we're here. It's not personal at all. Hell, they may not even be coming this way."

Sam tilted her head up to Jason, then glanced at Conor. "How's that any different? Whether it's personal or not, if they're coming this way we'd be in danger just the same. It doesn't matter if the person who kills me looks at me with hatred or indifference, I'm just as dead either way."

Conor sat down on the edge of the porch. "I agree with you there, Sam. To some extent, the motivation of your enemy doesn't matter. What does matter is that we have advance warning that they're coming and can prepare. I'm not waiting on them to get here. I'm going to *them*. I want to know exactly what we're dealing with before the threat ever reaches my backyard."

"I'm in," Jason said without hesitation. He didn't even need to know what Conor's plan was but he was certain he wanted to be part of it.

His eagerness concerned Conor. "Are you sure you're up to it, lad?"

Jason knew what he was referring to. It was hard to forget about his injuries, the severe beating he'd taken. "There's no pain anymore unless I touch my face, talk, or accidentally bite my tongue."

Conor smiled. "And how many times a day do you do one or the other of those things?"

"Pretty often," Jason admitted.

"I appreciate your enthusiasm but I'm not going to accept your offer yet," Conor said. "You need time to talk this over with your family. I'll be back this way tomorrow and you can let me know what you decided. Wayne and I are going to go ahead as a two-man team and try to intercept them so we can collect intelligence."

"Two man, one woman team," Barb corrected.

Conor ignored her. He had another plan and she didn't know all the details, although this wasn't the time to get into it. "My plan is to have a larger force, an army, leave one day behind us, the day after tomorrow, and catch up with us on the road. By then, Wayne and I will know if they're a threat. If they are, we'll have a plan for engaging them."

There were nods around the group. Their faces were dark with concern but understood that what Conor was proposing was probably necessary.

"If he goes, I go," Sam blurted.

Jason stared at her as if she were crazy. "Baby, I love you but this is no place for women. This is dangerous. This is fighting. *War*."

Sam's mouth tightened and she backhanded Jason in the chest with a balled-up fist. He took a step back, startled and rubbing his chest. She'd hit him right in the sternum with her knuckles, a spot where he was probably still bruised from the attack that left his mother dead.

"Ow, babe!"

Sam waved her fist at her husband. "Jason Jacks, I'll knock out the rest of your teeth if you ever talk to me like that again. This *woman* is just as capable as you are. Just as tough."

Jason gave Conor a pleading look. "Can you talk some sense into her? Tell her it isn't the place for her."

Conor gazed at Sam, then turned his eyes to Jason. "I'd take her over you at the moment."

"What?" Jason demanded. "Why?"

"Your blood is running hot from your injury. You're pissed off and blinded by it. Every time it hurts, every time you feel pain shooting through your body, you want to make someone pay. Am I right?"

"Well, yeah. Of course."

Conor jabbed a finger at Jason as if he'd answered his own question. "That's it, right there. Your anger affects your judgment. Sam is doing this for the right reason. She's trying to protect her family and her community, she's not out for revenge. Sam would listen and take orders. She would not put others at risk because of some vendetta. That's the kind of soldiers I need."

"If you go, we go as a team," Sam said, strengthened by Conor's validation. Jason opened his mouth to protest but she cut him off. "That's the *only* way either of us goes and that's final, Jason Jacks."

Jason, new to marriage and the ways of strong-minded women, tried to gain control of the situation. "Yeah, we need to talk about this as a family, Conor. We'll let you know tomorrow."

"And you'll be doing some listening," Sam said. "Not just talking."

Jason appeared sheepish. "I always listen to you, baby."

"Who's going to take care of me?" Johnny asked, a grin on his face, apparently trying to redirect the conversation. "I'm old and frail. What if I fall down and break a hip?"

Conor laughed. "A little snow on the roof doesn't make you frail. In fact, you're the person I worry about least. You're tough as kangaroo jerky."

Barb frowned. "Seriously, Dad? You've had kangaroo jerky?"

"Yeah," Conor admitted. "Not the worst meat I've ever eaten but among the toughest."

"What was the worst meat you've eaten?" Ragus asked.

Barb slugged Ragus in the arm. "Why did you have to ask that? You know he'll tell us and it will be stuck in our heads all day. Haven't you learned anything about him?" She went to plug her ears with her fingers but before she could Conor made his pronouncement.

"Rotten shark in Iceland."

Barb made a gagging sound and walked off.

"Rotten shark?" Jason repeated.

"Yep. It's the national dish. They consider it a delicacy. They age the shark for several months. It's bloody nasty."

"What does it taste like?" Sam asked.

"Imagine you pick up a fish off the bank of the Dismal River over here. Something that's been rotting in the sun for several weeks. You throw it in the blender with a hunk of Bleu cheese to get that ammonia taste and then let it firm up. That's what it tastes like. I just had a little cube on a toothpick and I can taste it to this day."

Ragus watched Barb wander around the yard, sucking in deep breaths, hands on hips. "I never figured her for having a weak stomach," he said, genuinely surprised. "I never figured there was anything weak about her at all."

"She wasn't always like this. Happened after the coon juice incident."

"Coon juice?"

"You don't want to know, Ragus. And a word of warning. It isn't something to tease her about. You even say those two words together around her and she'll pound your ass into a greasy spot in the dirt. No joke."

Ragus's expression made it clear that he understood the gravity of the situation. It was one thing to tease her but quite another to intentionally poke her in the most vulnerable spot.

"I hope we're done with that particular conversation," Barb said, walking back up to the group.

"We are," Johnny said. "It wasn't my cup of tea either." He was trying to make Barb feel better and she gave him one of her rare smiles.

Conor sighed. "I guess we need to get moving. There's plenty to do at home before we have to leave again. Doc Marty, you guys coming with us?"

"I guess so," he replied. "Shannon, you ready?"

She nodded and the two of them got up. Shannon hugged everyone while Doc Marty shook hands. Apparently, the time these two families had spent together had bonded them.

"So is there anything we should be doing in the meantime?" Jason asked.

"You should seriously talk about who, if either of you, is coming with the larger force the day after tomorrow. It's not just about who wants to go but about who can keep the farm running in the absence of the other. No offense to Johnny, but I'm not sure he's up to doing it all himself. If you both go and leave Johnny here by himself, do you think he's going to just leave things alone or is he going to try to take on more than he's ready to do? I'm not trying to tell you what to do, but consider all the options. Think it out thoroughly."

"We will," Sam replied.

Conor and Ragus were already on their horses when Shannon and Doc Marty came off the porch. Ragus waved and began walking his horse down the farm road. Shannon swung into the saddle and trotted after him, anxious to catch up since they'd been apart most of the day.

Conor stood waiting on Barb. "You coming or what?"

She appeared confused. "No, Dad. All my gear is here. This is where I'm staying, remember?" She could tell by the expression on his face that he hadn't.

"I'm sorry, sweetie," he said awkwardly. "I forgot. I'm so used to—"

"It's okay, Dad. I'll be here when you come by tomorrow. Do you need the packhorse?"

"No, you hold onto it for now." He waved to the Jacks family and moved to catch up with the others.

He was shaking his head, lost in a weird mix of emotions. He was frustrated with himself for having forgotten that the whole reason they'd come over here originally was to drop Barb off, which only drew more attention to it and made it all that more awkward. It embarrassed him when few things did. Barb hadn't been embarrassed, just uncertain of what was going on in his head. In truth, it had been many things -- The Bond, his mission, assembling an army. In that chaos, that maelstrom of thought, he forgot about her.

"You okay?" Doc Marty asked.

"I must be getting too old for this. I can't believe that just happened."

"That you left your daughter with another family or that you forgot you were going to do it?"

"I guess both."

"You've trained for a lot of things in your life, Conor. This isn't one of them. Nearly every other situation you've been in simply required that you fall back on your training and rely on it. Not sure you trained for this."

Conor knew he was right but he couldn't fall into the same trap he'd just chastised Jason for. He couldn't let his emotions impede his thinking. Barb's living arrangements were a done deal. They'd already worked this out. There were a lot of things that needed to be worked out. He needed to build gear lists, and figure out what supplies might aid the larger force coming behind him and Wayne, such as food and spare ammo.

More delicate than the nuts and bolts business of list-building was the matter of duty assignments. Not everyone in his circle would be going with them. There would most certainly be some hard feelings and some resentment. That was okay. He couldn't be concerned about that. He needed to put the best person in the best spot for them. He would have to think about who should go forward and who should be held back. He also needed someone to stay with the compound. He couldn't leave it unattended for long. By the time he reached the compound, he needed to have all of this ironed out.

27

By the time they reached the compound gate, Conor was handing out instructions. He sent Ragus riding ahead to have it open for them. The group rode through and came to a stop in the common area in front of the main living quarters. Ragus closed and locked the gate, then joined them, leading his horse behind him.

"First things first. Ragus, I hate to do this to you but I hope you know that it's a sign of how much I trust and respect you," Conor began.

"I know, I know," Ragus said. "I'm going to be guarding the compound, aren't I?"

"I can't force you to but I would certainly appreciate it," Conor said. "I'm not sure who else I would trust with the responsibility."

"I was hoping for more action, but I know you're pressed for time so I won't argue with you. I got this."

Conor smiled. "That's a sign of maturity, Ragus. That's exactly why you're the right man for the job." Conor didn't mention that he had considered leaving Barb behind to keep watch on the compound, but he was afraid that such an action might further isolate her from everyone else. If anything, she needed to be more involved with the other folks in the community and bond with them as a team. The best way for that to happen right now was for her to take part in this action with them.

"Anything I can do for you in the meantime?" Ragus asked.

"Check the condition of the shoes on the horses. You remember how to do that?"

"Yes."

"If any need attention, we'll leave them for Johnny and Jason to attend to. I can do a lot with metal but I'm a bit skittish when it comes to attaching it to a mammal with nails."

"I would beg to differ," Doc Marty said. "Are you forgetting Honduras?"

Conor held a hand up to quiet him. "Not the time, Doc."

"Sorry," Doc Marty replied.

"I want us to prepare for a minimum two week engagement," Conor said. "Food, gear, ammo for as many days. Go heavy on ammo in case there's a protracted battle. We'll need a field medical kit for the larger force following Wayne and me. Any questions, track me down."

Doc Marty had several but Conor had already rushed off. He went first to the larder where he kept his long-term food storage. He grabbed two sealed five-gallon buckets of pasta and two more of rice. He pulled his flashlight from his shirt pocket and scanned the rows of buckets until he found another bucket containing soups and stews. Rice mixed with soup and pasta topped with stew might not be culinary masterpieces, but it was filling and could provide the energy to fuel an army. Conor wasn't so concerned about this putting a dent in his provisions. He had received several pallets of food as part of his arrangement for putting a roof over Doc Marty's head.

It took him a couple of trips to get everything into the living room where he started his first pile, which would be everything he was going to set aside for use by the larger force. It was his intention that Barb be part of that force and that she be in charge of these supplies. If by some fortuitous turn he and Wayne didn't encounter The Bond on the road, they would bring them back home for another time. Same for the cases of ammo he tossed into the pile.

Once he had that pile squared away he began working on his own gear. He lived in constant readiness for moments such as this. It had been his way of life for over twenty years now and he felt at the top of his game. Despite his age, he was more prepared than he'd ever been. More skilled, more effective, and way more deadly.

28

Doc Marty had no plans to pack anything until he visited the outhouse. Jostling around on a horse all day had stirred his insides until he felt like a shaken soda can. Mission accomplished, he strolled back to the quarters he shared with Shannon. When he didn't find her there he paid a visit to the empty guest quarters where he'd set up a temporary infirmary. Conor had been reluctant to give up the space.

"I told Ricardo I'd put a roof over your head. I'm not allowing any of that eminent domain bullshit here. You've got your shipping container and your quarters. You get nothing else."

"What if you or, God forbid, Barb, comes riding in here with a bullet in you?" Doc Marty said. "You want me out there in that shipping container rifling through boxes for what I need to save a life? The longer that stuff sits out there, the greater chance for it to be damaged or misplaced."

Conor finally conceded. Despite his reservations about surrendering territory, Conor had to admit that what Doc Marty said made sense from a logistical and practical standpoint. Doc Marty knew Conor didn't like it though, and he found a small amount of glee in that. He still had a smile plastered across his face when he entered the infirmary. Then he saw Shannon packing her bag with supplies.

Her bag.

"What are you doing?"

She took a deep breath and let it out. "I'm getting ready for the mission."

"Getting that ready for me? Shouldn't those supplies be going in my bag?"

"No, I'm getting it ready for me."

"The hell you are! You're not going on this mission. You're still a kid."

Shannon continued packing and did not meet her father's eye. "I am most certainly *not* a kid. If you'd been paying any attention you'd have seen that I haven't been a kid for a long time, Dad. No offense, but my childhood ended when you taught me how to resist a kidnapping and how to clear the house for intruders each day when I got home from school. Not to mention what I've been through since we got dropped off here."

Doc Marty was hearing none of it. He kept shaking his head as if that action alone would change her mind. "I will not have my baby going off into battle under the care of the Mad Mick."

"I don't know that I could be in any better hands," Shannon replied. "He's quite capable and he wants to help people."

"That's not the point," he admonished, "and stop what you're doing." He made to grab her bag from her but she yanked it away. "He also gets people killed with that screwed up sense of honor and loyalty he has. You'd be putting yourself at risk for people you don't even know."

"Isn't that what you do for a living? Putting both your life and mine at risk for people you don't know?"

"Nowhere close," he said, fully aware that she was correct but unwilling to concede the point.

She nodded at him slowly, her gaze accusing, and he couldn't meet it. "I am not a damn child. I've been soaking up every ounce of medical experience you've given me over the years. I've read every medical book you brought with you because I wanted to be of use to these people. Because I knew I might have to save a life one day, perhaps even *your* life, and I wanted to be ready."

"There's more to it than that," he spat, flinging his hands around in frustration. "It's not all stories and books."

Shannon went back to packing. "I had my hands in Johnny Jacks' body – in his blood -- plugging bullet holes with a gloved finger. I've worked under pressure."

"Not *field* pressure. Not *battle* pressure."

"You think I'm not smart enough? That I'm not capable? Is that it?"

"You know it's not that, Shannon," Doc Marty said. "I don't question your abilities. It's just that you're too young and too inexperienced for what's out there waiting on you. This is life or death circumstances with no second chances if you screw up and no breaks to get your head together. It's ugly, brutal business."

Shannon finished filling her bag and moved on to loading a second bag she'd brought with her. "What you don't understand is that I've lived under pressure for years, Dad. I learned long ago that we were undercover and could be found out. I knew there were people who would kill us if they figured out who we worked for. I knew there were people willing to torture or kill me to get back at you. You don't think that's pressure? Do you know how many times I ran and hid because I imagined some random man on the street was after me? How many times I hid under the bed when UPS knocked on the door because I assumed it was the precursor to the door being kicked in?"

"This is a different kind of pressure. Can you look into a man's eyes, knowing that he's going to die, and that any supplies you use on him will be wasted? Could you leave him to die and move on to the next injured person because you might be able to save them? I pray to God you never have to know what that's like because it never leaves you. *Never*! You'll hear that dying man's cries for the rest of your life."

"I need to do this."

Doc Marty shook his head. "You're my daughter and you're all that I have left. You can scream and cry all you want but it changes nothing. You can even hate me if you want, but you're not going and that's final."

Shannon slammed her bag down, burst into tears, and ran out the door. Doc Marty called to her and started to go after her but stopped. He needed to calm down. She needed to calm down. Surely then she'd listen to logic.

Walking briskly across the compound, sobbing, Shannon ran into Conor on his way to the stable. He needed some saddlebags for packing gear. Being a father, his first reaction to a crying young woman was to run in the other direction but he held himself steady and went with his second impulse, which was to see what was wrong. He shot out an arm and gently snagged her bicep as she stormed by him.

"Easy there, Shannon. What's wrong?"

"My father won't let me go on this mission. He thinks I'm a baby."

"Dads can be like that," Conor said, unaware that Shannon was so intent on going. "You see what I just went through with Barb. We struggle. We care but we're all thumbs when it comes to handling the emotions of our daughters."

They talked for several minutes, Conor listening as she vented her frustration. He patted her back and told her it would be okay, which was the main tool in a father's toolbox.

"Will you talk to him?" she begged.

Conor squirmed uncomfortably. "I don't mind to talk to him, my child, but he's your dad. This is his decision, not mine."

"And I'll tell you what I told him. I'm not a kid. It's *my* decision. If I want to go, he can't stop me."

"You don't want to do it that way, Shannon. If you go, you want to do it with his support and blessing. You want to have him pulling for you. You don't want to part in anger. If something were to happen to either of you, that memory would be something the other would have to live with forever. That's a big burden to shoulder."

Shannon mulled that over and Conor could see he'd struck a chord. "I want a chance to help and this is a way I can do it."

"Let me talk to him," Conor said. "You go find Ragus. I'll come find you after we've talked." He sent her away with a hug and went to the infirmary.

He found a sullen Doc Marty sitting in an old wooden desk chair, elbows on knees, chin resting on his palms. Conor sat down in an orange cafeteria chair with rusty chrome legs.

"I just talked to an angry young woman," he said.

"A pouting child is more like it. She had the nerve to think she was going north with your little army."

Conor shrugged. "Maybe she needs to. Maybe it's time."

Doc Marty sat up straight. "Have you lost your fucking mind, Conor Maguire? You know what's out there. You know what a battlefield medic goes through. You want that for my kid?"

"I don't want the experience of the battlefield for anyone, but I promised the people of this community that I would protect them. The only condition was they had to be willing to help. I have no doubt that I'll have a couple of dozen men willing to go because they understand that obligation. I don't want to see any of them hurt or killed but we have to find out if The Bond is coming this way. If they are, we need to make them see the error of their ways."

"I don't have a problem with that. I helped you carve those stupid double 'M' symbols all over the damn place. I understand what this is about, but you can do it without my daughter. That's final."

"That's fine, as long as you understand you won't be going either."

"What?" Doc Marty asked in surprise.

"Can't risk it. While you're technically only a bloody dentist, you're the closest thing we have to a doctor around here. Plus, if I get killed, I need someone like you to take command of this bunch. They won't follow Barb yet. I'm not sure they'll follow Wayne either. You're it."

Doc Marty stared at Conor incredulously. "You would actually take my daughter into battle with you?" He couldn't fathom the idea. He couldn't believe they were even having this conversation.

"I've taken my own daughter into battle, Doc. It's never easy, but it was time for her to make her own decisions. Your daughter has a good basic knowledge of ditch medicine and she handles pressure well. She could do this, if you'd let her."

"Did you two conspire together behind my back to set this up?"

"No. I played no part in it. I didn't plan on taking a medic at all. We'd lose a lot of men that way though, if they were injured. If Shannon is up for this then I think we should give her a chance. We can't force them to be children forever."

Doc Marty got up from his chair and went to a cabinet on the wall. He removed a bottle of Scotch, a shot glass upturned over the lid. He set it down on the countertop and placed the shot glass beside it with a clink. He unscrewed the lid and poured a shot. Instead of drinking it, he held it out to Conor.

Conor started to refuse – he rarely drank – but he understood he couldn't refuse this. To drink this shot was the natural course of things. It was where this conversation, this transaction, had to go. He took the shot and tipped it back, closing his eyes in deference to the memories associated with the taste. Drinks to dead friends, drinks to celebrate making it home when the odds were against you, and drinks to toast the anniversary of a wedding that felt like it was a thousand years gone.

He passed the glass back to Doc Marty and watched him down his own shot.

"She's all I got, Conor."

"Same here, my friend. It's just Barb and me." Conor gestured at Doc to retake his seat. Conor brought the bottle, pouring Doc Marty a second shot.

Doc drank it and set the glass down heavily. "She's just a kid."

"They're all fucking kids," Conor said. "Barb, Ragus, Shannon, the lot of them. Not a one over twenty-five years old. But we're looking at it through the eyes of old men. Old protective fathers. How did you feel at twenty-five?"

"Like I could tear the devil's head off and piss down his neck," Doc Marty said with a bitter smile.

"And we did. We made our bones and these kids have to do the same. Crazy as it sounds, they could be the hope for the nation. Who knows what it's going to be like when we come out the other end of this disaster. They could be facing some totalitarian state. Americans might need people who can fight, who can slip between the cracks and lead a revolution if it comes to that. Our kids would be willing to fight, to bleed, and to die to make it happen because that's how we raised them. They know what this country is about and they won't settle for less."

"I'm not ready for this, Conor."

"Our parents might have said the same of us but we had our wars. We learned from those wars. Now we aren't just warriors but also teachers."

"I don't want to teach my daughter about war," Doc Marty said.

"Like it or not, if she's *your* daughter she's already a warrior," Conor pointed out. "That's why this has come to a head. She knows this is her war. Fighting for what's right, for her community, is her cause. She feels that in her heart. You can see it. Barb is the same way. They were raised with that sense of honor and those values. I'm proud of that. I'm proud of the kids we raised, two old bastards like us."

"And you want her to go?" Doc Marty asked.

Conor could read between the lines. What Doc Marty was saying was that he would forever blame Conor for her death if this ended badly. "This decision isn't on me, my friend. I won't make her go, but I won't allow you to go in her place. I've already explained why. She has to make her own way in the world and you'll have to accept that eventually. I will make you this promise though. I will watch her like she was my own. I won't hesitate to give my life for her."

"What if I forbid it?" Doc Marty asked.

Conor gave him a tired smile. "Then you'll lose her." He left the building, leaving Doc Marty alone to think.

Doc sagged into the old office chair, the world completely still around him. Maybe the Mick was right. If he protected her forever, Shannon would never learn her strengths. She'd never know what she was made of. If he was going to let her venture out then perhaps the time to do it was now, when he and Conor were there to watch over her. There would be a time when he was no longer there for her and he had to make sure she was ready for that.

He stood up and forced his legs to carry him toward the door. He was going to tell his daughter she could go and he hoped he didn't regret it. He was going to tell the only thing he loved in this world that she had his blessing to walk into the mouth of hell.

29

Conor was gathering a few of his better radios for the trip when he spotted his satellite phone charging in his Faraday room. On a whim, he took it outside and punched in a number. It rang several times before a voice answered.

"Conor Maguire," Ricardo said. *"I hope you're not calling to tell me that you've killed Doc Marty."*

Conor laughed. "Not yet, though he did suffer a bit for stealing my teeth that time."

"I expected as much. You calling to extort more supplies out of me for his rent?"

"Nope. Not that either."

"Then what can I do for you?"

Ricardo was Conor's handler, the closest thing he had to a boss. When he'd been recruited it was never as an actual employee of any agency or organization but as a contractor on retainer. They paid him money and favors to keep him loyal and to assure his availability anytime they needed a job done that required his special skills. He was always free to take outside work as long as it didn't conflict with the goals of his primary employer and as long as he was ready for work when they needed him. It was nearly the perfect job.

The same man, long dead now, who had brought Conor into the fold had also recruited Doc Marty. After his death they passed through a rapid succession of handlers, none lasting very long, until they landed in Ricardo's lap. He'd been running their operations for over fifteen years and they had a good working relationship. Indeed it was Ricardo who'd set Conor up in his mountaintop compound.

"We had some folks wander into our community yesterday. They'd had a run-in on the road with a group calling themselves The Bond."

"The Bond? Never heard of them," Ricardo said. *"Kind of stupid name. Doesn't exactly instill fear."*

"These guys thought The Bond were military at first. They were wearing uniforms and had military gear."

"Anybody can get that shit. Means nothing."

"I've not personally laid eyes on them so I can't attest to it. The informant said they were driving older military trucks. I suspect multi-fuel vehicles. That's what I'd be doing."

"Again, that doesn't mean shit. You can buy those things on the secondary market all day long for five to ten thousand bucks. They'll run on anything from vodka to camel piss."

Conor chuckled, then stopped laughing, wondering why he hadn't had the foresight to purchase one. "The only other bit of information was the witness said he saw what he described as a gang tattoo on one of the men."

"Hell, a lot of soldiers get tattooed. Means nothing."

"This guy was certain this was ink affiliating him with a gang in the Detroit area."

"Conor, I don't usually work with the military directly, but I do have a friend who's a JAG officer. He told me once about a case he was working, investigating street gang infiltration into military units."

"Why would those guys want in the military?"

"The obvious reasons. They wanted weapons and tactical training that they could take back to the gang on discharge."

"I've heard rumors about such a thing but I figured it was just that, a rumor."

"*Oh, it's real and it's fairly widespread. There's been gang-related violence on bases. Some of these folks can't leave the street behind even though they're supposed to be undercover and keeping their noses clean.*"

"So it's possible this could be a real military unit?"

"*Eh, it's doubtful it's an actual unit,*" Ricardo said. "*The odds of having a unit entirely built of gang members is pretty slim. It's possible, though, that soldiers with gang affiliations have bonded together into a unit.*"

"Damn," Conor muttered.

"*What?*"

"You hear what you did there?"

"*No.*"

"You said it's possible that they *bonded* together," Conor said. "I wonder if that's where that name came from."

"*Not a very tough name for gang members. You'd think they'd pick something that inspired terror like The Manglers, The Violators, or some shit like that. Either way, if you call me back with more info it's possible I could ask around.*"

Conor sighed. "I'm hoping my first contact with them will be my last."

"*I'm presuming that your intent is for lethal contact?*"

"You would be assuming correctly," Conor confirmed.

"*How about you make sure you bring yourself back in one piece, Conor.*"

There was something about the way Ricardo said it that made Conor suspicious, as if there were things left unsaid. "Why the concern, Ricardo?"

"*We can't get into it now but business goes on. There's a lot of activity out there, both in the United States and the world at large. There are things we've needed to do for years that we're well-positioned to do now because of a certain lack of oversight. It's interesting that one of the guiding doctrines in our business is that we don't want to do something that's going to make us the lead story on CNN. It's very freeing to not have that concern at the moment. It's kind of like the Wild West. I have a growing list of erasures.*"

Conor was intrigued but had other concerns at the moment. "How about this – if I survive, I'll give you a call?"

Ricardo laughed. *"Oh, you'll survive, Conor. I'm in contact with dozens of operators and I'm not sure any are thriving quite like you are. As that crass expression goes, you seem happier than a pig in shit."*

"Goodbye, Ricardo."

"Later, Mad Mick."

30

After a long talk, tears on both sides, and several hugs, Shannon was making final preparations to her gear. Her dad walked into the infirmary with a plastic tote.

"How's it coming, Princess?"

"I think I about have everything."

"I've got a few tips and additions," Doc Marty said. "Put this on." He pulled a Molle vest with hard plates from the tote and handed it to her.

She'd handled heavy plates before but hadn't worn them very often. "I thought I'd just wear my soft armor." She had fitted soft armor that was light and comfortable. Nothing like the heavy gear she was having to hold up with both hands.

"You can't wear the soft armor into battle. You have to wear the heavy plates. These are Level IV. Conor may be a crazy man but even he wears hard plates into battle."

She slid the chest rig over her head and her dad helped her fit it. "You need to familiarize yourself with the layout of the pouches. They're already packed with medical supplies. Besides what you have in your med packs, you'll be carrying chest seals, tourniquets, Israeli bandages, rubber tubing, clamps, and shears. You also have a headlamp and spare batteries." He went back into the tote and came out with a worn battle belt rigged with a thigh holster.

"Will I be using my own handgun?"

"Your Glock 19, yes. There's spare mags on the belt, located where you're used to finding them. Even though your primary mission is being a medic, you should never go anywhere without your sidearm. It's easy to forget your rifle in this situation. You'll lay it down to use both hands on a patient, then run to the next patient without remembering to pick it up."

With her dad's help, Shannon adjusted the battle belt and strapped the thigh rig in place. She let her hands fall to the various pouches, making sure she could find and open them easily.

"I'm not as knife-obsessed as Conor but a good knife is critical. There's a Donnie Dunn tactical knife on the belt and a James Huse push dagger on the vest. Make sure you draw and handle them before you need them. I know you're going to be focused on another mission out there, on saving lives, but things can change in a flash. One minute you're rushing to the aid of a fallen companion, then the next time you look up you're completely cut off from your unit. So you always have to be ready to fight, whether it's with a knife or a gun."

"I could really have to fight with a knife? Someone could get that close?" The idea hadn't occurred to her that she would actually get within blade range of a combatant.

"You can be overrun easily in the heat of battle. It's sheer chaos. That's why you're taking this instead of a rifle." He handed her a customized pump shotgun. The barrel had been shortened and it had a folding stock. "It's a twenty gauge so the recoil won't be brutal. There's spare buckshot in pockets spread around your vest to distribute the load. I've got more for your saddlebags. There's a sheath that will fasten to the side of your pack and allow you to draw the shotgun by reaching back over your shoulder. That keeps it handy but out of the way."

He helped her fit the sheath to her pack and watched her practice drawing the unloaded shotgun. They added her Glock 19 to the mix and he studied her draw, offering suggestions as she reloaded from the mag pouches. He quizzed her on the contents of the various pouches until she could accurately recall the contents of each.

"There's one more piece of advice," he said. "You'll have to find your groove out there. You'll have to be different than you are here. I can't tell you how to become that person. It's something you'll have to figure out in the heat of things. All I can say is that it's okay to become that person. You've seen Conor in action. He becomes a heartless berserker who has no limits on the battlefield, but that's not who he is with us and with his family. You may have to become something else too, so just remember that's okay."

"Got it, Dad," Shannon said, though she wasn't certain she really did. What he was saying was so vague and so out of context for her that she wasn't sure what it even meant. She had to assume it would become clear in battle.

"Oh and there's one more thing," Doc Marty said. "You *always* listen to Conor. I don't care how you feel about his orders, you follow them anyway. You don't think about it, you don't second-guess it, you just do it. I've been in the shit with the Mad Mick more times than I can even count. He's kept me alive and he'll keep you alive too. He's probably killed more people than the plague."

"You say that like it's a good thing," Shannon said uncertainly.

"In this case it is."

31

The Huntington, West Virginia, area had been good to The Bond. They'd done well everywhere they stopped but Huntington was the only place where they'd ever had goods delivered right to their doorstep like they'd put in an order at Amazon. They had no real plan of action when they hit town. They weren't sure if they were going to stay there or keep rolling down the road, then the lead truck lurched to a stop and Mundo broke radio silence.

"Hold the phone, boys. Anyone up for a good night's sleep in a real bed?"

"If you're suggesting a hotel, we haven't found one yet that wasn't trashed," Thomas replied. "They're all full of hookers, hobos, and dead junkies."

"What about a furniture store full of pristine, unsoiled mattresses?" Mundo said. "What's your fucking sleep number, T?"

Mundo pulled off the four-lane highway into the large parking lot of a clean but older furniture store. For whatever reason, no one had looted it or even broken a single window. The showroom windows were lined with beautiful mattresses in every size and softness.

"I bet they got clean sheets in there too," He-Man piped in.

"And comforters," Jawbone added. "I ain't slept under a comforter in a long damn time."

Everyone was as excited about the unspoiled furniture as they were about anything they'd seen in a long time. Even Thomas, as cool and staid as a snowman, broke a grin at the inviting scene. They had set up a hasty camp. Buddha Boy and Shootah had food remaining from the last stop. They set up their bulky camp stove with its encrustation of spilled food around the burners. Other men broke into the front doors with a crowbar and built a fire in the parking lot from whatever they could drag out the door, as long as it wasn't a mattress. Expensive dressers were smashed into dry kindling and they burned well. Bookcases and wooden coffee tables went next.

Thomas dispatched a pair of two-man teams to set up guard posts on the road in and the road out of their camp. Their routine was to put each guard post just out of sight of the main camp. That allowed them to turn away gawkers without letting them see any details about the main camp, such as the size of the force, what they were driving, or what kind of supplies they had.

Lawdog was in charge of leading a truck convoy outside the perimeter to perform a sweep of the area. They needed to know what the neighbors were like, whether the natives were friendly. It was likely that the noise, light, and smells of their camp would draw the attention of folks nearby at some point during their stay. It was best to be proactive about that. Sometimes driving their vehicles through the area and firing off some rounds was enough to dispel any interest by residents remaining in the area. The smart ones would usually decide it was best to stay low key and hope this new threat eventually moved on.

That didn't always work. There was a certain kind of neighbor that didn't respond with the appropriate level of fear. They didn't run and hide; they met The Bond with hostility and aggression. Thomas and Lawdog had learned that only one approach worked with those folks. They would inevitably present a threat. They would eventually challenge the presence of the newcomers. It was best to deal with them proactively and kill them before they had time to come up with a plan.

The gauge by which they measured the threat posed by locals was very simple. There was either a yes or a no decision to be made. Those who watched from behind curtains or scurried immediately from sight were allowed to live. Those who met The Bond with defiance were deemed to be a potential threat and dealt with accordingly. Lawdog usually gave the order if he was on point. The reaction of his force was to instantly open fire on the person eyeballing them. Once they were reduced to a bullet-riddled corpse, Bond soldiers would burn their house to the ground with everyone in it. If they couldn't determine which house the offending individual came from they would burn down several surrounding houses just to make clear their point. As the saying went, they painted with a broad brush.

On the evening that Pepe's group ran into The Bond, there were very few men remaining at camp other than the guards on the highway, the cooks, some soldiers performing camp security, and Thomas himself. It was almost completely dark, with the exception of the campfire and some lanterns set up by the men remaining at camp. The first indication of trouble came with the sound of gunfire.

The Bond camp was not immediately alarmed by the gunfire. They assumed it to be Lawdog's team dealing with an unwelcoming local. That happened at least once every time he took teams out. The camp security didn't even react. The cooks didn't break their routine. Then there were more shots and it began to sound like a battle rather than an execution.

Thomas raised his radio. "Thomas for Lawdog, Thomas for Lawdog. We good, man? You guys okay?"

"*Ain't us, Boss,*" Lawdog replied. "*You need us to come back?*"

Their exchange was interrupted by a frantic call on the radio. The voice was so high-pitched and terror-stricken Thomas couldn't immediately identify it, nor could he tell what they were saying.

"Slow down and identify yourself!" Thomas demanded.

"*This is Villain on the north guard post. There's a big civilian convoy rolled up on us and opened fire. I got a man down and I'm hit bad. We need help now."*

"*Coming back, T!*" Lawdog barked into his radio. "*Three minutes out!*"

"Get on that north position!" Thomas yelled to his security team. "Buddha Boy and Shootah, guard the camp."

"Roger that," Buddha Boy replied, turning off the propane camp stove.

Thomas ran toward the north position himself. There was more gunfire and the sound of squealing tires. There was the crunch of metal. It could have been vehicles hitting each other or vehicles hitting the guardrail. He couldn't see far enough to know yet.

Reaching the scene revealed chaos. Some of the civilian vehicles had headlights on, making a futile effort to get their vehicles turned. Others had seen the writing on the wall and abandoned their trucks, fleeing with only what they could carry.

"Light'em up!" Thomas bellowed.

The men did as they were told, shooting at the backs of the fleeing civilians, uncertain if they even hit them in the darkness. There was the roar of approaching engines from behind them and a flood of more men as Lawdog's teams arrived back from their patrol.

"You want us to chase'em down?" he asked.

"Fire on what you see but don't chase them," Thomas said. "We get men out too far ahead of the firing line and we're gonna shoot some of our own."

Lawdog relayed the orders to his men. "What about Villain?"

Thomas shook his head, visible in the light of Lawdog's head-lamp. "Ain't seen him yet."

"Over there," Mundo said. He pointed toward the front bumper of a pickup with both doors open.

"You check those vehicles, Mundo," Lawdog said. "Make sure there ain't no people hiding inside them." Lawdog followed Thomas to Villain's side.

Villain was stretched out in a pool of his own blood, illuminated by the stark beam of headlamps. He looked like an actor in the spotlight, performing a very convincing death scene. He wore a chest rig with no plates in it. A bloody hole in the vest bubbled and frothed as Villain struggled to breathe.

"He's shot in the lungs," He-Man said. "You want me to put a chest seal on him?"

Thomas stared at the injured man. "No point. What we going to do with him then? No ER, no doctor around. Can't fix it ourselves. He's fucked."

"You gotta help me," Villain said. "You can't leave me like this."

Thomas tipped the barrel of his rifle in Villain's direction and fired one round, then another. Villain arched his body and then it relaxed into death. "Consider yourself helped."

"Where you want us, Thomas?" Lawdog asked.

"Send a truck to the south guard post as reinforcement. Keep your truck here as a barricade. Send two more back to camp to establish an inner perimeter."

"What about Villain?" Lawdog asked.

"Take his shit," Thomas said. He was aware Lawdog was asking about burying their companion but that wasn't how they rolled. "I need to see what's on these vehicles."

Lawdog found Villain's rifle and then stripped him of his personal gear. He hated to see a fellow member of The Bond die but it was impractical to let good gear go to waste. They weren't Vikings. They didn't get buried with their shit. In fact, it was obvious they weren't likely to get buried at all.

When Lawdog was done he joined Thomas and Mundo at the abandoned vehicles. Mundo was playing a light around the interiors, running from truck to truck with a grin on his face.

"We got four trucks, four trailers, and a car. It's like Christmas," Mundo said.

"Indeed it is," Thomas agreed.

Lawdog leaned his head into the trucks and saw what the other men were talking about. These were heavy duty pickups with contractor-type caps and ladder racks on the back, each towing a trailer. Three were enclosed cargo trailers and one was an open utility trailer. Every inch of space was crammed with gear and it told the story of who these people were. This was a group who had decided to make a run for it. They'd packed everything with survival value into these vehicles and hit the road, headed for somewhere. They had food, spare fuel, weapons, and camping gear. Things probably seemed pretty good for them until a few minutes ago.

Then they ran into The Bond.

"We need to get this shit down to our camp. We can't watch it up here," Thomas said. "They might try to come back for it."

"They might come anyway, even if we move it," Lawdog warned.

"If they're dumbass enough to come into our camp hunting for it, we'll make sure they're nicely rewarded for their trouble," Mundo said. "Right, Thomas?"

"That's right, Mundo. All these got keys in them?"

"Two trucks have keys," Mundo said. "Two trucks and the car don't."

"Lawdog, get some men to move these rigs down to our camp and pitch everything out of them. Transfer everything from the trucks with no keys to the trucks we can drive. Once we have all the gear down at camp, send someone back to drain these fuel tanks."

"Got it, Thomas," Lawdog replied.

"Want me to go ahead and drive one of these trucks in?" Mundo asked.

"Go for it," Lawdog said. "I'll get the other one."

The men drove the two trucks to the furniture store. With the help of the other men, they unloaded them and unhooked the cargo trailers. Men piled into the trucks with them and returned to the scene of the shootout. The remaining trucks would not have been easy to move even if they had keys. One was hung up on the guardrail and another had jack-knifed the trailer in such a way as to bend the trailer fender into the tire, flattening it.

There was a lot of debate about what to do. Someone suggested unhooking the trailers and re-hooking them to the running trucks but that wasn't so easy. The hitches had locks that prevented anyone from unhooking the trailer. This hadn't been an issue with the trucks they had keys for, but was an issue for the ones in which the keys had been taken by the owner. No one was eager to offload all the gear and then have to handle it again to unload back at the camp. In the end, they opted for brute force. They put the trucks in neutral, hooked them with heavy towing chains, and tugged them loose. They dragged them back to camp where they could siphon the fuel and unload them at their convenience.

It was a big night at The Bond camp. The unexpected windfall made the men feel like they'd accomplished a lot with very little effort. It would make the coming days easier. They would loot the area for weapons and anything else that caught their eye but they would not have to spend as much time searching for food. The trucks were packed with it.

There were canned goods, dried goods, and even some freeze-fried stuff, though not in any quantity. These were not preppers, but refugees. What little long-term food storage they had was most likely part of their storm kits for the occasional blizzard or tornado that knocked power out in the north. There were lots of clothes. The men took any good socks they could wear but drew the line at wearing another man's underwear. That went into the fire, along with all of the women's clothing. They kept a few coats that were decent and a few pairs of boots, but their uniforms were part of their identity and they had no plans to stray from that. It was their strength. Their bond.

There were weapons and ammo too. In the first days of The Bond's journey, they kept every weapon they found, imagining a scenario where they might need them. They soon discovered this was impractical. At the rate they were acquiring weapons there would soon be the need for a tractor-trailer just to carry the guns they acquired. They didn't want to leave weapons behind though, not wanting to arm anyone who might use the weapons against them.

They assigned Droopy to the role of armorer. He was the one who made decisions on weapons. If they found a weapon better than that which one of the men was carrying, he would issue it and replace their weapon. They kept a supply of high-end optics, weapons lights, and other accessories as spares. Low end stuff got tossed.

When they found hunting shotguns, they effectively disabled them by beating the barrel against a rock until the barrel crimped closed. With revolvers, they took the cylinders and left the frames. With bolt-action hunting rifles, they removed the bolts. With cheap automatics, they removed the slides. The parts were scattered along their route and tossed off bridges into muddy rivers with the hope that they would never be reunited with their missing parts.

For a week they kept every AR and M4 variant they found, which quickly became impractical. With the rifles being so common, it made more sense to save the parts they might need. They kept magazines, which they loaded at night by the fire, usually while smoking pilfered weed. They kept the variety of springs found in the lower receiver and spare takedown pins. They kept a few mil-spec bolts, charging handles, and grips. The rest were scattered. By the time they reached Huntington, their system of weapons salvage functioned like a well-oiled machine. While going through all the vehicles, they piled the weapons by the fire to be dealt with after dinner.

Buddha Boy went through the food and made the meal decisions for the night based on anything perishable the stolen trucks carried. He had fresh, smoked pork roasts from the previous stop and they cooked some of the stolen food that wouldn't travel well. There was pasta in thin boxes and sauce in fragile glass jars. There were net bags of onions and sacks of potatoes. It was not a well-balanced meal, more like the kind of dinner a four year old kid might plan, but it was good and there was plenty of it.

In going through the trucks, Mundo found a bottle of Early Times whiskey he stashed away in his gear. Thomas had a zero-tolerance policy toward drinking. He'd killed a man on the spot for being drunk, but Mundo wasn't the only man to carry a bottle for a little nip on sentry duty. Those night watches could be long and boring. No one was ever dumb enough to make a move on their camp, so most nights were nothing but pacing around, trying to stay awake.

Thomas knew he could never enforce the same Draconian policy with marijuana. It was the thing many of these men missed most while they were in the service. They spoke of it with a reverent fondness. It wasn't easy to find but they found it. It was one of the things they asked for when they interrogated people. They offered hollow promises that they would go on their way without hurting anyone in exchange for weed or the whereabouts of people known to grow it. Although they always reneged on those promises, it was an effective search tool.

The night they arrived in Huntington the men were all smiles. Things had gone well beyond all hope. They had an excellent meal. They'd sorted their loot, keeping those things they needed and discarding the rest. They'd done the same with the weapons and had scattered the unwanted parts up and down the road, making a game of seeing what they could hit as they threw them for distance. They'd siphoned all the fuel from the unwanted vehicles and transferred it to their own. They had a supply of good weed from their stay in Chillicothe and passed joints late into the night.

"Need to get rid of those trucks tomorrow," Thomas said. "Can't have all that shit we ain't gonna take cluttering up our camp."

"We moving on tomorrow?" Lawdog asked.

"I see no need for that right now. This seems like a safe area. We've got plenty of food and supplies, got an amazing crib, and nowhere to be. Let's just hang and enjoy it. See the sights."

Catcalls went up from the men. They all knew this was code for "let's stick around and terrorize the community for fun." They loved their wild parties.

"Thomas?" Mundo asked.

"Yeah?"

"This may sound like a crazy question but it's been on my mind."

"What?"

"You mind if I light one of these fucking trucks on fire and send it rolling down the road? I've always wanted to do that."

The men erupted into snickers and laughter. They were used to Mundo's crazy ideas. He was always coming up with something over the top.

"You serious?" Lawdog asked.

Mundo nodded. "As a heart attack."

Lawdog shook his head.

"I'll make a deal with you," Thomas said.

Mundo was doubtful. "What kind of deal?"

"That idea of yours sounds like it's got trouble written all over it. What if the vehicle just rolls about ten feet and burns right there? Car fires are hot. It might damage our trucks. We might lose our fine accommodations for the night."

"I don't think that would happen," Mundo argued.

"But it could, right?"

Mundo nodded. "I guess so. What's the deal?"

"You can pull your stupid-ass stunt if you want to. Set a truck on fire, start it rolling, and jump up and down like a kid while it burns. But it needs to make it at least one hundred yards from this camp. Exactly one football field away. You think you can do that?"

Mundo chuckled. "Hell, I don't know. The truck would have to pick up some momentum and you'd have to hope it didn't run into something along the way. Hundred yards is a long damn way. What happens if it don't make it?"

"I put a bullet in your head. Kill you deader than hell," Thomas said.

Mundo's eyes went wide. They all knew Thomas was a hard man but this was new territory. "You serious?"

Thomas grinned. "As a heart attack."

Droopy hopped up from his seat in excitement. "I'm going to mark off a hundred yards with a flare. You taking this deal, ain't you?"

Mundo looked uncertain. "I ain't so sure. I thought it would be pretty damn funny to watch, but I ain't sure it's worth dying over. It was just an idea."

The men instantly started giving him shit, ribbing him about giving up so easily, and questioning his manhood.

"Alright! Alright! I'll do it."

"You sure?" Thomas asked. "'Cause I'm serious. You screw this up

– you don't make the hundred yards – and you gonna get a bullet in the head. No more Mundo."

"Yeah, I'm gonna do it," Mundo said. "Those the only rules?"

"Yep, the only rules. Don't screw up. You might be missed around this joint. Some of these people think your fool ass is funny. Me included." He stuck out his hand and Mundo shook it with determination.

The men were enjoying this exchange. Mundo was always running his mouth and giving people shit. They loved that it was being turned back onto him in a very serious fashion. They knew Thomas was serious about killing him. He didn't joke about shit like that. If Mundo took the deal and didn't live up to his end, Thomas would do exactly as he promised. To do any less would dishonor him in front of his men and he couldn't have that.

Mundo went from vehicle to vehicle, checking the condition of the tires and the steering. "Can I take a running one?"

"You said roll, not drive," Droopy pointed out, passing by with a flare. "Any dumbass can drive a vehicle a hundred yards and set it on fire."

"He's right," Thomas agreed, walking up, more men crowding around them. "I don't care if you take one with a key so you can at least unlock the steering, but it has to coast. You can't drive it. That's the deal."

"Can I change my mind?"

"Nope. We shook on it. You back out now, I got no choice but to kill you."

Mundo muttered to himself. He was easily agitated, always moving fast, talking fast, and cracking jokes. He wasn't making any jokes right now. He'd made a deal with the devil and had to see it through or pay the ultimate price.

"Okay, this one," he announced, standing beside a Ford F-150. "Can I at least unhook the trailer?"

"Got no problem with that," Thomas said.

Mundo stared at the truck for a moment. "You know what? Fuck it. I'm going to take the trailer too. If I'm going out, I'm going in style."

The men let up a collective cheer. This was the Mundo they liked to see. They might as well enjoy it since this might be his last performance. In the distance, Droopy struck the flare, held it up high for everyone to see, and then dropped it on the ground.

"You sure that's a hundred yards?" Mundo asked when Droopy made his way back. "That looks pretty damn far."

"It's a hundred," Droopy confirmed. "I counted. Both ways."

The men started piling around the scene, climbing onto vehicles to better see down-course. Some were placing bets with real money, which was pointless since it currently held no value at all. They liked the sound of it, placing fifty thousand dollars of useless money on a pointless bet. Mundo was pacing around, talking to himself and trying to get psyched up.

With a powerful war cry, Mundo launched himself at the Ford. He got his right hand on the steering wheel and his left on the door and heaved with all his might. The road was relatively flat but Mundo was blessed with a very gentle, nearly imperceptible incline which worked to his advantage. Still, he had to get the truck rolling under his own power and it took all he had. He pumped his legs, locked his arms, and cried out from the effort.

And it moved.

He grunted and roared. One leg slid out but he righted himself and kept at it, the truck gaining momentum bit by bit while the men were cheering and hollering. Thomas leaned back against the hood of another of the trucks, a joint hanging from his lips, and a smile on his face.

"He's going to make it," Lawdog said.

"He ain't there yet," Thomas countered.

It was in the wee hours of the morning, pitch black, and Mundo couldn't see anything once he was beyond the range of the men's headlamps. He didn't want to break pace to flip on the headlights, focusing instead on transferring his muscle power into momentum. A sudden grinding startled him and the door began to close shut on his body. He'd strayed too close to the guardrail.

"Shit!" he cried, leaping onto the truck's running board, then ducking into the cab, just as the door crushed closed. There was an earsplitting scraping sound.

When the truck hit the rail, the grinding of metal against metal sent sparks flying. The cheers of men erupted into the night. However this ended, it was a good show at the moment.

Mundo flipped several switches and turned several knobs before he found the headlights. When they sprang to life, cutting into the darkness ahead of him, he could see that he was riding against the guardrail. That friction was eroding his precious momentum. He steered away from the rail, getting all the tires back on the road, and aiming for Droopy's flare. He was nearly halfway there.

He rolled down the window and howled into the night. "Whoooohooooooooo!"

His audience loved it and they cheered in response. Mundo started patting his shirt pockets to find his lighter. Then he recalled that he'd passed it to someone to light a joint and they hadn't returned it. He smacked the steering wheel with his palms.

Damn!

People were always doing that shit! No respect for a man's personal property.

He switched on the cab light and didn't see anything. They didn't put cigarette lighters in them anymore. He checked the door compartments and the center console. Nothing. He couldn't go this far and screw this up. He couldn't put his life at risk for something this mundane and not finish it. The flare ahead was getting closer and closer. He didn't dare brake to buy himself more time.

He groaned in frustration and removed a flask of liquor from the cargo pocket on his pants. Careful not to spill any of it on himself, afraid that odor might make Thomas aware he'd had liquor on him, Mundo poured the alcohol into the passenger seat. It soaked into the cloth seat cover and ran into the foam padding underneath. Mundo had seen a couch burn once. The foam would go up like a bonfire.

Unable to find anything with which he could spark the fire to life, Mundo steered the truck until the flare was just to the left of the driver's side. He pushed open the door and gauged his speed. He only had one shot at this. As he closed in on the flare, he pumped his brakes once, then twice to bring his speed down enough to guarantee success.

He threw open his door and leaned out, holding onto the steering wheel with his right hand to keep him from falling. He dropped his left to the road and deftly scooped the flare into his gloved hand. The cheers of the men told him they'd been impressed by his maneuver.

"Damn right," he muttered. "You should be."

He yanked himself inside the cab, afraid that the weight of his body on the steering wheel might drive him into the guardrail again. If that happened with his body hanging out the door he'd be crushed, which was a hell of a lot worse death than being shot in the head. The sputtering flare was blinding, the sparks burning through his clothes.

He yelled and cursed, some it directed toward his own stupidity, before flinging the flare into the passenger seat. The alcohol caught fire and spread with a calm blue flame. He'd gone far enough. He'd passed his hundred yards and gone a bit past it. He didn't want to go so far that the men couldn't enjoy the spectacle he'd risked his life for. He grasped the wheel tightly, stomped the emergency brake, and spun the wheel.

The squeal of skidding tires silenced the onlookers. When the truck skidded broadside they could see the rising flames inside.

"I hope his dumb ass gets out of there," Lawdog said.

"I don't know how he's going to ever top this," Droopy said. "Crazy fool."

The driver's door flung open and Mundo sprang from the cab. The fire had accelerated faster than he'd expected and his radical steering maneuver had nearly thrown him over into it. The flames filled the cab and their brilliant orange light silhouetted Mundo's body. He raised his hands in victory and took a long bow.

The crowd, even those who'd lost some of their worthless cash on betting, cheered at his victory. No one wanted to see him die. Nothing ruined a good evening like seeing a teammate take a bullet, especially for something to trivial.

Mundo jogged all the way back, going directly to Thomas. "We good, T? I get to live?"

Thomas cracked up. "Yeah, you get to live. You crazy, you know? Risking your life for something like that."

Mundo shrugged. "I risk my life every day. At least I'd have known how I was going to die and that it would be quick."

Thomas pulled the joint from his mouth and handed it over to Mundo. He pointed behind him. "You missing your fire, man. You should at least watch it burn."

Mundo took the joint and nodded. He turned his back and stared at his fire, a broad grin on his face. Some of the men patted him on the back and congratulated him. Mundo let out another loud whoop that rang through the night.

32

Conor rode out of his compound before daylight. They'd firmed up their plans the previous night. Later that day, Doc Marty and Shannon were to depart for Johnny Jacks' house, where they would spend the night. It would put them closer to the firehouse on the day the larger force was to leave in support of Conor and Wayne. Ragus was to remain behind to keep watch on the compound, as much as he'd prefer to be involved in the action.

Tomorrow morning Shannon and Barb would go by the pastor's camp and then on to the firehouse, headed north with a force of volunteers from both Wayne and the pastor's camp. Doc Marty, much to his distress, would remain behind at Johnny's. It would keep him close enough to provide aid to the returning injured but would not expose him to unnecessary risk.

It was a cold morning, the nighttime temperature having dropped into the twenties. There was frost on every surface and Conor's breath froze, rising like fog in the beam of his headlamp. His horse was laden with his best gear. It was some of the same stuff he'd taken when he'd gone in pursuit of Barb after her kidnapping. The big difference then was that he'd not yet acquired a horse. He had to carry every bit of his kit on his back so he'd packed a lot lighter. Now he didn't have that restriction and he was free to go full Mad Mick. The bulk of the extra weight was ammo. He might not need much for the recon part of his trip but when the bulk of his force showed up for battle he had no idea how much they might need. He wouldn't have a plan for that until he got a better idea of what The Bond actually was. They could be trained, combat-hardened vets or they could be a bunch of clowns in stolen uniforms. He'd know soon.

Holstered on his battle belt, Conor carried a Glock 17 with a threaded barrel. Slung over his neck, he carried his battle rifle. It was an M4 variant that was not much different from an over-the-counter AR-15 except for the three position selector switch. He'd built the weapon around a Spike's Tactical lower receiver and the selector offered three engraved settings: Peace, War, and God Wills It. It was decked out with several other nice features, including a holographic sight that worked with his night vision, a targeting laser that offered both green and infrared modes, and a weapon-mounted light.

Also in his Eberlestock Gunslinger pack, strapped across his horse, was something he rarely brought out – his Accuracy International sniper rifle. The beast was nearly twenty pounds with an optic, ammo, and a bipod. It was chambered in .300 Win Mag and shot so damn well it made Conor surprise himself sometimes. He'd be the first to tell you that he was no sniper but there were times the job called for precision shooting. He kept the gun tuned, shooting it often enough that he was certain it would hit where he aimed it. Ballistic data for his custom rounds was taped to a scrap of paper inside the flip up lens cap. With that and his rangefinder he was usually good to go if environmental conditions were fairly stable.

He carried a bivy sack and a down bag for sleeping. He had trail food, which consisted of MREs, jerky, and energy bars. The larger force, Barb's group, would be carrying better provisions, but he and Wayne wouldn't be cooking. He had a lot more tactical goodies in his pack and saddlebags. Much of it he hoped he didn't need, including the combat tomahawk that he'd wielded so effectively when he'd rescued Barb. It had taken several good soakings to clean the thing of all the blood and gore. It had a lot of memories attached to it and they were all unpleasant. He carried it wrapped in a piece of red cloth like some especially powerful piece of dark magic that was only unleashed in the worst of times, which was perhaps a very accurate assessment of what the weapon was in Conor's hands.

The sun was up when he reached the spot where the ridge leveled out to farmland. Frost coated the land but the sun was heating it up, adding a reflective quality to every frozen surface as the frost began to melt. Whorls of mist rose from the ground. Conor stopped to take in the splendor of it. There was utter and total silence.

From the road, he heard no sound that was not of his own making. His saddle groaned and his gear creaked. His horse snorted, rattling its bridle as it shook its mighty head. This was not the first time he'd seen such beauty and experienced such peace on the way to do brutal business. It had happened so many times it almost seemed the way of things, that every eruption of violence was preceded by a calm so profound as to stop him in his tracks.

He'd found it in the deep jungle outside of Mosquito in Eastern Honduras, one of the most violent nations in the world, just before he detonated the explosive device that killed an uncooperative cartel leader. It was during a time when the CIA and the cartel often had overlapping interests. Then suddenly they didn't anymore and the drug lord had to go.

Conor again found it in the beautiful mountains around the Ma'in Hot Springs in the Madaba Governate in Jordan just hours before assassinating a terrorist financier with an exploding olive. It was an amazing device that utilized a pressure switch ignited by the man biting down on it. It wasn't large enough to vaporize the unsavory character but it created a traumatic wound from which the bleeding could not be stemmed.

He experienced the same thing on a beautiful beach at Phuket, Thailand, where he was tracking down a mercenary who'd disclosed Conor's participation in a job they'd done together. The guy figured he was far enough from the United States that Conor wouldn't hear about his loose tongue. He was wrong. Conor killed him by slipping a fake ice cube into his drink, the cube infused with a fast-acting poison. It happened in a club frequented by mercenaries, operators, and guns for hire. It was the kind of place where no one saw a thing, no one asked questions, and stepping over bodies didn't raise an eyebrow.

And you wonder why they call you the Mad Mick, Conor mused.

Fifteen more minutes of riding put him at the road by Johnny's house. The smell of wood smoke hung in the crisp air. A tendril of smoke curled from the chimney. Conor knew that Johnny was probably already up. Barb would be soon, if she wasn't already. Conor opened the gate and went through, the dog sounding an alarm at his arrival. By the time he reached the house, Johnny was on the porch wearing a flannel shirt, suspenders, and a big grin.

"Why aren't you inside by that warm fire?" Conor asked, climbing off his horse and tying it off near the porch.

"Wanted to see how you took your coffee."

"Black, thank you. Barb up?"

"Not yet, but I assume that she'll be rolling down those steps any minute since the dog started barking. She likes to stay on top of what's going on around her."

Conor nodded. "Noticed that, huh?"

"She's been with us less than twenty-four hours but yes. She's pretty..." Johnny struggled for the word.

"Switched on?" Conor offered. "Intense?"

Johnny snapped his finger and pointed at Conor. "That's it *exactly.*"

Conor climbed the steps, only bringing the M4 he was carrying. He propped it beside the door, removing his hat and gloves. "I can't stay long. I've got on too many layers for bandying about inside a heated house."

Johnny handed Conor a cup of coffee. "You think you're hot now? You'll be sweating bullets when you pour this down your neck."

"Thanks." Conor took the hot mug. "I just wanted to go over some details."

Footsteps on the stairs stopped Conor in his tracks. Barb bounced into sight, fully dressed.

"You sleep that way?" Conor asked.

Barb nodded. "Yeah, why?"

"No reason. I was just telling Johnny that I wanted to go over a few things about this operation."

"You want some coffee, Barb?" Johnny asked.

"Thanks." Barb smiled. "I can get it myself. I also brought some with me to contribute to the cause."

"That's always appreciated," Johnny said. "I saw a shirt once that said *I Run On Coffee and Hate*. Mine would be more like *I Run On Coffee and Bacon*."

Conor's mind floated to the coffee mug Barb had given him but he didn't bring it up. "I'm on my way to catch up with Wayne. He and I will try to catch up with The Bond and do some recon. I've got a good radio with me but it's of limited use in these hills until anyone is close to us."

"And you don't want me going with you?" Barb confirmed.

"I'd prefer you lead the larger force. It will be made up of folks from Wayne's camp and the pastor's camp."

Barb grinned wickedly. "Oh, they're going to love that. The pastor's folks are not going to want to take orders from me."

"I'll be talking to them on my way through this morning. They'll know the score in advance. They can either come with you or not. It's their choice and they have to live with the decision."

"I'll be gentle," Barb assured him. "Though I'd much rather be going with you and Wayne. I love sneaking around."

"Shannon will be coming with your group. If Johnny doesn't mind, I was hoping you could put Shannon and Doc Marty up for the night."

It was Barb's turn to appear questioning. "You sure Shannon is up for a trip like this?"

"Might be handy to have a medic," Conor said.

"We have Doc Marty," Barb said. "You think we need two medics?"

"Doc Marty isn't going."

"Okay, you've lost your ever-loving mind, old man. You're sending this teenager with me instead of a real doc? I hope to hell no one gets hurt."

Conor took a sip of his coffee. He was indeed starting to sweat, both from the caffeine content and the layers he was wearing. "There's several reasons for that. Doc Marty is a valuable asset to the community, perhaps too valuable to send off into combat. We did a lot of operations together over the years but the man is more of a white-glove operator than a grunt. He's kind of soft."

"So he just allowed you to send his daughter in his place?" Johnny Jacks asked. "That surprises me."

"More complicated than that," Conor said. "The whole thing was her idea. I just planned on you guys running with no medic but she was determined to go. There was a lot of drama and bullshit, but by the end Doc Marty understood this was important to Shannon. She wants to contribute. She needs to contribute."

"All these daughters rebelling on you old men," Barb teased. "We don't fit in your little molds and you start to lose your shit."

Conor ignored that comment. "I'm supporting her in this opportunity like I'm supporting you in taking on more responsibility. She'll need your support too. More than you've ever given her before." That wasn't asking for much, Conor knew, because she'd never really given Shannon any support before. She just barely tolerated her. Any support was an improvement over nothing.

"Understood," Barb said.

Conor hoped it was really that simple.

"Doc Marty and Shannon are welcome to stay here," Johnny said. "No problem. I'm out of beds but they're welcome to roll out sleeping bags by the fire."

"That's more than enough," Conor said. "Doc Marty will be staying with you a few nights since he's not going on the operation. I wanted to keep him in this end of the community so he'd be close if we had wounded who needed his attention. I also don't know what Sam and Jason worked out. Doc can lend you a hand around the place if one or both of them goes."

Johnny's smile disappeared and his mouth tightened. He took a sip of coffee before letting out a long sigh. "They're both going. I'm not happy about it but I understand. They can't sit this one out."

"I get that," Conor said. "Sam's in better physical condition but the boy is tough. They're a good team."

"He won't let her go without him," Johnny added.

"I need to get out of here," Conor said, delivering his cup to the kitchen. When he returned he patted Johnny on the back, then hugged his daughter. "Doc Marty and Shannon will be here tonight. They'll be bringing some food to fuel your people, more ammo, and some gear. You guys be careful. Keep your radio on and listen for us."

"Got it, Dad. Be careful."

"You know it, baby girl. If we're lucky, this will all be for naught. We'll get to Huntington and find The Bond went another way. You'll find Wayne and me riding home with smiles on our faces, singing a tune."

"I'm all for that," Johnny said.

"Only because you haven't heard his singing," Barb cracked.

33

Conor wasted no time at the pastor's camp. He'd been there enough that the sentry knew what he wanted, leaving wordlessly to get the pastor upon Conor's arrival. The pastor, clad in a red flannel jacket and orange hat with ear flaps, came to speak with him at the gate.

"Do you have volunteers?" Conor asked.

"Seventeen men."

"They need to head to the firehouse in the morning, prepared for two weeks in the field," Conor said. "My daughter Barb will be leading that force."

The pastor mulled that over a good while, finally settling on, "That's probably best."

Conor understood that the pastor could have stated it that way because he thought Barb was a murderous she-devil, thereby making her the most appropriate choice for leading an army. He could have meant a lot of things, but what was important was that they were sending men and those men would know Barb was in charge.

"Then I'll be leaving," Conor said.

"And I'll be praying," the pastor replied with a nod.

The next stop was Wayne's camp, and Conor arrived at the first sentry post with a stick of deer jerky hanging from his mouth like a cigar. The sentry waved him on without a word, barely taking his eyes off the jerky. Conor thought the man looked like a dog with a treat just inches above its nose, chin quivering and salivating. Not wanting to get ambushed for his breakfast, Conor stuck it in a pouch on the side of his plate carrier. While this pouch could have held a grenade, like the pouch beside it, or some other especially wicked piece of kit, it was Conor's snack pouch. It was packed with jerky, protein bars, and jellybeans.

He tied his horse off outside the barricade of junk cars and wove his way through the maze of an entrance, heading toward the fire circle. The firehouse was so crowded that men were always outside gathered around a fire. Sometimes it was alongside the river, other times in the parking lot. They were desperate to escape the congested interior where they spent too much time with both their families and the families of their companions.

This morning was no exception. They had no coffee or tea left but there was a steaming pot of an herbal brew suspended over the fire. The men stood watching the pot heat in silence. They had little left to talk about that had not been covered already. Without news and the latest television shows to spur conversation there was only the weather, and everyone was beyond sick of talking about that.

"I was hoping to see a Hardee's bag in your hand with coffee and biscuits," Wayne quipped when Conor walked up.

Conor turned his nose up. "Bloody hell, man, it'd be the fecking Bojangles is what it would be. Have you men never had a proper biscuit before?"

The men laughed. People usually had more of a routine around breakfast than they did for any other meal, likely because they weren't awake enough yet to make rational decisions.

"Bojangles, huh?" Wayne asked. "Never tried it."

"Damn right, Bojangles. And not with coffee, either. I recommend two bacon, egg, and cheese biscuits with a big honking vat of sweet tea the size of a human lung."

One of the men, a disturbed expression on his face, cleared his throat. "For those of us that have never seen a human lung…"

Conor held his hands apart, one above the other, like he was measuring the height of a squirrel. "About that feckin' tall."

"Got it," the man said, sharing a wary glance with his companions.

"The pastor is sending seventeen men," Conor said. "Add Barb and Shannon to that. How many do you have going with the team tomorrow?"

"Eleven," Wayne said.

Conor nodded. "The odds will suck but they always do. One gets used to it."

"I'm a little worried about leaving the camp without much protection," Wayne admitted. "They'll be vulnerable."

"Doc Marty will be arriving at Johnny's house tonight. He'll be staying there until we return. Let your people know he's available to assist should they need more manpower here. He's pretty resourceful. We've worked, uh…known each other for years."

"Well, since you didn't bring biscuits, I guess we might as well be going," Wayne said.

"At a minimum I can promise you a change of scenery," Conor said.

"Then let's get on with it," Wayne said. "I've stared across this fire at you peckerwoods long enough."

There were some good-natured jabs directed at Wayne. Conor stepped into the bushes, fought his way through several layers of clothing, and de-iced a circle on the ground while Wayne said his goodbyes. He was sitting on his horse, staring at the river, when Wayne joined him on his own mount.

Conor swung his horse to the west, headed toward Route 23. Wayne fell in alongside him, their horses at a trot. They exchanged no words. Conor knew where the man's head was at now. Saying goodbye to your family to go on an operation was never an insignificant thing. The odds of coming home, especially in current circumstances, were depressing to consider. Conor was probably a little more used to it than other men, having had to leave Barb behind since she was a toddler, even when she had no one in the world but him.

How he missed those days. If he didn't come home now, she'd be sad for a little while but she'd go on with her life. She'd probably find some poor man to marry and torment the way she'd lovingly tormented him. She'd be okay though. A man like Wayne, his family younger, their future uncertain, had a lot more to worry about.

Conor left him alone in his thoughts. He'd come up for air eventually.

34

The Bond stuck around the outskirts of Huntington, West Virginia, until Thomas got the prickling sensation on the back of his neck that told him it was time to move on. The bounty they'd obtained from the vehicles abandoned at their roadblock hadn't required much effort on their part at all. It was like a gift from whatever gods protected rogues, murderers, and thieves. They'd stuck around long enough to host several parties, something they rarely did since their parties had a way of turning public sentiment from fear to hatred. Perhaps that was what was triggering Thomas, the awareness that somewhere people were plotting against The Bond.

They had a nice meal that morning. Fried Spam, powdered eggs with hot sauce, and hash browns, all of it from the trucks that had shown up on their doorstep. They were eating in the furniture store, literally having breakfast in bed, though it was not so posh as the term implied. The men were propped up on the store's stock of mattresses, wearing their cammies and boots. They didn't care if they got the sheets dirty.

On one of their looting trips they'd found some of the propane heater heads that screwed directly onto propane tanks and had managed to heat the store's interior to a comfy fifty degrees. Because of that, no one was anxious to rush outside and start packing up camp. They'd been spoiled and had gotten soft.

"We leave today," Thomas announced as the men ate their breakfast.

"Awww, do we gotta?" Mundo whined, sounding like a kid asked to pick up his room.

"We do," Thomas confirmed. "I'm getting itchy about staying here and a man should always go with his gut. Learned that a long time ago. My gut says we been here too long."

"My gut's asking if we got more Spam," Droopy said, struggling to get up off the bed.

"Your gut's always asking for more," Mundo said. "Your fat ass eats like a whole football team at a buffet."

"This body is a temple, asshole," Droopy said. "Respect the temple."

"Hey, T," Mundo said, "we might get more miles per meal if we leave Tubby, I mean *Droopy*, behind."

"And we'd get a lot more peace and quiet if we left *you* behind," Thomas retorted. "Y'all got five minutes to finish up and get packing."

Grumbling, the men shoveled their food in at an accelerated pace. They were no strangers to having to eat quickly and had only become slack in that particular area since striking out on their own. Thomas was beginning to notice that, wondering if his force was losing its edge. He probably needed to rein them in at some point but it was a fine line. Push too hard and they might turn on him. Part of him wished Mundo had lost that bet the other night. If he'd killed the man in front of the group they'd remember that. They'd understand he had ice for blood and wouldn't tolerate any bullshit.

The furniture store also sold china and flatware. All week long soldiers of The Bond had eaten off fine china and expensive stainless steel, throwing the used plates into a pile outside the building when they were done. A few minutes after Thomas's warning to finish up, plates were clattering into the pile and the men were gathering their personal gear. When that was stowed, some helped Buddha Boy and Shootah take down the kitchen.

Packing was different now that they had an unanticipated surplus of gear. Some of the trailers that had been abandoned at the roadblock were better than the trailers The Bond was currently using. During their stay outside of Huntington they'd come upon a battery-powered grinder with a cut-off wheel and used it to cut off the hitch locks. They would leave two of their smaller trailers behind and take the larger twin-axle contractor trailers gifted to them by their victims. Several days of carefully going through the gear had allowed them to consolidate it down to the most valuable items. Everything else was left in a pile or burned.

"Who's doing the signature, Thomas?" Lawdog asked.

Thomas glanced around the group. While all of the men were busy, those who heard Lawdog's question did their best to appear even busier. No one, with the exception of Mundo, liked doing the signature.

Mundo was jumping up and down like a second-grader who knew an answer for the first time. "Pick me! Pick me!" he sang, playing it up.

Thomas grinned. "Always playing the fool, Mundo."

"But I do it right." He grinned. "When I leave the signature, shit knows it's been signed."

"Go for it then," Thomas said. "You only got fifteen minutes. Don't be starting some elaborate thing you ain't got time to finish."

Mundo frowned at the restrictions put on him. "That's like giving me the big box of crayons but saying I can only use seven of them."

"Fourteen and a half minutes," Thomas said.

Mundo kicked into gear, starting a timer on his watch. He recruited a couple of men nearly done with their tasks and put them to work for him. They were more than willing to help as long as he shouldered the creative burden.

With seconds to spare, Mundo backed away from the wall, threw his hands up, and yelled, "Done!" With that, he started jogging around like a running back who'd just scored a touchdown, doing a victory dance.

Thomas and Lawdog were leaned back against the fender of a truck, both scratching their chins like art critics studying a gallery wall.

"What do you think, Lawdog?" Thomas asked.

Lawdog raised an eyebrow and lowered his voice, adopting the tone he imagined an art critic might use. "I think the artist shows a newfound maturity. There's a boldness in his stroke and a confidence in his palette that is refreshing in someone so young. I think we're seeing a new talent on the brink of greatness."

"I would tend to agree with you, Professor Lawdog," said Thomas, "but I find the lineage of his work to be somewhat derivative. We are not seeing anything new here."

"Y'all like it or not?" Mundo asked, stepping to the side and gesturing at the wall with a sweeping flourish.

The plastic letters on the high storefront had been smashed free with an ax. Galvanized spikes thick enough to join landscape timbers had been used to crucify a dead man against the wall. He formed the letter "T" while the rest of the "he Bond" was spray-painted in graffiti-style lettering.

"Come on," said Mundo, "you gotta admit it's eye-catching."

"Let's go," Thomas said. "We need to get out of here."

"What? That's all I get?" Mundo demanded. He wasn't angry but putting on his usual comedy performance, playing the outraged and forever-wronged victim.

"You don't shut your mouth, we going to hang your ass up there as an exclamation point," Thomas snapped. "Now get in the damn trucks."

"Yes, sir," Mundo said, suddenly all business.

Show over, the men piled into the trucks, manning guns and slamming doors. Engines were started and the lead truck crept forward. When he confirmed that the others were behind him, the driver accelerated and they headed south on Route 23.

"Where we headed next?" Droopy asked over the radio.

"Kentucky," Thomas replied. "Possibly Paintsville, depending on how the day goes."

35

Conor and Wayne followed the paved surface of Route 23 when they had to, opting for the soft shoulder when they could to spare their horses. As the road cut through the steep mountains of southwestern Virginia and eventually Kentucky, the four-lane highway was sometimes jammed into a narrow ledge scraped into the mountain with no shoulder to either side. They were constantly on watch against being ambushed by anyone who might want their gear or their horses.

There was no avoiding people. In a land utterly devoid of flat ground, the areas most suitable for road construction were inevitably the most suitable for the building of homes and towns. Tiny hamlets and clusters of houses showed up frequently so the pair crept through them on high alert, using back streets when they could, constantly staying on their weapons, ready to fire. Without numbers to intimidate, they relied heavily on menace. They weren't guys open to small talk or barter.

The two men hadn't spent much time together before but had nothing to do but talk as they passed long hours together. Wayne talked about his family and his home in Michigan, about how his parents had been from Kentucky prior to moving north so his dad could work for General Motors. He mentioned that his dad ended up as a shop carpenter for GM, one of the highest paid and most desirable carpenter jobs available in the Detroit area. Wayne had followed in his father's footsteps, seeking one of those plant carpenter positions, but had been unable to get on at GM. He wound up applying his skills in the high-volume residential construction industry, which had declined at the same rate as Detroit itself. He'd wanted to leave for some time but was caught in the trap of making just enough money to keep going but not enough to escape the city.

Wayne asked Conor about his life and how he'd ended up in the United States, since his obvious accent left no doubt he was from elsewhere.

"My own tale is crooked as a dog's hind leg," Conor said. "I don't talk about it very much."

"Don't or *won't* talk about it?"

"Both."

Wayne gestured around them at the steep mountains and the rocky bluffs. There was nothing but woods and empty road in all directions. "What else do we have to do but talk?"

Conor relented, to an extent, and for the next two hours shared the highlights of how he ended up in America, leaving out the juicy parts. He mentioned nothing about his family's background in Ireland and said nothing of avenging his wife's death. He didn't mention his employer, Ricardo, and what his actual career involved. He passed himself off as a welder and fabricator, though Wayne appeared extremely doubtful about that line. Conor also failed to mention that most of the male influences in his life had been from Irish crime families. None of this explained his relationship with Doc Marty, his extensive arsenal, or his obvious proficiency at ending human life.

When he was done, Wayne laughed ruefully. "There may be some truth in what you're saying but there are so many gaps in that story. It's like seeing those top secret documents they show on television that are seventy-five percent redacted. There's no continuity. I got no doubt that the best parts of your story are being blacked out."

Without commenting, Conor pulled out his GPS to check their location.

Over days of riding and more redacted tales they passed through Pikeville, Kentucky, and small communities like Betsy Layne, Tram, and Watergap. Until they hit Prestonsburg, Conor was mostly concerned about the threat presented by residents of those tiny communities. Beyond Prestonsburg, he was more on edge, increasingly concerned about running into The Bond. The distance between the riders and the last known location of The Bond was closing. Men in trucks would have had plenty of time to continue down Route 23 if that was their plan. Conor and Wayne moved thoughtfully, watching for blind spots and signs of large encampments. On the south side of Paintsville, Kentucky, they found The Bond.

Conor and Wayne reached the outskirts of town in the late afternoon after a long day of riding. The sun was getting low on the horizon and they were already anticipating having to find a place to hole up for the night with no fire. The pair didn't know that The Bond had already hit town earlier in the day and established a camp at a car dealership. They were at that very moment going around and doing their "friendly neighbor" bit, introducing themselves to the locals. Had it not been for The Bond rolling out their version of the welcome wagon, which always involved a little gunfire, Conor and Wayne might have been unfortunate enough to ride right up onto one of their guard posts. It was a burst of thumping gunfire from a belt-fed weapon that got their attention.

Conor reined in his horse so violently that the animal backed up and spun. "Easy now," he whispered. He held up a hand toward Wayne. "Listen!"

"You're the one making all the noise," Wayne retorted.

Dismounting, Conor led his horse to the shoulder of the road. In the distance they could see the sporadic placement of rural homes transitioning into a more orderly system of streets and neighborhoods. A faint scream sliced through the cold, echoing through the hollows. It was followed by another burst from the belt-fed gun.

Wayne dismounted and joined Conor. "We need to find them and put a stop to this. They're killing people."

"How many did Pepe say there were?" Conor asked.

"Could be a hundred or more."

"Wayne, we're not ready to engage anyone. We need intel. We need to confirm troop strength and capability."

Wayne let out a long, tense breath. "Sorry. There's just something about hearing people needing help that makes it hard to stand back and do nothing."

"I didn't say we'd do nothing. We might be able to help the people of this town, but if we give away our presence now, we'll blow it."

"You're right," Wayne conceded. "What do we need to do?"

They moved off the road into the woods and found an opening in the trees. There was enough grass growing that it might keep the horses entertained for a while. They hobbled them and offloaded their gear. Conor didn't want to take a chance on all his goodies being stolen if the horses made too much noise and someone found them. The two men stashed their gear a short distance away, covering it with branches and leaf litter. When they were done, they moved on with just their rifles and Go Bags.

They returned to the road, crossed it, and jumped the guardrail on the opposite side. Below them was a steep hillside descending to a creek, across which were several mobile homes on a winding gravel road. Conor led the way, descending in a controlled slide on the slate and scree. Several times his momentum outpaced his feet and he had to sit down to slow himself. When they reached the bottom, they found themselves on a distinct trail that ran along the creek bank.

"Let's follow this for a while," Conor said. "I don't want wet boots if I can avoid it."

They made good time on the trail and eventually reached a point where the road swung to their side of the creek. At this point they weren't as concerned about making noise. They had a good view of their surroundings and the few dwellings they'd seen showed no signs of being occupied. Houses soon became more frequent and the roads turned into streets, demonstrating a planned orderliness. There were no alleys here, just a small town backstreet with scattered houses. In the distance they began to hear the rumble of idling engines. They picked up their pace and moved toward them. Before they reached the source, the noise began moving away from them, leaving only a keening wail of grief.

They slowed, moving with raised rifles in the shadows of houses and parked cars. Conor took cover behind an azalea bush and Wayne fell in behind him. They were at a wide, paved street lined with picturesque houses. They were older homes from the early twentieth century that had all been updated. They had crisp white trim, painted shutters, and brass hardware. Smoke rolling from chimneys told Conor that at least some of the houses were occupied. In the middle of the street, a grief-stricken woman had collapsed to her knees, mourning someone that lay splayed awkwardly in a puddle of blood.

"Stay here," Conor ordered. Moving from concealment, he crept into the street, scanning in every direction. If there were people living here, which there obviously were, there was no way they could have missed the show that took place here. There had to be people watching out their windows right now and they would be watching him move toward the woman. He only hoped that no one would drop him without warning, firing a shot from a window or around a corner. He was aware of what he looked like and that he was probably the kind of guy that you'd want to shoot without warning.

When the sobbing woman saw him coming toward her she let out a bloodcurdling scream, recoiling from him and scuttling toward the opposite sidewalk. Conor held up a flattened palm to her, a sign to calm down, that he didn't intend to hurt her. She wasn't buying it and why would she? Her eyes roved along his camouflage clothing and came to rest on his rifle. She didn't know him. Why else would he be there but to inflict more pain? To kill more people?

"I don't mean you any harm," Conor said.

"Haven't you done enough already?" she moaned. "You've taken the only thing that meant anything to me."

Conor shut out her pain. He wasn't there to provide comfort. He needed information or there would be a whole lot more people in the same world of hurt. "I'm not with those people. Who are they? Do you know anything about them?"

The woman eased over on her side, resting her bare cheek on the pavement, and staring at the body in front of her. Her voice was a moan, a song of grief. "I don't know who they are. We were just out walking around the neighborhood. They said they were new here and wanted to introduce themselves because we'd be seeing more of them. My husband asked them if they were from the Army because they were dressed like they were. They had Army trucks and Army guns. They said they weren't, that they were from something called The Bond." The woman dragged a curled wrist to her face, wiped at her nose, then rolled over onto her back. She closed her eyes and began sobbing again.

A flash of movement caught Conor's eye. He stepped to the side and spun, his rifle barrel coming to rest center mass on an elderly man with thick white hair, a burgundy cardigan, and corduroy pants. The man had somehow gotten to within a few feet of him. Where the hell was Wayne?

"You fucking freeze!" Conor growled.

The man halted mid-step and raised his hands above his head. His eyes crunched closed in anticipation of the gunshot he expected must be coming. "I don't mean you any harm. I just wanted to check on the girl."

Conor took in the man before him and lowered his gun. He had retired lawyer written all over him. "Did you see what happened?"

The man lowered his hands and nodded, his eyes glued to the sobbing woman. "Can I?"

Conor nodded, then waved for Wayne to join him. Wayne had somehow missed the old man but spotted Conor's wave. "Nice job keeping watch, Eagle Eye," Conor said when Wayne reached him. "You could have mentioned this guy running right up my arse."

"I didn't see him. I was watching windows."

The lawyer was at the crying woman's side, crouched, and

holding her hand. He tried to get her to sit up but she fought him, crying harder, so he let her be. He turned his attention back to Conor.

"This is the first we've seen of those people. My wife and I were watching from the window because we thought they were the National Guard or Army here to deliver aid or assess damage. No one was concerned. They did this after the flood of '77, coming through like that in big trucks. We saw Sondra and her husband talking to them. Everyone was smiling. Then they opened fire for no reason at all. You can see this man didn't have a gun. There was no reason to kill him. Why would the Army do that?"

"It's not the Army," Conor said.

The man appeared confused by that but stared at Conor with renewed interest, taking in his weapons and his gear. He pointed at Conor with a crooked finger. "Then are *you* the Army?"

Conor hesitated before responding. "You might say that, but probably not the army you're expecting. Have you heard of the Mad Mick in these parts?"

A flicker of awareness cut through the man's confusion. "Uh...yeah. Travelers passing through have mentioned some signs. They're supposed to be some hillbilly vigilante group guarding the area south and west of here. Are you part of that group?"

"It's a group of one," Wayne said, nodding in Conor's direction. "Crazy Irishman. That's him."

The man pointed at Conor, a questioning expression on his face. Conor nodded in response.

"Oh my," the man said.

"Do you know which way they went?" Conor asked.

The man nodded to his right. "That road takes you to Route 460 and on into town. I expect that's where they've gone."

Conor wanted to immediately set off in pursuit but understood their walking pace wasn't going to do the job. "Let's get back to the horses, Wayne. Going by the GPS, this town is kind of sprawled out with two highways passing through it. We'll exhaust ourselves chasing them around on foot. I've got a different plan."

36

The climb back up to the road and their horses was not nearly so easy as the scamper down. The loose shale was merciless, like some cruel surface designed to torture climbers. They slid one step back for every two forward. They were forced to sling their rifles over their backs and use bushes as handholds. Sweating and gasping for breath, they hissed curses when they had the extra air to do so. It was absurd enough to have been comical, the type of situation Conor frequently laughed at himself for getting into, but darkness settled on them, forcing them to climb by the light of their red-lensed headlamps. It wasn't funny anymore. If someone had them in their crosshairs, there would be no escape. It would be like shooting Dall sheep from a cliff face.

When they reached the top and slithered over the guardrail, the men crumpled onto the asphalt to catch their breath. Conor tugged off his headlamp, removed his fleece watch cap, and allowed the night air to cool his soaked head. He could hear his mother telling him he'd catch his death for such a thing. The night was indeed getting cold, and their exertion had masked how much the temperature dropped. It was probably right at the freezing point, and being outside in their sweat-soaked clothes could become a problem. They'd have to get moving at a gentler pace and allow their body heat to dry their clothes or they could be at risk for hypothermia.

Conor sat up, then staggered to his feet. His legs were shaky, cooked from the climb, and his arms were tired from hauling himself up on scrubby bushes. Wayne hadn't budged and Conor tapped him with his boot. "Get up, you bum. We can't afford to catch a chill. We need to keep moving."

"Just shoot me," Wayne groaned. "I feel like I did five hundred squats with a horse on my back."

"We probably should have thought it out better. Using the road to get back up here might have been a smarter option than backtracking, but that's on you."

Wayne frowned. "Why the hell is that on me?"

"Because I don't want to look like a feckin' idiot." Conor grinned.

Wayne shook his head, lolling it back and forth where it rested on the pavement. "And I thought you knew what the hell you were doing."

"Not always. Sometimes I wing it." Conor turned his cap inside out, putting the dryer side against his head. He replaced his head-lamp and clicked on the red beam, angling it down at his feet, then headed off for their gear cache, knowing Wayne would follow soon enough. In a few minutes the two of them were back on the road with their horses and gear. They set off in the direction of town, choosing to walk because Conor was afraid that sitting in his saddle might allow hypothermia to set in. He needed to keep the muscles working until things dried a little.

"I thought I was in decent shape," Wayne said. "I work outside and do manual labor for a living, but that climb kicked my ass."

"I don't know many folks conditioned enough to enjoy what we just did. Barb perhaps, but she's a glutton for punishment. I think the girl likes to suffer a little too much."

"I'm glad she wasn't here to see that. The only thing that could have made that climb worse would be her taunting us from the top of the hill like a drill instructor."

"I can think of other things that might have made it worse, my friend. Like being shot at, for example."

"You always make me feel better," Wayne said. "You're a ray of sunshine."

Conor smiled. "It's a gift."

Eventually they climbed onto their horses, switching from red-lensed headlamps to night vision. Conor also had a thermal scope in his bag of goodies but he couldn't wear the thing on a bump helmet like he could the night vision. He'd brought a bump helmet for Wayne too, sparing him the discomfort of wearing the skull-crusher headgear which was the other option if you didn't have a helmet. The skull-crusher was so named because the only way to get it tight enough that the heavy night vision gear didn't sag was to ratchet it so tight you could feel the seams of your skull threatening to break loose.

"This shit is amazing," Wayne said, ogling the sky and the terrain around them.

"You haven't used it before?"

"I've used it in the military but it's been a while. Not sure what I had was this good. It made everything green and this is white. Explain to me again why a welder has the latest and greatest night vision? And not just one set but two?"

"If I told you—"

"You'd have to kill me," Wayne finished. "I know. Why do I suspect you've used that line many times in your life and actually meant it?"

"If it makes you feel any better, I wouldn't *enjoy* having to kill you."

Wayne cracked up. "Oh yeah, that makes me feel much better. There's that gift again."

The highway ran high above the town but was descending as they moved. Most of the trees along the streets below them were hardwoods and had lost their leaves. This opened up lines of sight that the riders wouldn't have had months earlier. The hillsides around them had hardwood too, but also held a mix of pines, cedars, hemlocks, and evergreens that obscured sightlines in the deep forest. It was odd that there was a town down there in total darkness. The sight of a "dead" town was something it would be hard to get used to.

They could now see it wasn't totally dark. With the enhancement of night vision, they could see flickers of light at times. Conor was hoping to see a pocket of illumination brighter than the rest that might indicate a bonfire or lanterns. That could be the enemy camp they were searching for. So far he'd seen nothing like that.

The road was descending quickly and they'd be in town before they knew it. Conor didn't want to push into this unfamiliar town in darkness, not knowing what they might stumble into. Even if they could find a place to hole up for the night they might have trouble hiding the horses. He'd rather stop somewhere soon and crawl into his sleeping bag to warm up and shake the nagging chill. Tomorrow they could stash the horses in the woods somewhere and spend the day skulking around town.

"I've got a thermal scope in my saddlebags," Conor said. "I'm not sure it would give me any more information than this night vision though. I was hoping we'd be able to see their camp loud and clear at night. They're either further into town than we can see or they've got a dark camp tonight."

"I hope to hell those guys don't have thermal," Wayne commented. "I don't have much experience with it but I imagine these horses probably put out a hell of a heat signature. We'd really stand out."

Conor thought about that as his horse plodded forward. The loud clomping of shod hooves carrying in the night concerned him the most. This was a different enemy, a trained enemy. He began to feel really uncomfortable with the idea that the men they were pursuing had military gear and a military background. Why wouldn't they have night vision? If they had the same advantages he had, that meant he really had *no* advantage at all.

He was about to suggest they hole up for the night when a shot rang out. What Conor actually heard was a round impacting the guardrail ahead of them, followed by the echo of a distant rifle shot.

"*Run!*" he barked. It was a simple command but primal and direct, leaving no doubt as to what needed to be done.

The men spun their horses and fled back in the direction they'd come from. There was a second shot and a whine when the round ricocheted off the exposed rock face behind them. Dirt and rock shards rained down on the surface of the road. Whoever was shooting at them didn't have the rifle, the optic, or the skill required to make this shot. If he had, one of them would be dead by now.

"Get down, Wayne! Stay low on the horse!"

Wayne heeded his warning, leaning forward until the saddle horn bumped his chest plate, trying to make himself a smaller target. Aware that the element of surprise was gone, whoever was firing at them dumped their mag, replacing precision with volume of fire. Seconds later the shots died off and Conor rode alongside Wayne.

"I think they lost sight of us," he said. "They had time to change mags."

"That was fucking close."

"I should have anticipated that," Conor said. "I keep forgetting this is a military enemy and not just any bunch of rogue assholes. This is an occupying army and they need to be treated as such."

Wayne slowed his horse and Conor matched his gait. "You say that like you have experience dealing with a military enemy. What the hell kind of machinist are you again?"

"The kind who hates getting shot at," Conor growled. "The kind who takes it personally."

"Oh right. Just a regular old machinist. Before this trip is over, you and I are going to have a serious talk about your background."

Conor ignored the comment. "We need to find a good spot to hole up. If that was The Bond, they may come investigate what their sentry was shooting at. I would suspect they have night vision, but they might have thermal as well. We need to put a thermal barrier between us and the road."

"There were a few roads going to the uphill side of the highway," Wayne said. "Maybe we top this hill and find a spot on other side for the night."

"Let's do it," Conor said, nudging his horse into high gear.

37

Conor's synthetic-fill sleeping bag was heavier than a down bag but more resistant to moisture. He'd shoved it into a waterproof bivy sack before falling asleep, and was glad he had. He was covered in frost when he woke up. He'd stayed warm, the bag hooded over his head with only his nose and lips exposed, but he hadn't slept well. He was dehydrated and experienced several cramps overnight as a result. There was nothing like getting a cramp in a tight mummy bag.

He also didn't sleep as well on the ground as he used to, and blamed that on getting older. He'd launched into this mission just like his twenty-eight year old self would have, ready to sleep on the ground and spring out of his sleeping bag with a backflip the next morning. He clearly wasn't twenty-eight anymore, every pain in his body reminded him of that. He wished he'd brought his hammock. He might have felt a wee bit better.

He sat upright, the sleeping bag wrapped around him. Wayne was in the same state, propped against a tree, neither anxious to roll out into the cold morning.

Conor blinked at him. "Your beauty sleep didn't help you at all, Wayne. You're still ugly as a dog's arse."

"I'd give up some of my good looks to go a few years back in time. I feel like crap."

Conor thrust his bag down and climbed out of it. The days were short and it was light already. He needed to get this show on the road. "I'm with you, man. I feel like God ran a rolling pin over me last night, trying to crush me flat." He dragged on his boots, then stood and started pulling on the rest of his gear.

Wayne wasn't ready to take the plunge yet and continued to huddle in his bag. "This reminds me of deer hunting, only that's fun and this sucks. Oh, and this time the deer are shooting back. How's that for some bullshit? What's our plan for today?"

"I thought about that last night when I couldn't sleep. I've got a plan but I'm not sure you're going to like it."

"You're probably right," Wayne agreed. "I'm prepared for that."

Conor dropped to his knees and began cramming his sleeping gear into a stuff sack. "I want you to turn around, head back the way we came, and catch Barb's team."

Wayne stared at Conor like he was crazy. "Let me get this straight. You dragged my ass all the way up here until we caught The Bond, marched me up a mountainside, let me get shot at, and now you're sending me back?"

Conor yanked the drawstring tight to seal the bag, then crammed it into his Gunslinger pack. He pulled out two energy bars, tossed one to Wayne, and opened the other for himself. "Kind of sounds crazy when you put it that way, doesn't it?"

Wayne tore open his energy bar and bit into it. "Here's what I'm thinking," he said, mouth full. "We let our people catch up with us and we launch a surprise attack on The Bond. I don't think they'll be expecting that. If we lay enough hurt on those fuckers they'll turn and run. Even if they don't, it's not likely they'll continue heading in our direction. They'll go hunting for easier prey."

Conor made a pass around the area he'd slept, inspecting for anything he might have left behind. "There's a couple of problems with that idea. I think they're totally on guard against an attack like that. They have armed sentries watching the road with night vision.

Our people would be slaughtered. The other issue is that even if I did turn them around, we'd just be pushing them off on other poor, unsuspecting folks. After what I saw yesterday, I'm not good with that."

"So that's your plan?"

"I'm leaving my horse here and heading into town on foot. I'd like you to head back the way we came. At some point today or tomorrow you should run into Barb's group. Every half-hour I want you to put a call out to them on the radio. When you meet up, I have a list of things I want you to prepare. Then you just wait on me to show up."

"You're going to take on The Bond by yourself? Eliminate each and every man in that force with no help?"

"No, that's not the plan at all. I'm going to make them follow me. If we engage these guys head-on they'll annihilate us. They've got better guns than most of our people. More armor, more men, and more training."

"Not to mention they've got trucks," Wayne reminded him. "They can pursue us faster than we can escape."

"I've accounted for that."

"How can you be sure they'll follow you? Why would they break their routine for one man? You think you can be that much of an irritant?"

Conor smirked. "Barb doesn't get her personality from her mother."

Wayne's eyes grew wide. "Then you can definitely be that much of an irritant."

"Exactly."

Wayne climbed out of his bag, slipped on his shoes, and began packing his own gear. "So what do you want us to do?"

38

The pair split when they reached the highway, with Wayne riding back to rendezvous with Barb's force and Conor hoofing it into town on foot. Having learned from last night, he didn't hop the guardrail and descend the scree slope as they'd done before. Instead, he moved along the shoulder of the highway, keeping a hawk-eyed watch for anything out of the ordinary. At the spot where they'd come under fire last night, there were indications that large trucks had run onto the shoulder of the road as they'd turned around. Just as the two had expected, The Bond had come searching for them.

Conor had stashed his Gunslinger pack in the woods, a distance away from his hobbled horse. He'd have preferred to carry all his gear with him in case he needed it but that load on top of a Go Bag and a plate carrier with hard plates was too much. He'd be unable to maneuver, and if he fell onto his back, he'd be stuck like a bloody tortoise.

The town appeared deserted but Conor had been in enough war zones to know what was happening along those silent streets and in those quiet houses. By this point, months after the loss of power and resources, the town had probably lost one third of its residents to health-related causes, starvation, and violence. By spring that number would be much higher.

With cold weather settling in, people would be migrating to houses they could heat with wood. They would be pooling their resources, working together to stay alive. Clean water would be an issue, compounded by a lack of proper sanitation. Those unable to walk outside of town and haul back spring water would probably be drinking from the most readily available source of water—the river that passed through town. Contaminated with sewage, bacteria, and parasites, those who drank from it would eventually be sickened if they failed to properly filter the water.

Despite the cold morning, the lack of smoke coming from any of the chimneys in town told him something else. It meant that word had spread among the residents that they were living in an occupied city. Even towns in the midst of disaster developed their own communication networks. Information continued to travel even without telephones, the news, and social media. People gossiped in backyards and through windows. People met while fetching water or conducting discreet commerce. As people had done recently in Bosnia, Czechoslovakia, and Italy in World War II, they would stay holed up and hope these invaders moved on.

Because mountain towns ran along valleys they were often long and narrow, which meant that as long as Conor hadn't yet located The Bond, he needed to keep walking. It wasn't likely he would be passing by them without noticing because the town was only one or two streets deep to each side of the main drag. He'd be able to see their convoy even if it was off to the side. He considered climbing a ridge for a better vantage point but didn't want to expend the time or effort. He was too sore from yesterday's climb.

He decided to save himself some time by simply asking people if they'd seen the invaders. He tried to flag down the few people he saw moving about but they all ran when he hailed them. He could hardly blame them. In his gear, bristling with weapons, there was nothing warm and fuzzy about him. He saw no need to further terrify these already terrorized people by chasing them down.

The only people who didn't flee were those whose personal desperation blinded them to the threat posed by The Bond. These were the people who would normally be seen moving about in the same manner even in better times. The shuffling mentally ill, the drug-addicted, and those so poor they lived a hand-to-mouth existence. For some living with those conditions it may not have even been evident that the world had changed. Their lives may always have been on the precipice of an apocalyptic collapse, their burden ready to topple them into oblivion.

Conor saw such a being shuffling along a street. It was not evident until he got closer that it was a woman. Her face was dark and weathered in that look people got when they spent most days outside. She wore a crocheted yellow hat with a pink flower on it, the yarn stained, and the hat cocked at an angle that made Conor want to straighten it for her. She wore a shapeless, oversized sweater beneath a dark brown corduroy coat, green polyester pants that rose above her ankles, and ragged high-top tennis shoes that would have been no warmer in this cold than wearing plastic shopping bags on her feet. She appeared intent on passing by Conor without a word or a glance. Perhaps she didn't notice him, so accustomed to living invisibly in the world of normal people in their normal lives.

"Excuse me, miss," Conor asked.

She appeared startled by his invocation. When she looked at him, her eyes were yellowish, bleary, like an alley drunk. "I ain't got nothing to take, mister. Leave me be."

"I'm not here to rob you. In fact, I've got something for you if you'll give me a second of your time."

She glared at him suspiciously. No one ever offered her anything without conditions attached to it. She watched with interest as he fished an energy bar from the special pouch on his gear. He considered cutting it in half, wondering if he might run short on food and need it later, but she'd already seen the whole bar. If he was to put half of it back in his pocket she might just hold out on him, extorting the other half from him before answering any questions. He held it out to her.

She regarded it as she might someone showing her an abscess on their arm, her mouth crumpled and eyes narrowed. "That a candy bar?"

"Something like that. Take it. It's good."

She appeared uncertain but took it before he changed his mind. She struggled to unwrap it to the point Conor intervened, doing it for her and then holding it out as one might do with a child. She took a bite of it, chewed, and frowned. "It ain't exactly a Snickers, is it? Tastes like chocolate sawdust."

Conor smiled at her apt description. "It has a lot of protein. It will fill you up for a while."

She was doubtful. "I think I'd rather have a Snickers and take my chances with being hungry later." Despite her comment, she ate it. "Got anything to wash it down with? A cold Old Milwaukee beer?"

Conor smiled. "No, you'll have to keep looking if you want beer. Can't help you there."

"What about a slug from your water bottle?"

Conor studied her grime encrusted mouth, her tongue coated in white film, and the blackened nubs of her teeth. "Sorry, I have herpes," he said. "You shouldn't drink after me."

She recoiled in disgust and started to wander off, mumbling.

"Hold up," he said. "I want to ask you some questions. Have you seen some folks in town that look like they're from the Army?"

She stared him up and down before answering, as if this was a trick question. She was looking at a guy who appeared to be from the Army at that very moment. "Uh, yeah."

"Besides me?" he added, sensing where her mind was going.

"Yeah, them other fellers."

"Where did you see them?"

"They was riding around all over town last night. I hid and they didn't see me. I can be right sneaky. I climbed under the river bridge. Drink under there sometimes with the boys."

"That was smart," Conor said. "These men are dangerous and you don't want to let them see you. Have you seen where they're staying?"

She nodded.

Realizing she had no intention of elaborating, he attempted to draw out more information. "Can you *tell* me where they're staying?"

"Car dealership."

"What kind of car dealership?"

"New cars." She only knew of two kinds of dealerships, new or used. "They was a church near there that handed out food but they ran out. The scrap dealer that buys cans ain't open neither and that's how I make my money. Don't know why everything is closed these days."

"How far is the car dealership?"

She shrugged in an exaggerated way, rolling her shoulders nearly up to her ears.

"Can you see it from here?"

She turned and glanced back in the direction she'd come from. "You see that big blue sign?"

"That's it?"

"Nah, but it ain't far past that. A few minutes."

"I appreciate your help," Conor said. "You watch out for these people. They're bad. They shoot people just for entertainment."

She cackled, slapping at her thigh with a grimy hand. "Mister, this is Kentucky. People been shooting each other for entertainment since the second person got here."

Conor smiled at her joke, patted her on a thin shoulder, and hurried off.

He stayed off the road, moving across the lawns of homes and businesses. Head on a swivel, he constantly watched for any sign of a sentry post, a guard, or someone in military gear. "Stupid camo," he muttered. "Wish they were wearing something easier to spot, like prison jumpsuits."

As sometimes happened when he talked to himself, he was struck with a magnificent idea, but it would have to wait. He had to find them first. He lost sight of the blue sign the lady had pointed out but knew he had to be getting close.

The first sign of anything unusual was the smell of roasting meat. That smell instantly knotted Conor's stomach, wracking him with an intense craving. He could only imagine the number it was doing on the poor, starving people of this community. It had to be The Bond. Who but an invading army would have the audacity to cook in front of starving people with no concern for having their food stolen by a mob?

The torturous aroma provided some benefit. Conor homed in on it like it was a beacon, following it to the source. The closer he got, the worse it became. He felt like a drunk staggering into the Waffle House at 3 AM only to be further intoxicated by the aroma of greasy cheeseburgers, omelets, and waffles. He was nearly ready to take on the entire force just to steal their breakfast.

He looped around a fast food place, skirted a dumpster, and took cover behind a boxwood hedge. He was beyond the blue sign and had to be near the camp. Besides cooking food he could also smell a campfire. If the camp was that close, there had to be a guard post somewhere. He turned back in the direction he'd come from and could see the road into town snaking around the steep brown mountains. That was where he and Wayne had been when they were shot at last night. Where would the guard have been to see them?

There were some tall Victorian houses on the street. While they were tall enough that you could see the road from an upstairs window, Conor didn't think there was a guard there. A military guy would never pick a post that allowed him to only see in one direction like that. He'd have wanted something that provided more of a three hundred and sixty degree view, like an old school or a church.

Conor pulled a pair of binoculars from a pocket and scanned the area around him. Then he found it—a Presbyterian church with an old fashioned bell tower. The interior of the open tower was shadowed in the day but Conor focused on it, waiting for one of those shadows to move. When it finally did, he'd found his sentry. He also knew he was damn lucky to have made it this far without taking rounds. Had he walked up the road or sidewalk, the guy would have seen him for sure.

His first thought was to engage the sentry and quietly take him out. He could go to the church and do it with a knife or his suppressed Glock. If he did that, though, the camp would be on high alert tonight and that wasn't what Conor wanted. He had plans for them. Plans that required he get very close.

Aware that rapid movement drew the eye, Conor carefully plotted a path forward. His concealment was chosen to accommodate very slow movement. He didn't want to have to run. Until he was beyond this sentry he wanted to be able to move as slowly as possible. Although he hoped like hell there wasn't another sentry anywhere close, he would have to keep that possibility in mind.

It took him thirty minutes of stealth to move to a point where he was completely obscured from the church tower. By then, for better or worse, the smell of food was gone from the air, though the campfire remained. Conor wondered what these men did to keep themselves occupied between eating and killing innocent folks. He assumed they had to be scavengers, so perhaps that was their day job.

He didn't know how long The Bond had been in this town but the houses immediately surrounding the car dealership were in a different state than those he'd seen coming through town. There were belongings in the yards and doors left open. Conor couldn't tell if it was because the residents had fled in a hurry or whether Bond soldiers had ransacked the houses. If that was the case he didn't want to know what horrors might lay inside those homes.

Conor skirted them and climbed into a treehouse in the backyard of one property. It was sturdy enough to hold him and had a window facing out onto the car dealership. "Poor kid. Got a shitty view."

Back on his binoculars he found the camp to be different than he'd expected. He'd thought the soldiers might just pull up to the front and sleep in the snazzy glass-wrapped showroom. They were smarter than that. The Bond soldiers were using the service lot around back, with its chain link fencing, as their camp. The garage parking lot was filled with their trucks, which were late sixties and early seventies multi-fuel trucks.

The men were camping in the garage itself. The high roll-up door was raised and Conor could see their gear and at least one truck inside. Outside the garage area was an extended flat awning that ran along the side of the building, beneath which the men had a kitchen set up. A campfire burned on the concrete, blackening the steel awning above it. Some of the showroom furniture had been carried outside and set up around the fire. There were also a few office chairs and some coffee tables. It was a pretty nice setup if you were on that side of the fence.

Conor studied the men and the uniforms they wore. They were from different ethnic backgrounds and their uniforms, which appeared to be the real deal, had been stripped of identifying names or ranks. Most of the men were sitting down but four were standing with cups of coffee in their hands. Those four were all talking in an animated manner. Conor couldn't tell who was in charge but knew someone had to be. A group of men this size didn't function this smoothly without someone giving the orders.

This layout wasn't going to be perfect. His plan would require stealth and a good deal of luck. He also had some shopping to do before it got dark.

39

Conor didn't want to drive The Bond off and make them someone else's problem. He wanted to draw them into a well-constructed trap. He was aware he couldn't lure people after him by instilling fear in them, nor did he do it by angering them. He had to do it by humiliating them, make them so pissed off they became blinded by their rage and did stupid things. Pissing people off was right up Conor's alley.

To that end, after he'd located The Bond's camp he'd spent the rest of the day tracking down a sack full of goodies that would help him accomplish his goal. When he'd found everything on his list, he retreated into the woods and caught a little power nap.

When he woke from his nap he stowed his gear and ate an MRE. It wasn't selected because it was the most palatable option but because it was the heaviest food in his pack and he wanted to be shed of the weight. He readied the gear for his operation and then got moving. His first order of business was with the sentry in the church tower. He wanted to get close before darkness fell because he didn't know what technology the sentry had at his disposal. He expected the man had night vision gear and was uncertain about thermal.

Approaching the church was easier than anticipated. The sentry was using binoculars to monitor the town in a predictable pattern. He studied the view out one opening for several minutes, then turned clockwise and studied that view for several minutes. His continual rotation made it merely a matter of waiting until he turned away from Conor. Add to that, the church was surrounded by high, dense hedges that gave Conor an approach lane completely shielded from the sentry.

The arched front door was of oak construction, stained dark, and strapped with forged iron hardware. It wasn't locked but that wasn't entirely surprising. The Bond sentry probably didn't expect anyone to come inside unless they intended to relieve him. Conor intended to relieve him alright, although not in the manner the sentry expected.

It took him several minutes of careful searching with judicious use of a red headlamp to find the door that led to the bell tower. It stood open and a narrow set of winding stairs led upward. The stair treads were wooden and would likely creak as Conor ascended them. He took it slowly, staying as close to the wall as possible. The center section of the step, which got the most traffic, usually made more noise than either end.

The floor of the bell tower was the equivalent of five stories from the ground floor. Because the space allocated for the stairs was so narrow, there were four short landings required to ascend a single floor. That was a lot of careful walking. As a metal fabricator who'd made a set or two of steel steps in his life, Conor couldn't help but note how much simpler it would have been if they'd used steel.

Because there was no open center dropping top to bottom in this stairwell, Conor couldn't see until he got to the top that the trapdoor there was closed. It made sense that it would be. The floor of the bell tower was probably only six feet by six feet and leaving that door open in the dark would have been an invitation to step in it. Conor played his red beam around the space and familiarized himself with it. There was a rack of electronic equipment that replaced the old-fashioned bell. Most churches had a loudspeaker in their tower now and used recorded bells.

Conor knew he couldn't just throw open the trap door and storm the tower. The guy had a gun and would have the jump on him. He could also be standing on the trap door which would prevent Conor from even opening it at all. He studied the homemade ladder leading up to the trap door. It had been replaced at some point recently with a simple structure of two by four framing lumber fastened together with drywall screws.

A devious grin broke Conor's face as he removed a multitool from his pocket. After removing every single screw from the right side of the ladder, he retreated back a single landing.

"Yo, dude!" he called, then waited for a response. When there was no reaction, he repeated himself. "Yo! Dude! Open up!"

There was the sound of a chair being dragged across the bell tower floor and then the trap door was flipped open. Silence. The sentry must have been waiting for whoever called to him to come up. A light flicked on and shone through the opening, reflecting off the white painted walls.

"Hello?" When there was no response, the voice spoke again. "Hey, don't be fucking around. You know Thomas takes this sentry shit all serious."

Conor groaned, making it sound like he was injured. He needed the man to come down the stairs without getting on his radio and alerting the main camp.

"This ain't funny, man. You hurt?"

Conor groaned again, barely loud enough to be heard. He mumbled something indecipherable.

"Mundo, that better not be your dumb ass down there. If you're messing with me I'm going to throw you off this roof."

When there was no response, the man leaned down and played his light through the opening, examining all corners of the room. He saw no one and nothing out of place. Despite the screws Conor removed from the ladder, friction held each wooden step in place until the man put his weight on it. Then the step gave way, as did each below it, and the sentry noisily dropped the twelve feet or so to the floor.

Conor launched himself up the landing, hitting the switch on his headlamp as he went. There was loud cursing and the red light revealed the man writhing in pain at the base of the booby-trapped ladder. He sprang onto the man's chest and jammed a device against his neck, activating the plunger with his thumb. It was Doc Marty's creation, a modified auto-injector similar to what a soldier might use to administer a dose of morphine to himself after an injury. Instead of morphine, this one contained a Propofol and Fentanyl combination that produced a rapid anesthetic affect.

He'd once asked the Doc for some type of chloroform-type knockout drop only to find out that the immediate knock-out effect shown in the movies was fictional. There was no real-life equivalent. This injection was pretty darn close but required Conor hold the man down, mouth covered, until the drug took effect. When it did, Conor gave him a quick inspection to make sure none of his limbs were broken in half. Certain that he had no bones jutting through his skin, Conor grabbed him by the collar and pulled him down the steps to the ground floor.

He continued through the church, out the front door, and dumped the comatose man by a brown Dodge Aries. He had a bag of goodies shoved up under the car waiting on him. He removed a roll of paper towels and a spray bottle of window cleaner, then cleaned the dust from the hood of the car. When he was done, he dumped the remaining contents from the bag and got to work.

40

When he reached the car dealership, the only sentries Conor spotted on the inner perimeter were two sullen men standing at the gate leading to the service area of the dealership. Perhaps they were not happy about being late for dinner or missing out on the fireside festivities. The sentry Conor had taken out at the church had a PVS-14, now stored as a spare in Conor's Go Bag, but neither of these men had any type of night vision or thermal. Perhaps they weren't as well-equipped as he thought.

He slipped around to the rear of the fenced lot and used the bolt cutters he'd stolen earlier that day to snip a hole in the fence. When he was done, he carefully laid the cutters to the side and slithered through the opening. He pulled his gear in after him, then disappeared into the maze of vehicles.

The men of The Bond were eating dinner, the same cooked meat smell pervading the area and twisting Conor's stomach. He silently swore vengeance on them for making a fat boy's discomfort that much worse. Not only was he putting his life in danger to deal with this vermin, but did he really have to be crippled by hunger pangs while he was doing it? It was inhumane. That was okay though. He would have his revenge. He intended to be just as inhumane before this was over with.

The men talked loudly as they ate, telling stories and laughing. Somewhere music was playing. It was rap, which didn't help Conor's disposition. He never really cared for recorded music, preferring something live, with voices and instruments. The music and the casual attitude within the fenced compound told Conor that these men were comfortable. They didn't fear attack. They assumed the population was cowed and their sentries were more than capable of dealing with whatever threat might show up at their door.

Conor was about to show them just how wrong they were.

With the group's noise helping to cover his steps and the occasional bump of gear into a vehicle, Conor methodically worked his way toward the lead truck. It was the closest to the improvised kitchen and the fire around which the men ate. There were a few lanterns strung up and ambient light coming from the campfire so Conor flipped his night vision out of the way. He needed all the coordination and dexterity he could manage.

When he reached the lead truck, he moved into the gap between it and the truck behind it. He crept as far forward as he dared and removed two devices from the open flap of the cargo pocket on his pants. He'd staged them there earlier, not wanting to have to pull open the Velcro flap on a pouch. There was no stealth where Velcro was concerned.

He pulled the pin on the M84 stun grenade, reached out, and lobbed it into the campfire. No one noticed him but they all flinched when the device detonated in the middle of their fire circle, disorienting them with the noise and blinding them with the brilliant light. Landing beside the fire, it also blew sparks over the men, forcing them to swat at their clothing as the burning embers stung their flesh. Conor followed up with a smoke grenade to mask his movements. Chaos erupted, men toppling back in their chairs and scrambling for weapons that their damaged eyes could not see, cursing and falling over top of each other.

The noise brought the guards from the gate running to the scene.

Conor had expected this and was watching for them. They must have thought the cook stove had exploded. They weren't thinking "attack" and didn't have their weapons ready. Conor was ready for them. He put a bullet in each man's face, then dropped his rifle, allowing it to hang from the sling.

He climbed into the nearest truck bed. It put him above the men, looking down onto the scene. If they started firing in the smoke, blinded by the flash-bang, they would only be hitting each other. It was then that he opened up on them with the device he'd put together earlier in the day. Fully expecting the smoke grenade to obscure everyone's vision, he'd fastened his thermal optic to a full-auto paintball gun and he cut loose with no mercy.

The paintball gun sputtered and burped, pouring the stinging balls out at a rate of around twenty per second. Conor had no trouble spotting the men in his thermal and they paid the price. He aimed for faces and groins, vulnerable spots that had the men squealing, cursing, and crying. When he emptied the gun, he ripped his thermal loose from it and tossed it down.

He bolted for the grill, kicking and shoving, stepping on crawling men who assumed he was one of their brothers. He scooped up two steaks in a gloved hand and disappeared into the night cackling like a madman.

41

The vibe at the camp was kicked back. The Bond found Paintsville to be a very chill town–a very passive town–where they didn't anticipate running into any trouble at all. There were people living there but they were hiding. To The Bond, those people were like canned goods sitting on the shelf at the grocery store, just waiting for The Bond to put them in a shopping cart.

Their first evening in town they sent out emissaries to make their presence known. They killed a few folks, shot at things that caught their attention, and were back at their base in time for dinner. The rest of the team set up camp at a car dealership and established sentry posts along the road to either side of their base.

They were glad to be settled in a new town. Travel days made everyone anxious. There were frequent stops to remove disabled cars from the road. Every time they did this they imagined it might be a trap with locals hiding in roadside bunkers ready to open fire on them. There was also the fear that some random person with a rifle might open fire on them for the same reason they opened fire on random people–just for the hell of it.

Every new town brought a sigh of relief and the thrill of expectation. They imagined the fun they would have there, the women and the goodies they might find. It was a like a drunken teenage camping trip with a really cool chaperone who let you party as long as you didn't get out of hand. Everyone agreed that if Thomas would ease up on that rule about drinking he'd be the perfect boss.

Their second day in town they paid a visit to the houses closest to them. A few more people got killed and some loot taken but Thomas felt the day was a success. They didn't want anyone in the houses immediately around them anyway. It made them nervous, like they were being spied on. Since the residents didn't have the good sense to run, Thomas sent men to take care of them.

Another team roamed the town with the tanker truck. They were fortunate to find that a lot of the homes in the town used oil furnaces with tanks in the yard or the basement. They used their transfer pump to suck those dry. That fuel would top off the trucks and they'd go searching for more tomorrow to store in the tanker. There was such a wealth of fuel in the town that Thomas even had the men on the lookout for a fuel trailer that they could pull behind the tanker for additional capacity.

Spirits were high when they sat down to dinner that night. One of the men had killed an elk earlier in the day, cutting it into steaks and roasts. The smell was insane. Joints were passed, which only made the men more ravenous. Thomas agreed to let them play some music as long as they were reasonable with the volume.

"Hell, you worried about the neighbors, T? Shouldn't be. We killed them all," Lawdog cracked.

"I ain't scared of the people in this town but there ain't no point in broadcasting our position either," Thomas replied.

Lawdog gave a sheepish grin. "Sorry, I was trying to be funny."

"We already got one fool, don't need another. Right, Mundo?"

Mundo frowned, then smiled at Thomas. "We gotta be driving these people nuts with the smell of that meat. We should drive around after dinner telling everyone we got free food just to see if any good-looking women come out. That would save a lot of work. Make them come to us instead of having to run them down like rabbits."

"Going away party ain't until the end of the week," Lawdog said. "You know the rules."

"Why can't we have a welcome party too?" Mundo asked.

"'Cause too much partying will make you soft," Thomas said. "And everyone is getting too soft already."

Mundo didn't respond to that. If Thomas had any idea how much he really partied, especially that he'd been regularly drinking on watch, he'd kill him. He couldn't help it. Since he'd been around twelve years old he'd had a taste for booze and it had never gone away, despite some legendary hangovers.

Dinner was amazing that night. None of the men had eaten elk before. It was so good that they joked they should carefully guard Buddha Boy against injury because they had no cook skilled enough to replace him. They were laughing about this very thing when an object came sailing over some of the men's heads and landed near the fire. Before they even had time to consider what it might be, trash or an empty bottle, it exploded, blinding them with intense light.

Nearly all the men were affected, sitting so tightly together around the fire. Lawdog, Mundo, and Thomas, standing together, staggered into each other, rubbing their eyes. Shootah, also blinded, backed into the grill, screaming when he dropped a hand to the surface to catch himself. Thomas tried to shout orders but had no idea what to tell people to do.

"We're under attack!" he yelled, but it was nowhere near loud enough to be heard over the chaos.

There was a clatter and a hiss. Thomas recognized it as the sound of a smoke grenade. The men who could still see, whose direct line of sight to the flash-bang had been blocked by other men's bodies, were now just as blinded as their companions, unable to see through the dense cloud of smoke. Then there were two gunshots immediately alongside the group.

Thomas hoped it was one of his own men, someone able to see, who had been able to fire back at the attacker. "You get 'em?" he yelled.

There was a screech of pain. Thomas recognized the voice. It was Mundo.

"Fuck!"

Then there were more screams and a low sputtering sound, nothing Thomas recognized or had heard before. It was a rapid mechanical sound that could possibly be a suppressed full-auto weapon of some sort. There was screaming all around him now but not the screams of dying men. These were the screams of injured men.

Then he felt a searing pain in his neck, the sting of a projectile. A second hit him in the ribs. He twisted his body and caught a burst in the groin that doubled him over. He fell over a box of cooking utensils and hit the concrete hard. He couldn't see and scuttled backward until his head struck metal siding.

He was against the outside wall of the building. The sputtering stopped, then a clatter came over top of the groaning of his men. Something had fallen or been thrown down. He hoped it wasn't grenades. If so, they were dead.

Who had grenades besides them? Had this been one of his own men? Surely there was no one in this town with that kind of gear.

Then he heard the laugh. A cheerful, maniacal laughter disappearing into the night. He clutched his swelling groin and rolled over to his side.

42

As the smoke cleared, the men whose eyes were less affected by the flash-bang took up weapons and formed a secure perimeter. With Thomas not fully recovered, they fell back on their training. Others began caring for the fallen, trying to determine if their brothers were blinded by the flash bang or had been injured.

"Thomas! Where you at?" Droopy had been spared the direct flash of the grenade because of another man sitting in front of him. He was running around with his weapon trying to find his boss.

"Here!" Thomas called.

Droopy found him in a dark recess, sitting against the wall of the building, waiting on his eyes to start working again. The scene in front of them was gradually improving and he understood the effects weren't permanent. Droopy helped him to his feet. He kept an assisting hand on Thomas, trying to steady him, but Thomas yanked free.

"What the fuck just happened?" Thomas hissed. "Where were the sentries?"

"Whoever it was must have come in the back. We found a hole cut in the fence. The men on the gate came as soon as they heard trouble but they each caught a round to the face."

"Real rounds?"

"Yeah, they dead," Droopy said. "The rest of you got shot up with paintballs."

"Paintballs?" Thomas spat. He wiped at his shirt, feeling the sticky mess on his uniform. He blinked a couple of times and was able to make out rough shapes. Green blobs. The glow of the fire. When he could see well enough to make out Droopy standing before him, he grabbed him by the shirt and slammed him against the building.

Droopy started to shove Thomas away, but wisely restrained himself from putting hands on him. He gritted his teeth as Thomas, probably a hundred pounds lighter than him, repeatedly shoved him into the metal wall. He could smell Thomas's foul breath when the man got in his face.

"Was this one of our people?" Thomas demanded.

"I don't think so, T," Droopy replied.

"Was this one of *our people*?" Thomas screamed. His volume silenced the chaos in the camp and everyone stopped what they were doing. They understood his anger but it was never a good thing when Thomas got this mad. Somebody usually died.

"I don't think so," Lawdog offered, walking unsteadily toward Thomas. "None of our people would have done something like this. This wasn't a prank. We got two men dead and one unaccounted for."

"Who's unaccounted for?" Thomas asked, releasing Droopy and taking a step toward the fire. The movement caused a shooting pain in his groin. He flinched and grabbed for his swollen testicles.

"He-Man ain't answering his radio," said Lawdog. "He was on watch down at that church, up in the bell tower."

"Anyone have serious injuries?"

"A lot of swollen nuts," Mundo said. "What kinda sadistic asshole does something like this?"

"I didn't ask you!" Thomas barked. "I suggest you shut the fuck up."

Mundo limped away, trying to walk off the pain.

"We have a couple of eye injuries," Lawdog said. "Shot in the eye with a paintball. Some of them may be blinded in that eye, I don't know. The groin injuries aren't serious but they may be disabling for a few days."

Thomas was disgusted. They'd never come under attack like this before. No one had the audacity. "Lock this place down," he ordered. "Get two trucks together with people who can walk and see. We're going to check on He-Man."

Lawdog found Mundo and they put two ten-man teams together. They loaded the back of the trucks like they were cartel soldiers on patrol, everyone on their weapons and ready to shoot. Each truck had a man on the belt-fed gun. In their anger they wanted to start lighting the town up, blasting everything in sight, but Thomas made them hold off until they saw what awaited them at the church.

No one was ready for what they found. The trucks parked in the street, their headlights illuminating the church. Men with handheld spotlights played them around the scene, searching for anything of concern.

"I'll be damned!" Mundo said, hopping out of the truck. "Over here with that spotlight."

The men with the spotlights responded by directing the beams toward a car parked in the handicapped spot in front of the church.

"That He-Man?" Droopy asked, hopping down from the bed of the truck.

The spotlights converged on the car, as did the headlamps and flashlights of the other Bond soldiers.

"Y'all got to help me," He-Man begged. "I'm stuck."

Mundo started laughing at the sight. He-Man was sprawled over the hood of the car like he was about to be searched by the police. His pants were around his ankles.

"Are those Wonder Woman panties?" Droopy asked.

"They ain't mine," He-Man growled. "Asshole jumped me. He glued me to this car and I can't move. My hands and my knees are glued down. And these ain't my fucking underwears."

"That ain't even underwear," Mundo said. "That's like little girl panties. You some kind of freak or something." He doubled over with laughter but the motion caused his groin to ache. He straightened out, frowning.

Thomas stepped forward and took in the scene. "What the hell happened?"

"Somebody got to get me loose," He-Man said, louder.

"I asked you what happened," Thomas repeated.

"I heard a noise but I thought it was somebody come to relieve me."

"Was it time for someone to relieve you?" Thomas asked.

"Well, no," He-Man admitted. "But I heard a noise. I started down the ladder to check into it and the ladder was booby-trapped. The steps broke and I fell all the way down. Then some guy jumped on me and stuck a needle in my neck. He drugged me and I woke up like this."

"You know this guy?" Thomas asked. "You recognize him?"

"No, I couldn't get a good look. It was dark and it happened so fast."

"This guy that got past you killed two of our men. He could have killed all of us. Instead he just shot us up with paintballs like some sick bastard. He made punks out of all us. If you'd been doing your job we—"

"I *was* doing my job!" He-Man yelled.

"Not well enough. Not living to up to the standard. You know I got standards."

"I'll make up for it," He-Man said desperately. "I'll do anything you want. You name it."

"No," Thomas said, "you won't." He raised his rifle, flipped the safety, and dumped a dozen rounds into He-Man's flinching body.

The Bond soldiers didn't react. They weren't surprised. They'd all been expecting this, knowing how seriously Thomas took sentry duty. He had a zero-tolerance attitude toward failure and this was a significant fail. Besides, somebody had to pay for the indignity they'd suffered and there was no one else immediately at hand. He-Man would have to do.

"Mundo, take over this post. Fix the ladder. Whatever it takes. Just get your ass up in that tower and no one better get past you. Got it?"

"Yes, sir!" Mundo jogged off toward the church.

"Call back on the radio!" Lawdog called after him. "Before we leave, make sure you got his night vision and that it works."

"Roger that," Mundo replied.

"Get his gear," Thomas told Droopy. "Guns and ammo."

Droopy hurried off to do as he'd been instructed.

"We gonna bury him?" Lawdog asked.

"Hell no, we ain't gonna bury him," Thomas said. "We're leaving him as a message for this town. I want whoever the hell came at us tonight to know what we're capable of. If we'll kill one of our own for not doing his job, it might tell the people of this town a little something about how serious we are. If they're not scared, they better get that way real fast."

"Hey, Thomas?" Droopy called from the car.

"What is it?"

"You need to see this, man."

Thomas glared at Lawdog then strode over to the car.

"There's writing all over it," Droopy said, playing his light over the car.

Sure enough, there was a message written in Sharpie on the door of the car.

Thomas leaned over and began reading out loud. "Gentlemen, you have unwittingly crossed a boundary that you don't want to cross. Beyond this town is the territory of The Mad Mick. If you know what's good for you, you'll get back in your little green Army trucks and go back the way you came. If you continue south on this highway, I'll kill each and every one of you. Signed, The Mad Mick."

"What we gonna do?" Droopy asked.

Thomas stared at him like he was idiot. "We're packing up and heading south tomorrow. We're going to catch this bastard and make him pay."

"Tomorrow?" Lawdog asked. "We just got here, man."

"You questioning me?"

"No. I just wanted to be certain."

"You certain now?"

Lawdog nodded. "Yes, T. We head out tomorrow. We're going to find this Mad Mick and kill him."

43

After sprinting from the car dealership, Conor retraced his steps, knowing the path he'd taken was relatively safe. Once clear of the scene, he spread a bandana on the trunk of a car and laid out the hot elk steaks he'd snatched from the grill. He unsheathed his fixed blade knife and rapidly sliced the steaks into strips the thickness of jerky. When he was done, he sheathed the knife and pulled an empty plastic shopping bag from his back pocket. He usually carried two in his gear. They took up no room and could serve as gloves, socks, or for carrying things such as random elk steaks you might happen across.

He put one of the strips of meat in his mouth and groaned. That was some good stuff. The rest of the bag went into a dump pouch on the back of his battle belt. It would be easy to get to while he was on the move.

While he jokingly called himself a fat boy because he was so fond of his food, he did what he could to stay in good shape specifically for circumstances like this. He set out running at a jogging pace. Near the church where he'd taken out the sentry, he stopped to retrieve the rifle he'd taken off the man. The sentry had a decent scoped carbine, which Conor threw across his back, and an M9 handgun that was already stashed in his Go Bag.

Neither of the weapons appealed to Conor all that much. He had better gear than that. However, the weapons might be of use to someone back home who didn't have anything. He also hated the idea of leaving weapons behind so they could be used against him. No use arming the enemy.

Conor's system, if he had a choice, was not to exert himself so much that he'd been unable to fight if it came to that. He jogged until he began to breathe hard then he'd slow to a walking pace. When his breathing recovered, he was off running again. Although it wasn't the stealthiest mode of travel, his objective was to put distance between himself and The Bond. They would come after him, but he didn't expect they'd do it tonight. It would be tomorrow. They'd be unable to resist the challenge, the taunt he'd left them. They'd be unable to let go the insult of his attack on them. They would want to make an example of him, which was something he had no intention of letting them do.

It took him about an hour to reach his cache of gear. He paused there to rehydrate and finish the last of the magnificent elk dinner The Bond had been kind enough to prepare for him. He tracked down the hobbled horse using his night vision, speaking to it until the nervous animal calmed enough that he could saddle it. Conor imagined he looked a bit unnerving in his helmet, night vision, and assorted gear, like some insectoid creature stalking the horse in the dark.

When he had everything strapped onto the horse he led it out of the woods and back onto the road. He felt comfortable riding on the road under these circumstances. The Bond's trucks were loud. He'd hear them coming. He expected he'd have to ride all night. That was okay. He had a good horse, a full belly, and a pocket full of chemical stimulants if he needed them. He nudged his horse and they barreled off into the night.

44

Though everyone coming along with Barb's team understood that she was in charge, there was no honeymoon period. The folks from Wayne's camp were scared and wary, both of her and what lay ahead of them on their journey. The stiff contingent from Pastor White's group, while not openly hostile, was not exactly friendly. Everyone listened to her and did as she asked but there was no sense of camaraderie. There was nothing that bonded them together as a group, though she had hoped that marching off into the unknown would do exactly that.

Her strongest supporters were Shannon, Jason Jacks, and his wife Sam. It almost made Barb feel bad that she'd been so rough on Shannon. The nervous young woman had stuck by her side the entire time. Jason and Sam didn't question any of Barb's orders, displaying a complete lack of "attitude" with her that was refreshing. Barb was beginning to get a little taste of how being so hard on people could make it difficult to get their cooperation when she needed it. It wasn't like she set out to be a bitch with people, she just had this personality that needed room to express itself. When it did, it sometimes rattled everyone around her. Her dad once said that her personality had its own blast radius. She only now realized he was right.

Her group rode Route 23 on horseback, having secured enough horses and tack for everyone, leading four pack horses with food, ammunition, and various gear. They probably could have gotten by on fewer horses but they wanted spares in case a horse was injured and a rider needed to switch out.

Their trip retraced Conor and Wayne's route, though at a slower pace. At the end of the day, aching and exhausted, they set up camp under the awnings of secluded highway convenience stores or in abandoned industrial buildings. With the cold temperatures they wanted locations where they could have fires to warm the parts that chilled on the long days in the saddle. Barb had imagined they would begin to bond into a unit around the nightly fire but it didn't work out that way. There was never just one fire, each group preferring to stay with their own kind. Pastor White's group had their fire, Wayne's folks had another, and her small group had their own. It wasn't the way she wanted it but she didn't have any plan of how to unite them yet, and she figured it would only be divisive to force it.

Each night Barb made rounds to every individual fire. She complimented the riders on their endurance and the ground they'd covered that day. She attempted to make small talk, to learn about these men and their families, but those attempts fell flat. The groups fell silent at her arrival and pretty much stayed that way until she walked away. While not overtly hostile, they spared her no warmth. They didn't trust her and it made her think. While she didn't feel that she needed other people for anything in her life, she recognized there was a value in being able to inspire people to want to work with you. Her dad had that ability, but apparently it was not hereditary. None of these people would have ridden with her if not for her father.

On the second day of riding, the road began to trace the route of the fast-moving Levisa River. Barb found the sound of the water comforting and it added a new element to the scenery. They passed through the same small towns and communities as Conor and Wayne, receiving the same reception. No one messed with them; no one wanted to cross paths with them. People simply held their breath, hoping the riders moved on and didn't stop. That was what they did. They were not there to scavenge or make friends.

Most nights they camped between the tiny coal towns, not wanting to risk a group of locals perceiving them as a threat and taking action. After a few days on the road they closed in on Allen City, Kentucky, and spent the night in an abandoned service center for coal trucks. The shop area was large, though covered in a patina of coal dust and grease. They were pleased to find an enormous shop-built stove that burned both wood and coal, allowing them to heat their sleeping quarters for a change. They kept two men on watch that night to make sure the horses stayed safe, though no one was very excited about leaving the heated building. Barb dropped watch times to an hour per shift in the spirit of fairness.

The next morning, after the most comfortable sleep of the trip, Barb went outside to relieve herself and saw a man on horseback talking to the guards. Her hand dropped to her holster, gripping her handgun, and then the rider turned toward her. It was Wayne.

"Hey!" she said, relaxing and heading toward him. Her face clouded when she didn't see her father, her mind going to that place she didn't like it to go. "Where's my dad?"

Wayne smiled. "Easy now, Barb. Don't worry. He's fine."

She tried to recover from the burst of panic. "I wasn't worried about him. That crotchety old man is more than capable of taking care of himself."

Wayne dismounted. "I need to water my horse. You got a second? I need to speak with you in private."

"I have to take care of something first, but I'll meet you beside the river."

After taking care of her business behind a rusting truck body, Barb joined Wayne on the bank of the river. He was standing on a rock letting his horse drink from the cold water. "You ride all night?" she asked.

"No. I actually spent the night just up the road. Didn't sleep well, so I got on the road early. If I'd known you guys were here I'd have pushed on and met up with you. Guess I should have used the radio like Conor said."

"We slept pretty well here," Barb said. "We were able to heat this building. I'll have to physically drag everyone out of their sleeping bags this morning. No one's going to want to leave."

Wayne's horse stopped drinking, raising its head and allowing water to rain down from its mouth. "Are you done?" Wayne asked, and the horse lowered its head and started drinking again.

"So, we found these assholes who call themselves The Bond. Ran into them just up the road in Paintsville. Conor had a little something in mind for them, so he wanted me to come back and talk to you."

Barb frowned and shook her head. "We could have been there in another day or two, engaged them there as a group."

"I argued that very thing but he had other plans."

"What's he got in mind?"

"He wants them to chase him. He's afraid if we attack them there they might flee north and we won't be able to stop them, then they'll become someone else's problem. You know how he is about that. He feels like it's his obligation to protect people."

Barb smiled knowingly. "Well, he did put up those stupid signs all over the place," she said. "I guess if you're going to claim that the Mad Mick is protecting all the lands far and wide then you have some level of obligation to see that through. At least in my dad's head."

Wayne smiled. "I get the whole sheepdog protector thing but your dad takes it to a whole new level. He's trying to protect a patch of ground bigger than some states."

"My dad takes everything to a new level."

"Speaking of which, he's given me a list of things he wants us to prepare. I expect we'll probably see him by the end of the day, so we'll need to get cracking."

45

Conor didn't know what time The Bond soldiers would set out in pursuit of him but he made two assumptions. First, he had to leave taunting messages so they would know they were on the right track. Another pleasant by-product of those messages would be the fact that it would piss them off all over again. He was never afraid to poke the bear. Secondly, he would need to impede their progress when he could without spending too much time doing so. It was trucks against a man on horseback and he wanted to stay ahead of them if he could.

Taunting them was easy and only required some of the cans of spray paint he'd picked up along the way. He didn't have much artistic talent but he painted crude hands with upraised middle fingers on the sides of buildings and on cars along the route. Beside each drawing he would leave brief messages such as "A Present For The Bond" or "Turn Back Now!" He was aware it was childish, but he was trying to anger them on a primitive, immature level. He wanted their judgment to be clouded by hate.

In places where the road was partially blocked by cars, he tried to find ways to further block it, knowing The Bond would have to spend time trying to clear those jams in order to get their trucks through.

Sometimes it was a matter of attaching one of his handy explosive devices to the trunk of a tree and felling it to close the gap. While their trucks had winches and could pull the trees out of the way, it took time, delaying them. In other places he used explosives to dislodge precarious boulders from the mountainside and drop them into the road. Hopefully the time he gained with each of those impediments would keep The Bond from passing him on the road.

However, The Bond moved faster than Conor expected. They were an efficient team and knew how to work together. They also carried chainsaws with them, something Conor had also not expected. He was feeling pretty good about himself when he reached Prestonsburg, Kentucky. That feeling was short-lived when he heard the unmistakable sound of truck engines echoing through the hills.

He mumbled a curse but wasted no time questioning his misfortune. He kicked his horse into a gallop, searching for a spot to escape the confines of the guard-railed highway. He usually preferred to hide on the high side of the road, hoping for a vantage point that would allow him to better see what the enemy was up to. There were no exits to that side of the road, though, nowhere he could get a horse across.

An opening appeared on the downhill side of the road and Conor went for it, steering his galloping horse onto what appeared to be a driveway but turned out to be a gravel road. A sharp bend put him out of sight of the road. Rather than disappearing into the mountains he tied his horse off and ran back toward the road.

There was a flimsy plywood shack sitting where the gravel road met the highway. Parents built them at their own expense to prevent their kids from having to stand in the bad weather when waiting on the school bus. His mind racing, Conor flattened himself against the back of it, heart pounding, as the trucks got closer. He needed to slow these men. He couldn't let them get ahead of him.

He ripped open the long pouch to the left side of his plate carrier and slipped out a suppressor for his Glock. He rapidly unscrewed the thread protector, dropping it in his haste and letting it go. He twisted the suppressor on then removed the magazine of supersonic rounds from the handgun, stashing it in his dump pouch. He cycled the slide, ejecting the supersonic round in the chamber. He tried to snatch it out of the air all cool-like but missed it. So much for being cool.

He carried two mags of subsonic 9mm separate from his other magazines. He slammed one into the Glock and dropped the slide to chamber a round, then spun back toward the road. The structure blocked him from the view of oncoming drivers but would allow Conor to see them once they'd passed. Someone riding in a truck could only see him if they hung their head from one of the passing vehicles and he doubted they'd be doing that today. It was too damn cold to ride with a window down.

He braced his left elbow against the tiny building to stabilize himself, leveling the gun with the point where he anticipated the tires would be as the truck passed, staring down the tall suppressor-height sights. When the lead truck passed him, he tracked the front tire nearest him and began squeezing the trigger. It took three rounds before he hit his mark and the tire popped.

With the subsonic rounds, the report of each shot was diminished enough that he doubted these men could have heard it over the engine and road noise. They knew something was wrong, though. With the loss of a steering tire in a curve, the wheel itself hit the road surface and sparks flew as it ground along the asphalt. The truck wobbled as the driver stomped the brake pedal and the truck screeched to a stop.

Conor didn't stick around to watch. He was already on his horse and moving. He hoped the tire was damaged enough that they wouldn't know what had taken place, attributing it to debris or wear. It didn't really matter. Either way, this could cost them an hour by the time they pulled a jack and a spare from beneath the loads they carried in their trucks.

He was going to have to work fast. In the hour they'd be delayed, how far down the road would he actually make it? He had to negotiate woods to make his way back to the highway which would be hard on him and his horse. Then he might be able to put a couple of miles between them, but it wouldn't take The Bond long to close that distance in motorized vehicles.

When he finally rejoined the road, he'd burned twenty minutes of the possible hour he'd gained himself. This wasn't going to work. This wasn't nearly enough of a delay to benefit him. He wanted to buy more time for Wayne and Barb to carry out the list of things he'd asked them to do. As much as he hated to admit it, he might have to accept that he wasn't going to be able to get there ahead of The Bond.

Conor stood in the road, his horse heaving from the effort of their climb. There was no point in trying to put more miles between him and The Bond yet. His work here wasn't done. He was going to have to change his plan. He turned his horse and began walking it back up the road, toward his enemy.

When he came to the first road branching off the uphill side of the highway, he steered his horse in that direction. They soon ran into a yellow pipe gate and Conor knew he was probably on a gas well site. Perfect. He skirted the pipe gate and rode a little further. He stopped to consult his GPS and was satisfied by what he saw. He dismounted and walked his horse into the woods.

When he was at the right spot, he removed the Accuracy International sniper rifle from his large pack. He made sure he had all the rounds and support gear he needed for the weapon, then hurried deeper into the woods. Using his GPS, he was able to locate a rocky bluff that overlooked the disabled Bond truck. His binoculars revealed that the men were fighting to get the truck up on a jack. The road was steep and the weight of the truck and trailer combined pushed the jack over every time they made any progress.

This was the first opportunity he'd had to see the group as a whole. There were probably ten trucks, including a tanker for refueling between stops. He had to give them a nod for that. Men were everywhere, and though he couldn't count them he was confident in an estimate of between eighty to one hundred men. The fact there were at least two less than yesterday brought a smile to his face. He could have killed more of them but under those conditions he didn't have much of an advantage. He was determined to wipe them out but he didn't want to be killed in the process. Seeing how many there were now, he could see some advantage to paring their numbers down a little more before they reached Barb and Wayne.

The good thing about this situation below him was that the truck and trailer had completely blocked that lane of the highway when it wrecked. The men were trapped there. Even to turn their trucks around and flee in the other direction would require unhooking their trailers. There was no way they could swing the large trucks around for a U-turn in the tight confines of the guard-railed highway.

Conor found a good spot, took off his Go Bag, and set up the rifle. He unfolded the legs of the Atlas bipod and leveled everything, using the miniature bubble level mounted on his scope to make sure the rifle wasn't canted. He used a rangefinder to measure the distance to target and inserted purple foam ear plugs into his cold ears. He proned out behind it and got himself oriented to the field of view visible through the scope. A scrap of paper taped inside the lens cover and a second in a waterproof sleeve taped around the stock of the rifle provided him the ballistic data he needed. He inserted a magazine, then laid out three more in a neat row beside him. He chambered a round and exhaled.

He didn't consider himself a sniper. He was a technician, a tinkerer in tools of death. The technical aspects of this deadly art appealed to him. Adjusting the scope for distance, windage, and drop were very similar in Conor's mind to the way he'd read thousandths of an inch with a caliper or micrometer. It was like the way he adjusted a milling machine or lathe to remove hair-thin layers of metal. So while Conor may not have been a master at the stalking aspects of sniping, he was very technically proficient at getting shots on target.

When his breathing was slowed, he made a few adjustments to the scope, and determined which of the dots in his reticle was to be his starting point of aim. He clicked the safety off, the sound surprisingly loud in the silent winter forest, then he pulled the trigger.

BOOM!

The round missed his target, shattering on the bumper by the guy's head, spraying him with fragments. The man grabbed his face and fell over backward. Conor heard his scream even over the distance. He adjusted his point of aim in his head as he transitioned to the second target. He'd already planned the pattern in his head and knew where every round in this mag was going.

BOOM!

The second target dropped, Conor's shot coming so fast that the stunned men had not even figured out what was going on. When the second man dropped, The Bond soldiers knew what was going on. These were soldiers and they'd been fired at before.

BOOM!

Conor caught a fleeing man in the lower back, a spine shot that dropped him like a puppet with its strings cut. The other men had rifles out, trying to figure out where the shots were coming from even as they struggled to find cover. Conor knew logic would eventually direct those men to his position so he had to make as much of an impact as he could in a short amount of time.

BOOM!

He was dialed in now and struck a hiding man just above the elbow, the lower part of the arm barely hanging on by a strip of flesh.

BOOM!

He nailed a driver who was uncertain if he'd be safer in the cab or outside of it. His decision to stay inside was the wrong one.

BOOM!

He shot a man running for the shoulder with a weapon, the man dropping to a heap and skidding to a stop.

Conor emptied the mag, killing or disabling one man per shot. When the mag was empty, he decided he didn't have enough time to load another. There were men who'd slipped off from the group. They would be scaling the steep hill, intent on finding him, and he didn't intend to stick around for that.

He gathered his gear and sprinted for his horse. He stowed the rifle carefully, knowing he'd likely need it again before this operation was over. He mounted his horse and urged it back the way they'd come. They were around the gate and galloping down the road before anyone was even close to his position.

46

Thomas rushed around the scene, alternately cursing both his men and their attacker. They couldn't be certain whether the shooter was still active or not so no one was anxious to stick their head from behind cover. They'd seen what this shooter did with any body part exposed to his crosshairs for too long.

Thomas threw open a truck door and grabbed his radio from the seat. "Please tell me that you found this asshole. I don't hear any shooting," he said into his radio, his voice a menacing growl. "You better not let him get away."

Several moments passed before Jawbone's reply. He was panting, struggling for breath as they fought their way up the nearly vertical slope of the mountain. *"Negative...T...still...looking."*

Thomas grimaced and threw the radio back into the truck, sending it crashing into the dash.

"If they haven't found him yet, he's probably gone," Lawdog spoke up hesitantly. "Anyone with the smarts to set up something like this would probably have enough sense to not stick around too long."

Deciding Lawdog was probably right, Thomas broke cover and stalked toward the lead vehicle. He stepped right over the bodies of his fallen men, some dead and others receiving aid that would in no way prolong their lives. He crouched by the flat tire and studied it. He traced his finger around the side wall until he found a bullet hole. He'd seen shot up tires before, both in the Middle East and in Detroit.

"Dammit!" He stood up and slammed his fist against the truck fender. The whole thing had been an ambush, just like Lawdog suspected. He hadn't even put it together in his head. He thought it had simply been a flat tire and that they had the dumb luck to get shot at by some hillbilly hunter who saw them as the target of opportunity. He understood now that was not the case. This had been a setup, probably orchestrated by the Mad Mick.

"Thomas?" a careful voice asked.

Thomas spun to find an apprehensive Lawdog standing behind him. "What?"

"I need to know what you want us to do here, man. What's the mission? What's the plan?" Lawdog was afraid to take any action without speaking to the man in charge first. He didn't want to do anything that might set their fiery leader off. Sometimes it didn't take much, and when he did go off it could be like a bomb. No one knew what the blast radius would be or how many people might be impacted.

"We're going to find this bastard," Thomas declared. He pronounced each word carefully, as if it was the most obvious thing in the world

Lawdog was hesitant to go on but continued despite his reservations. "We need to be careful, T. He antagonized us, and that may have blinded us a little. We should probably have been on guard against something like this."

Thomas lost it. He closed the distance, throwing both his hands up and shoving Lawdog backward. "You saying this is on me? You saying this is *my* fucking fault?" He was yelling now.

Had anyone on the street ever spoken to Lawdog this way, those would have been his last words. He'd have been killed for the disrespect. Lawdog was no pushover, he was no punk, but Thomas was in charge.

"Whoa there, T. That ain't what I'm saying at all. I'm talking about all of us being on watch against stuff like this, me included. We're soldiers. We've dealt with this shit before. I'm saying we need to be more careful from here on out because we know what this Mad Mick is capable of."

"Mad Mick, my ass!" Thomas roared. "That guy needs to be more concerned about what *I'm* capable of. My name is gonna be the last word out of his mouth. When I'm done, the Mad Mick is gonna be Dead Dick."

Lawdog nodded. "We're carrying on then? Full speed ahead?"

Thomas hung his head to the side, then glared at Lawdog like he was an idiot. "Hell yeah, we carry on. Ain't you listened to a damn thing I've said?"

"I'm listening."

"Then y'all get that tire changed. Redistribute the teams and let's get the hell on out of here."

Lawdog hesitated. "What about the bodies, Thomas?"

Thomas shrugged. "I don't give a shit."

Lawdog stepped closer and lowered his voice. "Not all those bodies are actually *bodies* yet, T. Those people are still alive with limbs broke off, guts hanging out and shit. What we supposed to do with them?"

"Make'em dead."

Lawdog could see his boss's patience was wearing thin. Thomas was pissed off and Lawdog's questions weren't helping things. Part of him wanted to verify what his boss had just ordered but he understood the answer would be the same the second time. Thomas wanted them dead and it was his job to make them dead. He walked off. Thomas watched him go, his stare a challenge, a warning that he better be done with the questions.

Lawdog made the rounds and every man who was severely injured was sent on his way to Valhalla. He felt bad about it, looking at his fallen friends, his team members, as he pulled the trigger on them. He had a hard time meeting his own men's eyes but what was he supposed to do? They knew he didn't give the orders around here.

Let them stand up to Thomas and deal with the fallout. Then their asses would be dead too.

Besides, they didn't have a medic. All they had was first aid kits and a basic knowledge of how to use them. Everyone the sniper shot needed surgery and The Bond only offered one kind: 9mm brain surgery.

He performed the operation as quickly and mechanically as he could, then walked off to process what he'd done. He reminded himself this was not the first time he'd killed men he knew. He'd had to do it on the streets before. It was part of his life now just like it was part of his life then. It wasn't something he needed to feel bad about.

Satisfied that his orders had been carried out, Thomas went to the disabled truck and impatiently watched Droopy struggle to position a hi-lift jack at one of the vehicle's lift points. Thomas staring over his shoulder did nothing to help matters. The jack kept tipping over every time he tried to crank it.

Thomas finally shoved Droopy out of the way and took over. "Start loosening them lug nuts. You guys are useless."

Droopy did as he was told, fitting the wrench on the lug nuts and twisting them loose. Thomas eventually positioned one jack and then added a second to help stabilize the vehicle. He alternated, cranking one and then the other until the tire was clear of the ground.

At the other end of the convoy, a team of somber men were tossing the dead over the guardrail and into the thicket of roadside briers. Lawdog was standing to the side, smoking a hand rolled cigarette, when Mundo walked up.

"That a joint?"

Lawdog exhaled smoke into Mundo's face. Mundo was disappointed when the fragrance was that of plain old tobacco.

"That's some hardcore shit right there," Mundo said. "Capping your injured and tossing them over the guardrail for predators to munch on. Harsh."

"I ain't in the mood to talk, Mundo. What the hell you want?"

Mundo glanced around then lowered his voice. "What you think about that shooting?"

"The guy could fucking shoot," Lawdog said. "Sniper-level shit."

"You think it's funny he didn't disable any of our vehicles, except for the one he used to spring the trap?"

"I ain't really thought about that."

"I have," Mundo said.

"And what do you fucking think about it?"

"I'm just saying, if guys were chasing me and I could shoot like that I'd probably be disabling some vehicles. Shooting engines and shit. Trying to stop them for good."

Lawdog gave Mundo a frustrated look. "You got something to say, say it. I ain't in the mood for your dumbass games, Mundo."

"I just told you. If it was me up on that hill and I could shoot like that, I'd take these trucks out. He could have stopped us in our tracks but he didn't. Only reason I can think of to *not* take the trucks out was if you wanted them to keep on coming. He's just toying with us. He wants us to pick our asses up and keep going. He'd ain't done with us yet."

Lawdog took another drag off his cigarette and glanced nervously back toward the line of trucks. Thomas was laying into Droopy, trying to make the slow-paced man move a little quicker. "You best keep your mouth shut about these ideas of yours, Mundo. You start talking crazy shit like that and it's going to be your ass tossed over the guardrail. Thomas ain't in the mood to hear it. Trust me on that."

"That information wasn't for Thomas, my friend. Telling you what I'm thinking is all."

"Your ass best be thinking about getting back to work. Now leave me the hell alone."

Mundo held his hands up in surrender and backed away. He was giving Lawdog a look, though. It said, *don't blame me when shit goes sideways. I tried to tell you.*

Lawdog flicked his cigarette butt into the weeds. He was aware it could start a wildfire, and hoped like hell it did. Let the whole place burn down. He didn't care.

47

Conor was running on fumes. He'd taken Modafinil once in the night to keep himself going but preferred not to hit it again. He needed to reach Barb and Wayne, but pushing himself too far without sleep would only make his judgment erratic. It would put him, and possibly others, at risk. He had more explosives in his gear and considered setting more booby traps, ultimately deciding against it. That last attack should have slowed them some. He hoped they hadn't suffered so many losses they would turn around and go home. That wasn't what Conor wanted. He wasn't done playing yet.

He stuck to the roads as much as possible, always keeping his ears open for the sound of truck engines. They'd quickly make up the time once they got on the road again. He began working the radio. His were a little better than the discount store models used by hunters. They were law enforcement grade Motorolas but the transmission distance was limited by antenna size. Getting any signal out of these mountains was going to be impossible until he was right on them.

He didn't let that discourage him. At each rise in the road, at each peak, at each change in the topography, he was broadcasting. "Conor for Barb, Conor for Barb." The lack of response was no surprise but he fought to not become frustrated. He was aware that frustration was a characteristic of the utter exhaustion he was experiencing. He choked that frustration down and relied on his experience and training.

"Keep jabbering on the radio," he chided himself. "Don't turn into a weepy old bastard just because no one is answering you."

What Conor didn't know was that spot where he'd ambushed The Bond and Barb's camp in Allen City were only about seven miles apart. The problem in southeastern Kentucky was that there could be a lot of hills in seven miles, a lot of obstacles to radio waves.

"Conor for Barb, Conor for Barb."

No response. He checked his watch. It had been an hour since he'd launched his sniper attack on The Bond. He figured it would take thirty minutes to an hour to deal with the tire and their injured. He'd only come a couple of miles. If they worked quickly, they could be on him at any moment. That thought was not encouraging.

He hit a sign that welcomed him to Allen City. He noted it was sponsored by the local Lion's Club and the Rotary Club. Thank God for small town clubs putting up signs or no one in rural areas would ever know where the hell they were.

"Conor for Barb, Conor for Barb," he repeated.

There was a crackle. *"Dad?"*

"Barb!" Conor cheered. "Good to hear your voice, my child."

"Good to hear you too, Dad."

"Where you at?"

"Allen City on the Pikeville side."

"Then I'm just across town from you. Did Wayne reach you?"

"He's right here."

"Listen, we might not have a lot of time. I had a run-in with our friends from the north this morning. I expect they'll be on my tail soon. This is where the magic happens. Are you guys ready?"

"We've done everything you asked Wayne to take care of."

"That's good," Conor said. "Is Wayne around?"

"Right here, Conor," Wayne said into his own radio.

"I need you to head in my direction. I just passed a tiny little bridge that would be perfect for what we discussed."

"So head through town with the materials that we picked up?"

"Affirmative," Conor said. "As a matter of fact, bring a third person. We might need help."

"What do I need to do?" Barb asked.

"I need you to have your camp packed up and have your group ready to boogie when we get to you."

"What about finishing these men off here?" Barb asked. *"If we have them trapped in town, wouldn't it be like shooting fish in a barrel? We just pick them off?"*

"The casualty rate for something like that concerns me," Conor said. "I think this group is over ninety men strong. They have mortars, grenade launchers, and perhaps even rocket propelled grenades. They've got belt-fed machine guns and a shit ton of ammo. We're outmanned and outgunned. They would eat us alive."

"I hate to run."

"We're not running," Conor assured her. "This is a strategic decision."

"I still don't like it."

"You'd like watching your people die even less."

48

Wayne didn't waste time on a friendly greeting when he rode up on Conor. "You look like shit, man. Have you slept at all?"

He'd brought Jason Jacks with him, who nodded in agreement with Wayne.

Conor shook his head. "No time for it. I've either been engaged or on the run the entire time."

"You look like those meth-head mug shots you see on the news out of Florida," said Wayne. "Your eyes are all jacked up."

"Excuse me for not putting on makeup to make myself more presentable."

Wayne laughed. "What do we need to do?"

"Did you find the fertilizer?"

"Yep. Strangely, no looters were interested in carrying off bags of fertilizers. The stores had plenty of it."

"Is it the right kind?"

Wayne rode closer to Conor and pointed to a label on the bag. "This is the kind you said to look for."

Conor nodded in satisfaction. "Use the wrong mix and it won't work. The government made it a little harder for us to blow shit up."

"The nerve," Wayne said.

Conor was struggling to make his exhausted brain focus on the task at hand. He stared at the fertilizer bag like he was struggling to read it.

"So what's the plan?" Wayne asked, hoping Conor could get himself together enough to pull this off.

Conor snapped back to attention. "We're blowing up a bridge. Follow me." He nudged his horse into a trot, heading back the way he'd come.

Wayne followed, leading a pack horse with the fertilizer. Jason brought up the rear, his horse carrying both his personal gear and a special set of saddlebags Conor had requested. In a few minutes they were at the older bridge Conor had selected. Wayne noted that Conor was struggling, his thoughts not flowing at their normal rapid pace as he battled exhaustion. He rubbed his temples, as if that action would make the thoughts flow easier.

"I need that saddlebag," Conor said, gesturing to Jason.

He pulled the bag off and started to toss it to Conor. "No, lad. Don't throw it. It's got homemade Claymores in it."

"As in Claymore mines?" Jason asked, riding forward and passing the saddlebags off to Conor in a gentler manner.

Conor nodded. "As in explosives. As in big fucking boom."

"I rode out here with something like that on the back of my horse?"

"Perfectly harmless until it gets in the right hands. Or the wrong hands, depending on which side you're on."

Jason didn't look so convinced. Conor picked up the pace and began handing out orders.

"Jason, you haul those bags under the bridge. Wayne, I need you to come with me."

Jason didn't have to be told twice. A farm boy used to hard work, he heaved one of the heavy fertilizer bags over his shoulder and began working his way down the steep riverbank to the strip of shoreline beneath the bridge. Conor ran toward an older black Ford truck. It had a bed-mounted fuel tank, the kind farmers and construction workers used to refuel their equipment. Conor crouched and put two hands where the edge of the tank overhung the bed. He shoved upward and the tank rocked slightly.

"No matter how well you fasten these damn things down, they always loosen up," Conor explained. "At least mine always do."

"It's bolted down. You want me to look for a wrench?" Wayne asked.

"No time. Just find something we can wedge in here and pry it loose."

Wayne went right to the cab and flipped the seat forward. He found the jack and the lug wrench fastened behind it. He unscrewed the wingnut to release the lug wrench and used it like a crowbar to pry loose one side of the fuel tank, then the other. When they had it loose, both men lifted it up and walked toward the tailgate of the truck. They paused there, resting it on the tailgate for a second.

"It feels like it has a little fuel in it," Wayne noticed.

"I was hoping it would," Conor said. "We need some for the mixture."

With no need to be delicate, the men waited until Jason was out of the way and shoved the fuel tank down the embankment. It slid like a sled until it smacked into a boulder on the riverbank. Wayne and Conor scrambled down the bank after it and then dragged it into place beneath the bridge.

"Wouldn't happen to have a funnel on you, would you?" Conor asked.

Wayne pretended to check his pockets. "Sorry, fresh out."

"Then a soda bottle will have to do."

The men hunted furiously before Wayne located a muddy one on the creek bank and held it up for Conor.

"Sorry to be a bastard but a two-liter would make this faster."

"The story of my life," Wayne said. "Never big enough."

Conor laughed. It didn't take long to find another one, a two-liter. Conor whipped out his knife and sliced the bottle around the middle, creating an improvised funnel.

Wayne removed the fuel cap off the tank while Conor steadied the funnel in the opening.

"Snip the corner off one of those fertilizer bags. We've got to dump all that in here."

Wayne did as he'd been asked, using his knife to remove a corner of one of the bags and start the process of emptying it into the fuel tank. "This isn't going to be quick."

"Hence the two liter."

Jason came sliding down the bank and dumped another bag on top of the stack. "This is the last one."

"Good job, lad. Take over for me," Conor said. "I'll start getting the Claymore ready."

"Should you be doing that already?" Jason asked, concern in his eyes. "What if something bad happens?"

Conor chuckled. "Something bad *is* going to happen but hopefully not until we're long gone."

While he filled the fuel tank Wayne watched Conor lay out the contents of his boom bag. "I've used a Claymore a time or two and that doesn't look like any Claymore I've ever seen."

"This is a Mad Mick Claymore. It's limited edition –the 'must have' explosive of the season. If I want to add shrapnel there's a special sleeve that I slide over top of the device. It also has interchangeable firing modules so I just snap on whichever module fits the particular situation. There's a special pressure sensitive module, a timer module, a remote control module, and a tripwire module. This one's going to be rigged so a tripwire sets it off on a one minute delay."

"Shouldn't it go off as soon as they hit the tripwire?" Jason asked. "That would stop them in their tracks."

"No," Conor said. "I don't want them to turn around and leave. I want to keep pushing them forward while nibbling away at their numbers a little bit at a time."

Jason was doubtful. "That seems like a lot of trouble. My vote would be that we just turn them around with a good kick in the butt and send them on their way."

"You got any family in Ohio?" Wayne asked, knowing many folks in Appalachia did.

"Yeah, some."

"And you don't have any problem with this group showing up and killing some of them?" Wayne continued.

"I guess I see what you mean. If we fix this problem we might as well fix it for everyone and not just ourselves."

Conor pulled a roll of heavy fishing line from his boom bag and took off with it. He scrambled up the bank on all fours, then ran to the center of the bridge. He tied the loose end of the fishing line to the rail on one side and then ran across the bridge, passing the line through a gap in the railing. "I need you to catch this!" he yelled.

Jason appeared beneath him, hands extended. Conor dropped it neatly into the boy's hands. He started off the bridge, ready to make his way back down the bank when he heard the distant rumble of trucks.

"Shit! They're coming!"

"The trucks?" Wayne yelled back.

"Yeah. How much of that do you have left?"

"One bag," Jason replied.

"Get up here, Jason!" While Conor waited on the boy to get up the bank, he grabbed his rifle and Go Bag from his horse, then ran to Wayne's horse and did the same.

"What do you need?" Jason asked, appearing at Conor's side.

"I need you to take the horses. Get across town and don't let these guys see you. If they even get close, you get on a side street or you take off into the woods. However you do it, you get back to Barb. We'll catch up with you there."

Conor awkwardly made his way back down the bank to the bridge, his arms loaded with gear. He dropped it in a pile beside the fuel tank. Wayne was struggling to pour the last bag of fertilizer into the fuel tank, spilling some as the funnel refused to cooperate.

"You think this is enough?" Wayne asked.

"Enough fertilizer?"

"Enough of a boom."

"My Claymores are a little heavy on the C-4," Conor said, sounding like a grandmother sharing the secret ingredient in her sauce. "That alone may be enough to do the trick. Between that and the boost it'll get from the fertilizer bomb, I think it'll do the job. Let's hurry, though. We've got to hustle."

When the contents of the last fertilizer bag sifted out, Wayne tossed it to the side. Conor threw the funnel to the ground and put the cap in place on the tank. He hurriedly positioned his charge in what he felt was the optimal placement, then cut the fishing line and tied it to the pin inserted into his tripwire module.

"We gotta go, Conor." It wasn't just urgency in Wayne's voice, it was fear. The trucks were getting very close.

Despite his lack of sleep, Conor was finding focus in his task. He knew this work like he knew anything in his life and his hands moved almost of their own accord. He finished setting the charge and double checked all of his connections. He stood, straightened out, and stretched his back. "It's ready. Let's go."

Wayne didn't have to be asked again. He already had his Go Bag on his back and his rifle slung over his shoulder. The two men clambered up the bank and kept running. The trucks were not in sight yet but had to be close. Not minutes away but seconds.

"Side street!" Conor barked when they came to the first intersection. "Turn right!" He was afraid they would be seen if they continued down the main street and he couldn't take a chance on that. If The Bond caught them in the open with their heavy guns, he and Wayne would be trapped like cattle in a chute.

He noticed the street they were running down, lined with the normal shops of small town America, was named Elm Street. There was a flower shop, a barber shop, and a consignment store. There was an antique shop with a junky old lamp in the window. He wondered how many other quiet, peaceful Elm Streets were in small towns across the country. Thousands perhaps. He was certain about one thing; whoever named this picturesque little street never imagined a day where two men would be charging down it to escape an explosive device they'd planted in the path of a horde of nomadic post-apocalyptic warriors.

At the end of Elm they swung left on Front Street. Conor yanked his radio from the pouch on his plate carrier and keyed the mic. "Barb! Conor for Barb!" He held the radio in his hand, arms pumping as he and Wayne barreled down the street.

She responded quickly. *"I'm here, Dad. Is everything okay?"*

Conor struggled to talk and breathe at the same time. This wasn't just jogging, it was running for his life carrying forty pounds of gear. "We got...interrupted. Company is...coming. When you...hear...the blast, that'll mean...The Bond...crossed the bridge...into...town. We sent...Jason on with...the horses. Wayne and I...are headed...toward you...on foot. Not sure we'll reach you...before Bond does. Don't...wait."

"We got this, Dad. What do you want us to do?"

"Get your...people...in woods. Don't engage...Bond. Too dangerous."

"I could set a charge," Barb suggested. *"I know how. I've watched you dozens of times."*

"No!" Conor gasped. He wanted to say more but he couldn't keep this up much longer, trying to talk and run his fat ass down the street at the same time. "Don't engage...hide!"

"Got it, Dad."

49

As soon as she was off the radio with her father, Barb gathered her people together. She relayed the details of her conversation with him and explained that she needed everyone to cross the river.

"We'll be safer with the river between us and those trucks. I need you to go down there and find a good location for crossing. I want you to make sure everyone gets across safely. Help each other. My dad says these guys have heavy firepower and we need to keep our heads down."

"Just what was the point to coming all this way if we're just going to run?" asked one of the pastor's men.

"We're not running," Barb explained. "This is guerrilla warfare. We're outnumbered at least three to one. We're outgunned so significantly that it's practically muskets against tanks. We have to pick our battles and not get ourselves slaughtered. We can't help anyone if we're dead."

"Why don't we just hole up on the roofs of those buildings along the street? We could open up on them as they went by," suggested one Wayne's men. There was a murmur of agreement from several among the crowd, heads nodding in consensus.

"We're done talking about this," Barb said firmly. "Our enemy has machine guns. They have grenades and launchers. They probably even have capabilities beyond what we know about. We need more intelligence on this enemy before we put our lives at risk."

"I thought that was what your dad was doing?" said another of the pastor's men.

"And we haven't had a chance to hear what he has to say yet, have we?" Barb countered.

There was a powerful explosion that startled everyone in the group. People flinched and scanned about frantically.

"That's them!" Barb said. "They just triggered my dad's explosives. We have to move now!"

Then they could hear the trucks. Barb, and likely Conor himself, had figured the explosives would slow down the caravan of trucks. They would stop to check for damage and to check the road ahead of them but the opposite appeared to be happening. The sound of roaring diesel engines filled the small town, echoing off buildings and traveling up the river valley. They weren't stopping. They were surging ahead.

"What can we do to help?" It was Shannon, with Sam at her side.

"I need you two to get across that river and get hidden."

"We're not going without you," Shannon said.

Barb could sense their determination and saw it was pointless to argue with them. Like it or not, they were stuck at her side for the duration of this. "Despite what my dad said, I wanted to plant a charge to slow these assholes down but I don't think I have time."

"They sound really close," Shannon said. "I might have an idea, though, if you want to hear it."

Barb started to dismiss her. What could this girl have to offer? Then realizing that she had no ideas of her own, she decided what could it hurt? "What?"

"My dad told me about this really stupid trick that worked for snipers in the Vietnam War. It might work for these guys too. It's pretty simple but we'll have to work fast."

"What do we need?" Barb asked.

"A pen, an envelope, and a piece of string."

50

Lawdog and Mundo were in the lead truck when the convoy crossed into the small town of Allen City, Kentucky. After what happened to them a few miles back, with the sniper ambush on the highway, they were being as cautious as they could be at thirty-five miles per hour. Lawdog wanted to go slow so they could watch for explosives but Thomas wasn't having it. Lawdog could see clearer than ever that Thomas was blinded by vengeance. Mundo was right. All Thomas could see was this Mad Mick character being tortured to death in front of him. Lawdog had to wonder if Thomas wanted that more than he wanted to keep his men alive. It was beginning to feel that way. After all, Thomas wasn't in the lead truck with them. If they came under attack, it was probably he and Mundo that were going to get blown to Kingdom Come.

It didn't come down that way. Lawdog's truck was past the booby-trapped bridge, almost one entire block into town when Conor's bomb detonated. The blast was deafening and sent debris raining down on the entire convoy. All these men were combat veterans and immediately assumed one of the trucks had struck an IED. Men ducked, cursed, and swerved all over the road as they tried to figure out what was going on.

Mundo stuck his neck out the window and craned it around backwards. "I think he missed us! The son-of-a-bitch missed us."

"Any trucks hit?" Lawdog asked.

Mundo slithered back into the cab. "Don't look like it."

Lawdog picked up the microphone to check the status of the other trucks but was interrupted by Thomas on the radio.

"Any casualties? Any damage?"

Surprisingly, as the reports came in, it was just as Mundo had described. All of them had escaped injury.

"Should we stop to check the vehicles for damage?" Lawdog suggested. "We could have fuel tanks hit or tires damaged by shrapnel."

"That's a negative," Thomas snapped. *"Hammer down and keep moving. Get us out of this fucking town. If we got problems with a vehicle, we'll know soon enough."*

"Roger that," Lawdog replied, thoroughly chastised. He would have to think twice before making suggestions next time. He was supposed to be the second in command in this operation but Thomas wasn't having it right now. He didn't care what anyone thought about anything.

"You see what he did there, don't you?" Mundo asked

"What?" Lawdog asked, his mind still on the way Thomas had shut him down.

"He cut off our retreat. He nailed the back door closed so we can't get outta here."

"Who? Thomas?"

"No, dammit. Not Thomas. The Mad Mick."

Lawdog shook his head as if Mundo was telling him about a time he saw Bigfoot. "I don't want to hear any of that bullshit. I've got enough to worry about. You just keep your eyes open for tripwires or anything suspicious. If we hit a booby-trap because you're not paying attention, I'll kill you my own self."

"Whatever, man," Mundo mumbled.

They did as they were told, keeping their speed at a constant thirty-five mph through the abandoned town. The streets were mostly clear of vehicles which made it easy to maintain speed but Lawdog was worried. He was tired of this trip. He liked what they'd been doing back in the cities better. The pickings were easy. Nobody was getting hurt. Life was good. They were the baddest thing around and could have anything they wanted. Nothing wrong with that. It was the dream life.

"What the hell is that?"

Pulled from his thoughts, Lawdog scanned ahead of him, then to the sides, and didn't see a damn thing. "What you talking about?"

Mundo stabbed a finger ahead of him. "That! Right there in front of your face."

Then Lawdog saw it too. A string had been tossed over a useless power line spanning the main road. A white envelope hung from the string right at eye level, dead center in the middle of the road, spinning slightly in the breeze. Lawdog downshifted and coasted to a stop.

"What the hell's going on up there?" Thomas demanded over the radio. *"Why are you slowing down?"*

Lawdog picked up the microphone and pressed the transmit button. "Give us a second, T. There's something in the road we need to check out." Lawdog released the button and gestured at Mundo. "Get out and see what that is."

Mundo squinted at Lawdog. "So I guess *us* checking it out means *me* checking it out?"

"Of course. Now get moving before the boss starts bitching."

Scowling, Mundo got out of the truck and jogged toward the envelope, his rifle in his hand. Before he touched anything, he visually traced the string up the wire to make sure it wasn't attached to any type of unusual device, particularly the kind that might blow him up. He scanned the surrounding windows to see if he could spot anyone lying in wait for them. He saw nothing out of the ordinary, only his own reflection in grimy storefronts. He pulled his Leatherman tool from his belt and opened the scissors. He carefully approached the string, scissors extended, prepared to snip it. He moved slowly, anxious that the act of snipping the string might somehow trigger a massive explosion.

A honking horn nearly made him wet his pants.

"Move it!" Lawdog demanded. "Thomas wants to know what's taking so long."

Mundo dropped the Leatherman to his side. "Dammit, man, you almost made me piss all over myself. Don't do that again."

"Get moving!" Lawdog said. "If you don't hurry up, Thomas is going to be up here breathing down your neck."

Convinced now that he wasn't going to die if he cut the string, Mundo raised the Leatherman back up and snipped it, the white envelope dropping neatly into the palm of his outstretched hand. He held it before him in both hands and examined the bold print on the outside. "Take this to your leader," he read out loud.

Mundo obeyed, jogging double-time back through the convoy, arriving at the passenger side of the truck in which Thomas was riding. He hopped deftly onto the running board and presented the envelope at the window. "Your mail, sir."

"What the hell is that?" Thomas asked.

Mundo shrugged. "Beats me. It was hanging from the string in the middle of the road. It says it's for you." He held it up for Thomas to read.

It only took Thomas a split second to figure out the point of that message. Before he could issue a warning, gunfire erupted from the roof of a nearby building, pounding the cab of the truck Thomas was riding in.

The windshield shattered. Rounds punched holes where they could and pinged off thicker surfaces they couldn't penetrate. Thomas ducked instinctively, crouching below the dashboard, trying to put the engine between him and the shooters. The effort wasn't entirely successful. Way too many rounds were finding their way into the cab, buzzing around like angry hornets. The truck lurched and the engine stalled. Thomas glanced toward the driver, ready to tear into him for the rookie move but the driver was dead. He'd caught rounds in the neck and face. His face was shredded and blood soaked his uniform.

Thomas hit the latch on the door and shoved his shoulder against it until it sprang open. He threw his body to the side, half rolling and half falling out the door. It was a substantial drop and he hit hard but had no time to recover. Rounds hit the ground around him. At any moment those flattened projectiles were going to find his flesh and shred him like razor blades. He rolled hard, then scrambled to his feet and flattened himself against the building. Wherever those shooters were, he was out of their immediate line of fire.

His first thought was that it was the Mad Mick but this wasn't one guy. There were several guns firing. Several more people that would have to pay for this insult. With their primary target – him – no longer visible, the enemy rifles turned their attention on the lead vehicle. Thomas could see Mundo in the bed of the truck, crouched with the other men staring wide-eyed back in his direction. He had good reason to keep his eye on Thomas. He knew he'd screwed up.

Thomas drew his handgun and leveled it on Mundo. If he could hit him at this distance without wounding another of his soldiers he'd have killed him. This was all his fault. He should have seen through that trick. That was kindergarten-level stuff.

Now that he was getting the brunt of the fire, Lawdog had to do something. He stomped the pedal and accelerated the heavy truck to the extent that was possible, weaving from side to side in a futile attempt to evade fire. He immediately banged into a parked vehicle, unable to see through a shattered windshield. The soldiers in the bed of his truck aimed over the cab and returned fire on the distant rooftop. It was a couple of hundred yards away and they couldn't even make out what they were shooting at. One of them launched a grenade in that direction from his M203 but he aimed low and his target was at the far end of the effective range. The grenade blew harmlessly along the street, blowing out a shop window and knocking over the sign for an insurance company.

Another truck further back in the convoy made a sudden turn to the left and pulled off the main street. The maneuver put a brick building between them and the shooters, sparing them from further gunfire. Trucks further back followed suit, ducking into alleys and side streets. Men poured from those trucks, taking up weapons and dispersing along the streets.

"That way!" Thomas barked, gesturing wildly toward the shooters.

Lawdog had miraculously not been injured but he couldn't see a thing through the bullet-riddled windshield. He was trying to get his truck to safety, taking rounds and unable to escape the withering gunfire. Steering wildly, attempting evasive maneuvers the truck was too awkward to manage, he ran up on a fire hydrant. He tried to reverse off of it, but judging by the sound of screeching metal, only managed to do more damage to the undercarriage.

Thomas raised his radio. "You're only making it worse, Lawdog. Get out of that vehicle. Return fire! Quit running and fight back!"

Thomas was disappointed to see that Lawdog apparently had no more sense than Mundo. He couldn't be certain that Lawdog had heard his radio over the chaos because he continued to try and wrench the vehicle free. Finally the bolts beneath the hydrant sheared and it toppled over with barely a trickle of water. Still unable to see, being freed from the obstacle didn't help Lawdog. In another vain attempt at escape, he veered into a telephone pole which snapped off and dropped across the bed of his truck. There were cries from the men but any injuries didn't appear to be life-threatening. The passengers streamed from the vehicle, taking cover behind it and returning fire.

51

Conor and Wayne ran along the town's riverfront back street. The Bond trucks had passed them. They heard the sound of their engines echoing off buildings and there was nothing they could do about it. Just as Conor had expected, they were behind the curve, however, they could recover. Barb's team was supposed to be hidden safely in the woods along the route. The Bond would continue on their way. They would have to stop for sleep though. Conor would push through and catch up with them. He would stop them and finish the job. That certainty went out the window when the gunfire started.

Conor ducked into a loading dock and tugged Wayne in with him. He yanked his radio from his pocket and yelled into it. "Barb, what the hell is going on?"

Her reply was immediate and irritatingly calm. *"I took it upon myself to slow the enemy."*

Conor could sense the underlying meaning behind her tone. She knew she'd defied him but also knew that it was too late for him to do anything about it now. They'd just have to roll with it. She'd done that with him before, just never on matters of this scale. Through the radio, Conor could hear gunfire raging around her. "I had a plan, daughter. I made that clear to you. Engaging these people was a very bad idea. People could die because of this."

"Letting them get ahead of us was a very bad idea," she countered. *"We may never catch up with them again. That would have defeated the point of this whole mission, father."*

He took a calming breath. "There's a reason you kill a hornet nest by spraying it and then getting the hell out of there. Even if you have to go back a couple of times to kill them all, you don't get hurt that way. You know what happens if you poke the nest with a stick? They all come spilling out at once and you lose control of the bloody situation!"

"I see your point," Barb conceded. *"That's kind of where we're at right now."*

"No shit!"

Their conversation was interrupted by three men in full load-out emerging from a cross street behind Conor and Wayne. They weren't pursuing Conor but were likely attempting to circle behind Barb. Conor, already pissed off because of Barb's decision to engage The Bond, handed his radio off to Wayne and stepped clear of the loading dock. His rifle was already up and he snapped off three quick shots, hitting each of the three surprised men in the face. As they stumbled back, he tracked them, putting a second round into each man for good measure.

Conor stepped back into the loading dock area and snatched his radio from a stunned Wayne. He patted him on the back and gestured down the road ahead of them. "Let's move!"

Wayne raised his own rifle and flipped off the safety. Instead of running blindly to put distance behind them and The Bond, he moved cautiously, ready to drop anyone who stepped out in front of him.

Conor constantly swiveled between the view ahead of him and behind him. He keyed his radio. "Barb, we can talk about this later. You need to get out of there now. The town is overrun. Did Jason reach you with your horses?"

"Roger that. He's waiting behind the building. We're going now. We'll be

crossing the river behind our camp and waiting on the hill above the river. Wayne was at our camp this morning. He can show you where it was."

"If we don't reach you in thirty minutes, move out," Conor said. "We'll catch up on the road."

"If it comes to that we'll leave two horses behind on that hill for you."

Barb was waiting on his response when Jason opened fire from behind the building. She ran across the flat roof and peered over the brick parapet wall. Jason was leaning from behind the building and engaging a shooter hidden behind an old Subaru parked along the street. Barb pulled a grenade from her vest, pulled the pin, and embedded the grenade in the windshield of the Subaru. When the man raised his head to investigate, his top half was vaporized in a pink, frothy spray.

Barb faced her stunned companions. The two terrified women, Sam and Shannon, were doing an outstanding job. They'd done everything she asked. "Ladies, we have to go now. Let's move."

While those two negotiated the rusty fire escape on the back of the building, Barb addressed the panicked inquiries from her father. "Sorry, Dad. Had to deal with something. We're bugging out."

"Roger that. Be safe. And if I give you another set of instructions I bloody well expect you to follow them." Without waiting for a response, Conor pocketed his radio and devoted his full attention to the hunt for bad guys.

"Barb said they were crossing the river behind her camp. She said you would know where to go."

Wayne nodded frantically, never taking is eye from his optic. "We're close. A couple hundred yards."

"Don't let that distract you. That's room for a lot of bad shit."

"Got it, man. I'm on it."

They continued to move along the back street like a well-oiled machine. They hugged the back of old brick buildings, ready to take cover if things got hairy. The one thing they had going for them at this point was that The Bond was probably not after them specifically. Their focus was likely directed toward the team of shooters who had engaged them from the front.

Another pair of Bond soldiers popped out of an alley, well in front of Wayne and Conor's position. They should have paid more attention to their surroundings before skidding into view like that.

Conor whispered, "You take right. I've got left."

The two enemy soldiers did not even notice their pursuers, so intent on getting to Barb's position. That wasn't going to happen. Conor and Wayne opened fire. Both men flinched and fell but they weren't out of the fight. They twisted on the ground and shot back.

Conor latched a hand onto Wayne's gear and flung him toward the safety of a recessed doorway. He dropped to a knee, making himself a smaller target, and returned fire.

"Body armor!" Wayne bellowed.

Conor had seen that too, switching his selector to fire three-shot bursts. He dropped one man with a barrage that caught him in the armpit. Wayne dropped the second with a bullet beneath the chin. With the targets neutralized, Conor stood and gestured for Wayne to come with him. They paused at the fallen men.

"Keep watch," Conor hissed. "We've got people who need this gear."

With Wayne watching for bad guys, Conor retrieved the men's armor and weapons. It was an ungainly bundle but he was counting on the fact that they didn't have far to go. If he could get across the river with it, he could drape it over a horse. A shout in a nearby alley put them on guard.

"We need to go," Wayne said urgently.

"Over the guardrail. We'll follow the riverbank."

They sprinted toward the guardrail and climbed over it, their burden of rifles and gear clattering as they made their way down the steep bank. Someone, likely the Army Corps of Engineers, had covered the bank with large boulders to prevent it from washing away in floods. It made the climbing difficult. The rocks were slippery and there were plenty of holes just waiting to trap a limb.

"If I slip and break a leg just shoot me," Wayne muttered.

"Same here."

Taking to the riverbank had been a good call. By the time they reached the bottom, they could hear voices on the street above them. No one appeared to be thinking about what might be below them, and no heads appeared. Everyone was too intent on reaching the people who had been shooting at them. Conor prayed Barb was no longer there. The girl had had plenty of time to cross the river and take cover, but just because he'd told her to certainly didn't mean she would. They'd been down that road today already. All he could hope was that she learned from the experience.

52

"I got'em," Jason said, staring through binoculars. "They're on the riverbank."

He was watching the town from across the river, waiting to see if Conor and Wayne needed assistance. Conor had suggested, perhaps even gone as far as ordering, that they all pull back out of range of The Bond's guns, but no one wanted to go. Barb only managed to get some of her people to retreat when she reminded them they needed to get the horses to safety or they'd have a very long walk home. The rest, a little more than twenty men and women, were hunkered down in the wooded foothills above the riverbank. It would have been a decent hiding spot in mid-summer, the hardwoods fully leafed-out and the grass high. This time of year, only the broad trunks of oaks, maples, and poplars provided any cover. They would stop bullets but they didn't provide much concealment unless you kept yourself glued to the back of them.

Barb rushed to Jason's side and squinted toward the river, trying to make out the moving figures in the jumble of rocks. "The streets must be overrun with men or they wouldn't choose that route. That's slow going." The part she didn't mention was that it was probably her fault, because she'd poked the nest. If she'd listened to Conor the town would not be crawling with men now. They'd have gone on their way and they could have engaged them later under better conditions.

"I can see Wayne pointing out our camp. They're almost at the crossing," Jason said. "They're not the only ones."

Barb took the binoculars from Jason's hands, only asking for permission to do so once she already had them to her eyes. Sam was frowning at her abruptness but Jason just grinned. He thought Barb was funny but that might change after he had to live with her for a while.

Concerned about the proximity of The Bond soldiers on the road, Barb keyed her radio. "Barb for Conor. Barb for Conor."

Everyone around her listened for the response but there was nothing.

"He may have it turned off with so many bad guys around," Sam said. "Wouldn't want it giving him away."

Barb was glued to the binoculars, frowning and biting her lip from the anxiety that consumed her. "They're ready to go for it. They're going to cross," she said. "They can't see the men in the road above them. They can't see up over that riverbank. If they run out now, they're going to get mowed down." She handed the binoculars back to Jason.

"They're in the water," Jason announced.

Barb and her people had crossed on horseback. The water wasn't much above knee-level to a person, but it was frigid, fast-moving water, and the slippery rocks made it difficult to move quickly. There would be no running under those conditions. Once you were in the water and exposed, you were committed to the endeavor.

"They need cover fire," one of Wayne's men, a burly guy named Chuck, said. "We need to help them out."

"Then we need experienced shooters," Barb snapped. "We can't afford anyone shooting too low. We'll kill the men we're trying to help."

"It doesn't have to be accurate," Chuck offered. "Just has to make those bad guys run for cover."

"That's probably about four hundred yards," Jason said, shaking his head doubtfully.

"I don't remember the exact drop on a 5.56 round at that range but I'm sure it's a couple of feet," Barb said.

"We have a couple of hunting rifles in the group," Jason said. "There's several .30 caliber or better. They're a better option at this distance."

"Get them down here," Barb said.

Jason, Sam, and Chuck spread the word among the group and shooters came forward with .308s, .30-06s, and even a .303 Enfield. They dropped to the ground and leveled their rifles over downed trees. Barb was running a 1x6 scope with a combat reticle that quickly allowed her to determine range while looking through the optic. She chose to shoot from a standing position, bracing her rifle against a sapling.

"What's happening, Jason?" she asked.

"The men are still at our old camp. They're studying the horse tracks."

"What should I do?" Shannon asked Barb. She'd been silent until this point, afraid to leave the reassuring presence of the only people she knew among this group. She was just trying to stay out of the way.

"That shotgun you're carrying is wrong for this kind of fight," Barb said. "You just stand ready to provide aid if it comes to that. Be ready and be tough."

Shannon nodded. "Got it."

"They're following the horse tracks," Jason said.

"If they start following those tracks..." Sam began.

"They'll find Wayne and Dad in the river," Barb finished. There would be no way around it. Through her scope, she could see the two men in the waters of the Levisa River, struggling with their burden of gear, the current, and the numbingly cold water. She couldn't help but whisper them encouragement. "Come on, come on."

"I think we need to start blasting," Chuck said. "They're going to be seen and then it's going to be too late."

"No," Barb said firmly. "You shoot without my go-ahead and you'll be the first to die."

Seeing the expressions on the faces around her, Barb tried to reel it back in a little and explain herself. "On the off chance that they might slip across the river unseen I don't want to draw any attention to them. We wait until they've been spotted and we only react if we have to."

"It may be too late by then," Jason countered.

"Tell me something I don't know," Barb snapped.

Jason pointed at the river. "They're almost across. Just a few more feet."

Everyone shared the desperate urge to pull the two men forward, to make them move faster, but all they could do was watch helplessly.

Everyone froze when a single shot split the air.

There was a solid *whap* as the round struck Conor in the back. He arched, then pitched forward, falling onto the shore. His legs were in the water, his upper body on the muddy riverbank. He clawed at the ground, trying to pull himself forward.

Barb searched desperately, trying to locate where the shot had come from. It had not been the small group they were watching. The Bond soldiers standing around her camp, studying the horse tracks, were doing the same thing she was doing, trying to spot the shooter. They saw him at the same time Barb did. It was a solitary man standing back toward the center of town, hundreds of feet from her camp. He was at the guardrail separating the road from the riverbank, his rifle braced on the guardrail. He was lining up another shot.

Everyone, from The Bond soldiers to Barb's team, heard the echo of the man's shouted cry. "In the water! Crossing the river!"

"Fire!" Barb shouted.

She swung her rifle from the men at her camp and onto the man who'd fired on her father. She hastily gauged the distance and opened up, trying to disrupt his follow-up shot. Her target was at the limits of both her optic and her rifle but she rained rounds all around him. There were no hits but she'd put him on notice. He was scared. His only cover was the guardrail and he tried to make himself small enough to hide behind it but it was ineffective. Dead grass and weeds rose to cover everything below the guardrail but she was certain of where he was, even if she couldn't see him. She walked rounds into that grass until she was rewarded with a high-pitched scream.

"Got ya, bastard," she whispered as he rolled backwards and writhed on the asphalt.

She swung back to the group at her old camp. She desperately wanted to drop her optic a little further and check on her dad, to see if he'd crawled to safety, but she didn't want to take her gun out of the fight. Her team of long-range shooters with their bolt-actions was firing effectively and scoring hits but their rate of fire did not match that of the men across the river. With their full auto and select-fire weapons they could spray the hillside if they got the opportunity. Her team tried to prevent that, laying down shots with such precision that none of the Bond soldiers dared approach the guardrail either to send more rounds into her father or return fire on her team.

That moment of satisfaction, of pride in the effectiveness of her force, was short-lived when The Bond upped the ante. There was a *pop* and a *whoosh* followed by a powerful explosion as a soldier with an M203 grenade launcher brought it into the fight.

"Just what we need," Jason moaned.

The first grenades fell short as the man with the launcher struggled to get a shot without getting his head blown off. He found his groove, and soon had the range dialed in. Each successive grenade climbed closer to Barb's firing line.

"Keep your heads down!" she ordered.

Inspired by the explosions that the M203 was producing, other Bond soldiers began lobbing grenades blindly over the guardrail toward the river. Each explosion, slightly muffled by the water, sent plumes skyward like fountains. Though water would minimize their effectiveness, a grenade landing too close to Wayne and Conor would shred them in a way their armor could not prevent.

Barb scanned for the source of the grenades, hoping to focus her fire, but there were men all over the place now. Too many to keep up with. They were behind cars, shooting from the windows of buildings, behind trees, and flattened behind obstructions. How many more were there that she couldn't see?

Her team had to keep firing, had to keep pressure on these men, so that her dad and Wayne could get away, but their fire was less effective. The Bond soldiers were dug in and it was her team that was suddenly more vulnerable with grenades popping off and rifle rounds chewing up the ground around them.

Then it happened. A grenade landed just feet ahead of a downed tree providing cover for several of her shooters. When it exploded, there was the whistle of flying debris. That was followed by a scream and a chorus of shouts. One man rolled to his side, clutching his face. A second toppled over silently. Yet another was holding his mangled hand above his head and praying loudly.

Barb snapped her head toward Shannon and found the young woman paralyzed with fear. "You're on, kid! Go!"

Shannon's terrified eyes found hers. Barb didn't have time for reassurance and encouragement, but before she had to repeat herself the young woman choked it down. Shannon grabbed her bag and bolted toward the injured.

Rounds were zipping all over the place, shredding the bark off trees and dropping tiny limbs from above. The opposing force had Barb's group in their crosshairs and the tables were turned. This was when she'd start losing people. Maybe it was time to go?

With her head already out of the game for the moment, Barb chanced a glance downward to check on her father, terrified of what she might find. She imagined him in a bloody puddle, staining the water around him. She was pleased to find that this was not the case. He was gone. Wayne too. Her instinct was to search for him, to see where he'd gotten to, but she curbed that. Her dad would be fine. He was not in the open anymore. She had work to do and she needed to get on with it.

"There's more crossing downstream!" Jason yelled.

With no orders to the contrary, her remaining shooters directed their fire toward a second group of men downstream pouring over the guardrail. Some had already reached the river and were taking those first icy steps to ford the river. With all fire turned in that direction, the soldiers at her old camp seized the opportunity to launch their own offensive. She might not have noticed this immediately had one of the men not been so gung ho as to take a running leap over the guardrail. His foot sank into a hole between two boulders. His body had so much forward momentum that his leg snapped immediately, the knee hinging in an entirely new direction. The soldier hung there trapped and screaming until Barb mercifully euthanized him.

There were more targets than they could repel. They were in danger of being overrun. Barb either needed to call more shooters forward or bite the bullet and retreat. If those men climbed this hill and got in the woods around them, her people would be picked off one by one. It would be over.

Yet she was a fighter, not a runner. Perhaps it came from her lack of experience. Just as she keyed her radio to call more shooters forward, a dozen enemy splashed through the knee-deep water, retracing the path her father and Wayne had taken moments ago. She dropped her radio and turned her rifle on the men but never had a chance to fire. Just feet from the shore there was a massive explosion that dropped all of the men. Bodies collapsed into the water, the current pulling them away, and the water running red with their blood.

She understood now that her father had left the men a present before he made his way to safety. One of his little Mad Mick claymores with his special recipe of ball bearings, washers, and hex nuts. He hadn't had time to rig a trip wire so he must have triggered it remotely. That meant he was alive.

With this team eliminated from the fight, she directed all guns toward the second team attempting to cross. Taking the brunt of all the fire, those men could not find adequate cover and chose to retreat.

"We've got them on the run!" Chuck yelled. "Get 'em, boys!"

Invigorated that they were back on the winning side of things,

Barb's team was overtaken by a proficiency they'd not possessed earlier. They became more confident that they could win this battle. Rather than spraying rounds to keep the enemy from advancing, her shooters were in the zone and had their targets ranged. For every man who vaulted the guardrail to safety another caught a round and went down screaming.

Sam had been less confident of her shooting abilities at this distance. She'd been directing her fire at areas where there was a greater concentration of enemy, hoping her odds of taking someone out were improved. She put her rifle on safe and propped it up against a log. "Hand me those binoculars."

Jason dropped a hand and groped for them, then slid them through the leaves toward her. She pressed them to her eyes. Barb noticed her staring in a direction they hadn't been taking fire from previously.

"Are there more?" Barb asked. "Did they get around us?"

Sam stood up and rushed toward Barb. Jason grabbed her, trying to pull her back behind cover, but she slipped away from him. She handed the binoculars over to Barb and directed her where to look. When Barb got the binoculars to her eyes she found her father and Wayne in a draw about fifty yards away, working their way toward them.

They continued to take fire but it was more sporadic. Grenade fire had petered out. She suspected it was likely because they had expended the rounds they carried with them. These men had rushed into the fight and hadn't been armed up for a prolonged engagement. She was lucky. If they'd had their trucks with them, their belt-fed weapons at their disposal, this might've gone another way. Then, as if invoked by her thoughts, two diesel engines started in tandem. She sensed this was exactly what she had feared. These men were not running. They were bringing their A-game.

Barb shouted out orders. She radioed her people at the top of the hill to get the horses clear. She ordered Chuck, Sam, and the others to continue firing. She scanned down the firing line and caught Shannon working desperately with a severely injured man. Shannon gave Barb a pleading expression but Barb had no time to spare for her.

"Jason, you're going with me. We need to help my dad. The rest of you, start retreating up this mountain. Take turns laying down cover fire while everyone else moves backwards. If I'm right, we need to get the hell out of here immediately."

53

Conor struggled up the steep slope, his legs turning to rubber and threatening to give out on him. Although the blow from the round he'd taken had knocked him flat on his ass, he was uninjured. The two sets of body armor he'd stolen from the dead Bond soldiers had been tossed over his shoulder when he was shot. The bullet meant to kill him was buried somewhere in that stack of gear.

His elation at not having been killed though was short-lived. His clothes were soaked through from the thighs down and in the cold, breezy conditions it was extremely uncomfortable. While he didn't think he was at risk for hypothermia, it made for a really bad day. Add to it that he was chugging up an extremely steep hill loaded down with his personal gear, his boom bag, and the goodies they'd taken from the men they killed.

Except for the claymore he planted on the riverbank Conor and Wayne had mostly stayed out of the fight. They had very little cover and wanted to gain distance up the slope before they engaged the enemy. If they drew fire they had nowhere to go. He was impressed at the effectiveness of Barb's force. They'd done well to keep the enemy at bay despite the odds. It couldn't last though. Barb's people would be severely outgunned if The Bond could untangle their trucks and bring their best toys into the fight.

"The Bond is...running," Wayne gasped. "They're...turning them back."

Struggling under the weight of his gear, Conor found it nearly impossible to respond. He gasped, "No." He wasn't convinced they were leaving. This wasn't over.

Wayne simply shrugged rather than waste his breath arguing about it. He was convinced The Bond had enough and was going home. When he heard the diesel engines starting up he understood exactly what Conor meant. He was wrong. The Bond wasn't retreating. They were just running back to the house to get their big stick. When they got back the real ass-kicking would start.

"Must suck...to be right...all the time," Wayne croaked.

Conor shook his head wearily. There was a highlight reel of his failures running in his head at that comment. All the times he'd been wrong. There were so many he didn't have the wind to go into it.

"Dad!"

Conor snapped his head up to see Barb barreling down the slope toward him, Jason behind her. He didn't like this one bit. The move had left them both too exposed. It was entirely unnecessary. He'd have made it up there. Eventually. Besides not having the wind to reprimand her, he was aware that he would have done the exact same thing in her situation.

Jason ran to one side and Barb the other. They slung the personal rifles across their backs and offloaded Conor and Wayne's burdens onto their own shoulders. They didn't stick around for a mushy reunion and pats on the back. There was no time for that. With their fresh legs, Jason and Barb chugged back up the hill at double time, leaving Wayne and Conor shaking their heads.

"Youth..." Conor said, too winded to take the thought anywhere.

Wayne nodded, understanding every unsaid sentiment.

Shed of his burden, Conor did manage to find a second wind. The hills out of the river valley were nearly vertical. Standing upright Conor could almost hold his hands out in front of him and touch the slope ahead. Running was not an option. It was more like climbing stairs. He put everything he had left into it. If The Bond had the kind of goodies on those trucks that he imagined, they needed to get as far away from here as they could.

When they reached Barb's firing position they found a group standing around staring at Shannon. She was crouched on the ground beside a young man with a traumatic injury to his neck. His eyes were glazed over and bright arterial blood seeped from a wound Shannon was desperately trying to pack gauze into.

At Conor's arrival, Shannon gave him a pleading look. He was familiar with what that expression said. She was acknowledging that everything her father had feared was correct. Despite her certainty that she was ready for this, she was discovering she was not. She was completely overwhelmed and had no idea what to do. Certainly she understood what to do from a treatment perspective. She understood the basic methods for stopping bleeding when the wound allowed for it but found herself wholly unprepared for the moral, ethical, and emotional aspects of her actions.

"What do I do?" she begged.

Conor began issuing orders. He wasn't familiar with everyone's names but instructed two men to grab the injured man and begin making their way up the hill with him. The rest of the injured could walk and he directed them to get moving.

"Barb, get up that hill as fast as you can. Those trucks are bringing heavier guns. Get everyone on their horses and send them to the southwest."

"Southwest is the wrong direction," Jason said. "Home is toward the south, then southeast."

"I know but I was told these men had more mortars at one point. If they do they may start shelling this hillside when they get those trucks over here. Since they can't see us, they'll target the logical direction, which they might assume to be the direction of the high-way. We need to be going in the *least* logical direction, which is away from the highway. And we need to be going that way *now* so get moving."

They were approximately one hundred and fifty feet from the crest of the hill, where the horses, gear, and the rest of the men waited for them. As the group slowly worked their way up the hill, Barb was already on the radio handing out orders to her people. Conor was pleased to see the way she delegated. She hadn't really had the opportunity to assume this role before and she was handling it well.

"If we don't keep pressure on that wound, he's going to die," Shannon said. She was sitting on her knees, surrounded by scattered medical gear and empty packaging.

Conor dropped down beside her and urgently started packing gear into her medical bag. "He's going to die anyway, sweetie. You know that and I know that. There's no chopper waiting to take him to a hospital. There's no trauma center waiting for us back home. If he's alive when we get to the top of that hill, I'll be surprised."

Tears welled in her eyes. As a father, Conor ached for her. "What am I supposed to do with that?"

This was where Conor could have said this was what her dad tried to prepare her for, why he didn't want her to come. He didn't say that though. He didn't want to reinforce the notion that she wasn't ready for this. He didn't want her to feel incapable. He wanted to reinforce the notion that she could rise to this occasion. He wanted her to manage this situation and others like it in the future. This was a situation where being sheltered by a father could not help her. She needed confidence but she also needed truth, as harsh and ugly as it was.

"It's not easy and it's not pretty but you have to triage your patients according to who you can save and who you can't. As cold as it sounds, you have to save your supplies for the people you can fix. If that young man had been my patient, I would've pressed a trauma pad against his neck, held his hand if I had the time, and offered reassurance. You're a ditch doctor, not a trauma surgeon."

Shannon took a deep breath, wiped her eyes, and got to her feet. Conor was pleased to see that she maintained her composure. She didn't break down or give into any of the other flood of emotions she had to be experiencing. Although the father in him wanted to hug her, he restrained himself. She didn't need to be sheltered or babied; she needed support and information.

With the last of her supplies stashed in the med bag, Conor lashed it shut and grabbed her by the hand. He could hear a diesel truck moving along the riverfront street. He glanced back down the hill, onto the town, and saw two Bond trucks rolling beside each other. They were near the very spot where he and Wayne had crossed the river.

"Run!" Conor barked.

The pair took off up the merciless slope. He didn't pause to check behind him again but he could hear the shouts of men and the metallic banging of gear being shifted in the beds of the trucks. He couldn't swear to it but it sounded an awful lot like the rattle of ammo cans being pitched about. The same ammo cans used with belt-fed M60 machine guns.

As Wayne had mentioned earlier, it was hard always being right. It was awkward in the best of times but worse when you were correct in guessing the weapon being deployed to kill you. All speculation ended when Conor heard the unmistakable racking of the charging handle. They were about to be mowed down.

"Go! Go!" he shouted at Shannon. The crest of the hill was in sight. He keyed the mic on his radio. He was sucking wind, wheezing like a bad turbo, but he tried to form words. "Incoming...fire...now. Don't wait...on us."

Conor's full focus was on getting to the top of that hill without suffering a major cardiac event. His heart was pumping like a freight train, his ears ringing with it. Shannon was already there, bent over, hands on her knees and gasping for breath. Conor was just seconds behind her and patted her on the back, urging her forward. He couldn't stop to catch his breath or he might not get going again.

Chaos erupted behind them when the truck-mounted weapon opened fire on the position they held just moments ago. There was the enormous report of the rounds firing accompanied by the mechanical clatter as the gun cycled. There was a flat thump as the rounds impacted the hillside, chewing anything in their path to shreds. The Bond had either not noticed that their enemy had moved or they didn't care. He assumed that by this point they were probably tired of being kicked around and wanted to kill something.

Nothing could keep you moving like a machine gun at your back. Conor imagined he could actually finish a marathon with that kind of inspiration. On the rounded knoll at the crest of the hill, the terrain was more forgiving and the pair sprinted for all they were worth. They hadn't gone far before Barb came flying at them at full gallop, two saddled horses behind her. The terrified Shannon was on hers in seconds. Conor wasn't certain if she climbed aboard using the stirrups or simply sprang onto the horse's back, motivated by terror.

"Go!" Barb ordered, pointing Shannon in the direction the others had gone.

She did as she was told, bolting off on her mount. His legs spent from the climb, Conor hopped on one leg, chasing his circling horse with one foot in a stirrup, trying to find the momentum to spring onto its back.

"Do I need to get under your arse and shove?" Barb asked. "Get with it, old man."

Conor did not have the wind nor the energy to rebuff her comment, but the indignity of the insult must've provided some motivation because he grasped the saddle horn and swung himself aboard. He struggled to find his balance and get his right foot into the other stirrup. Finally squared away, he kicked the animal into motion. Barb accelerated past him and took the lead. Conor was pleased to find that they were on some type of logging road, a flat patch dozed into the mountainside but covered with leaves and dead grass. They could make good time here. They could escape.

54

The Bond's injured went untreated unless they were able to attend to themselves. All effort had been directed at taking the hillside. For the most part the men were acting of their own accord. During the initial attack, they leapt out of their vehicles with their weapons and minimal gear. Only a couple of them possessed the foresight to sling on their body armor. That was the reason so many of them lay dead now. Thomas was not happy about it. Most didn't have their radios either. The orders he shouted into his own, commands on how to best engage this enemy, had largely gone unheard and unheeded.

Had his men been listening, Thomas would never have supported a charge against that hillside. It was obvious they would lose too many men, which was exactly what happened when his men blindly jumped the guardrail and attempted to rush over there. It wasn't until an explosive device eradicated a dozen of his men in one fell swoop that they began to question the wisdom of their actions. It was only then that they sought out their leader and asked for direction.

Thomas was nearly blinded by anger, both at the enemy that had laid such waste to his troops and at his own men for allowing themselves to be killed. He was so angry at his own dead that he almost wished he could bring them back to life just so he could kill them himself for their ignorance. With the weapons and the training they possessed there was no reason they should have experienced such casualties. It was because they reacted like idiots. They were using their street minds instead of their military minds. Perhaps that was his own fault. He hadn't been enforcing discipline like he needed to be. They needed to be reminded they were soldiers now.

When his surviving troops rallied in a protected alley, he choked down his anger and started handing out orders. "Get a couple of those trucks over there and bring those M60s into play. If we can chew up that hill we'll end this thing. If you dumbasses had done that to begin with, half of you wouldn't be spread out dead all over the place."

Thomas had a lot more to say on that topic, but it would have to wait for another time. He would prefer his men be pissed off at the enemy and not at him. They needed to focus and get this shit wrapped up. It took the men several minutes to get a path cleared and bring the trucks around to the back street. Taking orders focused them. They were starting to function as a combat unit again and not like a bunch of knuckleheads planning a drive-by shooting.

While his men were getting the trucks into position Thomas watched the hillside. He had nothing to use but his naked eye. He'd been forced into a hasty retreat from his vehicle, diving out the door to save his neck. He didn't have his binoculars or any type of magnified optic on his weapon. He couldn't see anything on the hillside but one thing was certain. He was not facing a single enemy. If this was the Mad Mick, he was not acting alone.

Yet he couldn't be certain this was the Mad Mick. Could be that it was simply a bunch of pissed off townspeople who had enough of strangers showing up to wreck their town. Perhaps they'd taken a proactive approach and decided they would drive The Bond out of town before they had the opportunity to get into trouble. He might never know, but he would take measures just in case that was the situation. He would level this town before he left. He would burn it to the ground and he'd blow up what wouldn't burn.

When the M60 started firing it got his head back in the game. He found a pair of binoculars in the cab of a truck and scanned the hillside for any sign of the people who'd been shooting at them. He didn't see anything but he didn't tell his men to quit firing. If nothing else, that heavy gun sent a message. It let people know what was waiting on them if they messed with him.

"Hey, T!" one of the men called over the rattle of the machine gun.

Thomas cupped a hand over his ear to better hear what he had to say.

"You want us to drop some mortar rounds on them?"

His first instinct was to say no. Since he couldn't see the enemy and had no intelligence that would assist him in directing their fire, part of him thought they shouldn't waste the rounds. They might need them later. Another part of him thought this could serve the same purpose as the machine gun fire. Sometimes it was as important to send a message as to inflict casualties, though inflicting casualties was pretty damn nice too. So why not?

He grinned and nodded in the man's direction. "Light'em up!"

Two men teamed up on the weapon and had it set up in no time. Thomas went to their side and directed them where to send a round.

"We have a lot of these things," one of the men said. "We should use them before they go stale." The men didn't really think the rounds went stale. It was just true that all soldiers would prefer to use ammo rather than carry it around.

"Drop one on that first target I gave you," Thomas instructed. "Then drop a second fifty yards directly behind it. Put another fifty yards behind that. Three total."

"Roger that, T."

Thomas watched with the binoculars. He saw no signs of their attackers. He went to the machine gunners and signaled them to cease-fire. It was no use cooking the barrels. They didn't carry spares. He gestured at the mortar team. "Fire!"

They sent the first round. All the men watched with satisfaction as it blew a chunk out of the hillside, raining dirt and splinters all around them. When they were done, Thomas was going to send a team over there and they better find some bodies.

55

When the mortar fire ceased, Conor was certain The Bond was done with their random shelling. They'd gotten it out of their system. They had no targeting intelligence and their leader apparently had the restraint to know when it was time to stop. If he'd been trying to send a message, Conor received it loud and clear. He was certain of what kind of weaponry The Bond had now and that made it even more critical that he keep these people away from home. A mortar round on Wayne's camp could wipe out all his people and preparations. The same for the pastor's camp. Worse yet, if a round was dropped on Conor's precious compound the efforts of the last decade of his life would be reduced to rubble.

He directed Barb's group back in the general direction of Route 23 when The Bond quit firing on them. Deep in the forest they made camp at a clearing along a gravel road. A high chain link fence surrounded green pipes and panels of electrical switchgear. Shannon checked the wounded while Barb instructed the group to get several small fires going. They would put off less light than a large one. Even though they were in remote country, deep in the middle of gas company property, there was no use broadcasting their position.

The young man with the neck wound had died during their retreat and was tied across the back of his horse, a stained sleeping bag covering his body. Men from the pastor's group insisted on leading the horse out of a sense of duty toward one of their own.

"We should bury him here," Conor said.

"He needs to be returned to his people," a man named Jonathan insisted. "His momma will want to bury him in the family cemetery."

"That's a bad idea," Conor said. "By the time we make it home, that body is not going to be anything like the young man his family remembers. Better they remember him the way he left home. If you bury him here by this equipment it'll provide a good landmark and you can get his family back here to pay their respects."

"It don't seem right," Jonathan mumbled.

"It's not," Conor said, "but it's what has to be done."

He went to one of the packhorses and retrieved two folding Gerber shovels. He assembled one and handed it to Jonathan, then started unfolding the second.

"You bring these because you expected to dig graves?" one of the men asked.

Conor nodded. "Sadly, yes. Where do you think we should dig?"

They eventually settled on a location that was outside of the work zone and would provide easy digging. While Conor and a handful of men from the pastor's group dug the grave, others set about making a marker. They used a folding saw to cut two lengths from a tree branch. With a couple of wraps of paracord they formed a rough cross.

The Appalachian Mountains were nearly half a billion years old, though Pastor White would beg to differ. Over that time, most of the soil had eroded from the ridge tops, leaving only the thinnest layer. The men were only able to dig a little more than three feet before they hit a solid limestone sheet.

"Do we have to start again?" a sweating man asked. "I'm not sure I have another grave in me."

Conor sighed in frustration. "This entire ridge is probably just like this. I think we're going to have to go ahead and bury him, then cover the grave with rocks to keep out predators."

The thought of predators tearing into the grave didn't sit right with the men. A sour expression crossed all their faces, as if each man had shared a sip of the same spoiled milk. They all understood the truth of it though. It was a bad spot for dying. They'd all dug holes in these mountains before, whether it be hunting ginseng, burying a carcass, or digging to set up a moonshine still.

They gently placed the body in the ground and tugged the sleeping bag up over the dead man's face. They took turns shoveling dirt over him, then worked by headlamps to pile rocks over the fresh soil. The pastor's group insisted on saying a few words over the dead man. Conor was quite impressed at their restraint, having heard that they could often go on for hours until even the corpse was rolling its eyes and begging them to shut up already.

With their grim work behind them everyone gathered around the fires. Wayne and Sam had volunteered to do the cooking that night and put together a rice concoction. Tired and traumatized by the events of the day, no one realized how hungry they were until the food appeared before them. Then they couldn't get their cups, plates, and mess kits out fast enough. Soon they were sitting on rocks, downed logs, and their own packs eating as fast as they could shovel it into their faces.

"Do any of you know what this place is?" Conor asked, gesturing toward the fenced enclosure. "I've lived here for a while but I've not seen anything like this."

"It's the PLC panels," a man named Lonzo replied. "It's how they monitor the gas control valves from back at the office. It's your computerized controls."

"Did you work in that industry?" Conor asked.

Lonzo nodded. "For over twenty years. I built these panels and maintained them."

"In this area?"

"Here, home, all the way up into West Virginia. I've worked for a couple of different outfits."

"What happens to the gas in the line since we don't have power?" Conor continued.

"Well, none of this stuff right here works without power. All your communication and remote control capabilities are lost. Your prime movers, your compressors, can still work if you activate them directly."

"Even without power?" Conor asked.

Lonzo stared at him like he was an idiot. "The compressors can make their own power. They have generators built into them and they got fuel running right there in the pipeline. They draw off just enough gas to run. It's a pretty smart system."

"So the system works, you just can't control it remotely?"

"I suppose, but I've never tried to do it that way, except during the initial installation and startup. I've never come back and done it after it's all hooked up and running."

An idea formed in Conor's mind. He turned it around in his head and examined it from all sides like a 3-D model being manipulated in design software. Around him, exhausted people filtered off to turn in for the night. Conor had no idea what time it was and could not remember the last time he'd slept. Accepting that the day ahead of him was likely to be a beast he decided to throttle his mind back and turn in.

He unrolled his sleeping bag, stretching it out on the ground beside Barb's.

"So what's the plan for tomorrow?" she asked now that they were alone.

"I don't rightly know yet," Conor said. "But I'll be dreaming about it and I'll let you know in the morning."

"Sometimes, Dad, you're completely full of shit."

"There's some things in this world you can't explain, Barb. The working of my mind is one of them. All I know is that when I wake up in the morning, you'll have your answer."

"I think the lack of oxygen at this altitude is affecting your brain."

"Love you too. Good night."

56

It was a dark, cold night. Hours had passed since the early winter sunset. Thomas stood on the bank of the Levisa River watching the moonlight reflect off the rocks. He couldn't recall that he'd ever spent any time beside a river like this, listening to the water tumble over the rocks. It was relaxing, like a fountain at the mall. His relaxation was further aided by the joint pinched between his cold fingers.

The scuff of boots on asphalt caught his attention and he found Lawdog behind him. Other than to shout a few orders in his direction, Thomas hadn't really spent any time talking to Lawdog since things broke loose that day. The two of them needed to have a serious talk at some point but there was business to attend to first.

"What's the damage?" Thomas asked.

"Twenty-three men either died in combat or were made dead because we couldn't treat their injuries. We got two more so severely injured that they might make it or might not. I figured we were hurting for men at this point, so I didn't want to kill them if I didn't have to. The rest will make it."

Thomas nodded stoically while he absorbed the information.

"You may redistribute the teams as necessary," he said, turning back to the water.

Lawdog knew he'd been dismissed but he wasn't done. "Sir, the teams need to know how much effort to put into this camp before they set up. Is this a one night deal or are we heading out tomorrow?"

Thomas let out a long, frustrated sigh. In the low light neither man could read the other's expression. "The men want to know that, Lawdog, or *you* want to know that?"

"We *all* need to know that."

Reading between the lines, Thomas began to get angry. "So what you really feel you need to know is if we're staying here for a while or if we're heading out after the Mad Mick?" He was getting that tone that warned most men off. Tonight it wasn't working. Lawdog just wouldn't shut up.

"I guess. Or if we're headed in some entirely different direction?" Lawdog said. "I would assume that's an option. Hell, we could even head west. We can do anything we want to do."

"What *I* want to do is track down the Mad Mick," Thomas said. "Look, I know what you're doing. You're over here sniffing around like some mangy dog, trying to figure out if I'm ready to call off this mission or not. That it?"

Lawdog didn't respond. Thomas was right, though. That was exactly what he was getting at. The two men continued to stare at each other without being able to make out more than the vaguest silhouette. Without expressions or menacing glares this could go on all night.

Lawdog finally broke the silence. "Thomas, we've known each other long time. Do I have permission to speak freely with you?"

Thomas chuckled. There was a rhythmic grating to it, like a rusty chain being slowly pulled from a barrel. "Lawdog, this ain't the Army anymore. A man can say any fucking thing he wants to say. He can do anything he wants to do. That doesn't mean we're without consequences though. I can do what I want to do and die for doing it. You can say what you want to say, but you may have to answer for it. You feeling me? You make the call."

Lawdog kept going, which surprised Thomas. Lawdog was getting above his raising. Too big for his britches, as Thomas's grandmother would have said.

"I know the roots of this organization, T. I know where we came from and I been there since the beginning. I believe in this. Our roots are twisted together and that makes us stronger. That gives us the bond that you're so fond of. But we can't keep losing people at this rate. It's going to leave us weak. I think we're either going to have to take on more people or easier missions. One or the other."

"Both of which mean giving up on this Mad Mick, right?"

"I'm not sure he's worth it," Lawdog said. "Who knows if he's even real? He may just be some shit people make up, like Santa Claus or the boogeyman. He may be the scary face of a bunch of old hillbillies or coal miners that are running around driving off strangers. We don't even know who we're fighting. They know this country and we don't. We had superior firepower and more training. We should have dusted those assholes but we didn't find a single dead body over there."

"That don't mean we didn't hit anybody," Thomas said. "They could have carried off their dead."

"They might have but I bet they didn't carry off twenty-three dead."

That stung, and both men fell silent. The joint Thomas was smoking had gone out from his inattention. He pulled a lighter from his pocket and flicked it to life. Briefly illuminated in that warm flare of light, his face appeared almost disembodied, the only thing of substance in an enormous black void. Thomas took a hit and extended it to Lawdog.

"You've given me a lot to think about. Let's sleep on it and we can deal with this shit in the morning. I'm too tired for decisions."

Lawdog stepped forward and took the joint. He had to pinch carefully to avoid burning his fingers. He closed his eyes and took a big draw, anxious for the relaxation it would provide. It'd been a rough day and he was whipped.

The gunshot that shattered the night startled everyone except

Lawdog. He died so fast he had no time to be concerned. His last thoughts were of a good night's sleep before the bullet severed the connection between his spine and brain. He would have a good sleep all right. He would sleep like the dead.

Thomas picked up his joint from the ground and took another hit from it. He keyed the mic on his radio. "That was me. Shot at a coyote. No worries."

He briefly considered tossing Lawdog's body over the rail and into the water but that was an awful lot of effort with no benefit. He walked back to the fire. The circle of men were on edge from the gunshot and fell silent at Thomas's approach. If anyone noticed Lawdog's absence they had the sense to not comment on it.

Thomas pointed to Mundo. "You're the lieutenant now. Second in command."

Mundo's eyes widened. He understood what that meant and the potential consequences of that position.

Coyote my ass, he thought. Make the wrong call and he could end up like Lawdog.

He didn't raise his eyes from the fire. "Thank you, T."

He sure as hell didn't mean it.

57

Everyone was slow to wake at Barb's camp. Breakfast consisted of leftovers from the previous night's dinner. There was no coffee, only spring water they'd filtered into bottles. Conor was awakened by the movements around him. He was usually a light sleeper, one of the first up, but took this as an indication of how exhausted he truly was. He glanced around groggily and found Barb sitting on her sleeping bag staring at him.

"Jesus, it's like having a bloody cat, waking to find them staring at you. You never know if they're demanding food or trying to decide if they can eat you."

Barb ignored him. "So what did the great Oracle of Bojangles figure out in his sleep?"

Conor groaned. "I'm not going to repeat what my belly just called you. Why did you have to do that? You know how I feel about you bringing up the fecking Bojangles when I'm on the cusp of starving to death."

"I've got no biscuits to offer the Oracle but we do have some reheated rice available."

Conor sat up in his sleeping bag and rubbed his eyes, pulled his black toboggan off and scratched his head. He checked his watch. "I've wasted an hour of daylight."

Barb shrugged. "It's okay. I think these people needed to rest. Yesterday was a bit much for some of them."

Conor regarded his daughter. "What about you, lass? How you holding up?"

"Fine," she said simply, as if it were merely any other day.

Maybe it was just any other day for her. She trained obsessively, so the physical demands of the previous day would have been inconsequential for her. Additionally, growing up in his shadow, on the periphery of his world of paranoia and violence, none of the rest of it may have phased her either. She might have been the best suited of the group, aside from Conor himself, to experience days like yesterday with no lingering effect.

"You did well with your people," Conor said. "I haven't seen you working with them the entire time, of course, but what I saw was impressive. You gave orders efficiently and you didn't lose your cool. You got people to do what you needed without having to threaten them. That's certainly the best way to lead if you have that option."

"I lost my cool a couple of times and I'm pretty sure I did threaten a few of them, but enough about me. What's on the agenda for today?" She wasn't uncomfortable with the praise but she wanted to move past it. It was a waste of time as far as she was concerned.

Conor smiled. He was trying to compliment her but she didn't like him calling attention to her progress. "As a matter of fact I did come up with a plan. Once I get squared away I need to speak with you, Wayne, and Lonzo."

Barb raised a curious eyebrow at him. "Lonzo?"

Conor nodded. "The guy who said he had worked on gas wells."

"I know who he is, but why do you need to speak to him? Did it somehow come to you in your dreams that Lonzo was the missing piece of the plan?"

"You'll know when I've stowed my gear and watered the nearest tree. If you can go find those two and bring them back here without raising a lot of attention, you'll find out."

With a frustrated sigh, Barb pushed herself up from the ground and walked off. Conor attended to his business in order of urgency. He stowed his gear in his pack and refilled his grenade pouches from his saddlebags. He was thumbing 5.56 rounds into depleted magazines when Barb returned with her companions.

Conor was pleased that she chose not to openly display her sarcasm and frustration in front of the other two men. She refrained from addressing him as the Oracle, which he took as a sign that she was beginning to understand the responsibility that came with her role. She apparently grasped that, even among this crew of guerrilla fighters, she needed to be professional.

Conor got to his feet and slung his rifle over his shoulder, making a quick check to make sure he hadn't left any gear behind. "Let's take a little walk."

"I'm uncomfortable being singled out like this," Lonzo said. "I don't like keeping secrets from the rest of my group."

"There aren't any secrets," Conor said. "But I have a plan and it's not up for debate. Everyone has a role. Once you understand your role, we can tell everyone else. They all have a role to play. This ends tonight."

"What ends tonight?" Wayne asked.

"The Bond, my friend. The Bond ends tonight."

58

With a lighter load, their gear stripped to the basics, Barb and Conor rode hard toward the scene of their previous battle with The Bond. At the fastest pace they could push from the horses they reached the hill above Allen City in a little more than an hour. Just as Conor expected, their enemy had not left town yet. They would have to make sure they had collected all the gear from the dead. They would have to check the vehicles carefully to make sure nothing critical had been damaged in the gunfight. If a vehicle was disabled they would require a little time to transfer gear from that vehicle to an undamaged vehicle. At a minimum Conor knew that some windshields would have to be removed because Barb shot holes in a few of them.

Conor examined the scene through the optic of his Accuracy International rifle. Barb used binoculars. The Bond trucks were organized into a neat line along the riverfront street. Their tanker moved along the convoy, filling the individual fuel tanks. Behind the last of the trucks the men were assembled in a loose group.

"Looks like they're having a little meeting," Conor said.

"I bet they stayed at my old camp," Barb said. "That giant woodstove was a nice feature."

"Well, we know they can only go forward. The bridge I blew up was their only retreat."

"I'm sure there are back roads out of town," Barb said. "Some of them probably head north."

"I'm sure there are too. That's why we're here. Our job is to make sure they continue to move forward."

Conor had explained the details of his plan to her already. They were one of three teams carrying out assigned tasks as part of Conor's plan. Each had a very specific role that was crucial to accomplishing the mission. Conor and Barb's team was just the two of them. Their task required very specific skills and a good deal of risk. He didn't feel comfortable giving it to anyone else.

"So what do we need to do?" Barb asked.

"They're at least pointed in the right direction. That's a start. If they get ahead of us in those vehicles though, we'll never catch up. We need to put a few obstacles in front of them. Something that might slow their roll a little bit."

"That's hard on horses too. We can put plenty of obstacles in front of them. Drop trees, roll cars, whatever we find, but they'll get from obstacle to obstacle faster than us. Eventually they'll catch up and pass us, hopefully not killing us in the process."

"If they do get past us, the burden falls on Wayne's team. I think I might have a way to kill two birds with one stone though. I can piss them off and give them an incentive to chase us."

"Oh, I'm sure you can piss them off. It's a little talent you have, Dad."

Conor took offense. "Why, if that's not the pot calling the kettle black."

"I certainly inherited it from somewhere. It's genetics. You can't argue with science."

"More like you can't argue with *Barb*."

Conor laid out a hasty plan and received no objections from Barb. If she felt it was a harebrained scheme, she kept her mouth shut. From the scene unfolding below them, they knew there was little time before The Bond pulled out. If they weren't in position before those trucks started, Conor's plan wouldn't work.

As soon as Barb understood her role, Conor handed over his horse and began descending the same ravine in the hillside that had concealed him and Wayne yesterday, carrying only his Go Bag and his rifle. He had gravity on his side this time which helped tremendously. He was making a lot better progress going down than he'd made coming up.

In no time he was at the same spot along the riverbank where he left his little gift for his pursuers yesterday. The Bond, feeling no allegiance to their deceased, had not retrieved any of the bodies of the men Conor took out with his Claymore. Several had washed ashore or were hung up on rocks. The wounds on their bodies attested not only to the effectiveness of his explosive device, but also to an abundant and healthy turtle population. There was no way his bomb was responsible for the missing digits and bite marks.

Conor gritted his teeth against the impending cold and made his way across the shallow river. There were more dead men scattered along the steep rock embankment but he ignored them. They were far from the first dead bodies he'd ever seen and they were of much less concern to him than the live soldiers. One kind shot back, the other didn't. He climbed carefully, making certain his rifle didn't clatter against the rocks and that he didn't dislodge any with his feet.

When he reached the top he flattened himself against the ground and parted the dead weeds beneath the guardrail. The bulk of The Bond troops, gathered at the rear of the convoy, were out of sight. The only man Conor could see was the bored fuel attendant waiting impatiently for the slow twelve-volt pump to fuel the trucks. Concerned that the troops might be released from their meeting at any moment, Conor had no time to arrive at an elaborate plan for his next step. This situation called for quick and dirty.

He rolled to his side and opened a long pouch on his plate carrier. He withdrew his custom suppressor and threaded it onto his 9mm. He stood as quietly and carefully as he could then eased over the guardrail. Once on pavement he closed the distance between him and the truck in short order. He heard the distinctive metallic sound of the soldier tapping the fuel nozzle against the tank, getting out the last drops before he capped the tank.

Conor swung around the front of the tanker and leveled his Glock on the face of the confused fuel attendant. He had no time to react before Conor squeezed off a round. The man fell over backwards, the fuel nozzle clattering to the ground. The handgun was now too long for its holster and Conor didn't want to waste time unthreading the suppressor. He shoved the Glock through his battle belt and withdrew a Sharpie marker from the webbing on his plate carrier. He intended to leave a message on the dead man's forehead, as he was so fond of doing, but there was not enough undamaged tissue, so he slashed the man's shirt open and scribbled a message on the flesh of his stomach.

He made certain the fuel hose was secured and climbed aboard the tanker. While he'd driven one of these trucks before it'd been several years. He quickly familiarized himself with the controls and started the engine. He checked the mirrors and saw no one coming. It wasn't likely the sound of the engine would alarm anyone. They probably assumed it was the fuel tanker repositioning itself to fill another truck.

He'd forgotten how slow the damn things were. He accelerated and ground the gears as he shifted the five-speed. He checked his rearview again and found that the sound of his accelerating engine had finally garnered some attention. A few confused-looking men stood at the rear of the convoy trying to figure out what was going on. Conor knew they would figure it out soon enough. After all, he'd been kind enough to leave them a message.

Just beyond Barb's old camp, he passed her on the side of the road and waved. She gave him a thumbs up, then pushed a button on a remote control and detonated a charge. There was a sharp pop and two charges blew in tandem, dropping a pair of telephone poles across the road. He checked his rearview again and saw Barb hopping on her horse and galloping after him. The telephone poles would not be serious impediments, but they would slow the Bond enough to allow him to gain some distance.

The tanker was equipped with a winch and Conor stopped when he could to drag more debris into the road. He pulled leaning trees from the hillside, pulled trailers and cars into the road, and then tapped them with the rear bumper to wedge them into place. None of these barricades were meant to deter The Bond, merely to slow them. He wanted them to come after him.

He lost sight of Barb. Their plan was that she would travel by the road until she heard the trucks and then she was to disappear into the hillside like a ghost, taking Conor's horse with her. They had a secondary plan from that point. The Bond would be pinched in the middle with Conor irritating them from the front and Barb nipping at their heels like a Chihuahua.

59

It was Mundo who first noticed the roar of the tanker truck's engine. The guy was only moving twenty feet at a time. How fast did he need to go? Mundo took a few steps back from the group and craned his neck to get a better look down the row of trucks.

Thomas noticed Mundo's distraction and was not happy about it, especially after the poor performance of his troops yesterday. "Am I boring you?"

"No, T," Mundo replied, his attention glued to the tanker. "I'm just not sure what that fool is doing."

"I think he's turning the tanker around," Thomas offered. "Maybe you should just tighten your own shit up and not worry about him."

"No, T, something is wrong. He's still going. His ass is booking down the road."

Thomas moved to where he could see down the other side of the convoy. "Shit, is that a body on the ground?"

Thomas bolted toward the head of the convoy with his men in tow. They spread out to both sides of the convoy, their rifles at the ready. Everyone was scanning windows and searching beneath cars.

They were checking over the guardrail and staring toward the hill beyond it, where their enemy had retreated yesterday.

Thomas beat everyone to the body, recognizing that it was the man who should have been driving that truck. "Dammit!" He stalked off angrily. All his men standing right there, in broad daylight, and he lost a man and a truck.

Mundo flipped the dead's man's shirt out of the way, noticing the ink on the man's body. "What's that?"

"Looks like a tattoo, man," Droopy said.

"That ain't no ink. T, you need to see this."

Thomas stalked back over and read the message scribbled on the man's belly: *Go home, boys, before you piss me off, signed The Mad Mick.*

"Meanwhile that tanker is getting farther away and y'all ain't doing shit about it!" Thomas barked. "Get it back!"

Everyone flew to their positions. Engines were started and weapons readied. Before they could pull out, there was an explosion in the direction of the fleeing tanker.

"You think he blew it up?" Mundo asked into his radio.

"Negative," Thomas replied. *"Would have been louder."*

They quickly found the source of the explosion when they ran up on the two downed telephone poles. The men wasted no time there. One was immediately out of his truck and dragging the winch cable to fasten it to the first pole. He stepped clear while the driver winched it in, then directed a second truck to remove the second pole while Jawbone unhooked the winch cable from the first. Unfortunately for them, just getting the poles clear of the road was not enough to let them pass. The downed power lines were draped and tangled across the road. Mundo was able to snip them out of the way with bolt cutters but it took time. As soon as the lines dropped, the convoy charged through. The entire effort, though conducted as quickly as possible, took around fifteen minutes.

That was not to be their last obstacle in this pursuit. They found themselves unable to go a single mile without running into some roadblock the Mad Mick left for them. Several times, blinded by rage,

Thomas directed a driver to push obstacles from the road. It never worked. Every little trap was laid out to prevent that, like some maddening puzzle.

After four hours of travel they were no closer to securing their stolen tanker. Thomas insisted they had to be gaining ground. They had dealt with each obstacle as efficiently as possible. Surely they were cutting through them faster than the Mad Mick was putting them in place. Then they hit the coal truck and the whole thing ground to a halt.

Thomas could only imagine that the coal truck had ran out of fuel while traveling fully loaded. From the scene before him, it appeared that the Mad Mick must have transferred over enough fuel to restart the coal truck and raise the dump bed. He could have just dumped the load in the highway but he didn't. He'd raised the bed without opening the rear gate, raising the center of gravity and making the truck extremely unstable. From that point it appeared as if the Mad Mick had backed the tanker into the coal truck and rocked it enough that it had fallen over. Not only was the road entirely blocked by a load of coal, but by a coal truck laying on its side, the bed fully raised.

Thomas climbed out of his truck and ranted. He yelled and cursed, dumped a magazine of ammo at full auto, shooting into the woods ahead of them. When that failed to make him feel better, he dumped another. Only then did his calm rationality return to him. He took a deep breath and went to study the problem before them.

This would not be an easy job. It might take an entire day to remove this mess, but what option did they have? As Lawdog had suggested before his unfortunate demise, was it time to give up? Should they back the trucks down the road, find a place to turn around, and escape this Appalachian hellhole? He would study the GPS while his men worked. It was possible there was some other road that would circumvent this obstacle.

We can do this, he reminded himself. They were The Bond, the most hardened of the hard. While the Army showed up to rescue you, The Bond showed up to kill you and take your shit. While the Army showed up to defend you, The Bond showed up to crush your soul. That was exactly what they would do when they found this Mad Mick. They would crush his soul and every soul he'd ever cared about.

Then the first shot came.

60

Conor stashed the tanker truck behind an abandoned mobile home a mile past the overturned coal truck. He used his radio to coordinate a rendezvous with Barb and retrieved his horse. They put the second phase of the plan into action before The Bond came upon the substantial roadblock. It was critical they get into position because darkness came early in the steep mountain valleys. By 3 PM the sun was at a shallow angle and its light merely skimmed across the top of the ridges, leaving the bottomland in early darkness.

Route 23 followed the river but the valley broadened out there, spreading about one hundred and fifty yards at its widest point. The river bisected that bottom, and to either side of it were marshy expanses that would be difficult to negotiate on foot. It was a cold muck full of briers that would frustrate the most determined of men. Halfway up the slope of the opposite hill was an overgrown logging road. Two thick poplars had fallen across each other and created a fortified shooting position. From here Barb was facing a three hundred yard shot to the trap they'd created for The Bond. That was a comfortable distance for her. At that range she could do some damage. She was already wearing her bump helmet. If the fight went on into the darkness she could drop her night vision and keep shooting.

Conor had improvised a ghillie suit. It might not have been necessary in other seasons of the year where there was more ground cover, but it was in short supply now. He gathered what materials he could – broomsedge, dry grass, holly, and twigs with brown leaves. He fashioned an outfit he was halfway proud of until Barb started in on him.

"Is your new call sign Houseplant?" she asked.

Conor was lining up his own smart remark when they heard the sound of the trucks echoing through the valley. "Be careful," he warned, then he skipped down the slope toward the marsh. He wanted to shoot from a different position, spreading out their fire. From the valley bottom he would have less cover than Barb. Hopefully his ghillie suit would offer him some level of camouflage and not look like a houseplant sitting in a field.

They agreed that no one would take a shot at any target on their side of the river. If the enemy got that far, the rules would change immediately. At that point Conor and Barb were to meet at the horses and implement the next stage of their plan.

Barb, higher in the mountain and with a better vantage point, was the first to spot The Bond trucks. "Barb for Houseplant, Barb for Houseplant. I have a visual."

"Houseplant to Smart Ass, acknowledged. I can see them now."

Barb snickered to herself. She loved pissing her dad off.

"I count one less truck than yesterday," Conor said. *"We must have taken one out of the fight."*

"Roger that, Houseplant. Let's see if we can do worse today."

"Be ready to fire but hold for my order."

"Acknowledged."

They watched patiently through The Bond's arrival at the scene of the overturned coal truck. Conor was particularly proud of the obstacle he'd left in their way. It was a matter of simple physics. With no guardrail dividing the four-lane highway in this section, he'd managed to block the entire road with a single obstacle. In these steep mountains, there was no clearance to either side of the road for the group to pass.

Watching through the optic of his sniper rifle Conor was getting a pretty good idea of who was in charge. It had to be the guy who was so pissed-off, ranting and raving. Everyone was deferring to the guy, practically shying away from him. Conor had a clear shot at him. Part of him thought pulling the trigger would be the best move. Take him out.

It would produce the opposite result of what he was interested in though. He wanted to keep these guys here, consolidated into a single unit, so he could finish them off. He was fairly certain, seeing the leadership dynamic, that all these men only stayed out of fear of their commander. If he were to assassinate him, drop him dead in his tracks, the rest of the men would probably all go home. Just as he'd warned his group, they would become someone else's problem then and none of these men deserved to be turned loose on another community. They'd already been infected by power, knew that they could take what they wanted by force. They could take advantage of the good nature of the people around them. If they were allowed to escape they would form another entity just like The Bond. This was a virus that needed to be dealt with, once and for all.

While their leader threw his tantrum, the rest of the men formed a tight perimeter around the convoy with their weapons. While they were technically performing their duty, he could sense the undercurrent behind their actions. They were trying to stay clear of their leader, to avoid his wrath. Conor figured most of them probably wanted a cigarette but were afraid it might appear that they were shirking their duties. An unstable leader like this one might shoot them for the infraction. A man like that ruled by threat of violence. That was how he kept other hard and violent men working for him. That was how he cemented The Bond.

"Conor for Barb."

"*Go for Barb.*"

"I want you to target that cluster of men at the rear of the convoy. While you're focusing on human targets I'm going to try and disable some of those trucks. They're running old non-directional tires, so I should be able to punch holes right through them. I did it once before with a handgun. Once we start shooting it's going to be chaotic. If you see men branching out to launch an offensive you let me know. I'll do the same for you. If that happens, we retreat and meet up at the horses. Got it?"

"Roger that, Houseplant. Let's do this."

"Fire when ready."

Barb calculated the holdover on her reticle and aligned the appropriate dot with the chest of her intended target. Some of the men appeared to be wearing body armor but she could tell by the way his plate carrier hung this guy had opted to ditch the heavy plates. He would pay for his laziness. She squeezed the trigger and sent a round.

The man flinched, screamed, and dropped. By the time the men around him heard the shot and registered what happened, she put a round in the neck of the man standing beside the first. Bond soldiers were scattering in all directions. One had not taken cover but was crouched beside the dead bodies, studying the hillside where Barb hid. She made him pay for his boldness. She couldn't tell if he was wearing armor or not due to his stance. She aligned her crosshairs on him and sent three rounds, one after another, until he fell over backwards. She was not certain if she'd done damage or if the impacts had simply shoved him backwards so she aimed for a meaty thigh and put a bullet in it for good measure.

The truck body shifted without warning, startling the men hiding behind it. They didn't know what was going on and scurried from their hiding place as if the truck might overturn. Barb took the opportunity to drop another of them. She noticed the steady boom of Conor's high-powered rifle at that point. He was working his magic, moving up and down the line taking out tires. Occasionally, in his search for vulnerable rubber, his optic crossed the face of a terrified Bond soldier. Unwilling to pass up a target of opportunity, Conor hastily backed up and added a new orifice to the wide-eyed face.

When no more of The Bond soldiers presented themselves as

targets Barb aimed for the asphalt surface of the road, trying to ricochet bullet splatter beneath the trucks and flush the men out. It was an effective technique and drove limping men into the open. They tried to find better hiding spots, diving for ditches or flattening themselves behind the guardrail. Running from Barb was a mistake. In doing so, these men turned their bodies sideways to her, exposing a gap in their armor. She aimed high on their sides and dropped several more.

Time in a firefight could be deceptive. What had in actuality been around three or four minutes seemed more like twenty. Barb was late into her second magazine and she had no idea how many rounds Conor had fired. He was cycling that bolt as fast as he could work it. They could both hear shouting across the road, orders being given. Someone was attempting to make these men fall back on their training and do battle.

"They're organizing," came Conor's voice over the radio. *"Time to back out. Rally at the horses."*

"Acknowledged."

Barb rapidly swapped for a fresh magazine. All of her empties were already stashed in pouches. Aware that there were probably men with optics scanning the hillside for her and Conor, she retreated carefully. On the densely wooded hillside, with so many vertical trees, it would be quick lateral movement that would draw the eye. She did her best not to provide that movement. She walked steadily from tree to tree, pausing behind each new cover to locate her next position before moving again.

Frustrated that they'd been unable to spot her, The Bond soldiers began randomly firing at the hillside. The rounds were not close and did not appear to be targeted to any particular area.

"You okay up there, Barb?"

Barb keyed her mic. "I don't think they see me, Dad. I think they're just trying to flush up some movement."

"Watch the top of those trucks. At least three have ring mounts for heavy guns. If you see them put one in place, you run like hell. I don't care if they see you or not at that point. Just run."

"Got it. What's your ETA to the horses?"

"Ten minutes. All uphill."

"Roger that, Dad. Be careful."

"Houseplant out."

She smiled. He'd adopted the name.

61

Barb was waiting nervously at the horses when Conor showed up. He called to her on the radio as he approached the position to make sure she was aware he was approaching. He felt like he was dying of a coronary climbing the hill. The last thing he needed was to get offed by friendly fire at the top.

The sun had set somewhere far beyond their view and color was leaving the world. Everything became shades of black and gray. Long shadows lost their form, dissolving and seeping into the night. Barb had no trouble recognizing the man-shaped houseplant staggering toward her.

"Jesus, Dad, could you not have lost the ghillie suit? Surely the climb would be easier without that mess strapped to you."

Conor didn't respond. It wasn't rudeness but the fact that he had no wind left. He was puffing like a bellows. He dragged the large backpack off his hobbled horse and dropped it to the ground, putting the sniper rifle away.

"You gonna make it, old man?" Despite her snarky tone she was legitimately concerned. Her dad tried to keep himself in shape but these mountains were made for deer, not men. No one fared well chugging up the side of one.

When Conor had the rifle packed away he lashed it to his horse and hastily sucked down a few gulps of water, spilling it down his face and neck as he drank.

"Watering yourself, houseplant?"

Conor smiled but couldn't reply. He took another, more careful drink. When he was done, he concentrated on speaking. "You take...the horses. Go to Wayne...and Lonzo. I'll lead The Bond there."

"I thought *we* were supposed to lead The Bond there. You know, as a team?"

"It's going to be too dangerous in full dark. We'll lose track of each other. Somebody has to let Lonzo know we're coming and make sure the trap is ready."

Barb sighed. "You did see there's another fifty or sixty men left down there, right?"

Conor nodded, taking another drink.

"Sixty men against one wheezing geezer dressed like a houseplant."

Conor grinned. "I know. Doesn't hardly seem fair does it? Poor bastards won't have a chance in Hell."

"Should I warn them? Give them a chance to prepare for what awaits them?"

"I think not. We'll let it be a surprise, daughter. Besides, they had their chance to turn around and didn't take it. They've earned their fate."

Barb smiled at her father's optimism. She suspected it was his Irish roots, so used to being the underdog that the odds didn't concern him in the least. Whatever it was, she hoped she'd inherited a fair dose of it. She hugged her dad, their gear and weapons rattling together as they embraced. She removed the hobbles from the horses, attached a lead to Conor's, and then climbed onto hers. She dropped her night vision in front of her eyes and turned the knob.

"Be safe," Conor said with a wave.

Barb saluted. "Keep your branches low, Houseplant."

62

No longer burdened by the heavy sniper rifle, Conor moved easier through the woods. Barb was correct that the ghillie suit was a little awkward but he felt like he needed it. He was certain his opponents had night vision because he'd retrieved military-issue units from their dead bodies. He had no indication that they had thermal, so the ghillie suit would allow him to hide in plain sight. It would be perfect for what he had in mind for them.

He angled back off the ridge, not aiming for the trapped vehicles but for the road ahead of it. The Bond was stuck for the night. There was no way they had enough tires to repair all of the vehicles. He also expected they'd be reluctant to stand out in the open and work on them if they were at risk of taking fire. He wanted them to come out into the night and play. They just needed a little incentive.

He walked quietly since the sound of crunching leaves carried a long way in the darkness. Through his night vision he could see movement around the trucks. The men were active but they were quiet, and there were no campfires. He had clear shots at some of them but he didn't take them. He was here to play a different game this time.

He eventually worked his way into a position where he was high above the Bond soldiers on their side of the road. That would take them by surprise. He was close enough that they could hear him when he called to them. It was time to talk. To make certain he had their attention, he gave a long high-pitched rebel yell that cut the night like the slash of a machete.

It was so primal that it was not immediately recognizable as a human sound. He could imagine it chilling those men to the bone as they listened to it echo down the wooded valley, trying to figure out what it was. Even without words, the message was clear. They were no longer the hunters there. They were no longer the top-tier predator. There was something more dangerous and more violent out there in the night. The Bond was about to learn how far down the food chain they'd slid.

"Ahoy, assholes!" Conor bellowed, allowing his voice to echo dramatically before he continued. "You should've run when you had the chance. Now you're mine. You'll never leave here alive."

There was no response for a moment. Conor let them stew. He could imagine what was going on in the men's heads. He could sense the fear, the sensation of a claw tightening around their hearts. These were city men, unused to the woods and the wildness of the mountains. They were outside of their element and far beyond their comfort zone. They might as well have been on the moon.

"Is this the Mad Mick?" came a shouted response from the roadway.

Conor shifted positions again. When he replied, it was from a different place on the mountain. "The one and only. And who do I have the pleasure of speaking to?"

"My name is Thomas. And if you're such a badass, why don't you bring your army down here and take us on man to man? Why you hiding up there on the mountain like some kind of chickenshit?"

Conor moved again. "Oh, there's no army. There never was. That was just me and my daughter kicking your ass up and down the road like a tin can. I sent her on home. Didn't figure I needed her anymore since we cut you down to a more manageable size."

Men scrambled at Thomas's direction, trying desperately to find

Conor's location on the hillside but he eluded them, always a step ahead. They couldn't help but be terrified. In this alien country, perhaps this *man* wasn't even a man? Perhaps he was some kind of ghost, some kind of evil mountain troll who preyed on travelers, like something out of a fairytale or legend?

Thomas laughed loudly, making sure it rolled to fill the valley around them. He also had a sense of drama. "You that confident in yourself? I've got over a hundred men down here ready to shred you to pieces."

It was Conor's turn to laugh, loud and genuine, rolling through the mountains like the chilling cackle of a hyena. He'd changed positions again, the sound coming from a different direction than Thomas expected. "You *had* over a hundred men but I've probably killed half of them already. Just like I'm going to kill you."

It took Thomas some time to reply to that, so angry he could barely speak. "And just how you intend to do that?"

When the reply came, Conor was again in a position that was totally unexpected. He stood atop the bed of the overturned dump truck. He boldly faced Thomas and the rest of the Bond soldiers, appearing like some brazen mountain god in his ghillie suit.

"I intend to kill you one man at a time," Conor replied, tossing a grenade into their midst.

Conor leapt from the truck bed just before the explosion shook the valley. In the aftermath, while debris rained down on him, he heard Thomas's command bellowed to his troops.

"Get him!"

63

Barb stuck to the logging roads, staying high on the ridge. She constantly worked her radio, trying to find Wayne and Lonzo. After a little more than an hour of riding, she heard the sound of mechanical equipment running in the distance. She had to be getting close and began to work her radio in earnest.

"*Barb!*" Wayne replied over the radio. "*I was starting to worry about you guys. Is everyone okay?*"

"We're okay. Is everything going to be ready?"

"*It should be. Lonzo found the perfect place and everything is working just as expected.*"

"I can hear you guys but I can't see you," Barb said. "Can you flash a light or something?"

Barb focused on the area where the sound appeared to be coming from, though it was confusing the way noise bounced around. Eventually she saw a flash of light in the trees and headed in that direction. In another fifteen minutes, she had joined the men at a fenced enclosure that was much larger than the one where they camped the previous night.

"What is this place?" she asked.

"Some kind of pumping station for natural gas," Wayne answered.

"The engine you hear running is a compressor. It runs off the natural gas in the pipeline. That tank you see is the odorant that gives natural gas its sulfur smell. It's added right here at the compressor station."

"But they've turned the odorant off, right? Lonzo said that would make it undetectable."

"It's turned off. He said there might be some residual odorant in the gas already standing in the pipeline but that the odor would be faint."

"And the location? It's just right?"

"Relax," Wayne said. "Lonzo says it's perfect. He said the very thing we're doing is something they used to talk about on the job. You know the way bored employees sit around and talk about worst-case scenarios? Apparently, this was one of them."

Barb slid off her horse, tying it and Conor's to the chain-link fence. She stepped inside the enclosure and found Lonzo along with two other of the pastor's men, working in the glow of a red head-lamp. At her arrival, Lonzo gave her a brief glance then went back to his work. He seemed knowledgeable about the job but uncomfortable with the purpose of it. There were duties that he agreed to perform for the greater good but there were other aspects he refused to have any part of, insisting that someone else would have to be responsible for those. Barb assumed that duty would fall to her or Wayne.

"We may only have a couple of hours. Dad was poking the bear when I left. He and those men are on foot though. It will take them a little longer to get here."

Lonzo studied his watch. He glanced at Barb nervously, then back to his work. "I can only do what I can do."

"I have faith in you. My father had faith in you too. Is the gas flowing?"

"It's been flowing for hours," said Lonzo. "Just ain't sure it's going to do what you want it to do. Never tried something like that."

"We have a plan for that," Wayne added. "We have people surrounding the valley as a backup. I hope it doesn't come to that. The odds are a little better now that we've killed some of them but we're significantly outnumbered. Plus they're trained men fighting against our untrained men."

"You guys need to relax," Barb said. "My dad says it's good to plan, but don't waste time fighting the battle in your head before it actually gets here. It won't change the outcome."

"Your dad is a little too comfortable with taking lives," Lonzo said. "I think worrying about it is a natural reaction."

"There are times the world needs men like Conor," Wayne stated. "This is one of them."

64

Before the grenade detonated, Conor leapt from the bed of the overturned truck onto the sloped pile of coal. The fuse was a short one, the grenade blowing three seconds after he tossed it. In those three seconds, he heard men screaming, running, and even one dumb enough to shoot at him instead of taking cover. When it blew there were screams from the wounded and dying, the sound of men running in all directions. One voice, louder than the others, was barking orders.

Thomas was still alive.

Before bolting into the darkness, Conor leaned around one end of the dump truck and sprayed a half-dozen rushed shots into the fray. They weren't intended to hit anyone as much as to increase the sense of panic. Satisfied with his work, he retreated. As he moved, he scanned in all directions, his point of aim moving as he turned. He wanted them to pursue him but he was ready to drop anyone who got too close. Even over the chaos he heard the distinctive ratcheting sound of the charging handle on an M60.

Conor didn't hear anyone shouting orders to the gunner. Perhaps it was even Thomas himself who had leapt behind the weapon to chase Conor into the night. Either way, only seconds passed between his escape and the deafening rattle of 7.62 caliber slugs bouncing off the heavy dump bed and frame of the truck. Conor was already on the run, headed for his next position at the top of a rise along the road.

He paused there to fire a burst before ducking and sprinting away. He was performing now. This wasn't intended to be effective fire, merely to draw The Bond's attention and lure them in his direction. It had that effect. Conor could hear shouting as Thomas attempted to rally his troops. It took a significant effort since they were firing blindly in all directions, lost to the fear of this unseen enemy.

Thomas had never led men into combat outside of his role within The Bond. His understanding of battle tactics was a combination of the things he learned on the streets and what he learned under the command of other men in the military. This was like nothing he'd experienced before, like nothing any of them had trained for. Thomas was shoving men toward the fray, beating them on the back and urging them forward. When that failed, he made threats.

Part of the problem was not all of his men had night vision. The Bond had only procured around a dozen sets to begin with and they'd lost and broken a few along the way. Some of the men rushing out into the fight were wearing regular headlamps which not only made them targets but interfered with the effectiveness of the night vision gear.

While Thomas had managed to push nearly half his men into pursuit, it had required a monumental effort. When he finally found Mundo at the rear of the convoy, the man received the full brunt of his wrath. Thomas grabbed him by the collar and slammed him against the bed of one of the disabled trucks.

"You are my fucking lieutenant! You get out there and help find that bastard!" The glow of his red headlamp hit Mundo directly in the face and Thomas could see terror.

"You can't fight a man you can't see," Mundo said. "This is a suicide mission. We go out there after that guy and he's going to kill every one of us. We been walking into a trap this whole time and you never saw it. I knew it. Lawdog saw it and you killed him."

That statement inflamed Thomas and he drew his pistol, shoving it against the side of Mundo's temple. "You got two choices. You can die here or take your chances out there."

Mundo made his decision. He gritted his teeth. "I'll go, T."

Thomas lowered his gun and Mundo limped away before Thomas could change his mind. He had taken some shrapnel from the grenade. His unhurried pace angered Thomas. The pistol already in his hand, he raised it and fired a round, pinging it off the ground near Mundo's feet.

"Move faster!" Thomas's voice was like the throaty growl of a chained Rottweiler. Mundo obliged, stepping up his pace to a jog. Only when Thomas was certain that he had all of his troops in pursuit did he fall in behind them. He wanted a piece of the Mad Mick too.

They moved up the road like a unit on patrol. Thomas made an effort to organize them into what he hoped would be a more effective formation. He got his men with night vision gear out in front as scouts. The main body of his force was moving along under the light of their headlamps, though he'd finally managed to get everyone to switch to the red LED to preserve their night sight.

Well ahead of the pack, Conor had no intention of this turning into a foot race. He was too old for that. He was tired and he'd already soaked his clothes with sweat charging up and down the hills like a bloody mountain goat. He had no confidence in his ability to outrun these men if it came to that. Staying a comfortable pace ahead of them was dependent on him keeping them scared. Fear would slow them, make them hesitate.

Conor hoped to keep them together. The last thing he wanted to do was scatter the force or send them fleeing backwards. He decided he needed to get behind them so he could push them. Conor dropped a hand to his plate carrier and took stock of his grenades. He had one fragmentation grenade and two smokes left.

Certain that less than a minute separated him from the lead element of the Bond, Conor hastily taped a smoke grenade to the guardrail and ran a tripwire with Kevlar cord. His hope was that the Kevlar cord would be less visible in night vision or with headlamps than the fishing line he normally used. With his tripwire rigged, Conor hopped the guardrail and flattened himself against the embankment. He again installed the suppressor on his Glock. He checked the magazine and found that it was still loaded with the subsonics from when he'd stolen the tanker. From his Go Bag, he retrieved the thermal optic.

He peered through the weeds below the guardrail. He didn't move a muscle and his ghillie suit helped obscure him from the sight of The Bond's lead element. He counted a half dozen men, weapons ready, moving along with night vision. They really needed to work on their stalking game. Even if he hadn't been watching for them they gave themselves away with the scuff of their boots, the creak of their webbing, and the rattle of their gear. They were as loud as a herd of cattle.

Conor didn't move, barely breathing as the men neared him. They passed directly in front of him, giving no indication that they spotted the Kevlar tripwire. One of them noticed the pressure of the tripwire hitting his leg but it was too late. The hiss of the smoke grenade startled them, sounding like an angry snake. The grenade was on the guardrail opposite his position and it drew the team's attention in that direction. Smoke poured, enveloping the men before they could even decide what to do. They were scared to proceed into the unknown but equally terrified to retreat. That meant answering to Thomas.

Conor flipped his night vision out of the way and watched through the thermal. Smoke impairing the team's vision but did not affect Conor's at all. Through the thermal scope he could clearly see the men moving about as they spoke to each other, trying to determine a course of action. Conor decided he would help them along. He couldn't attach this optic to his pistol but he could hold it in front of his eyes and instinctively point his weapon at the men. That was exactly what he did, rapidly popping off rounds at the men standing less than thirty feet from him.

Those who were hit cried out in pain, startling the other men standing around blindly, trying to figure out what to do. They were afraid to return fire, afraid they'd hit one of their own since they couldn't see. Conor dropped four of the six and the remaining two scattered. They ran in the same direction and he chased them with rounds, catching one in the lower back and the other in the calf before his slide locked open.

The man with the calf wound took off his night vision, dropping it to the ground. He tugged a flashlight from his pocket and played it around frantically in the darkness and smoke. Men were dying around him and he didn't want to be one of them.

"Thomas!" he barked. "I need help!"

Through his thermal, Conor could see the man limping around awkwardly, holding his rifle with one hand as he played the light about uselessly. Conor shoved the suppressed pistol through his battle belt. He had more subsonic rounds in his Go Bag and regular rounds in his mag pouches but he didn't need a gun for this. The man turned slowly in the darkness, trying to watch all directions at once.

Zeroing in on him, Conor slipped his thermal scope into his dump pouch and eased forward. His hand shot out of the darkness and twisted the rifle barrel skyward. The injured man pulled the trigger and a three round burst sprayed into the air. Trying to wrench the gun from Conor, he dropped his flashlight, the beam playing across the leering face of the Mad Mick. It caught the flash of a knife blade as Conor swung, plunging it into the man's neck, and ripping it out the front of his throat. Conor sheathed his knife and bolted from the cloud of smoke.

Once clear, he dropped his night vision back down and sprinted into the darkness. He could hear the main body of Bond troops behind him. They'd encountered the fading wall of smoke and knew it carried bad tidings.

"It's thinning out," Thomas said. "Keep moving. I heard something."

Hearing The Bond leader giving orders Conor wondered why his terrified men didn't put a round in his head. It was a testament to the hold that he had on his team. Even when they outnumbered him to the same degree they outnumbered Conor they couldn't say no to him.

At the next bend in the road, Conor paused and checked his six. Through his night vision he could see the demoralized Bond soldiers examining his handiwork. The man who must have been Thomas retrieved all the night vision gear. He took a set for himself and handed out what remained. Two devices had been broken when the men had fallen onto the asphalt.

"Sucks for you," Conor muttered.

There was a crackle in his earpiece and the familiar voice of his daughter. *"Dad, where are you? Have you hit the steep section of road yet? Lonzo says you need to be looking for a wrecked beer truck."*

Conor was winded from his sprint to safety. He learned over the years it was hard to whisper when you couldn't breathe. He gave himself a moment to recover before responding to her. "I've started up the hill but haven't seen a beer truck yet."

"Lonzo says there's a wrecked beer truck halfway up that hill. When you reach the beer truck you need to get those men to follow you off on the secondary road to the right. It will take you downhill into a bowl-shaped valley that was created when they built the four-lane highway. There's an old gas station and abandoned restaurant down there that closed when the highway went through. You need to lead everyone down there and then get out. It's a dead end."

"Roger that," Conor gasped.

Not being one to linger over initiating action, Conor stepped out into the center of the road. He raised his rifle and fired off three quick rounds into the air. "This is your last chance," Conor bellowed. "Turn around now."

He didn't wait for a response. He sprang to safety behind the bend in the road as the Bond soldiers dropped to their knees and opened fire in his direction. They didn't even wait for Thomas's command. Dozens of rounds simultaneously ricocheted from the stone face of the road cut. Conor wouldn't wait around for them to get a better firing position. He was already jogging up the road, firing random shots to leave a trail of breadcrumbs for them. He didn't want them to lose their motivation. They needed to think they were closing in.

"Beer truck better be close," Conor groaned. "I feel like I've run the Boston Marathon tonight."

65

Thomas was furious that his men had let themselves be ambushed. He stalked around the dead and injured, tearing their bump helmets off and redistributing the night vision gear. He tossed off the black toboggan he was wearing and strapped a set onto his own head.

"We didn't see him, Thomas!" one of the men cried. He was writhing around on the ground trying to staunch the flow of blood from his side. Knowing how Thomas dealt with the injured, he wanted to make himself battle-ready.

Thomas didn't respond. Every minute they wasted there was another minute that bastard got ahead of them. This ended tonight. He'd already decided it was going to end. If they captured the Mad Mick alive, he was going to drag him behind the vehicle until he was dead. Once he was dead, they would continue dragging him behind the vehicle as a reminder to people everywhere they went. That was what happened when you messed with The Bond.

Taking measure of the size of his dwindling force, he understood that he had to beef up their ranks. They'd probably lost half their men tonight and a fifty man force was nowhere near as intimidating as a hundred man force. As a matter of fact, he'd go ahead and set a target for two hundred and fifty men. There would be no stopping them then. There would be no chance of another freak incident like this, a lone crazy man impeding their progress.

"Let's go," Thomas ordered. He tossed one of the bump helmets with the night vision to Mundo. "Put that on."

Mundo did as he was told, knowing that in his current state of mind, Thomas would shoot him for the slightest infraction. He too had been thinking about the future of The Bond and had come to his own conclusion – he was done with them. To hell with all the rules. To hell with Thomas. To hell with not being allowed to drink. To hell with his mission, and to hell with the Mad Mick. He was done with all of them. As soon as he had the opportunity he was jumping off this crazy train.

"Where you want me, T?" Mundo asked.

"You take point."

Mundo limped off, aware that he was being punished for what he'd said to Thomas earlier. Thomas was probably hoping he'd get killed. He halfway expected Thomas to put a bullet in him but he wouldn't have given him night vision if he was going to kill him. He'd wait until he took it off first so there was no risk of breaking it.

Staggering off into the darkness, his rifle raised, scanning nervously, Mundo heard Thomas giving more orders behind him. The men with night vision were being ordered to follow him. Mundo risked a quick glance backward. He wanted to put some distance between him and the main body of men, particularly between him and Thomas. That way if an opportunity presented itself, he could take it.

He was probably fifty feet ahead of the next man behind him, which he noticed happened to be Droopy. A short distance behind Droopy was another man wearing night vision. It may have been Shootah but he couldn't tell. Mundo noticed with some aggravation that Thomas, who had insisted on taking a pair of night vision, had flipped them up out of the way and was traveling with the main force of men. He was no dummy.

Mundo's calf was killing him. A fragment from the grenade had shredded the side of his calf. It was a nasty, painful wound but not life-threatening. If he could keep it clean and medicated he would survive. Despite that pain he limped on faster.

"Slow down," Droopy called to him. "We don't want to get too isolated from the main element."

"Fuck the main element," Mundo mumbled.

"What was that?" Droopy asked.

"I said your mama is big as an elephant."

"The only reason I don't shoot you is because I want to see the bug-eyed look on your face when I choke you to death."

"You too fat and slow," Mundo said, emboldened. "You'll probably fall over dead before we make it up this hill."

"You better hope so."

With this exchange, Mundo realized that Thomas wasn't the only thing he hated about this organization. He was tired of Droopy too. That hatred charged him a little and he walked even faster. He figured the faster he walked and the more insults he hurled, Droopy would be too tired to do much more than threaten him when they got to the top of this hill. If he could get him far enough away from the main group, he thought they could have some quiet time together and he could kill Droopy. He'd have to get the jump on him, but he'd love to see the expression of surprise on his face.

Mundo turned around to face Droopy, walking backwards up the steep hill. He was getting a second wind. "Hey, Droopy, I ever tell you about all the times I banged your sister?"

66

Conor was chugging like a freight train when he reached the beer truck. Apparently, it had run out of fuel on this section of road and been descended upon by thirsty hillbillies. The refrigerated truck had individual bays, each with a rolling door. Most of them had been pried open and a sea of beer bottles attested to the festivities that ensued. Conor could only imagine the expressions of glee on the men who found this gift from the heavens waiting on them.

He was glad to see the beer truck, although for a different reason. He felt like he had a pretty good lead on the men behind him but they had inexplicably increased their pace a while back. One minute they were a good eighty yards behind him and the next time he checked they'd cut that distance in half. At first he thought it was because the lead man had honed in on him, then he realized that wasn't the case. The lead man appeared to be walking backwards and was badgering the next man in line.

The elation he felt at finding the beer truck made him want to stop and lay down on the cold ground to catch his breath. This was another of those times where he understood that if he stopped he might not be able to get back up. To his right was an opening in the guardrail and a sign indicating that the road ended in a half mile. Hopefully the road wouldn't be the only thing ending in a half mile. Hopefully it would be the end of this brutal journey. Hopefully it would be the end of The Bond.

Conor cast a quick glance behind him and saw that the next Bond soldier was probably forty yards behind him. He shot through the gap in the guardrail and trotted a short distance down the steep gravel road. The downhill grade was a pleasant change but his legs felt like rubber and the ghillie suit made running awkward. He was afraid at any moment his legs would fold beneath him and he'd go tumbling down the hill like a heavily-armed tumbleweed.

When the beer truck was nearly out of sight, Conor yanked a length of paracord from his pocket. He tied one end around a bright tactical flashlight. When the first Bond soldier arrived at the beer truck, Conor turned the flashlight on and shined it at the startled man. While the man was temporarily blinded by the flare of light Conor took off down the hill. He dropped the flashlight and let the cord play out to a length of about twenty feet before the light started dragging behind him.

67

The flash of light to the face temporarily disoriented Mundo. It cleared quickly and he saw the flashlight disappearing down the gravel road. It was hard to get a clear picture, the light throwing off the way his night vision registered. He threw his rifle to his shoulder and fired three quick bursts toward the flashlight. He must have missed because it kept moving.

Mundo was preparing to unleash another burst when he was broadsided by what felt like a city bus. The bump helmet he was wearing wasn't properly adjusted to the size of his head and it went skittering up the road, taking his night vision with it. Mundo felt like a quarterback who'd been sacked even though he'd already thrown the pass. The breath knocked out of him, he rolled onto his back and could make out the hulking shape of Droopy overtop him. "What the hell, man?"

While the climb had exerted Droopy and he didn't have the wind to mount a response, the vague outlines of his profile showed he had a rifle leveled on Mundo's face. It appeared he was trying to make a decision at that moment. Depending on which way that decision went, this could be the end of Mundo's time on Earth.

"He's getting away," Mundo croaked.

"You think I give a fuck?" Droopy finally managed to say. "You was talking a lot of shit."

"What you think Thomas is going to say when he sees you chose kicking my ass over catching the Mad Mick? The guy is carrying a flashlight. You can see him running. You better decide fast, 'cause Thomas and the rest of them are almost here."

The ambient light from the multitude of headlamps was making Droopy's profile more refined. He turned his head to see the approaching group hurrying toward them, their speed increased by Mundo's shots. Droopy then whipped his head toward the gravel road where the flashlight was quickly disappearing down the road. He made a snap decision.

"Dammit, this ain't over," Droopy warned. "You better never turn your back on me again." With those parting words he bolted for the gravel road, pursuing the Mad Mick down the side road.

Mundo lay there in the dark for a second, his head rattled from hitting the pavement, his ribs aching with each breath. Then he realized he was completely alone. Droopy probably figured he would follow with Thomas's group. On the other hand, if Thomas didn't find him, he would assume he'd gone down the gravel road with Droopy. It was his turn for a snap decision. Before Thomas's group could reach him, he rolled out of sight and took cover behind the beer truck.

A bottle went rolling as he skittered for cover. He shot his hand out to stop it and was elated to find it was full. Unable to stop himself, he muffled the lid with his shirt and twisted it. The heavenly odor of beer reached his nostrils. He tipped the bottle up and drained it in a single, long gulp. The only nice thing about this cold night was that the beer was the perfect drinking temperature.

He groped around, his hand stung by shards of broken glass before he found another undamaged beer. He sucked it down with the same relish. He paused in his drinking when the clatter of footsteps told him Thomas's group had reached the truck. He prayed they stayed on that side of it. If Thomas found him hiding here with a beer in his hand, he'd shoot him in the head with no hesitation.

"Down there!" Thomas barked. "He's getting away. Go!" There was the sound of pounding boots as the men shot down the gravel road.

When they'd all left, Mundo sucked down that second beer and reached for another. He was like a man lost in the desert who'd found an oasis and couldn't stop drinking. Uncertain of how far away the men were, he placed his empty on the ground and found two more full ones. He needed to get away from this spot but he needed his night vision and his rifle first. Both had gone flying when Droopy bowled into him. Once he had his gear, he could grab some more beer and get out of there. He might even have time to get back to their trucks and grab some gear for the road.

He opened one of the beers and took a calming swig. He walked around the front of the truck. It was pitch black and he couldn't see a thing. Trying to recall his position relative to the truck, he groped around with the toe of his boot, trying to find his lost gear. In the distance he could hear yelling and sporadic gunfire as the men closed in on the Mad Mick.

"That you, Mundo?" came a voice from behind him.

The sound of that voice was like someone dumping ice water down the back of his shirt. He nearly pissed himself. In an instant, he knew what had happened. Thomas had left someone behind in case the Mad Mick doubled back. He should have considered that possibility.

"Who's that?" Mundo asked.

"It's Buddha Boy. What the fuck you doing back here?"

"I got blindsided," Mundo said, not mentioning it was Droopy who had done it. "My ass got knocked out."

"That a beer in your hand?"

Mundo knew that whoever this was had the advantage of night vision. They could see him but he couldn't see them. He needed to think fast. "I was thirsty when I regained consciousness. It was all I could find to drink. Want one? There's plenty."

"Nah, man," Buddha Boy said. "You best throw that shit away and get your ass into the fight. Thomas smells that, you're a dead man. Thomas misses you, you're a dead man. He don't like you anyway."

"Yeah, I get that." Mundo saw it all slipping away from him. He had his opportunity for escape. He could make this happen. This could be over. It was within his grasp and Buddha Boy was going to ruin it. He couldn't let that happen.

"Yeah, man, I'll do it," Mundo conceded. "My ribs are killing me. Bastard knocked me on my ass." He pressed his side like he was probing for a damaged rib. As he did, he removed the powerful LED flashlight tucked into his webbing. He'd been afraid to use it to hunt for his gear, concerned the beam would give him away, but now he felt he had no choice. He turned the flashlight toward Buddha Boy's face and thumbed the switch on the butt cap.

Buddha Boy flinched and made a motion to cover his optic. Mundo knew his eyes would be closed beneath the night vision. He took his beer bottle by the neck, smacked it against the bumper of the overturned truck, and closed the distance. He put a hand behind Buddha Boy's neck, trapping him, and ground the bottle into his neck. Buddha Boy staggered backward as Mundo released him. One hand yanked the bottle free, unleashing a torrent of blood. Although he tried to staunch the flow with a gloved hand, Mundo knew it was hopeless. Buddha Boy was a dead man.

In the fight, Mundo had dropped his flashlight. He picked it up and searched frantically for his gear. He needed to be done with this and get out of there. He spotted his night vision and replaced the bump helmet on his head. Fortunately, it was still working. He turned the flashlight off and stowed it on his webbing. Able to move freely in the darkness he quickly found his rifle and slung it over his shoulder.

He ran to the edge of the road, checked down into the valley, and saw that the men were in pursuit of their quarry. He should have plenty of time to return to the trucks and get some gear for the road. He felt a little bad about Buddha Boy. He'd never had a beef with the guy and he'd worked hard to keep them all fed. He paused at the body on his way by it.

Buddha Boy was still alive. Mundo couldn't see his eyes beneath the night vision gear but his fingers were moving as he tried to close the wound.

"I'm sorry, brother," Mundo said. "You were in the wrong place at the wrong time."

Buddha Boy's hand slipped from his throat. Mundo figured that was it. He'd lost too much blood and was gone. However, he had just enough life to release the retention on his holster and roll the Beretta M9 in Mundo's direction.

Mundo didn't notice the motion until a flash of light impaired his night vision, accompanied by a simultaneous searing pain in his inner thigh. He'd been shot. He reeled backward, dropping the two beers pinched between his fingers and the rifle in his other hand. He sat down hard, groping at the wound, trying to determine how bad it was. There was blood everywhere, black in his optic.

"You asshole! Why'd you have to do that?" Mundo screamed, trying to find something to shove into the wound. He traveled light because he didn't want the weight. He didn't have his blowout kit, his pack, or even his plates. He cut a quick glance at Buddha Boy to see if he was carrying any gear. Instead he found the M9 canted awkwardly in his direction.

Before he could pitch himself to the side there was another explosion from the weapon. He felt a hard punch to his chest and toppled over backward. There was searing pain and a whistle in his chest as he tried to breathe. He lay there a moment wishing those beers hadn't broken when he dropped them, then all went dark.

68

Conor charged down the dead-end road, leading his pursuers into the bowl-shaped valley created when the highway was built. He was fairly certain there was at least one man close behind him but they didn't have a direct line of sight to each other due to the thick woods lining both sides of the curvy road. The guy had taken some shots at him earlier but they'd been separated by the terrain for the last couple of minutes. Nearly at the bottom of the valley, when sucking in a breath, Conor caught the faintest whiff of natural gas and came to a stop.

He hadn't expected the gas to rise this high. The pumping effort must have been more effective than he'd imagined. He'd hoped it would be odorless if they weren't pumping the artificial odorant into it. Lonzo said he could shut that off, but it was too late to worry about that, since he had no control over it.

The flicker of flashlights and headlamps in the trees high behind him caught his attention. It meant the main body of Bond troops had topped the hill and were charging in his direction. He couldn't just stand around in the road.

"Dad, we can see The Bond. They're headed down into the valley," Barb confirmed over radio.

"Roger that," he replied. "I see them."

Conor's mind was occupied with how he was going to get himself out of there without alerting The Bond to his trap. He grabbed up the flashlight he was dragging behind him, turned it off, and shoved it into a cargo pocket. He still had his ghillie suit on and would have to hope that was enough to conceal him. He powered into the underbrush alongside the gravel road and started working his way back up, angling away from the road and path of The Bond soldiers.

69

"*Do you see him?*" Thomas demanded over the radio.

Droopy's knee was hurting from running downhill and he'd slowed to a limping walk. "I was following his light but I can't see him now. He's around a bend or something."

"*Find him!*"

Droopy gave a frustrated grunt and shoved his radio back in its pouch. "What the hell you think I'm trying to do?"

At the top of the hill, Thomas wasn't take any chances. "Go!" he barked, rushing the main body of his men down the road to assist Droopy in his search. They were so close. They had to keep the pressure on him. He pulled two men aside. "One of you circle left, the other right. Watch that he's not slipping away into the woods. Rejoin the group at the bottom."

He wasn't taking any chances. He'd learned his lesson. The Mad Mick wasn't some townie or some pissed off hillbilly. He was a formidable and dangerous opponent, but he'd pissed on the wrong tree. This ended now.

Thomas cut off his headlamp and studied the terrain through his night vision. It appeared there was no escape from the valley without having to climb back out. When the road was built, engineers had dammed one end of it to raise the elevation of the road, leaving this little pocket of isolated valley with only one way in and out. The Bond had the main route blocked. If the Mad Mick tried leaving by the woods, it would be slow going and produce noise that they could use to track him. He was not getting away.

Elated by his impending success, Thomas raised his face to the night and unleased a wolfish howl that rang through the hills. He would give the Mad Mick a taste of his own medicine. *Who's the predator now?* When he was done, he loped down the steep gravel road after his men. They weren't allowed to have all the fun. He wanted some blood too.

70

When Conor heard that howl he understood exactly what it meant. *Who's the hunted now, Mad Mick?* Conor received Thomas's message loud and clear. Despite the chilling nature of that message, it meant the leader of The Bond was involved in the pursuit. He was following his men into Conor's trap, which was exactly what he wanted, but there was one snag. He himself was in the trap too. He was not where he needed to be for the trap to be sprung.

Barb was constantly chattering in his ear, asking for updates on his position. He didn't want to speak out loud. He didn't know who might be out there in the night close enough to hear his voice. He focused on trying to climb as quietly as possible while maintaining a steady speed. Trekking silently was nearly a lost cause with the thick carpet of leaves and twigs underfoot. He could only hope that his enemy was drowning out his noise with their own steps, their chatter, and their labored breathing.

From above him, he spotted the erratic beam of a light bouncing from tree to tree as someone descended directly toward him at a very high speed. There was no time to run and nowhere to go. Had he been spotted?

Conor crouched behind an evergreen holly bush, focusing on total stillness. Whoever was headed in his direction was bounding down the hill, taking long strides to cover ground as fast as possible. That was good for him. They would be more concerned about trip hazards than studying greenery. Just in case, Conor slipped his hand to the grip of his combat knife. The man coming toward him would not have much control due to his speed. He certainly wouldn't be able to aim and shoot under those conditions.

The man didn't slow, running within a dozen feet of Conor and not even glancing in his direction. Conor let him pass, breathing a sigh of relief before standing and resuming his climb.

"*Dad, are you clear yet?*" Barb demanded.

"No, sweetie. I'm trying but it's slow going."

He could sense her frustration. "*You've got to hurry. Those men are near the bottom. They might smell the gas.*"

"I know. I smelled it when I got there."

"*Then we need to get on with this before they figure it out. Run!*"

"Give me two minutes to get clear, then light it up."

"*I'll check back with you in two minutes.*"

"No! This is an order. You spring the trap in two minutes. Don't worry about me. We blow this chance and we're screwed."

She didn't immediately answer and he wasn't going to waste time waiting on a response. He lowered his head and charged up the hillside like he was running a set of stairs. He checked his watch and noted when his two minutes would be up. He hoped she listened and did as he asked. If they had to engage these men in the woods it was going to be a nightmare. Barb's team could pull triggers all day but they were not trained for this to go close-quarters or hand-to-hand. They would lose a lot of people and perhaps even the battle itself. That was unacceptable.

He found the fastest pace he could maintain without losing his breath and went on autopilot. He was covering ground but had no idea how much. The end was not in sight, the lip of the valley obscured. All that lay ahead of him was more trees, more leaves, and more hill.

"One minute, Dad."

Conor pushed himself even harder. Soon he was gasping open-mouthed for breath, his legs weak, and weird lights flickering at the periphery of his vision. He wasn't going to make it.

"Thirty seconds," Barb said flatly.

He searched desperately for a place to hide, spotting a downed log. It was a massive oak several feet in circumference and wedged broadside to the slope. Whenever it fell, it started rolling down the hill before its progress was arrested by two standing trees. Conor dove behind it and flattened himself against the ground. He buried his face just as a shotgun-like blast cut through the night. Barb had fired the flare gun he'd given her.

Good, he thought. *She's doing what she was told.*

That was his last thought before the most powerful explosion he'd ever experienced shook his world. The ground shuddered beneath him. Trees cracked, splitting, and toppling. Weak limbs, debris, and stripped bark rained down on him. A heavy branch fell from one of the trees above him and would have crushed him if not for the log he lay huddled against.

Conor shimmied out from under the fallen branch and staggered to his feet. His legs were rubbery and trembled beneath him. Dirt and leaves clung to his clothes. Sweat ran down his back and he'd not caught his breath from his death march up the slope. He shoved his night vision out of the way and stared beneath him at the hellish scene. There were burning branches and pyres of flaming leaves. The abandoned structures at the bottom of the valley were completed flattened. Conor heard no screaming and no yelling. There were no cries for help. If there were men below him, they were dead.

It was over.

"Dad?" came a hesitant voice over the radio. *"You there?"*

"I'm here, Barb," Conor replied. "Un-scorched and in one piece."

"I wasn't worried."

He could tell she was lying. He'd heard the apprehension in her voice and it brought a smile to his face. It was good to have people in his life who didn't want to see him blown to smithereens.

"I'll meet you at the beer truck," he said. "Bring a horse. That's about as far as I'll be able to walk."

"Got it, Dad. See you there."

Conor picked up his rifle, checked the function, and confirmed the barrel was clear. He decided not to use his night vision. There was enough ambient light from the scattered fires started by the explosion. He could walk faster without the contraption on his face.

He set out at a brisk pace, walking sideways across the slope rather than climbing. He wanted to get to the gravel road and the easier hiking it presented. The only sound was the crackling of burning wood. There were no men organizing or tending their wounded. There were no taunts, threats, or yelling. Lonzo had been pumping natural gas into this valley for most of the day. Heavier than air, the gas settled there, awaiting the spark that would set it alight. That came compliments of Barb and her flare gun.

When he reached the gravel road, Conor was only about fifty yards from the top. He wasn't really a beer drinker but he was tempted to search the truck and see if any remained unbroken. His nerves were a frayed mess. He pushed on, climbing briskly. He was ready to be out of this hole and back with his people. Then they could wrap this up. In a few days, he could be home with his bed and his fire.

Conor staggered onto the pavement of Route 23. The smooth asphalt felt heaven-sent after what his feet and legs had been through on the steep hillside. "Barb, you here yet?" he asked into the radio.

"On my way, Dad. It's me, Shannon, Jason, and Sam."

"Roger that. I'm at the beer truck and I'm going to sit down for a minute. Or fall down. One or the other."

"Got it. There in a few."

Conor sat for a moment but his legs started cramping, so he got back to his feet and tried to walk it off. He understood from his cycling magazines that beer could function as a recovery beverage. Maybe he'd have one just for medicinal purposes. There wasn't enough light outside of the valley, so he used a small tactical light to examine the scene. He wandered around to the side of the truck and found two dead bodies, both Bond soldiers judging by their uniforms. He hadn't killed them, so this must have been some beef between the two men. Or perhaps Thomas had killed them. Men like those in The Bond would require a strong leader. This could have been how Thomas kept them in line.

Ignoring the bodies, Conor sorted through the remaining bottles with the toe of a boot, trying to find something that appealed to him. There were plenty of unopened bottles. He was surprised they hadn't frozen and broken but they probably would soon enough. He found a bottle of ale from a brewery he didn't recognize which was good, because most of the stuff he recognized was crap. It didn't have a twist-off lid which he took as a good sign. It just so happened that his Donnie Dunn knife had a bottle opener built into the pommel. God Bless that man for his foresight.

Just as he drew his knife he was struck with a powerful, full-body blow from behind, driving him hard into the side of the truck. The bump helmet protected his head but he struck his shoulder and was blinded by a wave of pain. He lost his footing when he stepped on a rolling bottle and went down in the pile of shattered glass. He could feel it slicing into his forearm and his legs as he sat down hard. He cursed from the pain.

He'd dropped his light but caught a flash of scorched camouflage fatigues from the corner of his eye as he twisted to face the threat. There was movement above him and he threw his arm up in a defensive gesture, blocking a blow from the stock of a rifle. Someone had tried to knock his head off like it was a tee ball on a stand. Conor latched onto the stock and tugged the rifle toward him, throwing his attacker off balance. His knife remained in his hand and he lashed out at the camouflaged legs with heavy slashing blows, the razor-sharp blade whistling as it cut through the air. Each swing of the knife twisted Conor's body, grinding the glass into him, and powering his fury.

The soldier let go of the rifle and staggered backward. Conor attempted to bring the rifle to bear. He saw the soldier going for his handgun, forcing Conor to fire off a burst before either of them were on target. The soldier dived to his right, away from Conor's line of fire. Conor chased him with rounds while staggering to his feet. He couldn't fight from his back. He needed to be mobile. Chunks of glass sliced through the palm of his glove, adding a new spice to the complex stew of pain simmering in Conor's body.

That second where Conor was transitioning from sitting to standing allowed the soldier to get off a single, rushed shot. The bullet punched through the refrigerated truck body only inches from Conor. Everything felt like it was moving in slow motion. The man had a clear shot because Conor was caught off balance and off target. He was a sitting duck, even if only for a second. The man's next round would hit him and he could only hope the armor caught it.

But the man's handgun didn't fire.

In a split-second Conor could see why. His attacker had his gloved hand too high on the grip and the glove had snagged the slide. It hadn't cycled and hadn't chambered a fresh round.

The man's eyes went from his M9 to Conor as he tried to figure out if he had time to manually rack the slide and get off a shot before Conor killed him. Conor knew he didn't. He was on target now and could squeeze off a round instantly.

"Are you Thomas?" Conor asked.

The man nodded, only his head moving.

"Thought so."

"Are you the Mad Mick?" Thomas asked.

Conor nodded.

"Somehow I knew that too. How'd you get that stupid name, anyway?"

Conor smiled. "If I told you, I'd...Oh, fuck it." He pulled the trigger and sent a three-round burst into Thomas's head and neck. He kicked the handgun clear of the body, then confirmed he was dead. He was, as Conor was fond of saying, dead as disco.

He heard hooves clattering toward him as he picked up the light. Everyone had their weapons at the ready, concerned they may have been too late. Conor held up his hand in a wave and made sure they knew it was him.

"I'm okay," he said. "Mostly."

Barb was off her horse and checking him out, Shannon at her side. They helped him pull off his glove and roll up his sleeve, examining the cuts from the glass.

"Make sure no one is alive down there!" Conor shouted to Jason and Sam. "Keep an eye out for survivors. I found one already. Or he found me."

"Is this your only injury, Conor?" Shannon asked.

Conor hesitated.

"She's your medic, Dad," Barb said. "You said she could handle this."

Conor took a deep breath. "Very well then." He turned around, unfastened his belt, and dropped his pants.

Barb played the light over the back of his sweating legs, tracked with watery rivulets of blood. Tiny shards of glass reflected back at the bright flashlight. "What the hell?"

Conor nodded toward Thomas. "He knocked me on my ass in all that broken glass. Not sure I can ride without getting some of it out. Hurts like hell."

Shannon gave Barb a reluctant look. "Well, he's *your* dad..."

Barb took offense. "And you're the bleeding medic!"

"I guess you could always hand the job off to someone else," Conor said. "But I'm pretty certain I can't reach them."

"Nah, we'll do it," Barb said. "Together."

Shannon nodded.

"Do we need to be concerned about the fires?" Conor asked.

"Already on it," Barb said. "The highway makes a fire break around most of it. There are logging roads around the rest that will serve the same purpose. I have men on them now raking leaves out of the way and watching for it."

"Lonzo did a good job," Conor said. "This is exactly what I was hoping would happen."

"He's not proud of the work," Barb replied. "He feels guilty."

Conor nodded. "I can understand that. It's okay. The world needs different kinds of people at different times. This time, the world needed our kind."

71

It turned out that Conor didn't have to ride home on horseback. They were able to salvage half of The Bond's trucks, including the tanker. They would distribute them to Pastor White, Pepe, Wayne, and Conor. The fuel would be split evenly. It was no replacement for what Pepe's group had lost on the road but it would be a start. They would have food, gear, and weapons. Conor had also claimed a portion of weapons and food for Johnny Jacks. He and his family had made a significant contribution to the effort of the mission.

It took them a good part of the next day to get the vehicles in order. They had to find enough tires for every vehicle and then transfer the gear they were taking to the working trucks. Some had to be carried on packhorses. Despite the difference in travel speeds, they did their best to travel as a group. The trucks would travel a couple of miles and then wait for the horses. No one cared because they ate well and their mission had been a success.

When they finally reached Wayne's camp, they lost a portion of their riders and a truck. The same happened when they reached the turn leading to Pepe's camp. They were met with grief at Pastor White's camp for the man they'd lost but there was a consolation in the fact that the man had died as part of a noble fight. They were pleased with the truck and its load of cargo.

"That will go a long way with my people," Pastor White said. "They're no strangers to making food last. It's how we all live."

"Your men did good," Conor said. "I know there's been tension but we worked as a team. We succeeded because everyone worked together. We couldn't have done it without you."

The pastor's response was tempered by his normal stoicism. He was reluctant to show pride in his men killing, reluctant to show joy when they'd lost a soul. It was his nature and Conor was learning that about him. He couldn't accept the bounty of the moment without acknowledging the suffering that led them there.

Jason and Sam rode ahead to warn Johnny that Conor was coming in a truck. They didn't want him to open fire on what he might take as an enemy invasion. He was pleased with the safe return of his son and daughter-in-law, shedding a tear at their happy return.

Shannon rushed to her father and hugged him tightly. That hug told the story and no words were necessary. Doc Marty knew by the way his daughter embraced him that she'd seen the things he warned against. She'd be different after this. It was inevitable.

"You okay, baby?" Doc asked when she finally pulled away from him.

She frowned. "It was awful. I had to pull glass out of Conor's butt with tweezers."

Doc Marty gave Conor a disturbed expression. "What the hell, man?"

Conor shrugged. "I couldn't reach them. What was I supposed to do?"

Doc patted Shannon on the shoulder. "Honey, if you're old enough to do that you're old enough for a drink. You're welcome to a shot of Scotch later if you want one."

"I might have to rub it in my eyes," she said, winking at Barb.

They unloaded the goods they'd set aside for Johnny, then helped him stash them in his storage areas.

"I think we better be going," Conor said. "Dark is closing in and I'm sure Ragus is about to climb the walls."

"Can we leave our horses here and come back for them tomorrow?" Shannon asked. "I'm saddle sore."

"That okay, Johnny?" Doc asked.

"Of course."

"Barb?" Conor asked. "You coming?"

She shook her head. Again, Conor had forgotten that she'd moved in with Johnny's family.

"Barb, you did well out there. If you want to come back home for a few days, back to your old room, that's fine."

"No, Dad, I'm good. I haven't even really had a chance to enjoy being out on my own yet. We rushed out on that operation before I even got settled in. How about I come see you at the compound tomorrow? I can bring your horses back to you then."

Conor nodded. He closed the distance to his daughter and hugged her tight. "I'm so proud of you, Barb. You know that, right?"

"I do. I'm proud of you too. I think I raised you right."

Conor laughed. "There are those who would beg to differ."

72

They radioed Ragus before they reached the compound, wanting to warn him that they were in a truck instead of on horseback. He was curious about that turn of events but they said they'd explain once they were home. Ragus was indeed glad to see people again, especially Shannon.

"I've been talking to the animals," he said. "I could swear one of the goats talked back."

"As long as it stopped at talk," Conor teased.

They had no interest in unloading the heavy truck. They were too sore and exhausted. Conor pulled it into one of the tall shop buildings where it would be safe until tomorrow. Desperate for information, Ragus peppered them with questions and Conor felt bad about blowing him off. After all, Ragus had really stepped up to care for the compound in Conor's absence. It was an important responsibility and he deserved to know what had happened.

Over a pot of hot tea Conor and Shannon recounted their trip for Doc Marty and Ragus. It was an emotional experience for the two who had missed the fight, both of them concerned that their family had been so exposed to danger. It took hours to relay the entire story and by then everyone was ready to turn in for the night. They all wanted to be back in their own beds in their own quarters.

"There's a fire going in your cabin," Ragus told Shannon and Doc Marty. "I kept it going the entire time you were gone. Didn't know if you had stuff that might freeze. Plus it would be warm when you got back."

Shannon rewarded him with a hug and a kiss on the cheek. The latter got a frown from her father who hadn't seen any public affection between them. Shannon caught the expression and frowned back at him.

"Oh, you think I'm old enough for a shot of Scotch but not old enough to kiss a boy on the cheek?"

"It's time for bed," Doc Marty said, getting to his feet. He wasn't ready for this.

Conor laughed. "I'm heading off too."

"You all go on. I'll secure the camp," Ragus said. "I'll bank the fire for the night, make a sweep around the property, then I'll be heading off to bed."

Conor smiled. "Thank you, lad. You're growing into quite the responsible young man. I didn't raise you but I'm very proud of you."

Ragus beamed as Conor headed back to his room. He was back in a few seconds with a sheet of paper. He held it out to Ragus.

"What's this?"

"Oh!" Ragus said, recalling something that had slipped his mind in the excitement. "That satellite phone of yours has been ringing like crazy."

Conor was concerned. "You didn't answer it did you?"

"No," Ragus said, as if the idea was absurd. "You've told me a million times not to. I just wanted to let you know as soon as you got back that someone must really want to speak to you."

Conor disappeared into the Faraday room and opened the satellite phone. There were dozens of calls from a single number, all Ricardo. Conor turned things over in his head. He was exhausted and in a lot of physical pain from the ordeal of the last week or so. He couldn't even count the various pains that tweaked his nerves like banjo strings. He planned on medicating himself and tapping out. But what did Ricardo want? Did he even want to know?

He punched redial and sat down in a worn desk chair while it rang. He leaned forward, resting an elbow on the desk and settling his weary head into his palm. Ricardo picked up the third ring.

"*Conor Maguire,*" Ricardo said. "*Where you been?*"

"I've been out. I saw that you called?"

"*Yeah, a time or two.*"

"Ricardo, I'm exhausted. I just wanted to see what was up since you've been bombing my phone."

"*Blowing up,*" Ragus mouthed from across the room. "*The expression is blowing up.*"

"Blowing up," Conor corrected.

"*It's about that thing you called me about,*" Ricardo said. "*I spoke to my JAG buddy. He said The Bond is an organization they're monitoring at some of the Midwestern Army bases. It's a loose alliance of soldiers with ties to street gangs. Supposed to be run by some character named Thomas Warner with ties to Detroit. Rumor is they've been stealing weapons to arm their old gangs.*"

Conor didn't know what to say. "Thanks, Ricardo. Appreciate you getting back to me on that."

"*That's all? I thought you would be interested in this information. You don't seem very excited about it at all.*"

"That was about a week ago. I just got home tonight from killing them all."

The line went silent for a long moment. "*Uh...okay,*" Ricardo finally said. "*But it was kind of large group. More than a hundred. How many did you get?*"

"All of them."

"*Hmmm...good to know. I'll pass it on to my JAG friend. That'll be one less thing for them to deal with when things get back to normal.*"

Conor didn't reply. This wasn't his business. He didn't wipe out The Bond for Ricardo or for the JAG officer or for the benefit of the government. He did it for his community. "Well thanks, Ricardo. I appreciate you getting back to me. I think I'm going to call it a night."

"*Oh, one more thing,*" Ricardo said, rushing to get Conor's attention before he could hang up.

"Yes?"

"*I've definitely got a job for you. When are you available?*"

"I'm honestly too tired to know, Ricardo. I'm exhausted."

"*I'll call next week. That be okay?*"

"I guess so," Conor said, smearing a hand down his tired face. "I should be healed up by then."

"*Good. We'll talk details next week. Be working on a price.*"

"It'll be high," Conor said.

"*I would expect no less, Mad Mick. Nighty night.*"

Conor clicked the phone off and dropped it heavily on his desk. He settled back into the chair. Who the hell said "nighty night" to an assassin?

"What was that about?" Ragus asked, stepping up to the door.

Conor was already asleep, slumped back in his chair. Ragus went to the couch and grabbed a blanket off the back. He spread it over his friend and turned off the lamp. "Good night, Conor."